There's Something About
ST. TROPEZ

There's Something About
ST. TROPEZ

ELIZABETH ADLER

St. Martin's Press ⚏ New York

This is a work of fiction. All of the characters, organizations, and events portrayed in this novel are either products of the author's imagination or are used fictitiously.

www.stmartins.com

Design by Sarah Gubkin

LIBRARY OF CONGRESS CATALOGING-IN-PUBLICATION DATA

Adler, Elizabeth (Elizabeth A.)
    There's something about St. Tropez / Elizabeth Adler. — 1st ed.
        p. cm.
    ISBN 13: 978-0-312-38514-9
    ISBN 10: 0-312-38514-5
  1. Private investigators—Fiction.   2. Television actors and actresses—Fiction.   3. Saint-Tropez (France)—Fiction.   4. Vacation rentals—Fiction.   5. Villas—Fiction.   6. Strangers—Fiction.   7. Murder—Investigation—Fiction.   I. Title.   II. Title: There's something about Saint-Tropez.
    PR6051.D56T48 2009
    823'.914—dc22

                                                                                        2009007676

10 9 8 7 6 5 4 3 2

There's Something About
ST. TROPEZ

ST. TROPEZ
SUMMER RENTAL

By month or longer term.

Charming traditional stone villa built around an ancient priory. Sunny terraces, mosaic-tiled swimming pool, arched courtyard with olive trees, lavish secluded grounds overlooking pine-treed hillside with direct view of the sea.

Five bedrooms, five baths. Beautifully furnished. Well-equipped kitchen. Staff available if required.

Perfectly private.

For brochure with photographs and further details, contact: MadameSusanneLariotCannes@wanadoo.france

Prologue

One cold spring morning in California, Mac Reilly was sitting on the deck of his small Malibu cottage with his feet propped on the guardrail, overlooking the glittering Pacific Ocean. A squall was building on the horizon and the windchill raised the hairs on his arms as he opened the large buff envelope with the French postmark, took out the papers and spread them out to read.

The letter was from Madame Suzanne Lariot, a rental agent, in answer to his inquiry about her ad for the villa in St. Tropez that he'd seen on the Internet.

Intrigued, Mac studied the glossy color pictures of the beautiful villa, Chez La Violette, with its arched colonnade, its turquoise pool, its limestone-flagged terraces with the white wicker loungers just waiting for that lucky holidaymaker to take the sun, hopefully with a chilled bottle of wine and a gorgeous woman by his side.

And Mac knew just the woman. You could get the wrong impression of Sonora Sky Coto de Alvarez, the impossible name bestowed on her by her hippie mother and her handsome Mexican rancher father, if you happened to see her in black leathers zooming down Pacific Coast Highway on her Harley, all long legs and sexy curves, but the fact was that Sunny, as she was always known, was also a graduate of the Wharton School of Business and ran her own successful PR company.

Sunny was girly and ditsy but she was also clever. She was funny and chaotic, and untidy. She was brave, as proven on certain nerve-racking murder hunts with Mac, yet she was also vulnerable and feminine. She was a terrific cook and a dedicated clotheshorse, beautiful when dressed up for a

ELIZABETH ADLER

date and gorgeous when undressed in bed. And unfortunately, she adored her little monster of a dog, a three-pound fiend on four paws, the Chihuahua known as Tesoro.

Mac had recently proposed marriage to Sunny. At least so she claimed, though Mac said he wasn't exactly sure he remembered. Anyhow, now she wore a heart-shaped pink diamond on her third finger, left hand, and a big smile on her beautiful face.

Truth was Mac kind of liked the way their relationship was now. Sunny had her condo at the Marina that she shared with the dreaded Chihuahua, and he had his little Malibu shack, stuck like a green barnacle onto the very end of posh Malibu Colony. And the other truth was that Tesoro maintained a running battle with Mac's own dog, a rescued one-eyed, three-legged mutt with a bad underbite that gave him a permanent smile. The dog's name was Pirate and he was Mac's pride and joy. And nobody came between a man and his dog. Not even Sunny.

Right now though, Chez La Violette seemed to Mac to be exactly what he and Sunny needed. To get away for a while, take things easy. *Be alone.* Malibu, and his small home were, for him, about as perfect as a man could want, but he'd been working doubly hard on his successful TV show, *Mac Reilly's Malibu Mysteries,* as television's private investigator, as well as on his "day job" as the real thing, *"Mac Reilly, PI to the stars,"* which is what the tabloids called him.

Time out was definitely needed to work out their lives and their future. St. Tropez seemed the perfect answer.

Picking up the phone, he called Madame Lariot in Cannes. Within ten minutes the villa known as Chez La Violette was his for the month of June, and for a great deal of money. But then, no one ever said St. Tropez was cheap. And it would be just him and Sunny, alone at last.

And the dogs of course.

The following day, Madame Lariot, in her tiny office on a Cannes back street, concluded her rental transactions, closed her laptop, put it in its bag, collected all the rental agreements in a folder and placed them in an airlines rolling carry-on.

She was a low-key unremarkable-looking woman who seemed addicted to her sunglasses. She was never seen without them. She fixed her brown hair, added a touch of oddly youthful pale pink lipstick and put on her unfashionable brown linen jacket.

Locking the door behind her, she took the creaking old cage elevator down, slipped the office key into the landlord's mailbox, went outside and got into her car.

She drove to the bank, checked that the money had been transferred, then closed her business account. She transferred the money again, this time to a private account, and was off to the airport. Madame Lariot was not the kind to waste time on people. In fact, Madame Lariot would allow no one to get in the way of what she wanted. She had always been like that. Ruthless.

1.

It was early June, the day before the longed-for vacation and Sunny was
packing, which meant that her apartment with its floor-to-ceiling windows
overlooking the Marina, was in chaos. Not that it was tidy at the best of times,
something that drove Mac crazy. The exception was the kitchen which was
as immaculate and scrubbed as an operating room.

Sunny had learned to cook from her Mexican grandmother (*Abuelita*'s
Christmas Eve tamales were a traditional treat never to be forgotten) and she
loved her kitchen. She loved cooking for Mac, always taking care to choose
a wine that would please a man who had by now become quite the connoisseur. And always taking care to wear something sweet and sexy that would
appeal to his heart as well as his palate.

When she'd first met Mac at the press party for his TV show, she'd found
herself looking at a rugged guy in jeans and a T-shirt, which she soon came to
know was his habitual attire, and whose intense blue eyes were taking her
in like she was the best thing he had seen all night. Electricity ran between
their fingers when they shook hands. It was, Sunny thought, as though they
were connected, grounding that electricity, sending a warm welcoming glow
through her body. That was two years ago now and they had rarely been apart
since.

Now Mac had become famous; his *Mac Reilly's Malibu Mysteries* TV
docudrama was shown around the world. He'd resolved some of Hollywood's
long-drawn-out mysteries, crimes of passion, money and violence and had
an almost uncanny ability to get into the mind of a criminal—or a killer. Plus
somehow he always managed to keep his sense of humor. Add to that, on

camera he was so darn attractive in his own beat-up, laid-back way, the way that Sunny found so endearing.

Mac also kept Sunny on her toes helping with his crime investigations. He made her feel as though he couldn't live without her. He made her laugh and he bought her flowers and, when jealous Tesoro wasn't around, they made better love that anyone had a right to expect. Life and love were like the same thing for Mac Reilly and Sunny loved him to pieces, though she did wonder how they could ever get married, because of their dogs. She was in her thirties and Mac in his forties. It was perfect timing. She would have given up the Marina apartment in a minute and moved in with him had their dogs not been so antagonistic. Still, she was forced to admit that Tesoro was the main culprit. Poor Pirate had learned to keep his distance when Tesoro curled her lip and bared her teeth in something that could definitely not be called a smile. And in fact, so had Mac, who had the scars to prove it.

Sunny sighed as she hefted yet another pile of clothes from the closet to the bed, already strewn with more than enough garments for a six-month stay and for every social eventuality. Why couldn't she ever make a decision, cut out two thirds and pack light, the way magazines told you?

Tesoro, sleek, chestnut-colored and pampered beyond belief, sat in the open suitcase, tense as a coiled spring, staring mournfully at her, afraid of being left behind in the kennels near the airport, where in fact she was treated like a princess and was said to have a good time. Of course she would never let Sunny know that. Tesoro knew how to lay guilt on her mistress, thick as hot cream.

"It's okay, sweetheart, this time you're coming with me," Sunny promised, depositing Tesoro in the smart Louis Vuitton dog carrier purchased at great expense the previous day. "After all," she said, "a dog can't go to St. Tropez in just any old carrier, now can she?"

She walked over to the windows and stood looking out at the forest of masts, pennants fluttering under a clear blue sky, still worrying about the packing.

Then the phone rang.

"Hi, babe, it's me."

Sunny smiled. "And this is the St. Tropez girl, ready to hit the beach and drink that rosé wine."

"Yeah, well . . ."

Sunny heard the hesitation in Mac's voice and frowned.

"It's like this, Sunny. I'm calling from the set. There's a few problems here and I have to reshoot some scenes. It involves rewrites and I'm not going to be able to make the flight tomorrow."

"*What?*"

"I can't leave tomorrow."

Stunned, Sunny said nothing.

"Look, I'm sorry, honey, but you know how it is. I have no choice. Here's what I thought. Why don't you go on ahead, take that flight anyway? Chez La Violette's ready and waiting, the housekeeper will be there so you'll be looked after, and I'll join you in a couple of days."

"A *couple* of days?"

Mac's voice had a sigh in it. "I'll do my best, hon, but there's no reason for you and Tesoro not to leave tomorrow. You have all the necessary papers for the dogs. You can get a head start on that tan. Look, I'll arrange for a limo to pick you up at the apartment. You can catch the Paris flight, then on to Nice. All you have to do when you get there is go to Hertz, collect the car and drive to St. Tropez. I'll give you the house keys and the rental agreement Madame Lariot FedExed me."

Sunny was silent until Mac finally said, "What do you think?"

She glared at him down the phone. "I'm thinking," she said, "about what to do with a man who backs out of a vacation trip at the last minute."

"Sun, baby, I'm not backing out. I'll be there in a few days."

"How many?"

"Two, three at the most."

"Okay," she said reluctantly.

"I'll be through here around nine. Can I come round and see you?"

"Meet me at Giorgio's," she said. "At least we can have a farewell dinner."

Even though she was miffed, Sunny made sure she looked good in a sleeveless white linen top and a narrow skirt with a clunky turquoise necklace and her signature red lipstick. Her cloud of softly curling shoulder-length black hair shone and her skin glowed golden in the soft light. She got there on time and sat, sulking, waiting for him.

Mac was half an hour late, hurrying into the small crowded Italian restaurant, dark blue eyes searching for her, pausing here and there on the way to her corner table to shake hands with Tom Cruise and Katie Holmes with Posh and Beckham at one table, and Sharon Stone, gorgeous as ever, at another. Everyone knew Mac from his TV show, and everyone liked him because he was up-front, honest and very good at what he did. Sunny's eyes met his across the room, and despite her disappointment her face lit up. Even tired, in a faded T-shirt and jeans and with the black leather jacket she'd bought him slung over his shoulder, Mac's long lean lived-in good looks turned her on.

He dropped a kiss on her hair then sat opposite and took both her hands in his. "Will you forgive me?"

"Hey," she said lightly. "It's not often a girl gets to go to St. Tropez on her own. You never know what kind of trouble she might get up to."

Mac shook his head, glad that she had seen reason and was accepting the inevitable.

"Too true," he said, as the waiter poured the decent Antinori Chianti that Sunny had already ordered. "You just never know. And anyhow you speak French."

"Hah, I worked in Paris for a while, but that was years ago. I've probably forgotten most of what I knew."

"I daresay it'll come back to you. When you're in France, I mean." Mac gripped her hand across the table. "You won't be alone for long, I promise." He was glad to see Sunny's face light up; the old sparkle was back in her eyes.

"I know, I know . . . you just love me too much ever to risk me being chatted up by gorgeous European men."

"You're right on that, baby."

Mac kissed her hand and they grinned at each other across the table.

"It's our last night together," she said, giving him a dramatic stare from under lashes that were so long and thick they cast shadows on her cheekbones.

He reached across and ran his finger gently over them. "You're not gonna cry on me are you, babe?"

The dramatic stare became a haughty glare. "Am I the kind of woman who cries?"

"Well, under certain circumstances . . ."

"Name them."

"Like, sometimes after we've made love . . ."

"Hah! That's an entirely different matter. That's . . . that's . . ."

"That's what?"

"That's pleasure," she whispered, her eyes now linked with his in that intimate gaze only lovers possess.

"Did I tell you you look beautiful tonight? Lovelier than I even remember?"

"You're just saying that to get off the hook."

"Will you let me off the hook then?"

"This time . . . maybe. But only this once."

"Good. Now can we get down to business and order the spaghetti with langoustines?"

Sunny sighed with delight. "You certainly know how to please a woman."

"It's my specialty."

"That and solving murders."

"Maybe that too."

"But not in St. Tropez." She was firm on that. "In St. Tropez we're on vacation."

"Of course." Mac took her hands across the table. "Pretty ring," he said.

"Soon there will be two rings."

"I guess you're right." Mac mentally crossed his fingers behind his back. He loved Sunny totally but this marriage business was another matter. Still, they would have to see what a stay at Chez La Violette and romance in the South of France would bring.

After dinner, driving his customized Prius hybrid, Mac followed Sunny in her Mini Cooper to the condo in Marina del Rey. No gas guzzlers for them. He parked next to her and they took the elevator to the ninth floor, necking passionately all the way.

"I'm gonna miss you, hon," he murmured, kissing her earlobes and feeling her shudder with pleasure.

He'd forgotten about Tesoro, who leapt at him as soon as he stepped through the door. "How could I forget you, you little savage?" he said, negotiating the foyer with Tesoro still sniffing at his heels. "Sun, what're you gonna do about this dog?"

He looked plaintively at her and she laughed. "Tesoro is my true love, aren't you, baby?" She got down on her knees and the dog deserted Mac, jumping into Sunny's arms and licking her face with enthusiastic little *yup*s of delight.

"You'll miss her when she's gone," Sunny warned.

"Wanna bet? And anyhow, you're not gone yet and I need to get close to you."

As though the dog had heard what he said, it turned its head and confronted him, still smugly ensconced in Sunny's arms, which was exactly where Mac wanted to be. Still laughing, Sunny carried the dog into the kitchen, took out a bag of treats and a large chew bone, and presented them to Tesoro. Tail wagging, the little dog sniffed, then tucked in.

"Happy at last," Mac said, taking her hand and leading her into the bedroom, meaning himself of course, as well as the dog. He stared dismayed at the small mountain of clothes still piled on the bed, next to an almost-empty suitcase.

"Your version of packing," he said stunned.

"Packing is a very personal matter." Sunny scooped the clothes carelessly off the bed and onto the floor, then she walked into his arms and tucked her head into his neck.

Her dark hair smelled like a fresh breeze and tickled his nose. Mac smoothed it gently back, enjoying its texture under his fingers. He pulled her closer. They stood, body to body. She tilted her head back, closing her eyes as he slid his hands up under her skirt, gripping her lace-clad buttocks, pulling her into him. She had recently taken to wearing lacy boy shorts instead of thongs and Mac thought how sexy they were as he slid his hands beneath the lace, hearing her sigh of pleasure.

"Beautiful," he whispered. "How beautiful you are, my Sunny, my most beautiful woman . . ."

She moved away, just a little, enough to allow her to fall back onto the bed, pulling him with her. Her white skirt inched up her golden thighs. The pale blue lace panties were just waiting to be taken off by Mac's trembling hands. He couldn't wait, not even long enough to remove all her clothes, or his.

"Do you want me, baby?" he whispered, pressing hard against her. "Tell me you want me."

"I do, oh I do," she whispered back. "Even if you are deserting me and sending me off to St. Tropez alone."

"What?" Mac pushed himself up onto his knees.

"Well," Sunny said, lying there, looking up at him, all big innocent amber eyes under the flutter of dark lashes. "After all, you won't be able to make love to me if you're not there, with me. Will you?"

"Two days," Mac groaned. "It's only two days, Sunny."

Her sigh echoed round the bedroom, the lashes fluttered dramatically. "It might as well be two weeks."

Their eyes met. They looked at each other for a long moment in silence. Sunny cracked first. A smile dimpled the corners of her mouth. "Just teasing," she said. And with a groan, Mac fell back on top of her, snuffling her neck, biting her ears, kissing her mouth.

"Will you let me make love to you, even though I'm deserting you in France for two whole days?"

"Maybe three," she reminded him.

"Aw, who cares," he said, quickly divesting himself of all his clothes. He had forgotten all about the dog. That is until a small whirlwind landed on his back, snapping at bits of him he would rather not have had exposed and sending him yelling away from Sunny and tumbling to the floor.

Frantically covering his private parts, Mac heard her laughing, as though it was the funniest thing she had ever seen.

"Bitch," he yelled at her. Then he began to laugh too. When he got to his feet and took a look, the dog was sitting on Sunny's belly. He could swear there was a triumphant look on its little Chihuahua face.

"I guess we have to wait till France," he said reluctantly.

Sunny was still laughing as she said, "I guess so."

2.

Nice, Midnight

Sunny was waiting impatiently at the Hertz desk in Nice airport. Her LA/Paris flight had been delayed five hours, she had missed the connecting flight and been forced to take a much later one. She seemed to have been traveling forever. Through the windows she could see palm trees bending in a wind that rattled the swinging doors. A storm was brewing. A *mistral,* the woman at the rental desk told her, shaking her head and rolling her eyes.

Tesoro whined miserably in her Louis Vuitton carrier perched on top of the *chariot,* as the French so charmingly called the luggage cart. Sunny was still clutching her tattered straw bag, veteran of many a trip, its handles tied together with a silk scarf to stop her last-minute stuff (which included clean underwear in case of lost luggage) from falling out. Sticking from the top was a very tired-looking sandwich, a large ham and cheese baguette picked up in Paris airport in the event of possible starvation. A paper cup of strong espresso was in her other hand and her "proper" carry-on bag, red with tan leather handles and a zipper so nothing *could* fall out, was slung over her shoulder and held her passport, money and other important documents, like the rental agreement and the keys to Chez La Violette, as well as a bag of M&M's and a volume of Proust (*Swann's Way*), which she intended for beach reading.

Her normally pulled-together appearance had disintegrated under the stress of what was now more than twenty-eight hours of travel. In jeans, T-shirt and a long fuchsia cashmere cardigan, with her black hair escaping from a hastily skewered bun and straggling over her eyes, hefting all her various bags and with the luggage piled in the *chariot* and Tesoro perched on top wailing mournfully, she looked like a traveling gypsy. Right now, it surely seemed a long way from the luxury vacation Mac had promised.

Outside, car keys in hand, Sunny breathed deeply, grateful for the fresh air, even though it was cold. An icy wind whistled round the corners sending clouds, puffy as gray cotton wool across the moonless sky. She unlocked the car and quickly piled the luggage into the trunk, then let the dog out.

Tesoro yelped and shivered, had a quick ladylike pee then scurried back into her carrier. Soon, Sunny promised her, they would be at Chez La Violette where all would be luxury and comfort with a warm soft bed for both to sleep on.

Punching the address into the GPS, she headed for the Autoroute du Soleil Est, just as the storm finally broke. Rain streamed across the windshield reducing traffic to a snail's pace. Still, she thought St. Tropez didn't look too far on the map. How long could it take anyway?

St. Tropez, 2:30 A.M.

Bertrand Olivier walked along the narrow muddy lane. The night was dark as a bat's cave and the rain slashed sideways, but Bertrand liked the storm. He liked the night. He liked to be alone.

He was wearing a camouflage-green hooded oilskin cape. His thick glasses were useless in this kind of rain but the heavy old-fashioned binoculars strung around his neck on a leather strap were fitted with small metal disks that protruded over the lenses like a pair of extra eyelids. They were all he needed to see with.

Headlights glimmered behind him. Caught off guard, he hesitated a second, then dived into the bushes, crouching low, watching and waiting for the vehicle to pass.

Sunny drove grimly along the muddy lane. It wasn't supposed to rain in St. Tropez, glamour spot of the world, and this was one of those torrential storms where you might expect to find Noah waiting round the next bend with his Ark.

"And trust me, Noah," she muttered through gritted teeth, "I'd be glad to see you."

The drive had taken forever, quite a lot of it on a curving, rural, single-lane highway. She was exhausted and wishing she had stayed in Nice overnight.

A mournful yelp came from the backseat. Tesoro was not used to being confined this long, even in a luxury Vuitton case. Plus to add to Sunny's misery her nose was running and she could swear she'd picked up a cold on the plane. Sniveling, and with Tesoro's yelps as a kind of chorus, she drove on.

The female on the GPS was talking at her again. *And in French* for God's sake. And by now she couldn't even remember her *droite* from her *gauche*.

Wait a minute though! What was that? She stamped on the brakes, sending the car into a mini skid. Was that an illusion? A mirage? *Or had she just seen a man standing in the road?*

Her heart thudded in her chest, her palms were clammy with sweat and she was suddenly very much aware that she was alone on this dark lonely French lane leading it seemed to nowhere.

She drove on. Her headlights swept the place where she'd thought she had seen him but there was no one. Heaving a sigh of relief, she thought longingly of the comforts waiting for her at Chez La Violette.

Bertrand Olivier stepped from the bushes. He trained his binoculars on the car, watching the red taillights receding in the distance. He could see that the driver was a woman. And that she was alone. He knew the only place she could be going on this road was to Chez La Violette. Bertrand knew it well, both inside and out. And he knew it was empty.

He began to jog toward it.

3.

Los Angeles

It was after five o'clock L.A. time and Mac had been working since six that morning. The unit was shooting at the big hangarlike studio out near Venice Beach. He was taking a break, downing a cup of coffee so hot and so tasteless he marveled that it contained caffeine, at the same time resisting the donuts and cookies whose sugar content might also have fueled his slipping energy level.

He was not the only tired one; the crew were flagging and the director was getting testy, but all were determined to carry on because there was a chance of getting the show wrapped tonight. The writers had come up with an answer to the problems they'd encountered, and now all Mac could think about was getting out of there and making the next flight to Paris. In fact he'd get a flight to anywhere in France if it meant getting closer to Sunny.

Despite his fatigue, he looked good, tall and slightly haggard in a sexy way with dark hair that fell over deep blue eyes that somehow, when he looked straight into the camera, which he always did in the opening and closing shots, seemed to connect directly with the viewers' own eyes, drawing them to him, the Hollywood PI in jeans and the black leather Dolce & Gabbana jacket Sunny had bought him and that had become his trademark look. Now, however, all he wanted to do was close those "magnetic" eyes (as the tabloids called them, making Sunny laugh), catch some sleep and get to France. He lay down on the sofa, eyes closed, thinking of Sunny and of the next shot.

"Reilly, there you are, you old bastard."

Mac raised his lids slowly and took in the man standing in front of him. He was short, broad-shouldered and muscular from lifting weights. His eyes were a light molten brown and his thick eyebrows almost met over his sharp nose. Despite being short, he had a commanding air about him, the demeanor of a man who knew power firsthand.

"Ron Perrin," Mac said. "When did you get out?"

"A few days ago." Perrin grinned. "Thanks partly to your good words about me to the prison authorities."

Mac got up and shook Perrin's hand. A year ago he had helped solve Ron's complicated trail of financial dealings, as well as a couple of murders in which Ron had been a suspect. Mac had found the true murderer, and Ron had done time for fraud, even though he claimed it was unintentional. Mac had straightened things out and at the same time, straightened out Perrin's complicated love life.

Perrin just happened to be married to a famous movie star, the girl-next-door blonde Allie Ray, and they used to live down the beach from Mac's place. Now, though, Allie had given up Hollywood and the "paparazzi" life and her Malibu Colony home, as well as the mansion in Bel Air. While Ron was in jail, she had bought a small vineyard in France, where she lived in a cottage, tending her vines.

Perrin said, "I called your assistant, Roddy. He told me you'd be here, got me a visitor pass. Thought I'd drop by and see you, let you know I'm out."

"A reformed character," Mac said.

"Maybe, maybe. I certainly had plenty of time to think things over. I lost a lot of money, had to get rid of a lot of baggage, but y'know I was able to keep the plane. It came in useful. Allie used it regularly, flew in every couple of weeks to see me. I think we're happier now than we've ever been. Or we will be once we're together again."

Mac hoped Ron was right.

Perrin said, "I knew your show would be finishing about now and Allie wanted me to ask you and Sunny to come join us in France. How about a little vacation at our vineyard in the Dordogne? You know it's not too far from Bordeaux and St. Emilion." Ron knew all about Mac's penchant for good wine.

"When are you leaving?"

"Any time you're ready. We can fly out of Santa Monica, easy."

Mac got up and gripped Ron by the shoulders. Looking into his eyes he said, "You don't know it, Ron Perrin, but you are the answer to my prayers."

Perrin shifted uncomfortably from one foot to the other. "Hey, you were the answer to my prayers, kiddo, a short while back. If I can do something to make up for that, just tell me what."

Mac brought him up-to-date with the story of the St. Tropez villa rental, how he had been delayed, and that Sunny had gone on alone.

"I need to leave tonight," he said. "If I can catch a ride with you I can be there almost before she has time to miss me."

Perrin high-fived him. "Consider it done. I'll take you wherever you need to go. Let me know your timing so I can file the flight plan. The Citation is ready when you are, Mr. PI."

"Tonight," Mac said. "Soon as I'm through here."

Now he knew he would see his Sunny again soon, everything was right in his world.

4.

St. Tropez, 3 A.M.

Sunny drove slowly up a small hill. Water flowed down it toward her. It was like climbing a waterfall. The GPS French woman was telling her she had arrived but peering through the deluge all she could see was darkness. Then a high wall. Then a pair of solid wooden gates. Shut of course.

Cursing, Sunny got out of the car. In seconds she was soaked, then the wind hit her, roaring through the treetops with a sound like an express train. Bending double she staggered toward the gates.

A decorative blue and yellow tile set in the wall announced that this was Chez La Violette. Well, thank God for that, at least she was in the right place. She tugged at the handles, twin wrought-iron circles clasped in lions' mouths, relieved when they opened.

She got back in the car and drove on. Storm-tossed trees bent over the driveway. A house loomed ahead. Not a light anywhere.

Lowering the window, Sunny stared at the darkened house. She was hours late but shouldn't the housekeeper at least have left a light on? Nervous, for a second she thought about turning round, driving back to St. Tropez town and finding a hotel, but it was the middle of the night and the storm was still raging, and besides the drive was too difficult, and anyhow she was exhausted. Retrieving the keys from her red bag, she hefted suitcases from the trunk, slung her straw bag over one arm, walked up the shallow steps, unlocked the door and stepped into a dark hallway.

Before she'd even found the switch the place was flooded with light. She blinked, half-blinded. When she looked up she saw a man crouched at the top of the stairs in a menacing martial arts stance, hands raised high over his head. And in those hands he held a sword.

Sunny did what any sensible woman would do under the circumstances. She turned and ran.

Terrified, she found herself under an arched cloister, skidding on the rain-slicked flagstones. Her heart thundered in her ears. She could hear him pounding after her, gaining on her. She skidded again, grabbed for a stone pillar, and fell.

The man was on her, she was facedown on the ground, hands locked behind her back. She was screaming but there was no one to hear.

"What the fuck were you doing in my house in the middle of the night?" The man's voice was rough with anger. *And* he was speaking in English.

Surprised, Sunny stopped screaming. "What do you mean *your* house? It's *mine*. I rented it."

"What?"

He seemed to think about what she had just said. Then he dropped the sword with a *clang*, let go of her hands and helped her to her feet.

She stood, shivering with cold and shock.

"Sorry about the sword," he said. "It's just a toy, part of a dress-up pirate costume. It was all I could find to defend myself with at short notice. I thought you were burglars."

Still shaking, Sunny took a look at him. It was too dark to make out his features but he was tall, wearing a T-shirt and workout pants, and he sounded American.

He picked up his sword, took her arm and led her back to the brightly lit hall. "You're wounded," he exclaimed, seeing blood on her hands where she'd thrust them out to stop her fall. "I'm sorry. Let me clean up those cuts, then you can tell me what exactly you meant when you said *you* rented the house."

From outside, Sunny heard a familiar wail. She'd forgotten all about Tesoro. She ran back to the car, grabbed the dog carrier and, praying she was doing the right thing, followed the stranger into the house.

3:30 A.M.

Hidden in thick rosemary bushes outside the kitchen window, Bertrand Olivier trained his binoculars on the scene in the kitchen. He was surprised to see a man there. A thrilled shiver ran down his spine when he noticed the sword on the table between them. Could the woman his prisoner?

She was drinking coffee—the can of Nescafé instant was on the table—and making a face as though she didn't like it. She looked wary but not afraid, and seemed quite calm for a woman possibly taken captive. Bertrand drew in a shocked breath though, when he saw that the palms of her hands were bleeding. The little dog on her lap sniffed the blood then turned away with a yelp so loud Bertrand could hear it through the closed windows. Bertrand's mother was English and he spoke that language and now he wished he could also hear what they were saying.

Sunny couldn't believe she was having a coffee with a man who, minutes ago she'd thought was about to kill her. They were sitting opposite each other at a large wooden table in a big dusty kitchen that seemed to belong to another century.

"I'd better introduce myself," the stranger said. "My name's Nate Masterson. From New York."

Sunny didn't like the way he was looking at her, with a half-amused smile on his lips. She knew she must look weary and wet and bedraggled but that was partly his fault. A New Yorker, huh? She might have known it. She took a sip of the coffee. No milk, no sugar. It tasted like hell but at least it was hot.

"Sonora Sky Coto de Alvarez," she introduced herself, giving him the full works. "From L.A. Usually known as Sunny. The only person who ever calls me Sonora is my mother."

Nate Masterson grinned. "May God forgive her."

Sunny suddenly realized she was looking at a very attractive man, maybe in his late thirties, brown hair cropped short, dark eyes over which he was now putting a pair of heavy tortoiseshell glasses that gave him an experienced, worldly look. He was tall with a muscular physique; obviously he worked out. The memory of him standing at the top of the stairs, menacing, powerful, holding the sword, made her shiver at the thought of what might have been.

Nate noticed the shiver. He said, "Look, you're freezing. Why don't you get out of those wet things? I have a bathrobe you can use."

Sunny threw him a wary glance, Oh, yeah, sure. She was not taking off her clothes even if she froze to death.

Nate smiled. "Trust me, rape is not on my mind. I simply don't want you to catch pneumonia on my watch."

She hugged Tesoro closer. The dog whined, not liking being pressed to her cold wet bosom. She said reluctantly, "I guess I can't just sit here all night dripping water all over your floor."

"*Our* floor."

"What?"

"Seems like this house may be yours *and* mine."

"What do you mean?"

"I'm willing to bet the rental agent has made a mistake and she's rented the property twice for the same month."

Sunny fished in her red bag until she found Mac's signed contract. She handed it over. "Doesn't that say 'for the month of June'?"

Nate read it, then got up, went to the sideboard and took out his own contract. "Ditto," he said, handing it to Sunny.

She read it, then read it again, stunned. She shoved her wet hair out of her eyes and glanced wearily up at him. "Now what?"

Nate checked his watch. "In the morning, which is only a few hours away, I think we should pay a visit to Madame Lariot in Cannes and ask her what she's going to do about it."

Sunny groaned. *Mac* should have been here to deal with this. What if Madame Lariot gave Nate Masterson custody of Chez La Violette? That would mean she and Mac—whenever he appeared that is—would be stuck in St. Tropez without a villa for a whole month. And this late in the Riviera summer-vacation game who knew what might be available. If anything. They would probably end up back in Malibu, with no vacation, no holiday romance, and no wedding.

Nate was still wishing she would change out of her wet clothes. She looked like a demented mermaid with her trails of long wet hair. Besides he didn't want a sick woman on his hands along with everything else. He said, "What are you doing here alone, anyway?"

Sunny twirled the pink diamond ring around her finger. "My fiancé was supposed to be here. He got delayed so I came on alone. He'll be joining me in a couple of days. I think," she added gloomily. Right now she was decidedly off Mac Reilly.

"Look here, Sunny Alvarez," Nate said, "you really have to change out of those wet clothes. For God's sake, what do I have to do to convince you I'm not about to attack you?"

Their eyes met across the table, his impatient, hers defensive. Then Sunny began to laugh. "All I need to do is take a look in the mirror, I guess."

He grabbed her two suitcases and led her across the hall into a large bedroom suite that made up the entire east wing.

"Violette's own boudoir," he said. "I preferred the gallery room at the top of the stairs."

He turned on a lamp then walked to the French doors and closed the curtains. Sunny took a look around.

It was a Hollywood movie set from the thirties, Busby Berkeley gone wild, all pale paneled walls, white-on-white silk and dove gray velvet, glimmering with chrome tables and mirrors and silver sconces. It evoked images of slender elegant women in bias-cut satin evening dresses, holding long cigarette holders and flirting with handsome tuxedoed men.

An enormous four-poster was made of a mosaic of tiny pieces of mirror glass, like an Indian maharaja's, so high, a set of wooden steps had been made to climb up to it, and the shredding silk coverlet was monogrammed with an oversized white *V,* for *Violette.*

An old desk in one corner was the only piece that looked real, as though someone, probably Violette herself, had designed it, or perhaps she had even made it, because all it was, was old planks, driftwood probably, weathered to a pale gray like the velvet sofas. It still held a white leather blotter and a letter stand with writing paper in that same pale gray stamped in white with the address, Chez La Violette, St. Tropez.

But a layer of dust lay over everything, the silver was tarnished, the once-elegant silk drapes fragmenting with age and the room smelled musty, as though the windows had not been opened in decades. In the rose-marble bathroom, there were rust stains in the black and silver claw-foot tub, and when the faucet was turned cold brown water gushed out. Heart sinking, Sunny realized this certainly wasn't the way Chez La Violette had looked in the brochure. Something was terribly wrong.

Putting aside any thoughts of a hot shower, she splashed her face with the rusty water, took a towel from the pile still stacked on the shelves and shook out the dust. Shivering, she dried her hair then ran her fingers through to untangle it.

She stood for a moment, listening to the rain drumming on the roof and the wind battering at the windows. Yet there was a stillness in Violette's room. A different kind of silence. Uneasy, Sunny looked at the dog, crouched on the white sheepskin rug emitting mournful little whines, the kind Mac said sounded like a police siren fitted with a suppressor. She bent to stroke her. "It's okay," she said, sounding uncertain. "I promise it will be all right, you'll see."

Quite suddenly a warm breeze filtered through the room, like a summer wind, bringing with it a faint flowery scent. It hung in the air for a moment, then it was gone.

The hair at the back of Sunny's neck prickled. She flung off her wet clothes, put on the white terry bathrobe and thrust her feet into the comfy old pink furry slippers that she never traveled without. She grabbed the ham and cheese baguette still in its wax-paper wrapper, bought what seemed like aeons ago in Paris airport, then with a doubtful glance around, picked up Tesoro and hurried back to the safety of the kitchen, where Nate Masterson had fresh mugs of hot coffee waiting.

One thing was certain: she was not sleeping in Violette's room.

Outside the window, Bertrand Olivier got her in focus. She looked better now. Her hair was a beautiful blue-black and her eyes were amber, almost the color of her dog, who to Bertrand's delight gave the man another snarl as he placed a fresh cup of the Nescafé instant in front of the woman. Now the man was offering her something from a bottle. Bertrand focused on it. Brandy.

He guessed the man was suggesting a hot toddy. Wasn't that supposed to get the blood flowing again, bring color to the cheeks? That's what his mother had told him, when she indulged. But Bertrand didn't want to think about his mother right now

He watched frustrated. He wished they would open a window so he could hear what they were saying. It was a pity the man was here though. His job would have been so much easier if he were not.

"That's better," Nate said with a grin Sunny felt must have charmed the pants off many a woman. It crossed her mind that, with Mac on the lam, perhaps she should be feeling lucky to be caught in a storm in a mysterious, neglected old villa in France, with a man as attractive as Nate Masterson.

He held up a large but half-empty bottle of Spanish Soberano brandy. "I found this in the cupboard. It tastes okay. How about a little in your coffee? Take the chill off things."

"That's your best idea yet. And I have the perfect accompaniment." She unwrapped the travel-worn sandwich. "You hungry?"

"Oh boy, am I!"

Sunny cut the baguette into four chunks and put it, still on its square of greasy paper, on the table between them. What with the coffee, the brandy, the food, it was getting to be almost cozy.

"So what do you do?" Nate asked. "Out there in the wilds of L.A.?"

"Oh, ooh, public relations. You know, getting clients recognition in the media, pushing them and their products, that kind of thing."

"That kind of *L.A.* thing."

"So what do *you* do anyway?" Sunny wished she didn't sound so defensive.

Nate sat back, sandwich in hand, thinking about it. "I do nothing. I quit everything that I am." He took a bite, thinking about what he'd just said, then corrected himself. "That is I quit everything that I *thought* I was; the Wall Street trader working every minute God sends and then some, stashing the purloined loot away like a squirrel stashes its nuts for that long winter hibernation. But I never got to 'hibernate,' I just kept on, summer and winter alike. I had no other life, just being the best at what I did, making money. Until one morning—one of those usual three o'clock mornings—getting dressed in my Wall Street pin-striped uniform, catching the latest events on the Asian market, my brain already running ahead to Europe and then . . ." He shrugged and took a gulp of coffee, pulling a face as the brandy hit his throat. "Well, you get the picture. It's kind of a classic: man sees his whole life run before his eyes like a bad movie, realizes he *has* no life, that money is not the be-all and end-all. That it's time for some real living."

"And now what?"

"Now?" Nate took another bite. "Now I have to find out what 'real living' means. I'm too used to work and solitude to thrust myself onto the world market. I need time to recuperate, figure out who I am, what I am, where I'm going. That's why I took this villa. It was better than a hotel, lots of space, I could be alone with my thoughts, do what I wanted, whenever I wanted."

"And then I came along."

"Then you came along."

There was a long silence. Then Sunny said, "Tell me some more about you."

Nate gave a self-deprecating little shrug. "Oh you know . . . I thought I might try my hand at that novel we all like to imagine we have in us."

"Perhaps you really have," Sunny said, but then she realized Nate wasn't listening. He was staring at the window, eyes narrowed. Tesoro turned to look then gave a sudden throaty growl.

Nate said, "I think there's somebody out there."

Scared, Sunny scrambled to her feet, but Nate was already heading for the door. It took him a few seconds to get the big old-fashioned iron key to turn, then he ran out into the storm.

Bertrand Olivier saw him coming and careened from the bushes, skidding across the muddy lawn at the side of the drive, dodging behind trees, finally hiding, panting, in a recess in the old yew hedge near the gates.

The footsteps had stopped. Bertrand knew the man was still standing there, searching the darkness for him, but he had the advantage of knowing the terrain. He knew this house and its grounds like the back of his own hand.

The man's footsteps retreated and Bertrand raced out into the lane before anyone could so much as catch a glimpse of his camouflage cape and the bulky old-fashioned bird-watcher's binoculars, bouncing on his chest.

He stopped near the gates though, looking longingly back, tempted to return, even though he knew there was a danger of being caught.

Nate had disappeared into the night. Nervous, Sunny paced the kitchen. She inspected the ancient range, all black and steel with massive ovens that she thought had probably, in Violette's day, been used to cook swans and larks or something equally awful and exotic.

It was obvious that no housekeeper had been near the place in years. All she found in the cupboards were a few dusty mugs and a couple of plates. There were no supplies, not even a box of cornflakes or dishwashing liquid. Yet the beamed kitchen had a country-style charm, with its low, wide windows and long refectory table, and the tattered blue-check curtain on a wire, hiding the space beneath the sink. Sunny tried to imagine it as it had once been, with a fire in the massive limestone grate, cheerful on a stormy night like this, and then in summer with the windows flung open to the sunshine and sea breezes. Perhaps Violette had held informal parties in this kitchen, fueled with wine and song with a crowd of friends gathered around the old upright piano that still stood in the corner near the fireplace, its lid now firmly closed, and covered, like everything else, in decades of dust.

She looked out the door and saw Nate walking toward her. He threw up his arms and shook his head.

"No one," he called out. "I guess I was mistaken."

Her huge sigh of relief made him smile. She held the door for him, waiting while he cleaned the mud off his shoes on the metal boot-scraper. The Chihuahua lurked behind her, growling.

Nate ran his hands through his wet hair then sat back at the kitchen table. "Some night!" he said, taking a look at the mermaid who, as she dried off, was becoming decidedly more attractive. Beautiful even. Pity about the fiancé. He said, "Tell me, how does the fiancé cope with Tesoro?"

"He doesn't." It was Sunny's turn to fix the coffee and she waited by the stove for the water to boil. There wasn't even a kettle and she had to use a little tin saucepan, which was almost all there was of the "*batterie de cuisine*" in the "immaculate French kitchen" promised in the brochure.

"Tesoro is jealous of Mac," she explained. "And besides, she hates Mac's dog. She won't even allow Pirate on the bed when I'm with him." She poured the almost-hot water onto the coffee grounds then carried the mugs over to the table. "That's the reason we're not married yet. Our dogs have to call a truce first."

"You can't be serious?"

"Of course I am."

Nate stared at her, stunned. He poured more brandy. "Okay," he said, "Tell me all about it, baby."

Looking at the beautiful Sunny across the table, for the first time in years Nate realized he was actually enjoying himself.

4 A.M.

New headlights flickered along the lane and Bertrand quickly ran and hid behind the big wooden gates.

The car overshot the driveway then, gears screeching, was flung violently into reverse. Tires squealed, as the big car jerked backward, narrowly missing the gateposts, finally swung between them, then screamed up the drive and came to an abrupt halt in a spray of gravel.

Bertrand saw it was a beautiful white Bentley convertible, mud-spattered and with a badly dented front bumper. Then a tall woman got out of it, cursing loudly as she ran through the rain into the house.

4 A.M.

The front door slammed. Footsteps crossed the hall. Nate and Sunny turned to look. A Sharon Stone look-alike stood in the arched entrance. She was wearing an expensive but badly creased white linen pants suit and red patent stilettos. Her blond hair was cropped short, her mouth was set in a tight line and her angry icy blue eyes took in the two of them, then the bottle of brandy and the sword on the table.

"I might have known it," she said, in a contemptuous English accent. "What else could I expect but to find the help boozing in the kitchen while I struggled with that bloody car?"

She tossed the keys to Nate. "You, go get my luggage. And you." She pointed at Sunny. "Pour me a double, plus put on another pot of coffee, then make sure my room is properly made up. The master bedroom, of course."

Stunned into silence, they stared back at her.

She stalked angrily toward them, heels clacking on the tiles. Her simmering temper had reached boiling point. "Well? Don't just sit there," she yelled. "Don't you know who I am?"

"No, I don't know who you are," Sunny snapped. "And what's more, I'm hoping I never have to find out."

The blonde's jaw dropped. Her angry eyes met Sunny's for a long moment, then suddenly she sank into a chair, all the stuffing knocked out of her.

"What the hell," she said wearily. "Just pour the friggin' brandy. I've left my husband. Left him—just like that! Couldn't take any more, even if he is as rich as all those Microsoft guys put together. I've driven all the way from San Remo in Italy in this bloody storm, smacked up the bloody Bentley, and I'm shattered."

Nate poured brandy into a mug and passed it to her. She took a gulp, gasped and said, "God, it's not even French." Then she took a proper look at them.

"I made a mistake, didn't I?" she said abruptly. "You're not the help." Clasping the mug of brandy in both hands, she heaved a sigh. "Typical of me. Jasper—the husband—says I'm always doing things like that. Embarrassing him. I told him if he wanted to be less embarrassed he should have married Laura Bush."

Sunny and Nate stared silently at her.

"Me?" she continued, taking another generous slurp of the brandy and holding out her mug to Nate for more. "Me? I am who I am. Which is more than can be said for Jasper." A sudden grin changed her from sullen rich bitch to mischievous girl. "Jasper Lord, hereinafter called 'the husband.' I can hardly bear to speak his name. Not that it's his real name of course. Oh no, he's really Mikel Markovich, but he's put all that Russian stuff behind him, hidden too far back for anyone to be interested in delving into his murky past.

"Anyhow, the Russian bastard is rich, he's controlling, he's crazy and he's violent. He'd have me locked up in Bluebeard's castle if he could. Oh, smothered in jewels, of course, and dressed in couture, available to be displayed at appropriate moments. But he picked the wrong woman. And that's why I left.

"Anyhow he wouldn't have come to this place with me. This is definitely not his style." She glanced doubtfully round the old kitchen. "Actually, I'm not sure it's *my* style. I thought it would be good to get away on my own for a while, away from the grand hotels where they all know me, away from the husband. Thought I'd lay low till all the fuss dies down, y'know what I mean?"

She looked expectantly at them. "So, who are you two anyway, if you're not the help? And what's the sword for?" She grinned mischievously. "*More* fun and games? And what kind of rental villa is this anyway?"

"Rental villa?" Sunny and Nate spoke as one.

"Hey, this is the right place, isn't it? Chez La Violette."

"You got it," Nate said. "Only trouble is—apart from the trouble you seem to be in already—that I also rented Chez La Violette. And so did Sunny. By the way, this is Sunny Alvarez, and I am Nate Masterson."

"I'm Belinda Lord. Oh God, I did make a mistake didn't I? But I have a signed contract."

Nate gave her a so-what look, and Belinda sighed again. "Looks like we're all in trouble, and anyhow this place is funky. What's with the dust and the mugs for the brandy? And where's the friggin' housekeeper anyway? I'd like to give her a piece of my mind."

"No housekeeper," Sunny said. "In fact you'll be lucky if you have a bed. I haven't checked but I'll bet there are no sheets."

"And I'll bet you're in the master."

Belinda looked very put out and Nate grinned. "First come first served."

"But I rented this place for three months," she objected. "The whole summer season. It cost me a small fortune."

"A small fortune that's now in Madame Lariot's hands, along with two more months' rent from us."

Belinda sagged back in the chair. She unbuttoned her crumpled linen jacket and kicked off the stilettos. "Jesus. You got any more of that brandy?"

"How about a cup of coffee instead?" Sunny said. She went to the sink, filled the saucepan again and put it on to boil. "We're getting down on the instant too, but there's part of a ham and cheese baguette left if you're hungry."

Belinda eyed the sorry-looking bits of sandwich adhering to the wax paper. "I'd rather starve," she said. And then she burst into tears.

Sunny rushed to her side. She put an arm around Belinda's shaking shoulders. "It's okay, really it is," she said gently. "You've just had a long night and a terrible drive in the storm."

"All those tunnels," Belinda wailed. "And those bridges with sheer hundred-foot drops just waiting for me and that friggin' Bentley. I thought my end had come, but I wasn't prepared to give the husband the satisfaction of disposing of me that easily. And now the husband will come after me, he'll find me, and then who *knows* what will happen. He'll probably have me killed."

Uneasy, Nate went to the stove and fixed the coffee. He put the mug in front of Belinda and glanced questioningly at Sunny. Sunny shrugged and went back to patting Belinda's back, soothingly.

"You're safe here with us," she told her. "It's all over, truly it is. Nate and I will look after you, won't we, Nate?"

"Sure," he said, not sounding at all positive.

Belinda sat up and mopped her eyes. Ignoring Sunny she gave Nate a long gaze and a watery smile. "Thank you so much," she said. "I always knew I could rely on a handsome American."

Bertrand wished he could hear what was being said but he could catch their voices only when they were raised. He knew he was in danger of being discovered again but he couldn't keep away. He was drawn to that warm, unknowing, intimate circle, framed like a scene in a movie by the kitchen light.

He decided they must be having an important secret meeting, driving through a storm, to their rendezvous, kind of like in the old French movie he'd seen where Jim Morrison and the Doors sang "Riders on the Storm." He could hear the music now, booming quite clearly in his head . . . "Riders on the storm . . ." It was his favorite.

His fingers holding the binoculars trembled, blurring his vision. Impatient, he reminded himself of his role. At night he was the explorer, the adventurer, afraid of nothing, of no one. His mission tonight was to observe, then to analyze those memories in his journal. A scientific record of the frailties of human nature.

For Bertrand, sleep happened when it happened, sometimes in his bed in the early hours of the morning, but more often than not in his "lair," atop a small hill overlooking the cove, sheltered from the hot sun by a small outcrop of rock where the tiny green lizards had by now come to terms with his presence, and slithered unafraid around him. They seemed to know that Bertrand would not harm them.

5 A.M.

The big red Hummer, gleaming with chrome extras, sloshed through the ever-expanding puddle in front of Chez La Violette's open gates, sped up the drive and came to a stop.

The three people in the kitchen glanced at each other.

"The rental agent," Sunny guessed. "Come to sort it all out."

"At five in the morning?" Nate shook his head. "I don't think so."

The front door closed quietly, footsteps crossed the hall, then a big, broad-shouldered man, cowboy hat jammed onto his head, strode into the kitchen, holding by the hand a pale pudgy girl, maybe eight years old, in a short fluffy pink tutu and a princess tiara.

"Hey, what d'ya know? A reception committee." He beamed at them. "What did I tell you, Little Laureen?" he said to the child. "They'll love you here in France."

The three stared at him, stunned into silence.

"Hi, I'm Billy Bashford, from Glitter Ranch, just south of San Antonio, Texas. Used to be called the B.B. and B Ranch, for my wife Betsy and myself, but when Little Laureen came along and turned out to be such a little sparkler, she decided she wanted to call it Glitter Ranch. So Glitter it is. Right, Laureen?"

He pronounced her name "Lore-eeen," but anyway the child did not respond. Instead she busied herself shaking raindrops out of her tutu.

"Sorry we're so late," he said, still with that cheerful grin on his square-jawed, freckled face, and still wearing his hat. "My pilot was diverted to Marseilles because of the weather. Shit, you don't get storms like this where I come from, well except maybe every other year." He strode over to the table and offered his hand to Nate. "I guess I can tell you don't know much about ranching and cattle though."

"Right." Nate shook his hand. "I'm Nate Masterson, from New York."

"But I do." Sunny held up the dog to show the child, who seemed traumatized. "This is Tesoro, and I'm Sunny Alvarez. I grew up on a ranch, near Santa Fe."

"No kiddin'? Then lady, we have something in common besides our beauty." Billy Bashford laughed heartily at his own joke and Sunny joined in. There was something immediately likable about the new stranger.

Billy took a long look at Belinda, crumpled and tearstained, then with a reverential expression he took her hand in both his and lifted it to his lips. "Let me tell you somethin', ma'am, nothin' is ever as bad as it seems."

"The name is Belinda Lord. And exactly how would you know that, Mr. Bashford?"

"Because I've been there, ma'am," he said. They looked at each other for a long minute, but Belinda made no further comment.

"Let me guess," Nate said wearily. "You've rented Chez La Violette for the month of June."

"Correct. Thought it'd cheer Little Laureen up, y'know, after her mother passed." Billy glanced round the suddenly silent table. "Hey, you guys, I didn't mean to spoil your party by tellin' you Betsy's gone. It's been over a year. It's a fact, that's all, and of course it's one Little Laureen here does not want to think about. She doesn't want to go anywhere, doesn't want to do anything, see anyone. That's why I took the villa, brought her to France, to get her out of herself. Right, Little Laureen?"

Laureen stared at Tesoro, then quickly down at her pink ballet shoes.

"We bought the Hummer specially. Red's one of Laureen's favorite colors. Brought my plane over and all her tutus. Laureen's a ballet dancer. Right, Laureen?"

The child stared silently at the floor.

Looking at pudgy Little Laureen, Sunny thought she had never seen a less likely ballerina. Her heart went out to her. She went over and took the girl's limp hand.

"Come, sit by me and Tesoro," she said gently, leading her to the table. "I'm sorry I don't have a Coke or anything to offer you."

The child hung her head, silent.

"What do you say, Little Laureen?" her father prompted her.

"Thank you," Laureen said stiffly.

The "sparkler" certainly was not sparkling now. She slumped in her chair, a vacant look on her face, as though she were not there. Or, Sunny thought, more likely didn't want to be.

"Better join us at the table too, Billy," Nate said. "It's time for a little storytelling of our own."

It turned out Billy was another fully-paid-up member of the rental scam.

By the time things were straightened out, explanations made, more instant coffee and brandy drunk, and a firm decision made to talk things over at an early breakfast in St. Tropez, they were all exhausted.

7:30 A.M.

Night had disappeared and the sky had turned a dark luminous gray. Bertrand knew it was time to go. Anything might happen; the girl might decide to come outside, explore the gardens and he'd be caught. Yet he lingered, fascinated.

What kind of a girl dressed like that? he wondered. Was she a dancer? And the man in the cowboy hat, who he guessed was her father, looked like those American country singers you saw on TV.

The cowboy laughed a lot too, yet when Bertrand focused his binoculars on him, he saw that his eyes were not smiling.

In fact Bertrand was concentrating so hard on the scene inside that he never heard the taxi crunching up the wet gravel drive.

The rain stopped, turned off like a faucet as suddenly as it had arrived. The clouds parted, pushed across the gray sky by the final gasps of the mistral as a petite young woman with heavy brown hair that swung when she walked, got out of the taxi. She paid the driver then, dragging her suitcase, walked into the house.

She stood framed at the arched entrance to the kitchen that Sunny thought had become like the proscenium arch of a theater, with different actors flitting on and off the stage. The young woman looked at them, brown eyes bugging, her expression somewhere between anger and despair. Tesoro growled, showing surprisingly large teeth.

"The hotels in town are full," she said. "Somebody told me you might be renting rooms here."

Faced with silence, a growling Chihuahua, and four pairs of astonished eyes and one indifferent—Little Laureen's—she shrugged, embarrassed. "Oh, well, I guess you don't. I mean this is, like, a private house, isn't it? And I've blundered in on you. Serves me right for jumping ship like that. . . . I mean, I just got off, you know, I'd had enough, enough of him—"

Nate held up his hand to stop her. "It's okay," he said. "We're all just glad to know you haven't rented this place for the month of June."

Her round brown eyes were bewildered and she looked as though she might burst into tears any second.

Jesus, Sunny thought, it's malcontents' paradise here.

Belinda Lord shunted her chair to one side to make room. "Come on in and join the gang. No coffee left but we're planning on heading into St. Tropez soon for breakfast. Anyhow, what's your name?"

"Sara Strange."

Belinda sniggered. "A name straight out of a porn movie, though I must admit you don't look the type."

Sara Strange frowned. "I've been getting comments about my name all my life," she said, wearily. "Even at school the kids used to say I was 'strange,' meaning weird. And anyhow I've never even seen a porn movie."

Belinda looked surprised. She said, "Trust me, you're not missing much."

Billy Bashford lumbered to his feet. "Pleased to know you, Miss Strange," he said, taking her hand and bending over it in a courtly fashion.

"Thank you." She stared uncertainly after him as Billy went round the table, introducing her to what he called his "new friends," and then his daughter, who refused even to look Sara's way.

Fatigue suddenly painted Little Laureen's face a minor shade of green and Sunny wondered if she was about to throw up.

"Little Laureen," she said, calling her by that title because her father referred to her like that, "it's been a long night. How about you and I go find the bathroom and freshen up?"

Without replying Laureen got up and went with Sunny, who carried Tesoro.

"You okay?" Sunny asked a few minutes later when the child emerged from the bathroom. "I thought for a while there you were going to be sick."

"I was, but I changed my mind."

So she could talk after all. "Feeling better now?"

"Yup." Laureen smoothed her battered pink tutu. She wore a white T-shirt under the too-tight satin bodice and the tulle skirt stuck out like a ruffle over the tops of her plump thighs. Her pink ballet slippers were spattered with mud. She glanced up at Sunny, who stood with her hands on her hips, watching her. "Thank you anyway."

"Hey, that's okay. You had a long flight, and then the drive. I know exactly how you felt. I did it myself."

"You did? Where did you come from?"

"California."

"Did you fly in your own Gulfstream?"

It was Sunny's turn to be astonished. "I flew commercial," she said. "With my dog."

"Your dog is cute."

"Do you have a dog?"

Laureen adjusted the princess tiara. "Nope."

Sunny sighed. The child simply wasn't letting her in. She wished she would not say just "yup" and "nope" but then she remembered there was no mother around to correct her, and Billy Bashford did not seem the kind of man to be aware of small things like proper speech. Laureen was wearing a necklace of fine silver mesh strands centered with a silver heart, that sat exactly in the fragile hollow of her throat.

"Pretty necklace," she said.

Laureen put up a hand to touch it, but said nothing.

"We're planning on going into town for breakfast," Sunny said. "I'll bet they make delicious crepes there."

"What's crepes?" Laureen crouched; her small pudgy fingers fiddled with the ribbons on her pink ballet shoes.

"Pancakes," Sunny said.

"I like pancakes."

"Well, that's good then, isn't it?"

"I guess so." Laureen glanced at Sunny's feet in the furry pink slippers. "You like pink too."

"I certainly do." Sunny felt at least she was gaining some rapport. "Better go back, they'll be waiting for us." She took Laureen's unexpectedly hot little hand in hers.

Sara Strange was sitting quietly at the table now. She was petite and kind of scrawny. Her hair cut in a deep fringe hung low over her dark brown eyes then straight as a die to her shoulders. She was not pretty but with her skinny ankles and twiggy arms there was a vulnerable air about her, as though she desperately needed someone to take care of her.

"It's like this," she was saying, leaning exhaustedly on the table. "I was on a seven-day cruise of the Mediterranean with my fiancé. Well, boyfriend really. I mean, like he still hadn't gotten around to buying me a ring. I thought it would be wonderful, y'know what I mean? Like, glamorous, all hot summer nights, champagne, that sort of thing, and when you're from a small town in Kansas that sounds, like, just plain out of this world. Especially when you've saved for a whole year for it. Not even a morning Starbucks if you know what I mean. And you'd be surprised how much you can save by just cutting that out."

She pushed her fringe out of her eyes looking at them. "Except my boyfriend thinks he's the playboy of the Western world, good-looking, a charmer, the kind who stares too deeply into every woman's eyes, like he really fancies them and he's passing on the message. Y'know what I mean?

"Anyway, I kept losing him on the ship, and on those shore excursions. I never knew where he was. Turns out he's been carrying on with this woman behind my back for the entire five days we were on the boat. Oh, everybody knew about it of course, the ship wasn't that big. Except me that is, until some of the other passengers felt they had to put me straight.

"Anyhow, last night he never even came back to our stateroom. I found out where the woman's room was, and of course he was there, in bed with her. So . . . I just threw my things into my suitcase and left the ship on the first tender."

She paused dramatically, then she said, "And the bastard had the nerve to stand there, on deck, begging me to come back, while the other passengers lined the rails, cheering me on."

She sniffed back a threatening tear. *"The bastard,"* she said again. "So that's why I'm looking for a room, and it can't be expensive because I don't have very much money."

Sunny shook her head, looking at the little crowd of misfits. She thought Mac was never going to believe what was going on here.

The night and the storm were over. Bertrand Olivier knew it was time to leave.

A short while later, back at his lair, he spread out his oilskin cape then lay down on it. He slept like a dead man on his rocky hillside, oblivious to the tiny lizards that, made bold by his stillness, slithered over and around him. One even rested for a moment, basking in the newly emerged sunlight on the pocket of Bertrand's blue cotton polo shirt, beneath which could be felt his beating heart.

It had been the best night of Bertrand's eleven-year-old life.

5.

It was morning. Still groggy from lack of sleep, Sunny stood with the others on the terrace at Chez La Violette, final mug of instant in hand, staring, disbelieving, at the devastation. In the dark and the storm they had not been able to see that the house looked nothing like the photographs. The terraces were overgrown with weeds, the trees and shrubs had gone wild, the unkempt lawns were a sea of mud, and the empty swimming pool was a wreck of broken tiles, awash in debris and stagnant water.

"Looks to me as though Madame Lariot has a lot to answer for," Nate said grimly.

"But what do we do now?" Sunny said. "We're too tired to go looking for her."

"And homeless," Belinda added bitterly.

"Well, I have to admit 'homeless' is a new feeling for me," Billy Bashford said, bewildered.

"Oh dear, oh dear, and I'm broke," Sara Strange wailed. "I should never have left that ship."

"Yes you should," Sunny said firmly. "You should never stay with a cheating bastard."

"That's cussin'," Little Laureen said loudly.

They turned to look at her, surprised that she actually spoke.

"I apologize," Sunny said. "I forgot myself."

"Laureen doesn't like cussin'," Billy said. "She hears it from the ranch hands though, it's just second nature to them, talking like that."

Little Laureen spoke again. "When are we going for pancakes?"

Billy's doubtful glance took in the group. "Guess I could probably fit y'all in the Hummer. Be the devil to park though, in them tight little streets, but I'll manage."

Sunlight streamed down from a suddenly clear blue sky and they turned grateful faces up to it.

"*Now* I'm in St. Tropez," Sunny said, hugging Tesoro closer. But to her surprise Tesoro gave a throaty warning growl, then flung a few high-pitched yelps into the air for good measure.

"What's with her?" Belinda complained, but Sunny was staring down the driveway.

From where they were standing they could not see the gates, but halfway to the house the drive curved past the terrace. And trotting up that drive came a dog. Ears perked, it paused here and there to sniff the exciting French aromas. Then it loped toward them. A familiar three-legged bouncing lope.

"*Pirate?*" Sunny shook her head. She must be delusional. She had been up for thirty-six hours. Or was it more? Apart from a nap on the plane she'd had no sleep, and she was beginning to feel a little woozy and as though her legs didn't quite belong to her. But Tesoro certainly wasn't hallucinating. That dog knew her enemy when she saw him.

Pirate spotted them, wuffed joyfully, galloped jerkily toward Sunny and flung himself on her.

"Baby," Sunny whispered. "Oh baby, how did *you* get here?"

"He came with me, of course." Mac strolled across the terrace, cool in white jeans and a black T-shirt. He set down his duffel and stopped in front of her, smiling.

Sunny did not return his smile. Nor did she throw herself into his arms. Instead she stared accusingly at him. "How did *you* get here?"

"We finished early. I hitched a ride on Ron Perrin's plane. He still has one you know, despite the jail time."

But Sunny wasn't interested in Ron Perrin right now. "You've no idea what I've been through."

Mac looked warily at her. She was definitely frazzled, not to say upset, and she was wearing her pink fuzzy slippers and a bathrobe. He took in the rest of the group: the athletic-looking guy in the workout pants; the tall, tearstained, good-looking blonde in bare feet and creased white pants suit; the brown-haired skinny waif with the serious eyes; the Texan with the cowboy hat; and the miniature ballerina, complete with tutu.

"Jesus," he said, astonished. "What's going on here?"

And then Tesoro bit Pirate and Sunny burst into tears.

9 A.M.

Sunny's nerves were jagged with fatigue and too much instant coffee, plus quite a lot of brandy. Everything had suddenly caught up to her: the long flights; the delays; driving through the storm; the scary image of the man on the dark lonely road; and the fright when she was chased by a stranger with a sword with no one there to call for help. Plus trying to cope with the disaster at Chez La Violette, *and* all these strangers with their own problems. She was flat-out exhausted. She knew she looked terrible. And she was mad as hell. Her teary glare said it all. Let the famous PI sort this one out. *She* had had it. Tears ran down her cheeks.

Billy didn't like to see a woman cry and the new guy seemed too stunned to do anything about it. He put a protective arm around Sunny's shoulders.

"Now let me tell ya somethin,' dude," he said to Mac. "This young woman's about had it. She's exhausted. Can't y'see she has no time for making small talk over tea and cookies? What she needs is a bed."

Sunny turned a grateful glance on him, then looked back at Mac from under her lashes. She wasn't too exhausted to check out his reaction to the big Texan with his arm around her.

"I'm Billy Bashford, this here's my daughter, Little Laureen. That's Nate Masterson, and there's Belinda Lord and Sara Strange. And you are?"

"Mac Reilly."

"The fiancé," Nate said, surprised.

If Mac was also surprised that Nate knew who he was, he didn't show it.

"And anyways, things are so crazy here at the villa Chez La Violette," Billy went on, "we're all wondering where we're gonna find that bed to lay our weary heads. If it weren't for Little Laureen, here, I'd be heading for that fancy hotel where Mick Jagger once got hitched to Bianca, the one with the Euro-trash nightclub. But of course that wouldn't be the correct place to take a little ballet dancer like my daughter Laureen."

"You're right," Mac said, still worrying about Sunny, who was keeping her distance, alternately mopping her eyes with her fist and glaring angrily at him. He wanted to go put his arms round her but her body language was definitely not encouraging. Besides, he still had no idea what was going on, nor why all these people were here. Bewildered, he took in the dilapidated pool, the rusting garden furniture, the weedy terraces and the muddy lawn. His questioning eyes met Sunny's.

She shook her head. "Don't even ask."

Mac nodded again. Whatever had happened he guessed he'd find out later. He said, "Sunny, we need to talk. Alone." He walked toward the house but Sunny did not go with him. This was definitely not good. Still, he thought he'd better take a look inside, check things out for himself.

A quick tour of Chez La Violette revealed more of the truth. Guilt overwhelmed him. He was the one who had rented the place from Madame Lariot without, for God's sake, even checking her credentials. This was his fault. He would take care of the rental agent later, but right now, since everyone was still standing around, gazing listlessly at the desolation, he guessed it was up to him to find them all a place to stay.

He remembered passing a hotel, a small place set back behind umbrella pines and bougainvillea. The simple wooden sign had said HÔTEL DES RÊVES, with three golden stars after the name. Mac liked the three stars, which in France meant a comfortable family hotel of good quality, though definitely not luxury. And he loved the name: Hotel of Dreams. He thought it appropriate under the circumstances. It seemed to him that right now they could all use a few "dreams."

9:15 A.M.

An old man on an ancient bicycle wobbled slowly up the drive of Chez La Violette. His wide face was weathered by sun and wind and his long nose had the ruby hue of good wine. He wore a very old Panama hat and the bright blue overalls of the French laborer. Blissfully unaware of the group on the terrace, he pedaled slowly on, whistling untunefully under his breath. That is, until Tesoro ran at him, aiming little snaps at his feet.

The old man flung his legs sideways into the air, the bicycle wobbled, his hat fell off and was snatched up by Tesoro, who ran wagging back to Sunny. Pirate, sitting at Mac's feet, watched warily, one ear up, one down, He knew never to trust Tesoro.

"*Merde.*" The old man ground to a trembling halt, staring astonished at the raggle-taggle group. "*Mais vous êtes qui? Et qu'est-ce que vous faites ici?* Who are you? And what are you doing here?"

"Nous sommes les locataires." It was Little Laureen who spoke—*and in French*—telling him they were the renters.

Astonished, they turned as one to look at her. Billy beamed proudly. "I had a tutor give Little Laureen French lessons for a couple of months," he said. "She's an awful quick learner, and see, the old guy understood what she said."

The old man was waving his hands in the air, yelling at the dog, galloping in the mud, the Panama hat still clasped between its jaws.

"Merde alors, quelle sauvage," the man yelled at the top of his squeaky lungs. *"Et vous, madame."* He pointed angrily at Sunny. *"C'est votre responsibilité. Calmez votre chien, et alors, donnez-moi mon chapeau."*

Mac caught Tesoro in midleap and wrestled the hat from between its teeth. The dog gazed innocently up at him. He could have sworn there was a smile on its face. He gave the hat back to the old man who inspected it carefully, pointing out the dog spittle and smeary teeth marks on the brim, the mud and the damage, tut-tutting and *merde alors*ing under his breath.

In hesitant French and with much pantomime, Mac finally made him understand that he would replace the hat.

"Mais ce n'est pas la meme chose," the old boy muttered, shaking his head. *"Ce chapeau! Ah, il y a longtemps ce chapeau appartenait à Violette. C'est irremplaçable.* It is not the same. Long ago this hat belonged to Violette. It's irreplaceable."

Sunny offered to shake his hand and apologize but he scowled and waved her away. Then Nate went over to try to help, and finally, with the occasional surprising French interjection from Little Laureen, they made him understand their position.

"Mais moi?" The old boy was beginning to enjoy being the center of attention. *"Je suis seulement le concierge,* I am only the janitor. I take care of Chez La Violette. And how is it possible you have rented it? It has not been lived in for many years, more years than I can count. Not since Violette went away and never came back." Crossing himself, he closed his eyes and added, "God rest her soul."

"Amen," Little Laureen said loudly.

Again all heads turned to look but ignoring them, Laureen gazed upward as though speaking directly to God, smoothing her by now ratty-looking pink ballet skirt, the tulle drooping from its contact with St. Tropez rain.

"Jesus!" Belinda said, surprised.

"Do not take the Lord's name in vain." Laureen continued to look at the heavens.

"Oh . . . my . . . God." Belinda couldn't help herself.

This time Laureen merely sighed heavily.

The old boy was still going on about how the house had not been lived in for many years, that the owner lived in Paris and as far as he knew had never even been here. He had come today merely to check on the storm damage.

Nate went back into the house and got the brochure with its glossy pictures. He showed it to the old janitor, pointing out the beautiful pool, the weedless terraces, the pristine white wicker furniture.

The old boy clapped a hand to his head. "*Ah, je sais, je sais.* Of course. But this was some years ago. A film company came here to make a commercial— for magazines and for TV, you understand?"

"A photo shoot," Mac said.

The old man maneuvered the brim of his Panama into shape then slammed it back on his head. He nodded vigorously. "*Oui, c'est ça. Photo shoot*, that's what they called it. They painted the swimming pool turquoise blue, *comme ça.*" He wagged a finger at the brochure. "They brought in chairs and tables." His finger wagged again at the picture. "They cleaned up the terrace, they even sprayed the lawn green. And then they brought in the pretty girls in bathing suits." His eyes gleamed at the memory and he chuckled to himself.

Mac knew only too well how easy it was to doctor pictures on a computer.

But now the janitor scowled suspiciously at them. "Nobody ever comes here. This house is haunted. *Naturellement*, it is the ghost of Violette. Nobody round here would so much as open the gates. Except me, of course. But that's because I am paid to do so. And I only ever come in broad daylight."

Sunny remembered the breath of warm air and the scent of flowers in the master bedroom, and the sudden sense that in Chez La Violette the mysterious past was very much present. She shivered and held Tesoro closer.

Mac asked the old man for the address of the Paris owner, slipped him fifty euros for a new Panama and thanked him for his trouble. Then he walked over to Sunny.

This time she let him put his arms around her. He looked deeply into her shadowed eyes and said gently, "There's this hotel I know down the road. The Hotel of Dreams."

Sunny shook her head, gazing tiredly back at him. "Let's just hope it's true."

And then Little Laureen said, "But what about the pancakes?"

6.

Mac was driving the rental Peugeot. Sunny, back once more in her damp jeans and T-shirt, was in the passenger seat. Pirate was on her lap, his head hanging out the window to capture every new aroma, while Tesoro moaned in the carrier in the back. Belinda and Sara followed in the beat-up white Bentley, then Billy Bashford and Little Laureen in the chrome-flashed red Hummer, with Nate Masterson on—surprise, surprise—the very latest yellow Ducati motorcycle, that he'd told them he'd bought online and had delivered at Nice airport.

Mac followed the leafy lane that led in the direction of St. Tropez. The silence between him and Sunny was thick as a woolly blanket. Apart from Tesoro's moans it was so quiet that through the open windows he could hear the sea, softly splashing onto an unseen shore. Sunny's profile seemed set in stone. He had never seen her like this. Well, perhaps not *never*, but rarely. It did not bode well.

"I'm sorry," he said. "Of course I would never have let you come alone had I known it was going to be like this."

"You have *no idea* what it was like." Her voice was cold, stubborn.

"I admit it. But Sun, baby, you must understand I would never have allowed this to happen if I were here—"

"But you weren't here."

She wasn't letting him off the hook and Mac guessed she was right. He gave up apologizing and tried pleading. "Tell me what I can do to make up for it. Just tell me, baby."

He glanced sideways at her. Was her mouth a little less set? Her chin at a lower angle? Were her lips curving into that half smile he knew so well? She had no idea how truly bad he felt about having sent her alone to the disaster that was Chez La Violette. *And* in one of the worst storms St. Tropez had seen in a decade.

"Just find me a room with a bathtub," Sunny said, softening. On quick reflection, she decided *technically* it was not Mac's fault. How could he have known the rental was a scam? After all, the others had been taken in too. She ventured a look at him. Their eyes met and the car swerved, causing a honking of horns behind.

"Sorry," Mac said again, but this time his grin was matched by Sunny's. "I'll make it up to you, though."

Sunny heaved a thankful sigh. She said, "Oh, Mac Reilly, you have no idea how glad I am to see you."

The Hôtel des Rêves was down a sandy white lane that ended in a clump of tall trees that must have been there for about a hundred years, and a small farmhouse that had been there even longer. Square-built of rugged stone, painted the color of fresh cream, small square windows deep-set in true old Provençal style, faded green shutters meant to close out the summer heat and the winter wind, and a roof whose old red tiles had turned a brownish pink. All it needed was a chimney on top from which a curl of blue smoke escaped.

Charm was the first word that sprang to Sunny's mind. *Real* was the second. After the nightmare of Chez La Violette, this was like coming home.

Over the years, the farm had been expanded—wings right and left and rows of French windows open to catch the breeze. Above, cheerful blue-striped awnings sheltered ample balconies, dripping with scarlet geraniums. A swimming pool gleamed, and down a small rocky incline Sunny could see the sparkle of the Mediterranean. The scent of the Gloire de Dijon roses climbing the portico mingled with those of verbena and jasmine and the clean scent of the sea. And to complete the perfect picture, a pair of white peacocks strutted toward them, tails spread like magnificent bridal trains. In back of them waddled a plain old brown peahen, but even she had her own kind of charm.

Holding hands, Sunny and Mac walked up two broad shallow steps. The wide glass doors stood open and they saw that the original farmhouse had been completely gutted. Now it was a single large lofty room open to the rafters and to the newer wings. In fact the whole place looked as though it had always been there. As though it belonged.

The hall was the same warm creamy color as the exterior, with that long row of French doors leading onto a flagged terrace where grass grew in the cracks. Squashy sofas in coral linen looked so comfortable Sunny wanted to dive right into one and sleep for about a week, and the simple country furniture had achieved the soft luster of age. Large lamps with chocolate linen shades cast gentle pools of light. At one end of the room was a bar with an old-fashioned zinc counter. At the other, floor-to-ceiling shelves held books and DVDs, with tables nearby for card games and chess, backgammon or jigsaw puzzles.

A small dining room opened onto a flowery courtyard with a fountain and more tables set with coral-pink cloths. And everywhere were great bowls of old-fashioned carnations, the deeply scented kind, picked fresh from the flower fields above Grasse and rarely seen anywhere else in the world.

It was the perfect small, unpretentious family hotel.

"Omygod," Belinda said, stunned. "All my life and all that money, and I've never seen a room as inviting as this."

Sara was nervous. "I know I can't afford it," she whispered, and Belinda snorted impatiently and told her to wait and see what it cost before she complained.

"Gee, this is great," Billy said appreciatively. "Beats the hell out of Chez La Violette."

Little Laureen, still clutching her daddy's hand, took a quick look around. Her face wore its usual impassive expression, as though she were determined not to allow anything to affect her emotionally.

The young woman behind the gigantic bowl of flowers at the reception desk wore a pink carnation in her tight blond chignon. She was pretty, with a charming smile that matched her attitude. The badge pinned to her crisp white shirt said her name was Caroline Cavalaire.

"Bonjour, messieurs, mesdames." Her voice had that sweet high French singsong that sounded so much prettier that just plain "Good morning, sir, madam." Sunny decided immediately she needed to learn it.

"Bonjour, mademoiselle, est-ce que vous avez des chambres à louer? Mac said. *"J'espère l'hôtel n'est pas complet par-ce-que nous n'avons pas de choix. La maison que nous louons n'est pas propre à habiter et nous sommes loins de la maison."*

Caroline Cavalaire looked surprised, then she laughed, and said in English. *"Eh bien,* well done, *monsieur.* I understood every word. You are without a home."

"Then you'll also understand why I'm praying." Mac stopped and waved an arm at the others. *"We* are *all* praying, that you might have *six* rooms?"

He glanced ruefully at Pirate, sitting quietly at his side, and at Tesoro, hunched in Sunny's arms. "We also have two dogs."

"No problem." Like many French hotels, the des Rêves welcomed dogs. "Though of course there will be a small extra charge." Caroline consulted her computer, fingers bouncing rapidly across the keys.

Sunny noticed that Caroline was wearing a beautiful ring, a square emerald offset with twin diamonds, large enough to impress, but since it was not on the third finger of her left hand obviously it was not an engagement ring.

"*Alors.*" Caroline looked up from her computer. "Yesterday an entire family party canceled due to the illness of the grandmother. Their misfortune is your good luck. But we have only *five* rooms, and of those only three are doubles. The other two are singles, at the back of the hotel but still with a pretty view of the courtyard where you can take breakfast and other meals. All have balconies and the doubles have a sea view. And of course, as it is the season, you must take *demi-pension,* half board. That means a larger price, but it does include breakfast and either lunch or dinner."

She consulted her computer again and came up with the prices. Mac asked the others what they thought.

"Three doubles," Belinda said. "One for me, one for you and Sunny, and one for the Bashfords."

"Little Laureen prefers her own room," Billy said.

"And I can't afford any of them." Sara's voice was flat. She wasn't into self-pity, she was simply stating a truth.

Belinda turned to look at her. "Tell you what," she said. "Since Little Laureen has to have her own room, Sara can bunk in with me. Cost you nothing, girl. I'll charge it all to the husband."

Sara's brown eyes bugged with gratitude. "Are you *sure*? I mean, a woman like you . . . Well, you know what I mean, a *rich* woman like you who is used to suites and all . . ."

"Let's just say I'm slumming, practicing for the future." Belinda's cheeky grin turned her from blond rich bitch to someone who might be fun.

"I'll take the other single," Nate said.

Pirate gave an encouraging *wuff.* Sunny eyed him doubtfully, then looked at Mac. "A *double* room?" she said. "And *both* dogs?"

He grinned. "Let's just look upon it as a test."

7.

Caroline Cavalaire pinged the old-fashioned brass bell on her desk and two young men, smart in white shorts and polo shirts, came to take their bags. Everyone handed over their car keys except Nate who went to unhitch his bag from the back of the Ducati.

Typical man, Sunny thought watching him. All he needed for a month was contained in that one small black duffel. Of course her own two bags were stuffed to bursting, while Mac's luggage was also a single piece, packed in haste and which, Sunny knew, would consist of T-shirts and shorts. Not to worry though, St. Tropez was known for its shops and she couldn't wait to get him into that South of France look.

The Bashfords had half a dozen bags while surprisingly, Belinda had had only a couple of large Vuittons. "I left in a hurry, all I had time for," she said. And the strange Sara Strange had just one small black Samsonite roll-on which made Sunny wonder how she'd ever planned to get through a cruise plus a week's vacation afterward. Sunny's shoes alone could take up that space.

The bellhops, known as Marco and Jules, led them up a wide wooden staircase with the dogs trotting after them, for once not fighting.

Sunny and Mac were shown to a spacious corner room with French doors leading onto a balcony and that famous sea view. It was simple and pleasing; just a double bed with plain white linens, a pine armoire, a couple of chairs, a small table, and striped cotton rugs on the wooden floor. The bellboy opened the shutters and the gauzy yellow curtains billowed gently in what had become a pleasant breeze.

Sunny smiled at Mac. "Let's forget Chez La Violette, I'll bet you there's a terrific bathtub here."

And of course there was. A corner tub, the vinyl type to be sure, but big enough for two and with a separate shower and double sinks.

Elated, Sunny grabbed Mac, waltzing round with him. *"Heaven,"* she sang, *"I'm in heaven, I'm so happy I can hardly speak . . ."*

Tesoro yapped jealously at Mac's heels as he pressed Sunny closer, and a discreet cough from the bellboy brought them back to reality

"Merci bien, Jules," Sunny called, in that new sexy French singsong, as Mac gave him his tip. Then the door closed and they were alone.

The dogs had priority; Sunny unpacked their bowls, filled them with food and water, put one set out on the balcony for Pirate and the other near the bedroom door for Tesoro, which was about as far apart as they could get. The dogs drank thirstily. Then she put Pirate on a chair out on the balcony and Tesoro on the bed and she and Mac walked into the bathroom, arms still round each other's waists.

Mac closed the door firmly, then turned on the taps. Sunny threw in a handful of the pretty pink bath crystals from the bowl beside the tub. Clouds of perfumed steam rose around them as they stripped off their clothes and kissed lingering.

Sunny stepped into the tub and sank into the bubbles, head thrown back, long dark hair floating round her shoulders. It wasn't the first time she had looked like a mermaid recently but this version was definitely an improvement. And it got even better when Mac climbed in beside her.

She gave him a lids-half-lowered glance. "I know lots of good games in showers," she murmured, "but I'm not so experienced in bathtubs."

"Better let me take charge of things." He pulled her closer. Then he lost his balance and both of them slid, sputtering, beneath the foam.

Sunny emerged first, gasping and shaking her head, rubbing water out of her eyes. "So much for the famous sexy TV private investigator." She laughed. " 'Every woman's Malibu fantasy. The man in charge. The guy who can do everything.' Except kiss a girl in a slippery tub."

"Get over here." Mac grabbed her again, running his hands over her familiar curves. And this time they had no trouble finding each other amongst all those scented bubbles.

"Let's begin where we left off," Mac said, remembering the night before Sunny left, when Tesoro had sabotaged their lovemaking.

"Yes," she breathed. "Now, right now, Mac." She was no longer tired and her hands were on him, on that firm muscular butt that looked so good in jeans. They were laughing as they skidded, clutching happily at each other. Making love in water was trickier than they had imagined. Somehow though, they managed it.

And they didn't even hear the mournful howl that came from the direction of the bedroom.

8.

Belinda Lord liked her double room though she was still pissed off about all the money she had paid for Chez La Violette. Still, the room was spacious enough, and simple, with its twin white beds and club chairs, and she liked the French doors with their green shutters opening onto a flowery balcony. A perfect place for a peaceful breakfast or a glass of wine while taking in the sunset.

For a moment she regretted inviting Sara Strange to share the room. Of course she had acted on impulse but there was more to it than that. Belinda had been in Sara's position; she knew what it felt like to be broke, to be cheated on, to have to go out and forge a life for herself. Only thing about Sara though, was Belinda was not sure she was the type to go out and get what she wanted from life.

Looking at Sara, still standing in the middle of the pretty room, brown eyes bugging with mixed apprehension and delight, Belinda sighed. She had too much on her own plate right now to worry about Sara. The girl would just have to get on with it.

She checked her phone and text messages. It was as she had expected. The mad Russian was even madder. He was too clever to threaten directly, knowing it could be traced and used against him in a court of law, but his entreaties to "come home, sweetheart, I miss you" held a note of menace that Belinda recognized. She closed her phone and sat on the balcony wondering what to do about it, and what would happen when the Russian husband caught up to her. A tremor of fear trickled down her spine.

"Is it all right if I take a shower?"

Sara's voice interrupted her downward spiral of thoughts.

"What? Oh, yes, of course it is. And by the way, I have first dibs on the bed by the window. Okay?"

"Of course. And I'll do your unpacking if you like. Anything you want. I can't tell you how much I appreciate this. *A good woman,* that's what my mom would have called you, and she knew what she was talking about."

Belinda laughed. "Then she'd have made a mistake this time, sweetie. 'Good' I am definitely not. Bad? Yes. Wicked? Maybe. And on any given day you will get bits of all those characteristics. Meanwhile, what are you going to do about the bastard boyfriend?"

Sara's lips tightened. "I'm thinking about that," she said uncertainly.

"Then keep right on thinking, sweetie, because there's only one answer and you know it. Meanwhile, take that shower please, and leave me alone with my thoughts. And trust me, your problems are minor compared with mine."

Sara wasn't too sure about that but she went anyway. Sara was the kind of girl who had always done as she was told.

9.

In the room next to Belinda's, Billy was arranging his new leather travel photo frames on the dresser. There were several pictures of Little Laureen of course, including one in her pink tutu, taken just a few weeks ago. And there was another earlier one on a chestnut-colored horse, bigger than a pony but not overly large, just enough for her short plump legs to manage.

Billy had never forgotten that terrible scene in the movie *Gone With the Wind,* when the little girl was thrown from the horse and Clark Gable had carried her lifeless body back into the house. He had always made sure his own daughter was mounted on the safest beast in Texas.

There was another photo of a younger, smiling Laureen in T-shirt and shorts perched on her mother's knee with a happy-looking Billy in his ten-gallon hat behind them, holding on to the back of the big old rocker that had been in his family for six generations and was a permanent part of their porch furniture. From the photo you could see that it was a big porch, wide with strong rails around it, all painted white and with cushioned swing chairs and chaise lounges in the vivid flowery patterns that Betsy, Billy's wife, had loved. Betsy had enjoyed color, that was for sure, and Billy had no doubt that was where Laureen had gotten her penchant for bright pinks and oranges. Little Laureen was definitely not a girl for white.

Of course there was his favorite picture of Betsy, his much beloved wife. Laureen looked a lot like her mother; a quiet face, never quick to show emotion. The same china blue eyes and long brownish hair, streaked by the sun. To many folk Betsy must have seemed a quiet, plainish-looking woman, but to Billy, who knew her so well, she was beautiful.

With Betsy gone Little Laureen was the most precious thing in Billy's life. His enormous ranch; his homestead; the helicopter he flew to survey his land and for hopping into the nearest town for dinner; the Gulfstream V that he rarely used but was there if and when he needed it, like for instance for trips into Dallas for doctors and hospitals when Betsy had gotten sick, but also just for fun if she'd wanted to go to the coast for a change. Things like that. Anyhow, now all of it was for Laureen.

One day Little Laureen would be no longer "little." She would be a grown woman with a mind of her own—which by the way she already had. Meanwhile, it was Billy's job to get her out of the post-traumatic stress state she had fallen into after her mother died of cancer, over a year ago. He had tried hard. Doctors had tried, psychiatrists, the whole damn works. And nothin' doin'. Little Laureen was still into that funk and Billy was hoping against hope that this trip to France would bring her out of it once and for all.

Billy stepped out onto his balcony and took a look around. He shook his head, marveling. The sea sparkled, blue as the sky only shinier, the air smelled of flowers and the sun shone. There was a swimming pool where Laureen could practice her dives, a tennis court if she cared to take lessons, and St. Tropez town was just down the road.

Billy was kind of glad Chez La Violette had turned out to be a dud. Had it not, he and Little Laureen would never have met all these nice folk. And there was no doubt the company would be good for her. And maybe for him as well.

Still, Little Laureen was on his mind as he walked across the corridor to her room to check on her.

Laureen was sitting on the bed in what was the smallest room she had ever seen. In fact the bed took up most of the space while her four suitcases took up the rest. She had to climb over the suitcases to get to the bathroom—which consisted of a tiny stall shower, a pedestal sink and a toilet—then climb back over the bed and the other suitcases to get onto the balcony.

A single night table held a lamp with a flowery yellow shade, and there was a narrow wooden armoire to hold her tutus. Plus a tiny table in the corner with the smallest TV Laureen had ever seen.

A painting of what she guessed was a Mediterranean beach scene, all blues and turquoises and yellows, hung over the bed, which had no pillows, just a strange, long sausage-shaped hard thing, guaranteed to break her neck. She wondered if the French were like the Japanese who, she had heard somewhere, slept with their heads perched on wooden blocks. It sounded horrible to her.

Still, it didn't matter. Nothing did anymore.

From outside her open window Laureen heard the clatter of dishes and the hum of voices. Her room overlooked the courtyard where people were already taking lunch. She thought again about the pancakes but somehow, now, she was no longer hungry.

Opening the first suitcase, she tossed the tutu collection onto the bed. Most were in shades of pink but there were a couple of orange ones, the color of fresh tangerines that were her new favorites. Since her mother died Laureen had taken to wearing the tutus full-time. No one knew why she did this, not even her daddy. It was Laureen's secret.

The tutus had caused quite a sensation in school until Billy had taken her out and hired a private teacher instead. The fact that he spoke French had been the bonus in Laureen's life. Of course she'd heard Spanish spoken every day around the ranch, where many of the workers and ranch hands were Mexican, and she had a working smattering of that language. But French was new. It piqued her interest—and that had sparked her daddy's idea that they should go to France for a vacation.

Now, he knocked on her door and called out, "All right if I come on in, Little Laureen, baby?"

Billy peeked in the door and took in the tangle of tulle on the bed, the open suitcases that took up most of the small floor space, the tiny TV and the old armoire. His daughter was used to a thousand-square-foot suite of her own. He shook his head, dismayed.

"It's okay, Daddy, I like it," Laureen said quickly.

Billy looked astonished, then pleased. He felt a lump in his throat as he gazed at his girl. Laureen with her pale round face, its bones lost beneath the pudge of youth, her blue eyes with their new habitual unfeeling expression, her long brown hair straggling limply over her shoulders, her legs with the dimpled knees and her plump hand holding the fairy wand, that Billy sometimes thought she might truly believe, with one special wave, would enable her dreams to come true, and bring her mother back.

Laureen had adopted the ballerina ensemble immediately after Betsy died and now it was impossible to part her from it. "Let her be," the doctors had told Billy. "It's a passing phase, a fantasy world that might help her get over it."

Billy hoped they were right and he'd simply let it go, providing her with the tutus and the tiaras and the ballet shoes and hoping for the best.

"Well then, hon," he said. "What d'y a say you take a shower, then you and I'll go downstairs and maybe meet some folks and have ourselves a bite of lunch?"

Laureen said, "I'm tired, Daddy. I think I'll just lie down and take a nap."

Billy looked worriedly at her from beneath knitted brows. He still wore his ten-gallon cowboy hat and Laureen had to look up and under it in order to meet his gaze.

"It's okay," she promised, "Truly."

"You sure, now?"

"*Daaaaaaddy . . .*"

Billy threw his hands in the air, giving up. "Well okay then. I'm not too hungry myself. Might do exactly what you're gonna do, baby girl, and take that nap." He held out his arms. "Come and give your old daddy a kiss then, before I go."

Laureen stood up on the bed. She put her arms round his neck and leaned against him, breathing in the familiar scent of his grassy cologne that always reminded her of the pastures at home where the horses grazed.

"Daddy," she said. "Don't the French have pillows?"

Billy checked the bed then said, "Let's find out, shall we?"

He called reception and asked Caroline Cavalaire the same question. Laureen could hear her laugh over the phone.

"*Oui, bien sûr.* Of course we do. The 'sausage' on the bed is called a bolster. In the daytime we keep the pillows in the armoire, and that's where you will find them."

"*Merci beaucoup, Mademoiselle Cavalaire,*" Billy said. And sure enough, there were the pillows, stashed in the armoire.

"Strange folk, these French," he said to Little Laureen, arranging them on the bed for her.

"Maybe," Laureen said.

When he had gone, she went to the window. Her balcony was so tiny there wasn't even room for a chair and only enough space for one person to stand.

Holding back the yellow curtains, she gazed down at the happy scene, catching snippets of French conversation. Watching. Listening. Longing. And crying silently.

It had taken Nate exactly five minutes to unpack his duffel and stow his possessions, which consisted of two pairs of surfer-style bathing shorts in a

Hawaiian print of dark blue with red hibiscus; half a dozen plain white Hanes T-shirts; two pairs of khaki shorts and one pair of J. Crew chinos with a bright yellow woven belt bought on impulse in the same store. There was a crumpled pale blue Brooks Brothers seersucker jacket, plus a French bicycle racer's outfit in snug yellow and black Lycra. A small leather duffel held his shaving kit and toiletries and he had not packed even so much as one pair of socks. Sandals and barefoot were Nate's aim and he intended to stick with that. He kind of missed the privacy of Chez La Violette, though.

Out on his small balcony he looked down onto the pretty courtyard where people were already drifting in for lunch. Ancient-looking waiters, who he thought had probably worked here all their lives, were busy carrying ice buckets on stands with bottles of that famous rosé wine he'd heard so much about. He couldn't wait to try it.

A quick shower, then in khaki shorts and a T-shirt he ran down the steps to join them. He chose a corner table where he could watch the action— couples of various ages, cool in summer pastels, all talking softly in that attractive French language. He decided on a lobster risotto then, suddenly famished, began devouring the basket of olive bread, slathering it with sweet Normandy butter. The waiter showed him the bottle of local rosé wine he'd ordered, so chilly that drops had formed on it and ran down into the surrounding napkin.

"From grapes grown just down the road, *monsieur*," the waiter told him.

Pleased, Nate thought all that was missing from the picture was Sunny Alvarez. He'd only met her less than twenty-four hours ago, but he couldn't get her out of his mind. He thought with Sunny beside him, life at this moment would have been perfect.

Taking his first approving sip of local St. Tropez rosé, iced and crisp and with a nice tang to it, he happened to glance up at the windows overlooking the courtyard. For a second he saw Little Laureen standing there. Then suddenly she was gone.

There had been something about her though, her stillness, her solitude, that was disturbing. He wondered uneasily what she was up to.

10.

Bertrand skittered into the Hôtel des Rêves, trying to look as inconspicuous as possible. The oilskin cape was wrapped tightly around his binoculars, hidden from view under his arm. His blue shirt was grass-stained, his shaggy blond hair was a bird's nest, and his sneakers were black with mud. Casting a nervous glance round the entrance hall, he made for the stairs.

"*Bertrand?*"

Caroline Cavalaire's voice stopped him in midstride. He turned reluctantly to face her.

"Bertrand! Just look at you!" Caroline spoke to him in French. "You look as though you spent the night in a field."

"Hmmm . . . I . . . I got lost . . . ," Bertrand improvised.

"And what do you think your mother would say if she could see you now?"

Bertrand stared at the floor, saying nothing. He knew his mother would hardly have noticed whether his shirt was clean or his shoes muddy. She would not have bothered even to question him about the cape and the binoculars. His mother lived her own life and Bertrand lived his. It was a fact that he had come to terms with long ago.

Caroline felt sorry for the boy. His oversized shorts sagged, his big owlish glasses slipped down his nose and his hair was in bad need of a cut. Bertrand had been coming to the Hôtel des Rêves since he was a small child and the regular staff knew him well. They also knew that his mother had run off with her latest lover, a man she had met at the Casino in Monte Carlo, leaving Bertrand alone at the hotel. Madame Olivier had been gone four weeks now, and the maids were keeping an eye on Bertrand while the fatherly waiters made sure he ate a good dinner every night. Not that it made any difference to his weight, Bertrand remained giraffelike no matter how much he ate. His bony knees stuck out of his shorts like mastodon bones. But the sad fact remained that Bertrand was eleven years old and he was all alone in a hotel.

"Better go get cleaned up," Caroline said again, giving him a forgiving smile.

Bertrand turned quickly up the stairs and bounced off Little Laureen, who was heading down, toes pointed out, ballet-style, a fresh orange tutu fluffing with every move. Laureen's princess tiara flew off and so did Bertrand's glasses. Then he dropped his cape and the binoculars fell out and landed next to the tiara on the bottom step.

The two stared at them. Then they looked at each other.

"Clumsy," Laureen said.

"Oh . . . *Je-je-je m'excuse, mademoiselle* . . ." Bertrand's nervous stutter was in full force.

"Why should I excuse you?"

Laureen gave him her implacable china blue stare and Bertrand quickly looked away. The binoculars were in full view of anyone coming through the hall or walking down the stairs. Their lenses with the protective metal "lids" seemed to be looking back at him and he knew this strange girl in the ballet costume must have seen them.

She had spoken in English and although Bertrand understood, he answered in French. "I-I . . . didn't see you." The stammer that seemed to happen whenever he was under stress was even more noticeable and he blushed.

Laureen's implacable gaze took in the binoculars, the big round glasses, the muddy sneakers, the baggy shorts, the knobby knees and the horrified pale blue eyes staring shortsightedly back at her. She looked again at the binoculars lying on that bottom step.

"Bertrand?" Caroline hurried over. "Oh, Bertrand, Laureen has come all the way from Texas." Caroline seemed either not to see, or to be ignoring the binoculars. "I thought perhaps you would make good companions for each other."

"*Je préfère* . . ." Laureen started in French, then got stuck. "I prefer my *own* company. Thank *you*," she finished in English. Then she kicked the binoculars daintily out of her way, picked up her tiara, perched it back on her head, tucked her hair behind her ears and continued to the door.

"Oh, by the way." She turned to look at them. "Can either of you please tell me where I can get a taxi into St. Tropez? And where I can get some pan-cakes?"

11.

Mac left Sunny sleeping, one arm curled beneath her head and Tesoro curved in the crook of her knees. She had a lot of sleep to catch up on, while he, thanks to the effortless and fast trip in Ron Perrin's Citation that had eliminated any airport hassle and delays, was fresh as a daisy.

It was time to confront Madame Lariot, though he didn't hold out much hope that she would be at the office address. He had not yet verified the amount stolen from the others but there was no doubt the woman had pulled off a massive scam. He'd bet it was at least half a million bucks and she was anywhere else but in Cannes.

Pirate ran down the corridor ahead of him, his big goofy underbite making him look the happiest, as well as the ugliest dog in the South of France. Not even a jeweled collar—which Pirate most certainly would have refused to wear—could have redeemed his looks. Fortunately Pirate seemed entirely unaware of any deficiency. Even the lack of an eye and a back leg did not faze him. Mac knew his dog and he knew that Pirate considered himself the norm. It was the other dogs that were different.

Ragged gray-brown ears perked, Pirate stopped at the top of the stairs to survey the little scene taking place at the bottom.

Mac was surprised to see Little Laureen without her daddy, and heading for the door. Caroline Cavalaire was with a stringy-looking kid who turned to look when he heard Pirate's *wuff*. Mac stared at the boy in surprise. He was spattered with mud, his long matted blond hair fell over his eyes and his shorts were held up with what seemed to be the remnants of an old silk tie. Suddenly the boy darted to the bottom of the stairs and picked something up.

Mac saw it was his glasses, that he now replaced on his nose, but Mac thought he'd also tucked something else under the old army surplus cape.

Sensing a new game, with a joyous *bark* Pirate bounded toward the boy. Balancing on his single hind leg, he sank his teeth into the cape and shook it vigorously.

"Non, non." Bertrand's voice rose in alarm. He held the cape up over his head but still Pirate bounced up and down after it, like a circus dog.

"Sit!" Mac yelled and, tail down, the dog obediently sat.

"Oh, mon dieu." Caroline fanned her face with her hand. "For a moment there I thought he might bite."

"Pirate never bites," Mac explained. "He simply wanted to play." He looked at the dog and said, "Pirate, go apologize for frightening people."

Head lowered, tail slowly wagging, Pirate inched on his belly toward Bertrand. When he got there, he rolled onto his back, paws waggling, goofy grin flashing.

"Ooh, mais ce chien est un charmeur. The dog is a charmer," Caroline said smiling.

Little Laureen came to take a look. "What happened to him?"

"A road accident," Mac explained. He did not tell her though how, driving over Malibu Canyon late one night, he had scooped the bloody and battered dog off the blacktop thinking it was dead. And how Pirate had opened an eye and looked gratefully at him. Of course then Mac was sunk. He'd taken off his shirt, wrapped the dog in it and driven all the way to the emergency vet in Santa Monica with the almost-dead dog on his knee. The vet amputated the leg, rescued one of his eyes and saved the dog's life. And Pirate had been Mac's best buddy ever since.

"Pauvre petite." Laureen knelt to stroke Pirate. She glanced at Bertrand, who was edging away up the stairs, hoping not to be noticed.

"So what about the pancakes?" Laureen called after him, but Bertrand fled.

"He's gone to take a shower," Caroline explained. "But I will ask the chef to prepare you some crepes. You can eat them out in the courtyard, and I'll tell your papa where you are."

She went back to her desk to call the kitchen and Mac took a long look at the little girl, kneeling on the floor next to the dog.

"Glad to hear you're going to get your pancakes at last," he said.

Laureen scrambled ungracefully to her feet, one hand on the silver heart necklace at her throat, the other smoothing her ruffled orange tulle.

"Goodbye," she said abruptly, and turned and walked over to Caroline at the reception desk.

"Would you ask them to send the crepes to my room, please?" she said. Then she walked back to the stairs, avoiding Mac's eyes.

He had time to notice, though, that Little Laureen's own eyes were swollen and red. It looked very much as though she had been crying.

12.

Cannes, the diamond city of the Mediterranean coast, glittered in the washed-clean summer day, as Mac nosed the Peugeot along the crowded Croisette, stopping every few feet to allow holidaymakers loaded with shopping bags to dart across. The sea was a smooth blue sheet on his right, the beaches were crowded and on his left the white terraces of the grand hotels buzzed with late lunchers and champagne drinkers.

He parked in the massive Gray d'Albion multistory lot then flagged down a taxi. Madame Lariot's office was a long way from the chic seaside area and its glossy name boutiques, set back on a treeless street of narrow four-story buildings with dusty windows and littered entrances, many of which had office FOR RENT signs in front.

Asking the driver to wait, Mac studied the names next to the set of brass buzzers outside the front door. There it was: *4ème étage. Lariot. #401*. He pressed the bell and waited. As he'd expected there was no answering buzz to let him in. No doubt Madame Lariot, or whatever her real name was, had long since flown the coop. He pressed the bell for the concierge.

An impatient female voice floated into the air. *"Qui est là?"*

"Je cherche Madame Lariot."

"Lariot? Pas ici."

Mac summoned some French words and strung them together to ask where Madame Lariot had gone, only to be told the concierge had no idea. Lariot was gone and that was final.

He wrote down the address and phone number of the rental company whose board was outside then took the taxi back to the Hôtel Carlton.

It had often been said there was no better place to observe life than the Carlton's terrace, made world-famous by the Cannes Film Festival. Now it was a mecca for international travelers, and for glamorous women on the lookout for adventure and stardom and handsome young men on the lookout for success. Royalty, of the real princess kind as well as film royalty, gathered there to take in the scene over a glass of Krug. The espresso was strong, the cappuccino topped with the softest *crema,* and the waiters knew everybody, and probably everything.

With Pirate at his heels, Mac edged his way through the crowd, managing to secure a tiny table shaded by a blue umbrella, with a fine view of the passing scene on the Croisette and of the beach beyond. He ordered a Stella Artois and a *croque-monsieur,* the French version of a toasted ham and cheese, and also a bowl of water for the dog. Then he took out his phone and called the number of the rental office.

The voice of the man who answered held a weary note. Mac couldn't blame him. Renting cheap offices to fly-by-nights could not be a rewarding occupation. He told the man who he was looking for and was informed that Lariot had left and no he did not know where she had gone. She had paid six months' rent in full and had departed a few weeks before the rental term was up.

Mac took a sip of his beer, served in a tall glass so cold it chilled his fingers. He asked if Madame Lariot had left a forwarding address, knowing the answer even before it was given. His next question was trickier.

"Did she pay by check?"

"Of course. Everyone does. No one deals in cash in the office rentals business."

"Then, *monsieur,* you must have an account number, and also the name of the bank."

There was a long silence, then the man said stiffly, "I cannot give out that information."

"Then allow me to explain the circumstances." Mac proceeded to fill him in on the rental-scam story.

There was another long silence. "This is none of my business," the rental agent said, guardedly. "I do not want to be involved."

I'll bet you don't, Mac thought. He said, "*Monsieur,* let me explain. It's a question of you giving *me* the name of the bank and that account number, or giving it to *the police.* The choice is yours."

Another silence. The waiter delivered the *croque-monsieur* and Mac took an appreciative bite. He'd forgotten when he last ate.

"I will get the information for you," the rental agent said at last. "One moment please."

Phone to his ear, Mac sipped his beer, enjoying his sandwich and the passing parade. He knew it was wrong but anyway he gave Pirate a chunk of the sandwich. The dog wolfed it down in a single gulp then looked hopefully for more. A few minutes later the agent got back to Mac with the information.

"Now there will be no need for the police to contact me," he said, sounding worried.

Mac assured him he was correct. He didn't add that at least for now it was. Later, who knew?

Meanwhile, he had what he wanted. The sky was blue, the breeze was soft and the sun shone. He was in the South of France and pretty women in summer dresses were stopping to coo over Pirate and tell Mac how cute he was, while at the same time giving him the eye. Mac smiled back and thought guiltily of Sunny.

On the way back to the hotel, he decided that later he'd call his assistant, Roddy, in Malibu and get him on the trail of the Lariot bank account, and also have him check out the Paris owners of Chez La Violette. Then he'd think about whether to go to the police.

Tomorrow, he'd pay a second visit to the villa, find out what was really going on there, and exactly what was so wrong about a house in a prime South of France location that no one had visited it in years.

13.

Sunny woke to Tesoro's worried snuffles in her ear. Through the half-closed shutters she could see the sky was the vivid electric blue of evening. She had been sleeping for hours and poor Tesoro must be bursting. Quickly pulling on shorts and a T-shirt, she pushed her hands through her hair, grabbed the dog and ran downstairs. No one was in the hall and she hurried down the drive-way and out into the lane, where she bumped into Pirate, head up, nose alert for new sniffs. And of course behind him strolled Mac.

"Hey," they said simultaneously.

Mac said, "When I got back you were so out of it I figured you'd sleep all night."

"Tesoro woke me. I thought she must be desperate."

"Don't worry, I already walked her half an hour ago."

Sunny snuggled into his arms. "Is this really *us*? *In the South of France? Together?*"

He pretended to glance behind him. "I don't see anybody else."

"Then kiss me," Sunny said. So he did.

Arms still round each other, they strolled back to the hotel while Mac told her the story of his Madame Lariot office visit.

"I've left messages for all our 'International Misfits,' summoning them to a breakfast meeting at eight tomorrow morning at the Café le Sénéquier in St. Tropez."

"*Eight o'clock?*"

"Eight," Mac said firmly. "We can't miss a minute of St. Tropez."

"I guess not," she said, sounding doubtful. "But what about Chez La Violette?"

"I need to find out why Lariot chose the place and if she had any accomplices. I also want to know why it's not been lived in for years, a villa in a prime location like that."

He stopped and took Sunny by the shoulders, looking at her. "Tell you what, why don't you and I go there now? Check what state the place is really in, see if there are any clues about Lariot. Just you and me?"

"And the ghost of Violette?"

He gave her a little shake, trying to get some sense into her. "Forget what that concierge said. There's no such things as ghosts, it's real live people who cause all the trouble. People like Madame Lariot."

Sunny glanced down at her shorts and T-shirt; she hadn't even brushed her hair. "I can't go like this."

"Why? Afraid Violette'll complain?" Mac asked, making her laugh.

They collected the Peugeot and drove back down the lane. The double wooden gates to Chez La Violette were closed, and when Mac got out and tried to open them he found they were swollen by last night's rain and would not budge. He got back in the car and drove slowly along the perimeter of the grounds. With a large villa like this, there was bound to be a tradesmen's entrance.

He found it fifty yards down the lane, almost hidden by a thicket of overgrown bushes. Green paint was peeling in chunks off the gate and a broken padlock hung from the arrow-shaped iron latch. The padlock chain had been cut.

They were in a kitchen garden with small plots divided into squares by low box hedges, in the French style called *parterre*. Gone-to-seed lettuces still grew there, and courgettes rampaged over everything, their yellow blossoms half-hiding little clumps of wild strawberries. Espaliered peach and pear trees lined one sunny wall, though there was no fruit, and vines with bunches of hard green grapes already pecked over by the birds, sagged from wire supports. Four narrow gravel pathways, just wide enough for a wheelbarrow, led to a centered stone fountain, its carved cherubs green with lichen, its swans'-head spouts silenced forever.

A sudden wind rustled through the tops of the trees with a shushing sound that sent a matching shiver down Sunny's spine. She had been in situations like this before with Mac, in houses that had given her the creeps, that had sent messages to her that at the time she had not understood, until disaster had fallen, that is. Now Chez La Violette made her nervous. She checked the dogs. Animals were supposed to be the barometers of anything untoward, like creepy situations and earthquakes, but they seemed okay, trotting in front of them on the path that led to the back of the villa.

The sun was going down quickly and the sky began to darken. Sunny clutched Mac's hand. "Why do I always agree to accompany you on wild-goose chases in the middle of the night?"

"It's not the middle of the night. Besides, I've got my flashlight."

Of course he had! Sunny knew Mac always carried that pencil-light thing that lit about six square inches in front of him and that left her in the dark.

Surprisingly, they found the kitchen door unlocked.

Mac opened it and Pirate loped eagerly at first, up the steps, then suddenly hung back. Sunny glanced nervously at him. Was he proving her theory correct? She picked up Tesoro. "You first," she said to Mac.

He stepped inside and switched on the light. He said thoughtfully, "Now I wonder why, when nothing else about this place functions, the electricity is turned on?"

"The gas too," Sunny volunteered. "The stove worked. I boiled water for coffee on it."

Everything was as they had left it: the rinsed coffee mugs on the wooden drainer; the Nescafé tin next to the empty Soberano brandy bottle on the tiled counter; chairs pushed haphazardly back. Then why did Sunny have the uneasy feeling something was different? She took another careful look round. She couldn't put her finger on it but something bothered her. Mac was already climbing the stairs that led to Nate Masterson's turret room and she hurried after him.

The circular room was meant to look like a cabin on a boat, with round windows like portholes, and a large *oeil-de-bœuf*, a bull's-eye window opposite the bed, from which you could see the sea. It was a simple guest room with a white iron bed and white-painted cabinets, fashioned to fit the curve of the pale blue walls.

Downstairs again, they checked the large sitting room that led onto a terrace at the rear of the house. The furniture was covered in dust sheets and only the three Murano chandeliers, feminine confections of crystal and pink glass roses, glimmered with life.

Quite suddenly the shuttered house with its covered furniture seemed to suck the breath out of Sunny's lungs. Claustrophobia threatened. She ran back outside and stood, arms folded over her chest, gasping in the fresh sea air. Chez La Violette seemed to breathe mystery and secrets that she wasn't sure she wanted to know.

"Mac?" she called, suddenly aware she was alone.

"Over here, hon." His voice came from inside the house.

She walked back into the hall, remembering Nate brandishing his sword at the top of the stairs. Come to think of it, where was the sword? She had last seen it on the kitchen table right before they all left.

"Mac?" she called again.

"Here." His voice came from the direction of the bedroom.

Picking up the dog, Sunny tiptoed through the hall, asking herself impatiently, why, for God's sake, she was walking on tiptoe in an empty house.

The door to Violette's boudoir stood open. It was dark. She called Mac again, running her hand down the wall, blindly searching for the switch. A lamp flashed on and Sunny jumped. *She had not touched the light switch.* Telling herself not to be so silly, that it must be Mac, that he was probably in the bathroom, she waited.

The bathroom door swung slowly open. Her heart beat so loudly she could hear the blood thundering in her ears. Her voice quavered as she said, "Mac? Are you there?"

There was no reply, but the musty room was suddenly filled with that same sweet scent of flowers. Sunny closed her eyes, unable to move.

"Here I am, honey," Mac said from behind her. She leapt about two feet in the air. "I went to check the basement, lost you for a minute."

She sagged against him. "Don't ever do that to me again."

"Do what?"

"Don't ever leave me alone in this house again."

Mac looked at her, puzzled.

"Do you smell the flowers?"

"What flowers? I don't see any."

"No! Do you *smell* them?"

He sniffed. "No, honey, I don't. And nor do you. This place is getting to you. Come on, let's go."

He stopped to switch off the light, aware of Sunny's eyes on him.

"Mac, I swear I didn't turn that lamp on," she said. "It went on by itself."

"Old houses," Mac said easily. "The electricity can be a bit uncertain."

They walked back into the kitchen. Something about it still bothered Sunny but she was anxious to get out and waited on the steps in the dark for Mac, breathing that soft moist air that smelled of green growing things and wild strawberries. *Living things.*

It wasn't until they were in the car and driving back to the hotel that she remembered what had bothered her in the kitchen. "It was the piano," she said.

Mac glanced at her. "What about the piano?"

"The lid was up. I could see the keys."

"So?"

"Last night that piano lid was down. It had been down for a very long time. There was dust all over it."

"Okay." Mac gave her a so-what smile.

Sunny stared straight ahead. She said, "Not one of us ever touched that piano."

14.

At eight o'clock the following morning Café le Sénéquier was not crowded, merely a few local coffee drinkers, newspapers to hand, croissants ready to be dunked, indifferent to the glittering array of expensive yachts moored directly across the road. Farther along, the *livrarie* had its magazine stands out and the tourist boutiques were washing down their sidewalks prior to setting up their racks of chiffon scarves and bead necklaces, T-shirts and flip-flops.

The Sénéquier waiters in white shirts and black pants with the usual white apron wrapped around the waist, polished the zinc bar and wiped off tables in anticipation of the rush that was to come. Some took a quick break, edging out into the narrow side street where cars barely made it past, perching on a bit of crumbled sidewalk, snatching a fast cigarette.

Sunny and Mac chose to sit toward the back of the terrace where it joined the open-fronted café proper, arranging the red chairs and grouping three small café tables in readiness for the "meeting" of what Mac described as "a bunch of international misfits escaping from their real lives."

Tesoro settled on Sunny's lap blinking in the sunlight, while Pirate took a quick sniff of every chair then slunk under the table at Mac's feet. For a moment, perhaps because they were in foreign territory, there seemed to be a truce between the dogs.

Sunny wore white shorts and a red T-shirt, her long dark hair was tied back with a red silk scarf and there were large gold hoops in her ears.

"You belong in St. Tropez," Mac said admiring her and nuzzling her cheek. She smelled of some old-fashioned perfume, Mitsouko he remembered, spicy and sweet at the same time, and her skin was velvet under his lips.

"You look pretty good yourself," Sunny said, thinking that in fact Mac looked exactly like himself in his usual Malibu day attire of shorts, favorite old T-shirt—this one faded after many washings from black to gray—dark hair rumpled, blue eyes narrowed in appreciation. She twirled the pink diamond ring. "Don't forget you asked me to marry you."

"And *why* would I forget? Hey, maybe we could ask a captain on one of these fancy yachts to do the honors? That's legal, isn't it?"

"Only if you're at sea." Sunny knew all the facts about getting married.

She gazed at the yachts being scrubbed down solicitously by what she noticed were very able-bodied young crew members.

The white Bentley convertible screeched to a sudden halt in front of the café and Belinda leaned her blond head out. "Hi," she yelled.

Heads lifted from newspapers and croissants stopped halfway to mouths as the customers took a look.

"Hope we're not late. I'll find somewhere to park this and we'll be right with you."

With a casual wave of the hand, she made an illegal left turn, almost colliding with a car coming out of the narrow one-way street. She gave its driver the finger and Sunny caught a glimpse of Sara sitting bolt upright, eyes wide with terror as, with another nonchalant wave, Belinda swerved again, then sped off down the port, only this time, thank God, in the right direction.

The coffee arrived, steaming hot and darkly rich in thick white cups, along with a basket of croissants and a bowl of water for the dogs, just as the red Hummer sauntered slowly past with Billy still in his cowboy hat at the wheel, and Little Laureen, a blur of orange tulle beside him. After them came the yellow Ducati with Nate Masterson, stunning in skintight Tour de France yellow and black Lycra with a yellow-striped black helmet and large goggles.

"Exactly like a bumblebee," Mac said with a grin.

It was ten more minutes before all the Misfits finally straggled into the café, grumbling about the lack of parking space in St. Tropez.

"What do you care?" Sunny exclaimed. "Take a look at where you are. Look at the view, take in those multimillion-dollar boats, the port, the clear blue sky. Feel the sun warming you, smell the aroma of good French coffee, just taste these croissants . . ."

Belinda pulled back a red chair and plumped into it. "You should have been a poet, girl," she said to Sunny. Pulling off the small crusty bit at the end of croissant, she bit into it. "Mmmmm, heaven," she sighed. "Why could I never get a croissant like this when I had a private chef and a houseboy to serve me breakfast? I think I'm learning how to live again."

"That's not a bad idea." Nate took off his helmet and goggles, then put on a pair of large sunglasses, the kind that changed intensity depending on the light.

A cautious guy, Mac thought, watching him; the kind of man who thinks out his moves before making them. Unlike Belinda, who was impetuous and probably foolhardy, and was very likely in deep trouble with the dangerous Russian husband.

Little Laureen had taken the seat next to Sunny. She leaned over to pat Tesoro. Her father sat down next to her and Sara took the final red chair next to him.

Waiting till last, Mac observed of Sara: never quite sure of herself, always worried that she might not be welcome. He wondered if she had anything to say for herself now that the boyfriend affair was over. Or was she as dull as she seemed?

They had yet to see Billy without his hat. Mac thought it might be a disguise, it shaded Billy's eyes and hid the way he really looked, as well as his thoughts.

Billy called the waiter over. "Decaf everyone?" he asked.

"Oh for God's sake," Sunny said. "This is *France*. Have the real thing. Enjoy yourself."

"Y'think so?" Billy looked doubtful. "I mean, it'll be all right?"

"You can go back on the decaf when you get home," Belinda said. "Meanwhile, what's Little Laureen going to have?"

"Pancakes, please." Little Laureen spoke up. "I mean, *Crêpes, s'il vous plaît*," she said to the waiter, who smiled at the odd little girl in her ballet frock and princess tiara and promised to see what he could do.

Laureen carried her wand today. She placed it carefully on the table, smoothing it with stubby fingers. Sunny noticed her bitten nails. She felt sorry for her.

The coffee came quickly: cappuccino for Sara; triple espresso for Belinda; café crème for Nate and regular black for Billy. "Tastes better than the local brew," he admitted, drinking it down fast and signaling for a second cup. "Mind you, they're a bit short on quantity. I mean, why don't they give you a nice tall mug?"

"A Venti, like at Starbucks," Sara agreed, sipping the cappuccino and getting a milky mustache that she seemed unaware of.

The noisy *blah blah* of police sirens cut through the quiet morning, and Sara gave a panicked little shriek as three police cars, lights flashing, zoomed along the port.

"Cops," Billy said, seeming surprised to find them in St. Tropez.

"*Les flics,*" Little Laureen corrected him, smoothing her wand.

"*Mais la petite est correct.*" The waiter smiled benignly at her. "*Les flics—*the cops." He set the dish of crepes on the table. "*Eh bien, mademoiselle, vouz parlez bien français.*"

"*Merci, monsieur.*" Laureen stared doubtfully at the crepes. They were wafer thin and sprinkled with lemon juice and sugar. "Are these French pancakes?" she asked in English.

"*Mais, bien sûr, ma petite. Tu ne les aime pas?*" The waiter looked troubled.

"I'll try," Laureen conceded, though there was a worried crease between her brows. She missed the maple syrup.

"What's with the cops?" Belinda asked the waiter.

"Ah, *madame,* it's the robberies. Another took place night before last, the night of the big storm. It was not discovered until now, and this time there has been a murder."

Sunny could almost see Mac's ears perk up. "Oh, no," she groaned. "You promised!"

But Mac still couldn't resist asking the waiter where the crime had taken place and if he knew what had been stolen.

"It was in Ramatuelle, *monsieur.* And it's the same as before. Artworks. The expensive kind collectors like to spend their money on. There have been five robberies along the coast now, and all of them seem to have taken place when the owners were away."

"But surely they had excellent security?"

"*Mais bien sûr,* of course, but somehow the alarms seemed to be turned off and the staff away for the night. It is very suspicious I think."

"I think you're right," Mac agreed, with a grin. "You might even call it 'a pattern.'"

"None of our business," Sunny said firmly.

"*Les crêpes sont bonnes,*" Little Laureen said to the waiter.

Billy beamed proudly at her. "See, Little Laureen, after a month you'll be speaking like a native."

"And maybe after a month Mac can get us our money back from Madame Lariot," Belinda said, helping herself to a second croissant and thinking the hell with the diet. So what if she couldn't get into the new Chanel? She wasn't likely to be going anywhere fancy in the near future. She signaled the waiter for more coffee.

Mac leaned his elbows on the table, catching their eyes, letting them know this was business.

"Okay, so I went to see Madame Lariot yesterday. Of course she was no longer at that address."

"She'd flown the coop," Sunny butted in.

"As expected," Mac agreed, going on to tell them about the Office for Rent sign and the information the rental agent had given him.

"My assistant tracked down the address of the bank in Cannes. The account had been closed."

"Of course it had," Nate said impatiently, as though events were not going fast enough for him.

"A question," Mac said. "Are you all prepared to go to the police about this?"

"Are you out of your head?" Belinda dropped the croissant, shocked. "The Russian will find me in a minute if I go to the cops."

"He's hardly likely to miss you sitting in the Sénéquier in St. Tropez and driving that bloody great Bentley," Sunny said.

"True." Belinda sank back into the narrow red chair, worried. "But, hell, I can't hide all my life, can I? I mean, I've got to get on with things . . ."

"But no police?" Mac asked.

She shook her short-cropped blond head. "Definitely no police."

"What about you, Nate?"

Nate took off his refractive sunglasses. His eyes met Mac's. "I'd rather lose the money than go to the cops and deprive Mr. Private Investigator here of the chance to solve the crime."

Mac shrugged. Nate was obviously challenging him, but he merely said, "Then I'll do my best," noticing that Nate had turned to smile at Sunny. He guessed he had competition on his hands as well as a crime.

"And you, Billy?"

"I'm with the others. I'd rather lose the money than mess with French cops. *Les flics*," he added, giving his daughter's shoulder a conspiratorial squeeze. He said, "See honey, I caught on to the lingo."

Laureen blushed, her father embarrassed her. She had not finished her pancakes.

"So it's agreed we all go along with whatever Mac decides to do," Nate said.

"I'm just grateful you found the Hôtel des Rêves," Billy agreed.

"And maybe the hotel's name will turn out to be true." Sara spoke up for the first time, surprising them. Suddenly her eyes bugged even wider. "Oh, no!" she cried.

Sunny followed her gaze to the man already pushing his way through the tables. He was good-looking if you liked that sort of thing: the too-long black hair slicked back Euro-trash style; the extra-large sunglasses with the big D & G logo on the sides; the linen shirt half-unbuttoned to show his suntanned chest; the large gold watch; the white loafers; the faded jeans.

Belinda said, "I can tell the breed at thirty paces. The guy's a shit."

He stalked up to Sara and put a hand heavily on her shoulder.

"Bitch," he hissed. "I saw you, driving around in that white Bentley. Who the fuck d'you think you are? Humiliating me in front of everybody. Do you know I had to leave the ship, thrown off by the fuckin' captain . . . said he wouldn't tolerate that kind of behavior on his ship? Well fuck him, and fuck you, Sara. You're not gonna get away so easily, trust me. I'll get you for this, you skinny little bitch. It's the last time you'll do this to me. Get it? *The last time, Sara.* Next time you see me you'll wish you never had."

Mac got up. He removed the fiancé's hand from Sara's shoulder. "I heard that," he said. "And so did the others. We are what's known as 'witnesses,' my friend. And let me tell you the St. Tropez cops will not take kindly to men who threaten women."

"*Les flics,*" Little Laureen corrected him.

"Fuck off, all of you." The fiancé had a snarl on his swarthy face that Sunny thought was decidedly not attractive.

"Time for you to leave," Mac said. Billy got up, they each grabbed an elbow and marched the fiancé out of the café, watched delightedly by the waiters and the other customers.

Belinda saw the tears rolling down Sara's face. "Oh get over it, woman," she said, exasperated. "Don't you see he's not worth it. None of 'em are," she added, signaling the waiter for another triple espresso, her third this morning. She caught Sunny's amazed look and said, "How the hell else am I to get through the day?"

Sunny went and sat next to Sara. She offered her a Kleenex and said comfortingly, "Trust me, he's not worth a single tear."

"But I'm so humiliated," Sara wailed.

"How can you be?" Little Laureen said. "He curses. He's a nasty person."

Belinda smiled. "Out of the mouths of babes," she quoted, just as Mac and Billy returned.

"I doubt he'll be bothering you again, Sara," Mac said.

"No siree," Billy added with a smug grin.

Nate turned away, embarrassed by Sara's tears. "So? Is this meeting over?"

"Not quite," Mac said. "I found the Paris address for Chez La Violette's owner. Since there's a chance he's involved with Madame Lariot, I thought I'd go there, find out what's going on."

Sunny groaned, seeing her St. Tropez vacation disappearing, but then Mac said, "How'd you fancy a romantic night in Paris?" And this time she smiled.

"You're a trouper, dude," Billy said. "I for one surely appreciate it." He flashed Nate a meaningful glance.

Nate frowned but also said a grudging thanks.

"And you might as well use my plane," Billy added. "It's sitting right there now, at Nice airport. All I have to do is call my captain and tell him to prepare for takeoff to Paris, and to look after my friend."

Mac said, "Thanks, Billy. I really appreciate that."

"And I certainly appreciate what you're doing, Mac," Belinda added. She surveyed the table. "Meeting over?"

"Finis," Little Laureen, the French speaker, said.

"Then Sara and I have a little shopping to do," Belinda decided. "After all, a woman can't go round looking the way you do, Sara, and hope to attract the right sort of man, now can she?"

With an astonished look on her still tearstained face, Sara followed Belinda obediently out of the café, trailed by Nate, who headed for his Ducati with the intent of exploring the coast.

"What say we go back and hit the beach?" Billy said to Laureen.

She frowned. "Must we?"

"You betcha," her daddy said.

Watching them all walk away, Mac said wonderingly, "How did this happen to me? I came for a private little vacation alone with my woman and now I find myself in charge of four strangers who want me to find out who took their money and why."

"And also, while you're at it, find their souls for them," Sunny added, shrewdly.

Pirate, who always knew when it was time to go, emerged from under the table, tongue lolling, eye bright, ready for action, while Tesoro gave a sharp yelp, looking up at Sunny, who looked at Mac.

"How about that night in Paris?" he said.

"We're taking the dogs of course."

"Not this time, hon. We'll get someone at the hotel to look after them."

"But Tesoro . . ."

Mac gave her that familiar exasperated Tesoro-or-me look. "Come on, Sun, baby, we need to be alone. Just you and me in Paris."

"Oh, okay," Sunny said, already feeling guilty. But then she smiled. "Hey, the two of us. In Paris! How bad can that be?"

15.

Back in her hotel room Sunny stared at the pile of clothes she'd strewn across the bed. What, she wondered, did a girl wear to Paris on a warm June night? Answer: the little black dress of course. Plus if it was cool, the white silk jacket that fit snugly over it and tied prettily at the waist. And with, naturally, the new red-suede five-inch heels while praying she didn't fall over. Of course she could go with the three-inch Manolos but the new red were more funky, a little "gladiator" in style with straps that wrapped around the ankles. Definitely sexy.

And for daytime? Black pants, a white shirt, a jeans jacket, with of course, comfy black flats. And—how could she not? The cavernous new ice gray Alexander McQueen handbag that was almost big enough to hold her entire Paris wardrobe.

"All the better to shop with, Little Red Riding Hood," she told herself looking at the huge bag with a pleased grin, completely forgetting that this was not a pleasure trip and that they were going to spend most of their time searching out Chez La Violette's owner and on the trail of Madame Lariot.

With the thought of a beautiful hotel room complete with soft lighting, a little music and a view of the rooftops of Paris outside their open windows, she added a small pile of sexy underwear, then managed to tuck the lot into a regulation-size carry-on bag.

Pleased with herself she looked across at Mac who was still on the phone trying to find a hotel.

Mac glanced at the bed piled with her usual chaos. He shook his head. "Sonora Sky Coto de Alvarez!" he said, exasperated.

She held up a protesting hand. "No, no, wait . . . let me tell you I have *two whole outfits* in this *one* small bag . . ."

"What about the rest of the stuff on the bed?"

Sunny scooped some up and pushed them back in the armoire. "There." She grinned at him.

Mac sighed. Sunny never changed. Meanwhile, he was still on the phone, searching for a hotel. "Looks like every tourist in the world comes to Paris in June," he grumbled. "Every hotel is booked solid."

Sunny sank back onto the bed, the vision of her sexy night in Paris fast disappearing. Still, the alternative was pretty good. "We can always go to the beach instead." She unzipped her bag. "I'll get my bathing suit."

Mac shook his head again. "We have to track down the villa's owner. I'm convinced he has something to do with the scam. We'll just get to Paris then see if we can find a hotel."

Sunny gave him a don't-do-this-to-me look. She said, "Give me the phone." Dialing information, she asked for the number of the Paris Ritz. When she was put through, she asked to speak to the manager.

"Tell him it's a friend of Allie Ray calling," she said. "My name is Sunny Alvarez."

She winked at Mac. Allie Ray was a world-famous movie star and a name to be conjured with. Plus Allie Ray *was* Sunny's friend. In fact she and Mac had saved Allie's life. Sunny knew Allie would welcome them using her name.

"Madame Alvarez, how can I be of help?" The manager came on the phone.

With a smile in her voice, Sunny charmingly explained her predicament. "I'm here in France to see Allie," she said. "I know how upset she would be if I couldn't find a room at the Ritz."

"But *madame,* of course there is a room for you. The Ritz will welcome you as one of its own. And please, give my best regards to Miss Ray. Tell her we look forward to hosting her here at the Ritz next time she is in Paris."

There was a smug pleased-with-herself look on Sunny's face this time as she gave Mac back the phone.

"Name-dropper," he said.

She gave a little shrug. "What's the use of knowing names if you can't drop 'em?"

He was laughing as he threw an arm around her shoulders and wrestled her backward on top of a pile of clothes. "I'd make love to you if we didn't have a plane waiting," he said.

Sunny put her hands on either side of his face, smiling up at him. She rubbed her nose against his, then put her lips over his. "Let it wait," she murmured, sliding down beneath him.

16.

Bertrand's room was marginally larger than Laureen's but it looked quite different. A folding table set up under the window held an old laptop computer as well as a small radio-CD player that blinked the time in luminous green numbers. A little pile of clean clothes had been left by the maid on the chair a few days ago and would stay there until they were used up, to be replaced by a fresh set, because Bertrand couldn't be bothered with cupboards and drawers. He did keep a few bits in the old pine armoire though, not because he was tidy but because they hid his late-night attire: the camouflage cape and the old binoculars.

He was sitting in front of the computer, pecking at it two-fingered style, inputting information he considered important, like the events that had taken place at Chez La Violette the other night, and the strange people who had arrived in the middle of the storm.

"Riders on the storm . . ." Jim Morrison's low voice seemed almost to whisper from the tiny CD player. The music swooped around the tiny room. "Riders on the storm . . ."

Bertrand was wearing only a pair of his usual oversize shorts held up with the worn striped-silk tie that had been his father's. Bertrand didn't remember ever seeing his father, though his mother had told him that he was exactly one year old when the father left them.

One was too young to remember much, wasn't it? Bertrand had asked. But his mother had replied it was a pity the father hadn't left sooner then Bertrand would not have had to worry about remembering him at all, and nor would she.

Bertrand had found the tie at the bottom of a cupboard. He had put it in the drawer where he kept a small cardboard box with holes punctured in the top and two green caterpillars that he fed with nasturtium leaves picked in the park near where he lived, in St. Cloud, just outside of Paris.

Eventually, the caterpillars died, and for a long time Bertrand didn't even look at the tie. Until one day he couldn't find his belt and since his shorts were falling down because he was so skinny, he used the tie instead. To his mother's chagrin, he had worn it ever since.

Outside his window the sun blazed down, filtering through the leaves of the trees in the courtyard into his room. The hotel was quiet and he knew everyone must be either at the pool or on the beach. Bertrand never did that. His body was alabaster white and he might have been living in Siberia for all the sun he got.

His long hair, blond and lank, slid into his eyes. Irritated, he got up, went to the bathroom, took a pair of scissors and lopped jaggedly across his forehead. He stared at the result in the mirror. He shrugged. At least it wouldn't get in his eyes anymore. Adjusting the pale plastic glasses with their thick lenses, he went back to his work. Then he heard something.

He sat up straight in the chair. He looked behind him. He listened. There it was again.

In the crack beneath the door he saw a small black nose. Astonished, he flung the door open. A scraggy gray-brown, three-legged, one-eyed dog sat back on its haunch and gave him a grin. Bertrand had never seen a dog that could smile. Nor had he ever seen a dog with only three legs. And only one eye. Nor a dog this ugly. He felt an instant kinship.

The dog trotted past him, leapt onto the bed and lay down amid the tangled sheets. It sat there, panting slightly, then it put its nose between its paws, looking as though it meant to take a nap.

"Pirate? Pirate? Where are you?"

A woman's voice came from down the corridor. Still standing by the open door Bertrand thought quickly. He was in a dilemma. He couldn't just close the door and shut the dog in. And he couldn't ask the woman to come into his room to get the dog.

"Oh, hello." She was standing by the open door. "You haven't by any chance seen a dog have you? A three-legged dog?"

It was the woman from Chez La Violette! The one he'd thought was a prisoner, but later had decided she was there for some important secret meeting.

"Le chien est ici, madame," he admitted reluctantly.

Peeking in, Sunny saw Pirate on the rumpled bed. "Oh, I'm so sorry." She rushed in and grabbed the dog. "I apologize for Pirate."

She stopped and took a proper look at Bertrand, all bones and glasses topped with a mop of blond hair that looked as though it had been cut with a blunt lawn mower.

"Hi, I'm Sunny." She offered him her hand.

Bertrand glanced suspiciously at her from behind the glasses. He didn't speak to anyone if he could help it but now he had no choice.

"Bertrand Olivier." He took her hand and made a formal little bow over it.

Sunny had never met a kid that bowed. "Hey," she said, sympathetically because the boy was obviously so nervous. "Are you staying at the hotel with your family?"

"With my mother," Bertrand said stiffly. He did not want to explain that his mother had left him there and that no one knew where she was. She had called him once. She was in Italy, she'd said. But now he was panicked because he knew the hotel bill had not been paid. What if she didn't come back? Would they put him in jail? But this was not this woman's business.

"Pirate likes you," Sunny said. Then with sudden inspiration and because she felt the boy's loneliness, she said, "Tell you what, my fiancé and I have to go to Paris for a couple of days. We're leaving Pirate here. We've asked the staff to look after him, they have a sort of a kennel in the back, but because Pirate likes you—I mean, he *chose* you, came to your door right?"

"Right," Bertrand said, still wary.

"I thought you might like to take him for walks."

Sunny looked hopefully at him. Everyone knew small boys and dogs were meant to be together. "The staff will be responsible, though," she added, because after all, he was just a kid.

"I understand," Bertrand said. "I will be happy to take Pirate for walks."

Secretly, he was thrilled, already thinking ahead to nighttime when he and his new dog would prowl the world together. "If Pirate likes, he can sleep on my bed," he added generously.

Sunny beamed, still a bit worried, because the boy was kind of odd. "That's good then," she said in French. "Just ask the manager for Pirate. Any time. Okay?"

"Okay." Bertrand watched her and the dog walk back down the corridor, then he closed the door and returned to his computer.

When Sunny got back to their room, she found Mac flinging a few things into his duffel, watched nervously by Tesoro.

"I just met this strange boy," she said. "Pirate was curled up on his bed as though he belonged. His name is Bertrand Olivier. I told him we were going away and said if he liked he could take Pirate for walks."

"Okay," Mac said.

There was a knock at the door. Mac went to open it. Little Laureen stood there, still in the orange tutu of the day.

"Oh, hi, Little Laureen." Sunny smiled, surprised.

"Hi." Laureen stared down at her feet in their scuffed ballet slippers. "I know you're going to Paris," she said, "and I wonder if you would please let me look after Tesoro." She looked up, her usually blank eyes beseeching. "She could sleep on my bed," she added quickly.

"Why, Laureen, I think that's a wonderful idea," Sunny said. "Don't you, Mac?"

"Oh, sure," Mac said, sounding doubtful.

"Now I know I won't need to worry about Tesoro," Sunny said, hoping once again she was doing the right thing. "And I know she likes you, Laureen, because I saw she let you stroke her."

"She knows I will look after her," Laureen said solemnly. Then with a brief wave of her hand and a lingering look at the small dog, she flitted back up the corridor to her own room.

"I thought Billy and daughter were going to the beach," Mac said, watching her go.

"Somehow I don't think Little Laureen is quite ready for the beaches of St. Tropez yet," Sunny said thoughtfully. "Let's hope Tesoro will help bring her out of herself a bit."

Mac sighed. Personally, he wasn't too optimistic about Tesoro's magical abilities with people.

17.

Sara Strange sat, shoulders drooping, on the edge of her bed gazing at the heap of shopping bags with names like Blanc Bleu, Cavalli, Erès, Sergio Rossi; names she had only ever seen in magazines. Belinda was taking a shower: "washing off all that fitting room sweat" was the way she had put it. She had told Sara they were going to the beach and that she was to wear the new Erès bikini.

"I've never worn a bikini before," Sara had protested in the store when Belinda had forced her into the dressing room with half a dozen tiny garments to try on.

But Belinda had only laughed. "Aw, come on, even in Kansas they must wear bikinis," she'd said. And then, when Sara was still struggling into the lavender-striped one, Belinda had peeked in and said, "Sara Strange where have you been hiding that body! The boyfriend definitely did not deserve it, you've been giving it away as a gift, girl."

Blushing, Sara had said she didn't feel comfortable in the suit but Belinda had summoned the saleswoman and said they would take these two, plus the turquoise caftan and the white pareo.

"Belinda, I can't afford them," Sara had wailed. "And I can't let you pay. Really, I just can't . . ."

"*I* am not paying. *The husband* is. And since he's about on par with the boyfriend, we're a team. Right, Sara Strange?"

Belinda had high-fived her. Sara wasn't quite certain how high-fiving worked and she'd been a bit clumsy about it, making Belinda laugh some more.

They'd bought shoes in Sergio Rossi and Belinda had kindly allowed

Sara to get the wedge heels instead of stilettos. They were toweringly high but at least she had a chance of being able to walk in them. And nothing sensible like black. These were apple green, kind of a snakeskin, and they tied in pretty bows round Sara's ankles that Belinda said were certainly skinny enough to be able to wear them.

They had "picked up" (Belinda's term for "bought") a little Cavalli silk dress with ruffled puffy sleeves—"to hide your twiggy arms, m'dear"—and a sort of cardigan wrap in silk that draped at the front to go with it, and all the color of fresh apricots.

"Shouldn't we get green to match the shoes?" Sara had asked but Belinda had said firmly, "No 'matchy-matchy.'"

By then Sara was getting a teeny bit fed up with what Belinda said, and was wishing, like Dorothy in *The Wizard of Oz*, that she was back in Kansas. But then Judy Garland wouldn't have been traipsing every morning to a safe job at the hospital where she worked as head of admissions in the surgical center, stopping off first for her daily Starbucks—or at least she had until last year when she'd begun to save for the cruise. And now that she thought about it, why had her boyfriend *not* had to save for that cruise?

In fact, he had not seemed bothered by the cost at all. And he had not even bought her an engagement ring, simply told her they would get it when they could afford it. Oh, yeah, like when? Sara thought now.

In fact she was also wondering why Mr. Handsome-Smoothie-Charmer-Womanizer had bothered with her at all. Except of course, he had lived for free in her small one-bedroom apartment for a year, while he traveled "on business." And "To save money to buy a house when we get married," he'd said.

Now Sara was asking herself why women always found out too late that they were being used. In fact she'd seen less and less of the fiancé—all that "business" traveling—as the year progressed, and if she had not personally booked and paid for the cruise (he'd promised to repay her), she knew now he would not have gone with her.

"Fool!" she said out loud, agonized. "You fucking little fool."

She had never in her life used the F-word before and she stopped, shocked.

"Did I just hear you say *fuck*?" Belinda stood at the bathroom door clad in a white bikini that was, Sara thought, even smaller than her own.

Belinda laughed and said, "Well, I guess that's what's known as progress." She checked Sara. "We should have picked up a pair of beach sandals for you."

"I have my flip-flops."

"I'll bet you do, and all the way from Rexall drugstore for two dollars and change. Lucky for you they're fashionable right now. Okay, so come on, get ready. We're off to the beach."

Reluctantly, Sara picked up the two bikinis.

"The stripy one," Belinda decided.

It was the one with the smallest triangle of a top, and Sara shuffled the thin fabric through her fingers, looking miserable.

"Don't worry, you'll be taking the top off anyway," Belinda said.

With a shocked gasp, Sara retreated into the bathroom. She closed the door firmly behind her. She was *not* taking off her top. *Never. Not in this world.* Her mother would *kill* her. No! She would wear the turquoise caftan over the bikini and her big straw hat and pray that no one would so much as even look at her.

When Sara finally emerged, Belinda was waiting, tapping her gold-sandaled foot impatiently.

"Jesus, I thought you were getting ready for a ball." Her sharp blue eyes appraised Sara, head to toe. "Pretty good," she decided, nodding. "In fact a definite improvement. Right?"

"Right," Sara admitted, though she still didn't quite believe it.

"Well then, let's go. We'll have a late lunch at the beach. We'll toast the husband in St. Tropez rosé. Or maybe champagne?" Belinda thought about it. "No, champagne can sometimes give you a headache in the sun. Rosé it is. After all," she added, beaming at Sara and linking arms with her, "the old bugger's paying for it, isn't he?"

18.

Billy, hat still rammed over his eyes, was propping up the bar at Le Club 55, usually known as Le Cinquante-cinq.

"Another beer, Texas?" The barman held up a second bottle of Kronenbourg.

"Why not?" Billy agreed, smiling his big friendly smile.

It was impossible not to like Billy Bashford. He was so outgoing and easy and so curious to know about this, to him, new country and its people. He marveled at the crowded tables, shaded under swags of white canvas propped up by leafy tamarisk trees whose leaves fluttered in the gentle sea breeze. He was amazed that it was heading up to three o'clock and all these folks were still eating lunch and drinking wine like it was twelve noon. Hell, back home, they woulda been finished by twelve-thirty max. A quick sandwich, a beer and back to work.

Of course they were probably on vacation and slept real late, but Billy had had nothin' since that coffee and croissant at somewhere round eight that morning and boy, was his belly rumblin'.

"Think I could get me a table?" he asked the barkeep, who nodded and summoned the maître d', who in any case turned out to be the owner, and who said, Five minutes, Monsieur Texas, and you shall have your table.

That was okay with Billy. Or least it was until he spotted Belinda Lord making a grand entrance, trailed by the Strange girl hiding under a straw hat that was almost as big as his own. Sara looked different. She was wearing something pretty, though her twiggy arms and legs still made her look like the eternal waif, while Belinda had a white bikini under her gauzy see-through caftan and it didn't take a connoisseur to know she had a great body. In fact Billy had never seen a woman quite like Belinda: gleaming, tanned, smooth as silk. Sure they had great-looking women in Dallas, not that he got there often because despite his wealth somehow he and Betsy had never moved in that glossy society league.

"Down-home folk" is what we are, Betsy had always said, and it was the truth. For Billy there was no place quite like his home, though sadly, with Betsy gone, it was not like "home" anymore. Now, its heartbeat was missing.

"Well, well, Billy Bashford." Belinda slid onto the barstool next to him. Leaning toward him she deposited a quick kiss first on one cheek, then the other, then back again. "For your information, Billy, that's a true 'French kiss,'" she said with that grin that lit her face like a lamp on a dark night.

Blushing, Billy got quickly to his feet and offered Sara his seat. He was nervous around Belinda.

"No, no, please." Sara hung back and Belinda said impatiently, "Oh for Christ's sake, Sara, you're like that ladies' companion in the old movie *Rebecca*, before she married Laurence Olivier and became Mrs. de Winter. You have to stop it. When a man offers you his seat you take it." She thought for a moment then added, "Unless he's a complete stranger of course, then you'd have to suss him out first. No more trash, right?"

Sara slid meekly onto the barstool, still warm from Billy's ample behind. "Thank you," she said to Billy.

"You're welcome, Sara. Now, what can I get you ladies? A martini? Champagne?"

"Let's order the Château Minuty rosé," Belinda said. "It's always good. And since we're about to have lunch, why don't you join us, Billy?"

He beamed at her, delighted. "Well, thank you, I would be pleased to join you," he said formally. "But lunch is on me."

"No it's not. It's on the husband." Belinda's voice was crisp and cold at the edges. "I'm spending as much of his money as I can while I still have the opportunity. After that I'll have to go to court to get any and believe me, it will not be easy. That bastard will threaten me, he'll scare the hell out of me, and probably try to kill me. But damn it, I've paid my dues, I'll get him where it hurts most."

Sara's brown eyes bugged with shock. "Belinda, he won't really try to kill you? I mean not *really* . . . ?"

"Oh yes he will. Of course I won't allow him to succeed, but I'm gonna have to watch my back, as you Texans say." She gave Billy a little nudge in the ribs.

He grinned back at her, perplexed. "I don't think we're about to let that happen to you, ma'am," he said solemnly. "Not with Mac Reilly and myself around, we're not."

"Plus Nate Masterson," Sara said, spotting him in the crowd.

"Oh my God, and in his bumblebee outfit." Belinda laughed, watching Nate who was standing on the wooden boardwalk at the tree-lined entrance. He still had on his helmet though now with the goggles pushed up, and was wearing the tight yellow and black Lycra bicycle-rider shorts and shirt that gripped his body like a second skin. She had to admit though it did offer a girl a rather tempting glimpse of what lay beneath: hard and muscular and in fact very attractive.

"Nate!" Billy yelled to him and heads turned to stare. "Over here, Nate." Billy walked over to meet him. "Come join us for lunch. We're about to try a bottle of that South of France rosé everybody talks about."

"I tried it yesterday. I can recommend it." Nate took off his helmet and goggles and put on his horn-rimmed glasses.

Belinda thought that now his top half looked like a New York businessman on holiday and his bottom half like a competitor in the Tour de France.

"Hey," she said, that mischievous grin flashing again. "Why not join us, Nate? Then we can talk about everybody else."

"There's nobody else to talk about, we're all here," Sara said. Then realizing who was missing, "Oh, but Billy, where is Little Laureen?"

"My girl decided she didn't want to come to the beach. I got the whole darn works ready for her." He waved a hand at the golden sand beyond the restaurant where tiny waves lapped at the shore and tanned bodies reclined on beach mattresses, attended by young men in white shorts, who brought them drinks and set up lunch so they never even had to move.

"But my baby doesn't want to be here. She wants to stay in her room. Or down in the lounge, watching French cartoons, or maybe doing a jigsaw puzzle and hoping, I believe, to take that little Chihuahua for a walk. I asked, 'Laureen, will you be okay on your own?' And she said, '*Daddeee,*' the way she always does when she gets pissed off at her father. So I made her promise not to leave the grounds and not to go swimming in the pool alone. And not to go down to the beach either, not without me along." Billy shrugged. "What more can a daddy do, I ask ya?"

"Not much," Belinda agreed. "Besides, you need a little grown-up time, on your own. And Laureen needs a little downtime from you, Big Daddy."

Billy managed a grin but his thoughts were still on Laureen. Pulling himself together, he said, "So what d'ya say, Nate? A couple of bottles of that nice rosé to start?"

"Why not," Nate agreed, as the waiter came to show them to a table at the edge of the beach, where the waves plopped softly and the sun tickled its way through the mesquite trees.

Belinda, who knew what was what around here, ordered the crudités platter for them all. When it came it proved to be an entire perfect cauliflower with whole tiny carrots and red peppers and little tomatoes and cucumbers; in fact all kinds of superfresh veggies, picked that very morning.

Nate, sophisticated New Yorker that he was, had expected to see the vegetables already cut into strips and florets, but at Cinquante-cinq you broke off bits of the crisp cauliflower yourself then dunked them in the freshly made aioli mayonnaise. And you spread your still-warm bread with butter so good that when it hit the crust it melted into a sweet creaminess.

The cold Minuty rosé slid down almost too easily and even Sara was on her second glass before she realized it. A further bottle was ordered, along with striped sea bass grilled to perfection and with a subtle perfume of fennel about it.

"You know what?" Sara said, and Nate noticed that her cheeks were flushed and her eyes sparkled. "We're all having fun," she said surprised.

"Thanks to Chez La Violette," Billy said.

Belinda raised her glass in a toast. "To Madame Lariot, without whom we might never have met."

"To Madame Lariot," they echoed, pleased with themselves.

Two hours or so later, Belinda gathered up her bag and Sara. Heading for the beach, she declared, "I always feel good about closing a joint. Come on. We've gotta sleep off that wine."

Belinda took off her caftan but kept on her top. Sara kept everything on. The four sat in a silent row on their mattresses, staring out at the sea, marveling at its different hues, from cobalt to turquoise, from sky to aquamarine to crystal.

"I wonder." Nate broke the silence. "How Sunny and Mac are getting on in Paris."

19.

Paris on a still June night was everything Sunny had imagined. The trees were in bloom, the Eiffel Tower glittered in the distance and the cafés were crowded. Unfortunately Mac had said there was no time to be wasted and she'd barely had a minute to check into the Ritz and check out the room, all swagged yellow silk and Louis-the-something furniture, plus check out the famous Bar Hemingway.

"Not even a quick glass of champagne?" she asked plaintively.

"There's no such thing as a 'quick' glass of champagne," Mac said. "At least give yourself time to enjoy it."

"I will if you will?" she said, but her hopes were dashed when Mac asked the doorman for a taxi, which came far too promptly.

And now Mac wasn't even looking at her, nor at Paris, which was flying past the taxi window like a dream sequence in a movie. He was on the phone with Roddy, his assistant, in Malibu.

Roddy was on the deck at Mac's Malibu house. He said to Mac, "You wouldn't believe how great it is out here today."

"Yeah. I would."

"Only ten in the morning," Roddy went on, "and already seventy-five degrees. The surfers are out there riding the waves and no doubt wishing they were bigger, and by the way your windows need washing again."

Mac sighed. At the beach, the windows always needed washing. Roddy was in his thirties, slim, compactly built, bleached blond and gay. And he could talk the hind leg off a donkey. "Get on with it, Roddy," he said.

He could sense the grin on Roddy's face as he said, "Just wanted to make you jealous . . ."

"Did you forget? I'm in Paris?"

"That's *why* I wanted to make you jealous. Hey, next time you head off to Europe you'll need your assistant. Right?"

"For God's sake, tell me what's up."

"What's up is Mr. Krendler is rich. As in *really* rich. The address I gave you is in one of the best *quartiers* of Paris, the Champs de Mars. Full, so I've heard of BCBGs—"

"What the hell are BCBTs and why do they matter to me?"

"*Bon Chic Bon Ton,* or in other words, rich well-brought-up yuppies with ancient family credentials."

"And Krendler?"

"A mystery. Big house but rarely seen out in public, except for visits to the opera. He's by way of being a fan, and also a big contributor to their fundraising, though he never attends their functions. Nor does he accept kudos for his good work."

"Hmm." Mac didn't like the sound of that. "Then he's either a born-again angel or he's hiding something."

"Like what?" Roddy said.

"That's what I'm about to find out. I'll call you later."

Mac rang off. He glanced at Sunny, who was staring eagerly out of the window. She had lived in Paris for a short while, years ago, and now it was all coming back to her. Her face was alight with pleasure, and Mac's heart melted all over again, as it had a thousand times since he'd met her.

"There's this little place I've heard of," he said, taking her hand. "Le Comptoir du Relais in St. Germain. It's *the* hot dinner spot and not easy to get into, but I had the concierge get us a reservation."

"Clever boy." Sunny snuggled her head into his shoulder.

The cab was pulling up in front of a tall imposing house overlooking a leafy square.

"Posh," Sunny said, admiring the slate blue mansard roof with its protruding top-floor windows shading what she told Mac no doubt had once been the servants' attics.

"And maybe still are," she added thoughtfully as he rang the bell. The door was opened promptly by a manservant in an immaculate white jacket and white gloves. Mac thought that even in the grander bits of Malibu you'd be hard-pressed to find menservants in white gloves.

"Mr. Reilly and Ms. Alvarez for Mr. Krendler," he said. "He's expecting us."

"Certainly, sir. Would you please come this way."

They followed the English butler through a lofty hall whose grand onyx staircase curved four stories upward to a trompe l'oeil ceiling with painted cherubs in a cloud-wisped blue sky.

"A bit over the top," Mac muttered. "Couldn't fancy that over our bed in Malibu."

Sunny was thrilled to hear him refer to his bed as "our bed." Hope sprang eternal.

The butler led them into a salon of gilded splendor. The walls were paneled in what the French called *boiserie,* a painted wood, in this case, an icy shade of pale green picked out in gold. Sunny remembered that the walls of Violette's boudoir were similarly paneled. It must be a French thing. And she would bet those huge chandeliers were Baccarat. The furniture looked flimsy and uncomfortable, in the period of Louis XVl, and heavy dark green silk curtains almost covered the windows leaving the big room in a kind of twilight.

"*Monsieur, madame,* please take a seat." The butler did not even crack a welcoming smile. "Monsieur Krendler will be with you shortly. Meanwhile may I offer you some refreshment? Tea, coffee, something to drink?"

"Tea would be wonderful," Sunny said, deciding on an impulse to test him, see how long it would take Mr. Superior English Butler to get her a cup of tea.

"And *monsieur?*"

Mac shook his head. "Nothing thanks."

Sunny perched on the very edge of a stiff pale green brocade sofa. In her little black dress and sexy red heels with her long glossy hair pulled into a sleek chignon, back straight, knees properly together, she was trying to live up to her surroundings.

Mac said, "You look like a Victorian schoolmarm."

"And this room is like an opera set."

Silver-framed photographs were dotted on a black concert grand piano. Sunny recognized Maria Callas with a pout in her eyes and on her large mouth. "To Joel Krendler, with gratitude," Callas had signed it. Of course there was Pavarotti and others Sunny didn't know, but who no doubt were famous because it didn't look as though Mr. Krendler knew anybody in the opera world who was not famous. Oddly, a life-size bronze of a greyhound stood in front of the ornate green-marble fireplace, above which was a grim oil painting of a murdered stag in what looked like the Scottish Highlands.

There was a tap on the door and a white-uniformed maid entered bearing a galleried silver tray complete with a delicate Limoges tea service: paper-thin pale green cup, matching teapot, creamer and sugar bowl. A tiny fleur-de-lys silver spoon tinkled prettily against the china as she set the tray in front of Sunny.

"Madame," she said, poker-faced.

Sunny said thank you and watched her walk quickly away.

"Nobody smiles around here," she whispered to Mac.

"Perhaps because they're afraid of their employer."

"Still, full marks for service," Sunny added. "That took exactly four minutes."

Mac looked at his watch. "And Mr. Krendler has now kept us waiting exactly nine minutes."

In fact Mr. Krendler kept them waiting exactly twenty-five minutes before the tall double doors were flung open by the butler.

Mac concealed his surprise. Krendler was in a wheelchair. No wonder he rarely went to functions and was almost never seen out and about.

Krendler was sixtyish, a handsome bull of a man who even in his wheelchair emanated that sense of power that meant nothing was closed to him. Mac knew this was a man who could have—and probably had—anything he ever wanted. Immaculate in a navy pin-striped suit, white shirt and dark green tie, he had still a touch of the athlete about him, and with his lion's mane of silver hair, his pale skin, piercing dark eyes, prominent nose and cold stare, he could have easily taken on the role of Don José, the brutal soldier in the opera *Carmen.*

Krendler ignored Sunny, sitting with her cup of tea on the pale green sofa and looking in fact, with her black hair and luminous amber eyes, as though she could have played the role of Carmen opposite him.

Instead he looked at Mac. "Mr. Reilly."

He spoke in a low voice with a slightly sibilant accent. He was not French, Mac decided at once.

"May I introduce Ms. Alvarez." Mac was not allowing Krendler to get away with such discourtesy.

Krendler inclined his head slightly toward her, but his eyes remained on Mac.

"I've watched your TV shows," he said. "We get them here, in France, you know. I found them very entertaining. Very astute. I think you are a clever man, Mr. Reilly."

"Thank you, sir," Mac said. "But anyway, the show is meant to be entertainment."

Krendler nodded. "I understand what is meant by 'entertainment,' though personally I'm more interested in the arts."

Sunny took a sip of her tea. The spoon rattled in the silence and she hastily put it back on the tray. She'd bet nobody in this house ever disturbed the master.

Krendler's full attention was on Mac and she took the opportunity to have a closer look at him. There was something odd about him, though it was hard to tell exactly what in the semidarkened room. She peered closer. Could it be? She glanced at Mac, wondering if he had noticed.

Krendler maneuvered his chair closer to Mac, indicating he should take the chair next to him.

"You are here only because of your show, Mr. Reilly," he said. "Normally, I do not entertain people I don't already know, nor do I encourage publicity."

"Then I thank you for taking the time, sir." Mac decided to get quickly to the point. "I'm here to talk about Chez La Violette."

"That old bugbear." There was almost a groan in Krendler's deep voice. "I knew one day it would come back to haunt me."

Sunny spoke up, surprising herself. "*Haunt* is an odd word to choose for Chez La Violette."

For the first time, Krendler looked at her. He seemed to appreciate what he saw because he said, "It was originally owned by a woman as beautiful as yourself, Ms. Alvarez."

Sunny was surprised he had even remembered her name, he'd ignored her so completely. She felt herself turning pink. Damn, she never blushed. This man was unnerving her.

"Thank you." She put her pretty Limoges cup back on the galleried silver tray, managing to spill its contents. She stared anguished at the tea, dripping all over the place.

Krendler said to Mac, "Would you please push that bell by the fireplace? Edwards will take care of the mess."

Mac pressed the bell and gave Sunny an encouraging brows-up grin. The butler was there in a second which made Mac wonder if he'd been listening at the door.

"Why did you say you knew Chez La Violette would come back to haunt you?" he asked.

Krendler's fingers drummed the arms of his wheelchair as he thought about the question. "I bought Chez La Violette ten years ago," he said finally. "Immediately before the accident. After which I became confined to this wheelchair. I knew the villa was in bad shape but the location was charming, there were plenty of rooms and the grounds were perfect for entertaining. Almost as soon as I bought it part of the roof collapsed and had to be replaced. The chimneys were found to be out of line and needed restructuring. The walls were cracking. It had taken me four years to battle through France's Napoleonic Code to get full title to the property and now it was falling around my ears."

He looked at Mac. "You understand the Napoleonic Code? Where a property by French law is left not simply to one person, but to an entire family, maybe even to generations of a family. Each one has a share and each one has to be tracked down and persuaded to part with his share in order to make a whole title."

His dominating dark eyes met Mac's again. "Not an easy task, I can assure you. And now you come to me with more troubles?"

Mac told him exactly what the trouble was.

Krendler listened, then said, "I lost interest in Chez La Violette. I've not seen it since I completed the purchase. To tell you the truth I wanted to put it out of my mind because it seemed from the day I bought it, everything in my life went wrong. Chez La Violette became a kind of jinx, you might say."

"Then why not sell it?" Sunny asked the logical question.

"Simply put, my dear Ms. Alvarez"—Krendler's voice was smooth as silk as he gave his full attention to her for the first time—"simply put, it's because I was afraid even to think about it in case something else went wrong. Isn't there an old English saying . . . 'Better to let sleeping dogs lie'? That is exactly the way I feel about Chez La Violette."

"And what about the ghost of Violette?"

Krendler's dismissive half smile put Sunny in her place as a silly fanciful woman. "I find people will believe exactly what they want to believe," he said.

He turned to Mac. "As for the rental scam you're involved in, all I can tell you is that I know nothing about it. That problem is for you to solve, Mr. Reilly." He gave him that hard penetrating stare again. "After all," he said, smoothly, "that's your job, is it not?"

Mac gave Sunny a quick sideways glance that she knew meant let's get out of here. She got to her feet, smoothing down the skirt of her little black dress. She was glad she had worn the kinky red suede gladiator sandals with the towering heels that made her legs look great. Give this hard old bastard something to stare at, which she knew he was doing from under hooded eyelids.

"Thank you for taking the time to see us," Mac said, taking a final glance around the elaborate, yet cold, room. It felt like a room that had never been lived in.

This time Krendler rang the bell for the butler. "Good luck with your detecting, Mr. Reilly," he said, and they both caught the mocking tone of his voice.

He did not offer to shake their hands, but Sunny could feel his eyes on her as she walked out.

"Don't like him," she said, relieved as the big front door closed behind them.

"Whatever makes you say that?" Mac said and they both laughed.

It was a perfect night. The trees in the square whispered in the breeze and darkness settled like a velvet blanket over the beautiful city.

Arms round each other's waists, they flagged down a taxi, kissing some more as it sped toward their dinner destination.

"*I* know something about Mr. Joel Krendler," Sunny said at Le Comptoir over a welcome glass of Ruinart champagne. "He was wearing makeup. Pale foundation, the thick stage kind, and even"—she paused, glass half-raised to her lips—"even *eye shadow! purple!*"

"Now I wonder," Mac said thoughtfully, "why he would do that."

20.

Le Comptoir was casually modern, with a few tables spilling onto a small terrace and a well-known chef who promised a more daring take on the usual bistro fare. Sunny liked it. "No fuss," she said. "No excess, no black-framed Paris photos. And the champagne's good."

But Mac's mind was still on Krendler. "Did you notice anything peculiar about that house?"

Sunny dredged quickly through her memory of the ice green room. "Was I supposed to?"

"Krendler had bad art on his walls. Like those copies of Chinese mandarins you can buy in Hong Kong's Stanley Market for a few bucks."

"I like those."

"There's no accounting for taste."

"What else?" She took another sip of the Ruinart, liking it even more on the second taste, and glancing at the neighboring tables filled with attractive well-dressed people, into their own conversations and the food.

Mac said, "You'd expect a Monet or two, or a Damien Hirst, not that dim Victorian Scottish landscape over the fireplace, complete with the dead deer, and a few modern 'daubs.'"

Sunny shuddered prettily.

"And how about that life-size bronze of the greyhound?"

"Probably in memory of his dog," she said, all sympathy.

"The guy's either a cheapskate or a fraud. You tell me which." Mac stared expectantly at her.

"Er . . . well . . . hum . . . it's like this . . . Truthfully, I don't know."

"And nor do I."

Sunny breathed again. "Oh, thank God. For a minute there I thought you expected me to solve the mystery of Mr. Krendler."

"Why do you think he's a mystery?"

"Jesus!" Sunny glared this time. "You're the detective, not me."

Their eyes met, his thoughtful, hers irritated. Then he laughed. "Sorry, babe. But that's a very expensive house in a very pricey bit of Paris, with a butler and a maid, and who knows what else."

"Perhaps the man simply has no taste," Sunny said, helpfully. "Y'know, maybe he's just an opera buff. You saw all those signed photos of celebs."

Mac's brows furrowed again as he tasted the Sancerre he'd ordered. He accepted it with a mere thank-you to the waiter, instead of with his usual discriminating comments. Mac was a serious wine buff; he was here in Paris drinking French wine and he wasn't even noticing it. Sunny knew something was definitely up.

"To Violette, who brought us together in France." She lifted her glass eliciting a smile from Mac, and took a sip of the flinty-edged white wine. "A very good choice, *Monsieur* Reilly, TV Private Investigator extraordinaire."

Mac gave her a keen glance. "So how do you think Krendler *really* knew about my show?"

Sunny heaved a sigh. He wasn't about to leave this alone. "Why not exactly the way he said? Anyway, how else could he have known?"

"Google."

"But why?"

"He wanted to know what he was in for if we met. Was the TV detective going to interrogate him about Chez La Violette and his connection with the rental scam?"

"Of course you were. But now we know he's too rich to bother with a minor financial fraud like that."

Mac thought for a bit then said, "Did he really think we wouldn't notice the eye shadow?"

"Probably. That room was a sort of twilight zone, I could barely see him. But wait a minute, don't actors use blue eye shadow to make themselves look ill? Sort of Elizabeth Barrett Browning consumptive. Or Camille?"

"You mean Krendler wanted to look more frail than he really is? And anyhow, who is he *really*? And *when* did this accident occur? And what *exactly* happened? There's something not right."

"But his story is so plausible," she said. "The accident, the trouble with Chez La Violette, the jinx—"

"A hard-edged businessman like Krendler talking about 'a jinx'?" Mac raised a skeptical eyebrow. "I doubt 'emotion' has ever played a role in the man's life. And anyway, how did he make his money? What about wives, ex-wives, children?"

"Dogs," Sunny added, helpfully.

Mac gave her an approving nod. "Dogs can tell you a lot about a person. Take Tesoro, for example."

"Must we?" Sunny definitely did not like the direction this conversation had taken, but Mac was laughing at her.

She was getting rather tired of Joel Krendler and she studied the menu instead, pleased it was a gastronomic "tasting" menu so they didn't really have to make choices, they could simply relax and enjoy. But now, to her annoyance, Mac had taken out his iPhone and was text-messaging.

"This is not what we came to Paris for," she complained.

"Just getting Ron Perrin onto a bit more research on Krendler. I figured billionaires always know about each other."

"Ex," Sunny said.

"Okay. Ex-billionaires."

Mac concluded his message. "And you're right, this is not what we came to Paris for."

Sunny said softly, "You know what? We have a wonderful room all to ourselves at the Ritz."

"With no dogs fighting."

"How about that?" Sunny's smile lit her face in the way Mac loved.

"Of course we have to go for a walk later," he said.

"The river Seine, Notre Dame . . ."

"Montmartre, the Latin Quarter, the Folies-Bergère."

They were laughing and Joel Krendler was temporarily forgotten as the waiter served a delicate cream of celery soup with foie gras and truffles, then topped up the wineglasses.

All was right in their Paris world.

Much later, they were back in their room at the Ritz. A bottle of champagne, the Heidsieck rosé Sunny liked, was chilling in a silver bucket, but they weren't looking.

Mac ran his hands over Sunny's hips. Thrilled, he realized she was wearing a garter belt. He hitched up her skirt. Fishnets! Oh. My. God.

She posed in front of him, hip jutted, long legs even longer in five-inch

red heels, and with that delicious gap between stockings and black silk panties. He couldn't wait to get his lips on her.

"Like it?" she asked with a cheeky grin, tossing back her hair in a mock-
abandoned gesture and pouting sexily.

Mac groaned, reaching for her.

She held him back with one finger. "As good as a Pussycat Doll?"

"Better." He was on his knees in front of her. She was looking down at
him, smiling that secret smile. There was a gleam in her eyes that Mac knew
meant Love me, baby, it's all I want, you are all I want.

He said the words for her, sliding off the black silk boy shorts, slipping
the straps of the matching bra from her shoulders. He almost didn't know
where to start, her body was so tempting.

He needn't have worried. Sunny simply took over where he had left off.

"Clothes," she said, scattering them to the wind. "Clothes are only the
temptation. *No* clothes is the reward."

And then she proceeded to give him his reward.

21.

From his table in a shadowy corner of the dining room, half-hidden by a potted palm tree, Bertrand kept an eye on his fellow hotel guests. Not that there was anything particularly fascinating about any of them, except for the mysterious group from Chez La Violette, the Riders on the Storm, as he liked to call them. But anyway they were not here tonight.

Most of the hotel guests were family groups who kept to themselves, though their young children eyed Bertrand sneakily, giggling behind their hands, and people at neighboring tables glanced his way, talking softly to each other. Everybody knew Bertrand's story and he knew they were speculating about his mother.

He stared fixedly at the basket of bread on his table. He did not want their sympathy, nor their curiosity in the guise of friendship. By now he was used to being alone. He didn't care. He had his own secret world when he was free from their prying eyes and pitying looks, prowling the narrow daytime streets of St. Tropez and emerging at night from his bedroom window, fluttering like a bat in his dark cape.

On those nights, when he was alone, prowling, observing people through his binoculars, he found a kind of freedom. He was seeing how "real" people lived. What they were really like, those proper families, in houses they called "home," with mothers and fathers who were there every night, and brothers and sisters who yelled at each other and played and who never had to worry about what their mother was up to and whether she would return to pay the hotel bill and collect him.

He was Bertrand the Observer. Sometimes though, he imagined he was the Terminator, Arnold Schwarzenegger, or Harry Potter, or even Johnny Depp, Pirate Scourge of the Caribbean. But right now he was just hungry.

Bertrand wrote all his observations in his journal. A "Scientific Experiment" he called it. It made him feel special. Superior even. For once in his life he felt better than other boys.

"Bertrand?"

His head shot up.

The chef in his whites, tall hat perched on his lofty forehead, a smile hidden behind his fluffy black mustache, placed a dish in front of him. He beamed sympathetically at the lonely boy. "I made it specially for you."

It was a whole spiny Mediterranean lobster, the kind without claws and whose meat, Bertrand knew, was the sweetest. He took a deep breath of pleasure. It was the best treat anyone could have given him.

"*Monsieur de la cuisine,* I am thanking you from my heart," he said, speaking in French of course. Then, "And from my stomach," he added with a grin that lit up his face so that for once he looked like the eleven-year-old he was.

"Enjoy, enjoy," the chef said. Gossip amongst the staff was not good. Madame Olivier had not been in contact and the hotel bill was growing daily, but no one was prepared to see the boy starve and everyone looked out for him. Soon, however, something would have to be done, and that might involve calling the child safety authorities.

He patted Bertrand's head, frowning as he noticed the newly jagged fringe of blond hair, shaking his own head muttering about bad parents as he turned and walked away.

Bertrand tackled the lobster. The back was already cracked open and he scooped out the tender white meat with the special little fork, not even bothering to dip it in the melted butter or the garlic aioli. He liked it pure. Closing his eyes he let the flavor hit him.

In no time he'd finished the lobster and was thinking about ice cream for dessert, worrying a bit about the cost. As though reading his mind, a waiter scooped the empty plate from in front of him and replaced it with a bowl of his favorite mocha-hazelnut.

"Spoiled, that's what you are," the waiter said with a grin.

Bertrand thanked him. He decided he would eat it very, very slowly, make it last as long as possible.

The perfect summer day was fading gently into night. It was that magical moment when the sea and the sky seemed to meld into a backlit neon blue and life was suddenly stilled. Even the birds had stopped their calling and were headed home, and the two white peacocks trailed silently across the lawn, drooping tails sweeping behind them like the trains of wedding dresses. A lone sailboat, a seventy-footer, Bertrand estimated, rolled gently in the nearby cove and as he watched a man climbed into its dinghy and made for the shore, the harsh *phut phut* of its engine shattering the silence.

Bertrand wished he had his binoculars so he could read the name on the boat. He watched as the dinghy came alongside the hotel's small wooden jetty and the man climbed out, tied it up then headed up the path to the Hô-tel des Rêves. A couple of minutes later, he strode into the hotel and into the dining room.

He looked to be in his forties, tall and handsome, dark hair tinged with silver, suntanned and outdoorsy. He nodded a pleasant *bonsoir* to the other guests, as was the French custom, then took a seat at a table in the courtyard, where Bertrand could still see him. A waiter hurried to him with a menu and the wine list. The man ordered something and the waiter went away, then came back a few minutes later carrying a drink on a small tray.

Caroline Cavalaire came into the dining room. She had finished her work shift and had on her dark blue jacket, though she had taken off her name badge. Bertrand watched her walk over to the man from the sailboat and shake his hand. She was smiling and obviously knew him well.

Bertrand wondered who he was. He was not French, probably Italian. He decided he would check out the sailboat and went back to his ice cream.

A couple of minutes later the normal dining room buzz of conversation suddenly ceased. Bertrand glanced up, puzzled.

The girl in the short orange tutu stood in the entrance, feet in fifth ballet position, the tiara that spelled out "Princess" perched on her head, a tiny Chihuahua clutched to her chest.

Bertrand remembered only too well how he had bumped into her and dropped his binoculars. He blushed at the memory. He had seen her a second time, though then she was with her father, who he'd heard call her Little Laureen. He thought she looked petulant and sulky and just knew she was spoiled rotten. *And oh my God she was heading toward his table!*

Little Laureen stopped a couple of feet away. She looked directly at him. Bertrand looked silently back. He was definitely not going to say hello. He did not want to know her. He did not want to be her friend. In fact he never wanted to see her again.

Little Laureen wished she could see the boy's eyes but those dumb glasses hid them. Why didn't his mother get him better ones so he didn't have to look so stupid? And he was sullen too. Just look how he avoided her eyes. And really *skinny*. Still, he was the only "interesting" kid there. All the others were just the regular little monsters you met in school, always screaming and yelling and pulling faces and always wanting to know too much. She'd bet this boy wouldn't want to know too much. And she liked that.

"*Bonsoir. Je m'appelle* Laureen," she said.

Bertrand swallowed the nervous lump in his throat that threatened to render him speechless. Head down, he nodded. "*Petite Laureen,*" he said finally.

Laureen took another step toward him, still clutching the Chihuahua, who tonight sported a brand-new jeweled red collar.

"How did you know that?" she said in English.

"I heard him talking to you."

"Daddy?"

Bertrand nodded.

Laureen stepped closer. She was actually at his table now. Bertrand considered getting up and running but decided it would cause a commotion and he didn't want to draw attention to himself. Reluctantly, he allowed himself to look at her.

She wasn't pretty, but then nor was he. It was something they had in common. And there was something else about her that struck a familiar chord. An air of loneliness? But how could it be? She was here with her father, and now also that whole bunch of Riders on the Storm.

His eyes widened in shock as Laureen pulled out a chair and plumped down opposite him, settling the dog on her lap.

"Could I have a taste of your ice cream?"

Her smooth round face had that indifferent expression as if she did not care one way or the other.

Bertrand pushed the bowl over to her. The ice cream was melting rapidly and she dipped a pudgy finger in then licked it.

"Good," she said.

She still did not smile and neither did he.

Then, "Why are you here alone?" she asked.

Bertrand shut his eyes, as though a great pain had run through his head. The worst had happened. She had gotten to the very core of his despair.

"No one ever asks me that," he managed to say after a long silence during which Petite Laureen sat patiently stroking the little dog.

"No one ever asks me either."

Bertrand opened his eyes again. He took a cautious look at her. "But you are not alone."

"Yes I am." Her china blue eyes looked straight into his. "Because my mother is dead you see."

Bertrand saw the quick flash of pain in the blue eyes that he thought were the only pretty thing about her.

He said, "And *my* mother has gone away. I don't know if she'll come back." He coughed loudly, wishing he had never admitted it. But *she* had admitted the truth, hadn't she? And he could tell she wasn't the kind who went around talking to everybody.

Laureen dipped another finger into the melted ice cream. She licked it off, thoughtfully.

"Where's your father?"

Bertrand explained quickly that he did not have one.

They sat in silence for a few minutes. They were both aware of the eyes of the diners at neighboring tables on them. Laureen turned her head and gave them her best intimidating stare. Then abruptly, she pushed back her chair and said, "*Eh bien,* Bertrand Olivier. You speak good English."

Bertrand felt that awful blush again. "My mother is English," he muttered.

Looking at him, Laureen recognized a fellow sufferer. He was as lonely as she was, and she knew it was because of that loneliness they had both chosen to be different. Both were hiding their sense of loss: she the mother who had died, and he the mother who had simply left him behind. They were alike.

"*Au revoir,*" she said. And with a flutter of orange tulle and the little dog clasped to her chest, she stalked past the curious diners and out of the room.

A short while later, from the dining room window, Bertrand spotted her walking the Chihuahua slowly down the path that led to the beach. The tiny Chihuahua seemed to float ghostlike behind her in the blue dusk. She looked as lonely as he felt.

Bertrand got up and ran to the kennel to pick up Pirate. It was time to take him for that walk.

22.

First though, Bertrand had to go back to his room for the binoculars. He did not take the cape, simply tucked the binoculars under his arm as out of sight as possible.

The barman gave him a wave as he trotted across the hall and down the front steps with Pirate limping excitedly next to him. He headed along the same path Little Laureen had taken. It led to the beach which he knew would be deserted at this time of night and he quickened his pace.

When he got to where the path ran down the gentle incline to the sand, he put the binoculars round his neck, opened up their metal "lids" and focused on the dinghy. It was still tied to the jetty. He quickly scanned the horizon for the sailboat. It was lit up, flags flying, and its name was *Blue Picasso*. Next he scanned the beach. There was no sign of Laureen.

Pirate pulled on his lead, snuffling in the grass above the cove, and Bertrand followed, up the small incline, letting the dog take him where he wanted. The cool night air was pure, breathing it felt like drinking clear spring-water, and around the point the lights of St. Tropez town sparkled like Little Laureen's tiara.

Finding a pebble he dribbled it along, pretending it was a soccer ball and that he was David Beckham, the soccer "star" of Europe. But he was clumsy, his sneaker skimmed over the top and he lost the pebble in the darkness. Then he saw her.

She was sitting at the water's edge, staring into the dark blue night. She was hunched over, arms wrapped around her knees. As though she had a pain in her stomach, Bertrand thought.

He stood, watching her until Pirate spotted the Chihuahua, a small indistinct blob at Little Lauren's side. Pirate gave a low growl.

Laureen spun round, eyes wide with fright.

"Oh," she said recognizing him. "It's you."

Bertrand did not mention having seen her walking along the path to the beach and that he had followed her. "Why aren't you with your father?" he said instead.

She turned back to her contemplation of the sea. The waves shushed softly at her feet and the Chihuahua whined pitifully. Laureen scooped it up and held it close. "Daddy's gone into town with the others. I told him I wanted to stay here."

"Alone," Bertrand said.

She gave him a long look over her shoulder but did not reply.

In the semidarkness Laureen thought Bertrand's huge pale-rimmed glasses gave him the look of a spacewalker. Blind and blundering. And what were those things strung around his neck?

"Are those *binoculars*?"

Bertrand patted his chest. "They are."

"They're weird."

"They were custom-made. The lids protect the lenses. They were used for bird-watching many years ago. They were probably used in World War Two by the airmen who parachuted into enemy-held France. These were brave men's binoculars."

Laureen said nothing and Bertrand guessed she must be impressed. "They probably belonged to an American airman," he said, inventing as he went along. "He probably used them to help capture a whole town and saved the lives of many of my countrymen."

Laureen stroked the dog. "Probably," she agreed.

Bertrand slid down the slope, dragging Pirate. He walked through the sand to where she was sitting. He heard Tesoro's warning growl and Laureen telling the dog to be quiet.

"You say *Tais-toi*," he told her, squatting in the sand a few feet away, afraid to get too close in case she told him to go away like most kids did. "That means 'Be quiet' in French."

"It means "Shut up,'" Laureen said.

He stared at her, surprised that she knew. "That too, but it's not polite to say shut up."

Pirate rolled in the sand then got up and began briskly to dig a hole, though he had trouble because of the missing leg and fell into it.

"Poor thing," Laureen said.

Bertrand thought her orange tutu must be full of the sand kicked up by Pirate now. "Why do you wear that ballet dress?" His voice had a squeak of nervousness. He was not used to asking people personal questions but he needed to know.

Laureen stared at the waves. She touched the silver Tiffany heart at her throat. Changing the subject, she said, "My mother gave this necklace to me." She turned her head to look at him, her hand still on the silver heart.

Bertrand nodded. He understood that it was special. A memory of her mother.

"Where did your mother go?" Laureen asked.

He shrugged, trying his best to look nonchalant. There was a long silence while they looked at each other. Laureen had told him about her necklace. She had been honest and now Bertrand knew he had to do the same thing. "She's just gone," he said.

"Gone where?"

Bertrand's stammer gave his anguish away. "I don't know. Maybe Italy. With a man she met here."

"You mean she just went? And left you here *alone*?"

Bertrand turned his face away, unable to look at her.

Laureen guessed he was fighting tears. "I'm sorry," she said.

Bertrand didn't know whether she meant she was sorry for asking, or sorry his mother had gone, and he did not reply.

"We're kind of alike," Laureen said. "You and me." She thought for a bit, then said, "I don't even know your name."

"Bertrand."

"Where did you get the binoculars?" she asked after a while.

"I stole them. From Chez La Violette."

"Are they your most treasured possession?"

He nodded.

"Why did you go to Chez La Violette?"

Bertrand shrugged. "I was exploring. I do it all the time. At night, when I can be alone. I observe people, what they do, who they are. And how strange they are."

Laureen's china blue eyes widened. "You go *spying*?" She stared at him. Then, "You're weird," she said.

Bertrand felt the blush burn his cheeks. He had said too much, trusted too far. Scrambling to his feet, he marched clumsily back through the sand, tugging Pirate after him.

"Sorry. *Je m'excuse, Bertrand.*"

Her voice filtered after him into the night. But it was too late.

23.

When Mac and Sunny got back to the hotel, the dailies were stacked on the wooden rack by the reception table, *Nice Matin* and the local St. Tropez gazette, as well as the Paris papers. Mac stopped to look at the blazing headlines. FIVE HUNDRED THOUSAND EUROS OFFERED FOR SOLVING LOCAL MURDER AND ART THEFT.

Caroline was not on duty this morning, another young woman had taken her place, petite and dark-haired with that superb olive skin and dark eyes typical of the Mediterranean, where for hundreds of years Italy and France had coexisted.

The name on her badge was Renée. Mac went over and asked if she could tell him what the article said.

"But of course, sir. It's Mr. Reilly, isn't it? And Miss Alvarez." She gave them the same big smile Caroline had.

"What it says is that Monsieur François Reynaud, the owner of the house where the murder took place and whose valuable paintings were stolen, is offering a very big reward for the capture of the killer of his friend and return of the stolen paintings. He says the stolen artworks are valuable but not as valuable as the young life that was also 'stolen.'"

Mac said, "I heard there have been other robberies, along the coast."

"Yes, but none before with a shooting." Renée shuddered.

Mac turned to look as he heard a masculine voice saying, *"Bonjour, madame."*

Sunny was gazing up at a good-looking guy, tall, suntanned and Eurosmooth in that sleek athletic way of a yachtsman or a polo player. He was dressed simply in shorts and a striped polo shirt and wore a thin gold watch, light-years away from the heavy Rolexes usually seen around. There was something about the man's simplicity that let you know he was rich.

"Bonjour." Sunny was giving the guy that upward flirty glance that sent a pang of jealousy directly to Mac's heart. He told himself to quit with the caveman reaction and pretended to read his newspaper, though of course he was still listening.

"I haven't seen you here before," the man was saying. "Are you staying at the hotel?"

Sunny said she was. Then with a glance in Mac's direction, she added, "I'm with my fiancé."

He lifted a hand in a polite salute to Mac. "I hope you're enjoying your vacation, *monsieur.*" He offered his hand. "Gianni Valenti."

"Mac Reilly." They shook hands and Mac said, "Then you're staying at the hotel too?"

"I'm on my boat, the *Blue Picasso.* You can see it out there. The draft is too deep to moor closer. I come in on my dinghy for lunch or a drink, dinner sometimes, and maybe some company. It can get a bit lonely on a boat."

Looking at the big sailboat floating gently on the swell, Mac thought it was unlikely Valenti would be lonely for very long. Women must be dying to get on that boat with him.

"You must come out sometime, both of you and have a drink." Valenti showed a perfect set of white teeth in a smile that would have made a Hollywood starlet envious, yet Mac could swear they were natural. Either that or he had the world's best cosmetic dentist.

"I'd like that."

"Give me a chance to show off my boat." Valenti turned to Renée. He gave her his thoroughbred smile. "Caroline is not here today?"

"It's Caroline's day off, Monsieur Valenti."

There was a sudden commotion and everyone turned to see what was happening. Pirate cantered lopsidedly across the hall, emitting something between a woof and a squeal of delight as he hurled himself at Mac. Behind him came Little Laureen, holding Tesoro tightly to her chest.

Laureen's tutu was raspberry color today, the satin bodice a little too tight, the drooping tulle skirt ankle-length for a change, and she was wearing flip-flops instead of the ballet slippers.

Sunny wanted to hug her but the distance Laureen placed between herself and other people made her hold back. Meanwhile Tesoro was giving her that same blank look as Laureen.

She said, "Thank you for looking after Tesoro so well."

Laureen stroked the Chihuahua's sleek brown fur then passed the dog re-luctantly back to Sunny. Then Bertrand came running, calling Pirate's name. He stopped when he saw them. His big glasses slid down his nose as he hung his head. "I lost him. I'm sorry."

Mac said, "It's okay, you didn't lose him. Pirate lost you."

Bertrand nodded, but he looked ashamed at letting Mac down.

Valenti nodded and with a wave went on his way.

Little Laureen looked longingly at the Chihuahua, then she too turned and walked away. Bertrand picked up a copy of the local newspaper and fol-lowed her into the garden.

"Well, *they* seem to have found each other," Sunny commented.

"A perfect match," Mac agreed, as the odd pair drifted slowly down the path to the beach, trailed by the perfect pair of white peacocks.

24.

"Maybe I could help him," Mac said to Sunny.

They were back in their room, unpacking, which in Sunny's case consisted of shifting her clothes from the bag onto a chair. Mac, of course, had hung his up right away.

Sunlight filtered through the half-closed green shutters and the scent of Provençal lavender wafted delicately as Sunny flung herself against the pillows, rescued by Mac from the armoire.

"Help who?"

"Mr. François Reynaud, the art collector with the murdered friend."

Sunny hid her face in her hands, groaning. "You promised no murders on this vacation."

"It's not exactly *my* murder. I'm just interested that's all, thought I'd give him a call . . ."

"You don't have his number and a man like that's not likely to be in the book." Sunny crossed her fingers, hoping she was right.

"I already thought about that."

"*When?*" They had only been in the room five minutes.

"Walking up the stairs. I'll bet Allie Ray knows him, and if not then Ron Perrin will know somebody who does. I told you before, billionaires always know each other." Mac had his iPhone in hand. "I'll get Allie to call him, give him my name and number, tell him I'd be pleased to help in any way I can."

Exasperated, Sunny flung herself backward, arms and legs askew. It was a done deal. Murder, as well as a rental scam, was now part of their summer vacation.

"You look like a snow angel on that white bed," Mac said.

"I'd rather be a beach bum. I've got the best bikini in the world and I haven't even had a chance to show it off yet."

"Soon, I promise. Oh hi, Allie, it's Mac. Yeah, how are you? Up to your eyes in manure? Well, that makes a change for America's Golden Girl. You're growing delphiniums and lupines. *And* clematis and passion fruit, as well as the vines? So what's Ron up to while you're doing all this gardening? He's the manure carrier. Plenty of horses round there huh . . . Well, that must be a fragrant job for an ex-billionaire. Right, *and* a jailbird, but you're right, it is better than doing time. When are we coming to visit?" He glanced inquiringly at Sunny who nodded back at him, pleased. "Pretty soon, we'll get there, Allie. You know we miss you."

Sunny noticed that Mac said "*we* miss you" but she knew he meant *he* missed Allie. The two had become very close when Allie had turned to Mac for help, a couple of years ago, in Malibu. There was no need for jealousy though, Allie was also her friend now, and Mac was always loyal to his friends.

She listened as Mac asked Allie for the favor and Allie agreed to pass his message on to Ron. She said she knew he must know about Krendler.

"Sunny sends love." Mac finished the call and closed his phone.

"Done deal?" Sunny asked.

"Let's wait and see." He came to lay on the bed with her, an arm flung over hers, his leg pressed against hers. "Did I ever tell you I love you and that you are the most understanding woman I ever met?"

Her heavy-lashed eyes swiveled his way. "I am?"

"Sun baby, you have to understand, it's what I do. I can't help myself."

"Kind of like a murder 'addict,' you mean?"

Mac sighed again. "Hey, I'm just a curious guy, I need to know who done it." He leaned on one elbow, looking at her. "Besides, I hate the idea of some poor young guy getting shot just because he happened to be in the wrong place at the wrong time."

"Why not let *les flics* take care of it?"

"Sometimes an outsider can give an overview, see something they might not."

The phone rang and Mac grabbed it. "Monsieur Reynaud, thanks for calling me back. At the Villa les Ambassadeurs at three. I'll be there, sir."

Mac looked at Sunny. He lifted a shoulder in an apologetic shrug. "Want to come with me?"

Despite herself, Sunny was intrigued. Mac had set something in motion and she knew there was no going back.

"Don't I always?" she said.

25.

François Reynaud's villa was more of a palace, a two-story building in the old Provençal coral-roofed style with Moorish additions. Marble pergolas were tiled in Spanish *azulejos* in the distinctive blue and white, and ink blue pools and streams meandered through gardens shaded by umbrella pines and cedars, down to an immaculately raked sandy beach. There was no hard-faced butler to open the door here, only a middle-aged Spanish woman in a white smock who greeted them with a smile and led them to where Monsieur Reynaud sat at a table overlooking the beach.

He got up to greet them, a smallish man, thin from what looked like a lifetime of smoking, and older than Mac had expected, probably in his late seventies.

"Welcome, Mr. Reilly." He shook Mac's hand, his expression serious.

"Thank you, sir. May I introduce Miss Alvarez, my assistant. And fiancée," Mac added.

Sunny took a seat at the table next to Mac. Reynaud sat opposite, sharp dark eyes watching them from behind steepled hands.

"Five hundred thousand euros is a lot of money, Mr. Reilly," he said.

Sunny felt the heat flare in her cheeks. Oh, God, Reynaud thought Mac was after the reward.

Mac nodded. "I appreciate that, sir. And if I am able to help you find the killers, I'd be happy for you to donate that sum to a local charity."

Reynaud pressed a bell to summon the manservant from the blue-tented beach bar. "I can offer you fresh lemonade," he said. "Maria Dolores, my housekeeper, makes the best in the world with lemons from our own trees. Of course in winter, when the weather turns cold here in St. Tropez, they are moved into the warmth of the conservatory to preserve them. Rather like myself," he added with a self-deprecating smile.

The young man in a blue-and-white-striped T-shirt, served the lemonade and offered a napkined basket containing small pastries.

"*Tartes tropéziennes*," Reynaud explained. "The local specialty."

Mac refused but Sunny, who had never been known to turn down a sweet or a chocolate, took one. When she bit into it, it was light and flaky with a delicate flavor of almonds.

"This is delicious." She beamed her pleasure at Monsieur Reynaud.

"You can buy them in town," he said. "At La Table du Marché on rue Georges Clemenceau." He sipped his lemonade then asked Mac exactly what he knew about the murder.

"Only what I read in the newspaper. To tell you the truth, I was drawn to the case because the victim was your friend. I imagined how you must feel, inviting him here . . . and then this."

François Reynaud studied Mac's face for a long moment, then he said, "I heard you were a good man, Reilly. From Allie, of course. She told me how you had helped her and Ron." He flung his hands in the air and added with a smile, "Of course, Ron is another matter, but also a man with a good heart, as Allie has come to recognize. Meanwhile, let me tell you how this happened.

"The victim's name is Thierry Sage. I was in Zurich when he called and told me he was going to be in the South. Thierry's father was a dear friend of mine. We did business together—I was in the aircraft industry for many years, and I had known his son since he was a boy. Of course I offered Thierry my guesthouse, said he could have the use of one of the cars and that Maria Dolores would be here to look after him. The young man who served us, is a staff member on my yacht. One or the other of them always comes here to attend to me when I'm in residence. I gave him leave to go back to the yacht that week, and said I would call for someone to come out here when I returned. So it was to be just Maria Dolores and Thierry here alone.

"Maria Dolores told me that, earlier, she received a phone call from a young woman who'd applied for the job as assistant housekeeper. The woman said she had no transportation so Maria Dolores arranged to meet her on the yacht in Monte Carlo. A long drive for her, but she was pleased to do it if it meant getting the right person to work here at the villa. Needless to say, it turned out to be a ploy to get Maria Dolores out of the house. The woman did not show up. And Thierry was alone at the house when the robbers struck."

"What about the security system?"

"It had been tampered with from inside. The main computer is in a closet in the front hall."

"Had there been workmen in the house recently? Men you didn't know?"

"No one. Though I did give a party a week earlier."

"How many people?"

"Oh, eighty, maybe a hundred."

"And you knew them all personally?"

Reynaud threw his hands in the air again. "Mr. Reilly, this is the South of France, you give a party for friends and they bring friends. That's just the way it is around here. People know each other. It's casual."

"Could we take a look at the guesthouse?"

Reynaud closed his eyes, a look of pain crossed his face but he summoned the waiter again and asked him to show Mac the little house. "Forgive me if I do not accompany you," he said.

The guesthouse was a white L-shaped building, entered via a wrought-iron gate in the shape of a peacock's tail painted green to match the hedge of ficus trees, clipped to flat perfection, that formed a small courtyard. Inside it was simple: just one long low room with the beamed ceiling painted white and a wall of glass overlooking the beach. The furnishings were blue and white with a seashell theme, very low-key vacation-home style. There was a single large bedroom, a sumptuous bathroom in pale tumbled marble, and a wrap-around terrace with that glorious view.

"It's perfection," Sunny said in a whisper, mindful of what had taken place here only a few days ago. But still she couldn't help thinking that this place was exactly what she had envisioned when Mac told her he had rented Chez La Violette.

The guesthouse had been cleaned and the victim's possessions removed. Mac knew there was nothing to be found here.

"The actual crime took place outside, sir." The young waiter led them to a walkway at the side of the house. To the right was the main house and beyond it a helicopter pad with a Sikorsky parked on it. To the left, a wooden jetty stuck out into the water. A speedboat was tied up to it. A Riva, Mac noticed. And also, next to it, a perfect vintage-wood-hulled Cigarette boat.

"It's Monsieur Reynaud's favorite, sir," the waiter explained. "He's by way of being a boat fanatic. He particularly likes the vintage wood, says the workmanship is miraculous."

He walked them about halfway up the path. "This is where the unfortunate event took place, sir." He pointed to a sheltered spot behind an oleander hedge.

Sunny noticed the oleander was still blooming, great white blossoms, like a bridal bouquet. Or a funeral wreath. She quickly took Mac's hand and felt him squeeze hers slightly.

They stood for a minute, silently looking round, then they walked back to the table under the trees, a walk that in fact took them almost five minutes. This was a big spread.

Reynaud gave Mac a quizzical look. "Well, Mr. Reilly?"

"Thank you for allowing me to see that, sir. I'm sure the police already took notes on everything."

"Everything."

"And no doubt they asked you for the party guest list."

"They did. I anticipated your question and I have a copy of it here for you." Reynaud pushed an envelope across the table. "Of course the police have checked every name on the list, plus the friends of friends who accompanied them, uninvited, and who were therefore *not* on the list." His sharp dark eyes watched as Mac put the envelope in his shirt pocket. "So now what, Mr. Reilly? Do you have any clues?"

"Sir, I do not. All I can tell you is I'll be thinking about this. Something may come up, something unexpected. That's usually the way it happens."

"Then I wish you luck, my friend." Reynaud got to his feet and shook Mac's hand again. "And I thank you for trying."

He stood, watching them go. "Take care of that beautiful young woman," he called after them.

26.

Bertrand and Laureen walked down the path to the beach. There was no need for questions. They were alike, both outside of normal society. They understood each other.

"I miss the dog," Bertrand said in French.

"Me too," Laureen answered in French. It was like a kind of bond between them, this dual language thing.

They sat on the beach, backs propped against a convenient spur of rock that Laureen complained was a bit scratchy but had the advantage of hiding them from the view of the other beachgoers, sprawled on striped mattresses, intent on getting as much sun as possible. In the distance the peacocks squawked their quarrelsome cry and pelicans glided past in tight squadrons, occasionally upending and diving as one into the sea. Gianni Valenti's sailboat had gone but a fleet of smaller boats, white sails bellying in the breeze, drifted past, while closer inshore speedboats flew by, noses uptilted in front, spray flying behind, en route, no doubt, to one of the chic beach cafés.

Laureen was sitting bolt upright, legs stuck out in front of her, raspberry tulle skirts fluffed up like a fan, wiggling her plump toes in the warm sand. Bertrand was in his usual uniform of old polo shirt and droopy shorts but had kept on his sneakers, and both of them wore battered straw sunhats with wide brims, "rescued" as Laureen termed it, from the small pile she'd found on the stand in the hall. Laureen had a new way of being "light-fingered." The hats were too big and Bertrand wore his on the back of his head; Laureen's was tilted over her eyes.

She said, "I'm sorry for what I said. About you being 'weird.'"

"That's okay."

Laureen peeked from behind her rock at the half-naked bathers wading into the sea that glittered silver and aquamarine. Closing her eyes again, she sniffed the air, so different from the green smell of the ranch and the arid aroma of the chaparral. French air smelled of a flower Belinda Lord had told her was jasmine and of the clean tang of salty sea, of hot baked sand and the coconutty aroma of suntan lotion. It smelled of coffee and something cooking that she didn't recognize coming from the Beach Bar but that wasn't hot dogs or burgers. France tasted different, even their pancakes and their ice cream. And the French looked different. She couldn't quite put her finger on how, but definitely "different," though not in the way she did. *She* was unique. If her mother was looking down from heaven Laureen was quite certain she would be able to pick her out from the crowd anywhere in the world. Even in France. That's why she wore the tutus, to make it easier for her mother to find her.

Opening her eyes, she glanced at Bertrand, who was sitting, knees hunched, glasses slipping down his nose, reading the newspaper he had picked up at the hotel.

He looked up and met her eyes, then tapped the headline with a long thin finger. "They are offering a reward to anyone who catches the art thieves."

Laureen lifted a surprised eyebrow; what did this have to do with her?

"Five hundred thousand euros," Bertrand added, awed.

Turning back to his newspaper, he reread the information, then sat back against the rock, skinny legs stuck out in front of him, like Laureen. He said, "Five hundred thousand euros is a lot of money. Mr. Reynaud must be very rich."

Laureen had paid thirty euros in St. Tropez for Tesoro's red jeweled collar. Her daddy had said it was a lot of money, something to do with "the exchange rate," but she'd told him it was worth it for Tesoro, and besides he could take it out of her allowance. Not that her allowance was very big; Daddy said he needed to keep her on a tight rein, like a pony, so she would know the true value of money.

Bertrand was silent, staring out to sea. A passerby strolling along the beach saw them and laughed, calling out to them that they looked like a pair of rag dolls dumped on the sand, bringing them abruptly back to embarrassed reality.

Bertrand had been thinking about his mother, who really was hardly a mother at all, just some woman who, as she constantly complained, was burdened by having to look after him. That five-hundred-thousand-euro reward could pay off the terrifying hotel bill. He could live here at the Hôtel des Rêves forever. *That reward could buy his freedom.*

Bertrand gave Laureen a penetrating look from behind the pale plastic glasses and she realized suddenly that his eyes were blue too, though paler than her own. They spoke their usual mixture of English and French, though Bertrand's English was superior.

"We could do it, *petite Laureen,*" Bertrand said. "We could catch those robbers."

"*We* could? But how?"

"I know everyone round here. I see everything."

"You mean with those weird binoculars?"

"They are valuable antiques. I told you the story."

"You told me you spied with them."

"Only for my Scientific Experiment. One day it will be useful, a study in"—he grasped for a phrase—"in human relations."

"All my relations are humans." Laureen was always practical.

He dismissed that impatiently. "Not *relatives* . . . relations . . . how people behave."

"How do we get the reward?" she asked.

"The artworks have not been found. It was very rainy that night. You remember, the night of the big storm?" Laureen nodded again. Bertrand said, "How could the thieves run away with big paintings in that rain? They would have been ruined." Laureen nodded again, eyes wide now as she realized where he was going. He added, "If it were me, I would have hidden them right there, where they stole them from."

"But the *flics* would have found them by now."

Bertrand saw his theory disappearing under her logic. "Maybe not hidden them right there at the house they stole them from," he conceded. "But somewhere near there."

"In the rocks you mean, like in a cave . . . ?"

Bertrand didn't think there were any caves near St. Tropez, but he said yes, perhaps in a cave, though it would have to be a dry one.

"What we need to do," he said, "is keep a watch on everybody."

"The way you do now."

He nodded, trying to think of what else they could do to catch the thieves. "We must be like James Bond," he decided.

"Secret agents, you mean?" Laureen was already imagining herself in her best tutu, the orange one, creeping through a dark cave, binoculars trained on the stolen paintings, glowing expensively as bats flew all around them.

"I don't mind bats," she said to Bertrand, who gave her a funny look and told her there were no bats in sea caves, maybe an occasional octopus though.

His eyes clouded as he thought about it. "But they couldn't keep paintings in a cave near the sea, they would be ruined. It would have to be something waterproof, solid, and very secret."

"Like a storage facility?" Laureen knew all about "storage facilities." They had one on the ranch where the workers' families kept things that wouldn't fit into their houses and that they didn't want to get rid of.

"We'll have to go out at night, searching," Bertrand decided.

"Okay." Laureen was game. She would say good night to her father, then sneak out.

Bertrand looked at the tutu. "You'll have to wear dark clothing." Her pudgy fingers skimmed across the raspberry pink tulle. She said nothing. "Otherwise you can't come," he added firmly.

She gave him an anguished look and he said, "Oh, okay, I'll let you wear my cape over the tutu."

Laureen breathed again. "When do we start?"

"Tonight. At midnight. I'll be waiting for you at the gates."

Bertrand did not have a plan but he knew he would think of something. The two of them would traverse the back lanes, keeping an eye out for suspicious persons and secret storage facilities.

They were so caught up in their plans that neither of them remembered that the robbers were also killers. And that one man was already dead.

27.

Nate parked the Ducati near the carousel in the place des Lices, where the big market took place every Tuesday and Saturday morning, bringing swarms of gourmets for the wonderful produce, much of it grown locally by smallholders, as well as for the bargain cashmere sweaters and linen dresses, sandals and faux jewelry, Panama hats and "Souvenirs de St. Tropez." Today though, there was no market and it was almost empty, just a few moms whose children were riding the carousel, and a woman in jodhpurs and a red shirt leading a large black horse around the back of the buildings on the opposite side to Le Café, which was where he was heading.

His head thundered from too much red wine followed by a great deal of brandy, imbibed the previous night in the trendy Bar du Port in the company of Billy Bashford. It had been worth it though; he had enjoyed himself, girl watching and even flirting which was not hard to do since the women in St. Tropez all seemed to be dedicated flirts. In his view though, none of them compared in looks or charm, to Sunny Alvarez. He still treasured the memory of the hours spent alone with her at Chez La Violette, and he almost regretted that the villa had turned out to be such a dog, though he had to concede the Hôtel des Rêves was pretty special, and certainly more comfortable.

He took off the goggles and the helmet, running his fingers through his dark hair as he strode toward the café. He spotted Belinda Lord, sitting at one of the tiny tables on the terrace, watching him. There was a mocking smile on her face that made him uneasy and he glanced down at himself, checking if something was wrong.

"Well, well, if it isn't the bumblebee." There always seemed to be a laugh in Belinda's low throaty voice. "Come join me, Nate, why don't you?"

"Thanks." He pulled up a chair next to her and they sat side by side, looking out onto the square. The leaves of the plane trees fluttered as the wind picked up, blowing away paper napkins and sending the waiter, cursing, running after them.

"I recommend the espresso," Belinda said. "And looking at you, I'd guess you needed it. First though, you'd better try the 'secret ingredient.'"

Nate raised an inquiring eyebrow, but Belinda held up her hand. "It's a certain cure for what, if I'm not mistaken, is ailing you."

Signaling the waiter Belinda ordered coffee and a Fernet-Branca. When it came she shoved the small glass in front of Nate, who picked it up and gave a sniff.

He pulled his head back, stunned. "Jesus."

"Aw, come on now, be a big boy. Take your medicine."

Her nose crinkled as she laughed at him, her ice blue eyes full of mockery. With her blond cropped hair, smooth tan skin and long legs in white shorts, she looked the epitome of the South of France woman.

Nate threw back his head and tossed down the "medicine." "Jesus," he said again, coughing. "That's terrible."

"We all have to suffer for our sins." Belinda patted his knee soothingly. "And trust me, in ten minutes you'll be a new man."

He gulped down the espresso and ordered another. "I wish it were that easy."

This time Belinda's eyebrows raised. "Really?"

Nate put on his glasses and gave her a long serious look. "I came here to find out who I am."

"Hmm, a mistake many make here in the South of France. Myself included. Once upon a time."

Nate waited for Belinda to expand on that but she did not, so he said instead, "Where's Sara?"

She groaned. "It's like we're joined at the hip, Belinda and Sara, the new duo." She shrugged. "I lent her the Bentley, told her to go for a drive, practice becoming a rich woman."

"You lent Sara *the Bentley*?"

Nate had a sudden vision of Sara, bug-eyed behind the wheel of the expensive car, maneuvering slowly along the crowded quai Suffren with a pileup of stalled cars behind her, drivers honking angrily.

"Hey, I already smacked it up, what's another dent or two? Though come to think of it, Sara will be ready to kill herself if she gets as much as a speck of dust on it."

"So tell me exactly how she's going 'to become a rich woman.'"

"Same way I did, by marrying it."

Nate made no comment but Belinda sensed his disapproval. "Listen," she said, "I gave value for money. I was a loving wife, I was chic, always perfectly made up and ready to hit the town in whatever city in the world, even though sometimes, *many times,* I would rather have curled up with a good book and a cup of tea." She watched Nate from narrowed eyes. "Didn't expect me to say that, did you?"

Nate shrugged. "I don't like the idea of women pursuing men for their money."

"Oddly enough, I didn't. It was Mikel who pursued me."

She called for croissants. Biting off the crisp end piece, she ate one thoughtfully.

"I only like the corners," she told Nate. "Wasteful, I know, but I'm making hay while the sun shines, as they say. Actually, I wonder who *did* say that. Anyhow, pretty soon I'll have to start practicing to be poor again and eat up all my crusts."

"Poor *again*?" Nate helped himself to a croissant. The headache had receded and he felt better.

"You are looking at a former suburban hairstylist—we called ourselves hairdressers in those days, an Essex girl made good. Sort of like in that old movie *Educating Rita.* You remember, the one with Julie Walters? Though now I think about it I don't think she was a hairdresser."

"Do you always talk in old-movie speak?"

"Hey, don't knock it. That's where I spent my life. I *lived* those movies. It's where I got my education, in the cinema, 'movie houses' you probably call them." Nate smiled but didn't correct her. "I've been everybody from Pretty Woman to Marie Antoinette." She met his eyes again. "Trust me, Nate Masterson, I can be anybody you want. That's part of my success with men."

"You don't think much of yourself, do you?"

"On the contrary, I've learned my worth—and it's not my weight in gold. Though I do *like* the gold," she added wistfully, as though seeing it disappearing before her eyes.

She signaled the waiter for a brandy, sipping it thoughtfully, her eyes still on him. "Feeling better?"

"Surprisingly, yes. I am. Thanks to you."

"Tricks of the trade," she said. "So what about you?"

"What *about* me?"

She looked him up and down. "So who are *you*, Masterson, anyway? Besides the Wall Street confidence trickster."

"I was not a confidence trickster."

"They are *all* confidence tricksters. Or else gamblers. And you avoided my question."

"I guess I am what I am. Rich enough, successful enough . . ."

"And a lonely man."

Their eyes linked. "That too," he said quietly.

"I told you people came here to find themselves."

"A mistake you said you had already made."

She leaned over, touched his hand. "I don't want you to make that same mistake, Masterson. You know, you're not so much different from Sara. Neither of you knows how to go out there and get what you really want."

Nate laughed. "My trouble is I don't *know* what I really want."

"Then it's time we found out." Belinda eyed him up and down critically again. "First thing, you have to lose the Lycra. Come on, Masterson, we're going shopping."

And, just as she had with Sara, she swept up her purse and Nate and headed for St. Tropez's best boutiques.

28.

In fact Sara was not stuck circling the port and the narrow back streets of St. Tropez, she had decided instead to be really adventurous and drive to Cannes. She had no plans on what to do when she got there; in fact all she knew about Cannes was what she had observed on TV's *Entertainment Tonight* about the film festival. She had seen the famous Hôtel Carlton with movie actors milling around, and now she wondered how it would feel to arrive there in the great white Bentley, hand it to the valet parker, sweep up the steps and order a glass of champagne, turning all heads as though she were someone important.

Of course, she couldn't do that, though. Or could she?

Sara thought quickly about the amount of money in her purse. It had to last her until her return flight to Kansas, ten more days, and even though Belinda was paying the hotel and had told her to stop worrying about money, it was still very much at the forefront of Sara's mind. She lay awake in bed worrying about the problem, while Belinda snored softly in the bed opposite. Of course Sara would never mention the snoring to Belinda, it might upset her. Belinda had such a perfect image, blond and sexy and glamorous as any movie star. Belinda would have been right at home on the terrace of the Carlton.

Steering the Bentley slowly through the notorious summer traffic at the St. Tropez roundabout, Sara was aware of heads turning to look at the beautiful car and to see who was driving it. She glanced down at her simple white cotton dress, passed on to her with Belinda's usual generosity. She knew from the label it was an Italian designer, and she was wearing her green snakeskin ankle-strap wedges. Her shoulder-length brown hair had achieved a new sheen from the South of France sunlight and she wore no jewelry and no makeup save for a tangerine lip gloss. In fact, she almost looked like a woman who owned a Bentley like this. A woman who could drive up to the Carlton's doors and hand the keys to the valet and order a glass of champagne on that terrace.

Winding slowly along the two-lane road, at last she came to the Autoroute du Soleil. She thought that in the South of France even the freeways had glamorous names, like this one, the Route of the Sun. Turning onto it she drove sedately east, heading for Cannes. The GPS system told her exactly where she should get off and it wasn't long before she was driving along the famous Croisette, taking her time, passing the Palais des Festivals and the old town, gasping at the incredible yachts moored side by side for what seemed miles. And there was the Hôtel Carlton, beckoning this new Sara Strange like a beacon from a lighthouse.

Almost without thinking, as though she had been programmed in fact, Sara stopped the car, handed it over to the valet, who bowed his head deferentially and called her *madame*, then she walked, knees trembling, up the steps onto that famous terrace.

The waiter showed her to a table near the back and in French she asked for *une coupe du champagne rosé*, pleased with herself for placing her order in French. She had learned by keeping her ears and eyes open around Belinda and the others, who all seemed so worldly-wise about everything, and rosé champagne was the most glamorous drink she could imagine.

The waiter placed a glass on the table, showed her the chilly bottle so she could read the label, Piper-Heidsieck Rosé Sauvage, then filled the glass. He set down a small dish, bowed, called her *madame* and departed.

Sara took a sip, eyes closed, savoring it. "Heaven," she said softly. Aware she was talking to herself she sat up straighter and took a look at the other tables. There was a happy hum of conversation interspersed with bursts of laughter. Everyone seemed to be having a good time, but Sara was too nervous to really enjoy herself. She was a woman alone, deserted by her boyfriend— "the bastard" as Belinda called him. She wasn't rich like these people. In fact she had almost no money and even the dress she was wearing was a hand-me-down.

She took another sip of the champagne and nibbled on something delicious. She felt a long way from Starbucks in small-town Kansas.

A chic woman in a white linen shirt and tight white pants paused on her way past Sara's table. "Hey, great shoes," she said with a smile and Sara found herself smiling back. *"Merci,"* she called after her, then realized the woman was American. Ah well, at least she had a couple of words in French now: she knew how to order a glass of champagne and how to say thank you. As Belinda would have said, what more did a girl need?

Half an hour later, when the waiter had come by to ask if she would care for another glass and Sara had said *non merci,* she fumbled in her purse for the correct money, leaving a small tip in the saucer provided, unnecessary she knew because the tab almost always included the gratuity, then made her way slowly back across the terrace and down the stairs.

Her Bentley was parked right in front between an apple green Lamborghini and a custom Maserati convertible in dark blue with quilted tan leather upholstery. They were the most beautiful cars Sara had ever seen.

The valet smiled into her eyes as he held open the door. Blushing, Sara quickly adjusted her sunglasses, overtipping him lavishly. He had seen her coming and the engine was already purring. Slipping the car into gear she turned to smile at him, but he had turned away and was talking to two thickset men, in white linen jackets, waving his arms and obviously explaining something.

Conscious that she had been drinking, only one and certainly not over the limit, nevertheless Sara drove carefully, drifting along the Croisette to the very end, then circling reluctantly back to the autoroute. It was, she thought dreamily, an adventure she would remember in those long winter months sipping her morning decaf skinny latte and keeping her jacket buttoned against the cold. Somehow her Toyota Corolla would never seem the same.

She first became aware of the car cruising behind her, maintaining the same speed she was, as she approached the St. Tropez exit. Puzzled, she checked it out in the rearview mirror. A big silver Mercedes 600. She told herself they were simply heading to St. Tropez like everybody else. Still she pressed her foot down a little harder and the Bentley surged forward. The Mercedes stayed right behind her.

It was afternoon and traffic was light. Sara was afraid to drive faster on the narrow curving road and she maintained her cruising speed, from time to time glancing in the mirror. Was the Mercedes really *following* her? She dismissed the idea, asking herself why they should.

The road widened slightly next to an area where trucks were able to pull to one side and allow the piled-up cars behind them to pass. Just as she approached it the Mercedes swung out from behind. It drew alongside, almost touching, forcing her into the narrow lay-by.

"Oh my God." Sara stomped on the brakes, shocked. "Oh my God . . ."

She threw a terrified glance at the Mercedes. The two men in white linen jackets from the hotel were running toward her . . . Were those guns gleaming in their hands?

In a split second all the lessons she had ever learned from TV about car hijacking ran through Sara's head. . . . She knew she would be dead if she stayed here. . . . Flinging the Bentley into gear she screeched round the Mercedes and out of the lay-by onto the road. The big car swung violently and she fought to bring it under control, not even taking time to look in the mirror and see if they were coming after her. There was a roaring noise behind her and a loud honk from a *camion,* a sixteen-wheeler, almost in her rear window. She breathed again in relief. There was no way the Mercedes could get past it.

Wiping the sweat off her forehead with the back of her hand, she said out loud, "Oh God, thank you, thank you. . . ."

And then the tears came.

29.

Billy Bashford was finding France lonelier than he had expected, his inner loneliness only accentuated by the fun-loving young people in St. Tropez, hedonistic, uncaring and somehow joyous in a way he had not felt in a long time. Driving the Hummer along the Old Port he wondered if he would ever feel that way again, the way he had when he first met his Betsy.

Now Betsy had been fun-loving too, not like these people, but in her own way. She had told him on the day they met that she was an observer in life rather than a participator. "I'm a quiet woman," she'd said seriously. "A schoolteacher."

Billy had almost expected her to say she taught an old-fashioned prairiecabin school but in fact Betsy taught in a tough urban ghetto in Fort Worth, and what's more, she cared deeply about "her" kids, as she called them. "They never had a chance," she said, "and I'm trying to give them one."

After they were married, a mere six months later, Betsy had carried that promise through, and she and Billy had endowed a foundation giving Texas inner-city children full college scholarships. Several thousand had benefited so far and in Betsy's memory, Billy had endowed a new scholarship fund for those who went on to further education, a master's degree, or even, in two cases so far, a Ph.D. Betsy Lowell Bashford's name would live on and Billy was forever grateful for that.

He was grateful for his daughter too, so unlike her mother in character, though not in appearance. As a young child, three, four, Laureen had been a dimpled charmer, bright-eyed, and as Billy put it, bushy-tailed, always up to mischief, always curious, always running, jumping, riding her horse. Laughter had rung round their front porch and through their hallways. God, life had been good then, he remembered as he headed for the St. Tropez parking lot.

The town was crowded of course, as it always was, and the pedestrians, in the way of all holidaymakers, took no notice of the rules, spilling off the narrow sidewalks into the road, almost under his wheels. A bunch of cute girls skipped out of his way, peeking in at him through the open window.

"Hey, Texas," the prettiest one yelled. She was wearing tiny yellow shorts and a bikini top, and her long blond hair floated sexily around her suntanned shoulders. "Like the hat! What're you doing tonight?"

She spoke in French and of course Billy did not understand a word but he got her meaning. Looking at her he was almost tempted, but he remembered he was here for Little Laureen and merely smiled and waved.

Laureen was a problem. Not only was she refusing to go to the beach with him, or even the pool, and in fact had agreed to go into St. Tropez town only once, and that was because she'd wanted to buy a collar for the Chihuahua, but today she had simply disappeared after breakfast.

She'd said she was going for a walk but the new woman at the reception desk told him she had gone off with young Bertrand Olivier, and Billy had panicked. He had no idea who Bertrand Olivier was, nor what he was doing with his daughter. Then he'd spotted the two of them sitting on the beach, heads together—Laureen in a sunhat he knew was not hers—poring over a newspaper like coconspirators. They had jerked apart guiltily, scrambling to their feet, when he'd called out her name, then the boy had tucked the newspaper under his arm and mumbling something about lunch, had taken off.

"Weird kid," Billy had said to Laureen, and she'd told him, defensively that Bertrand was okay. His mother had simply dumped him here, she said. He was alone . . . and anyhow . . . Her sentence had drifted off vaguely but Billy had understood.

Saying no more, he'd taken Laureen by the hand and the two of them had strolled the beach for an hour, Billy chatting to her about the sailboats, the pelicans, the good smells coming from the Beach Bar. Later, they'd had lunch together, he the grilled fish and Laureen french fries and a strawberry smoothie. Then she said she was tired and was going to her room. Left to his own devices, Billy had driven into St. Tropez and now he was circling the lot trying to park.

He'd just found a spot and was walking across the street when he saw the Bentley careen round the corner. He wasn't surprised, Belinda was a terrible driver. But then he saw it wasn't Belinda, it was Sara Strange. And, just for a change, she was crying. But this was no ordinary crying. There was a look of complete terror on Sara's face.

He stepped off the sidewalk to flag her down and she almost ran him over, braking as he leapt out of her way.

Billy took one look at her, then said, "Get out of the car."

Sara got out and stood obediently next to the Bentley.

Billy opened the passenger door and pushed her inside, slammed her door shut, then walked round to the driver's side and got in. Ignoring the curious onlookers staring at the expensive Bentley and its occupants, he drove off along the port.

After a while he shot Sara a keen sideways glance. "So what's up?" he asked, but all that happened was she began to cry again.

Billy drove aimlessly on, waiting for the storm to subside and the sobs to be less frequent. After a while she calmed down a little. He was out of town by now, driving along the beachfront in Ste. Maxime, then Juan les Pins. He pulled into a parking spot alongside the beach, got Sara out of the car, took her by the hand and led her across the road and down the steps to a café. It was little more than a hut really, selling suntan lotion and kids' beach balls, but it also sold simple snacks and drinks.

He put Sara at a table on the wooden platform overlooking the water, then went to the bar and ordered brandy and a Coke. He set the brandy down in front of her and said, "Okay, drink up. Then tell me what happened."

Her eyes were swollen into mere slits. "I already had a glass of champagne."

Billy wondered who she'd been drinking with but he pushed the glass toward her and said, "Just drink it, then talk."

Sara drank obediently, pulling a face but managing not to cough. She glanced at him again. "I was almost killed," she said.

"You mean you almost crashed the car?"

"No. I mean shot," she said.

Billy glanced quickly round to see who might be listening. Was he dealing with a crazy woman?

"They got me at a rest area," she said, gulping the brandy now. "They came at me with guns—"

"Listen," Billy stopped her. "Why not think it through, then start at the beginning?"

So Sara did. When she had finished she sat looking at Billy as though he had all the answers. And in some ways he had.

He said, "You were driving Belinda's car. Remember, she told us the husband would come after her, try to kill her? And I," he added also remembering, "assured her that would not happen, not with me and Mac Reilly around to protect her. Jesus!" He pushed the Stetson back on his forehead, stunned that Belinda's prediction had almost come true. He knew the thugs had recognized the Bentley and followed Sara intending to find out where Belinda was. And with the guns he had no doubt they had meant business.

He said, "Where's Belinda now?"

"In town. She was going shopping, said she would get a taxi home."

Billy's first instinct was to call Belinda and warn her but then he realized it would scare her. Instead he got Mac on his cell, told him there was serious trouble involving Belinda, quickly explained what had happened and asked him to meet them back at the Old Port. He said he would need someone to drive Belinda's Bentley back to the hotel so Sunny should come too.

Mac said they would be there right away and Billy drove back to the Old Port parking lot, hovering round until he saw the silver Peugeot with Mac at the wheel.

"I'll take the Bentley," Mac said. "Sara, you go with Sunny, and we'll all meet back at the hotel."

Sara's watery glance was grateful as she got into the car. With Mac and Billy around she felt safe.

Belinda had intended to take a taxi back home, but Nate had offered her a lift and the stores had promised to deliver their shopping bags, so she accepted. Anyhow, the Ducati was more fun. Her arms were wrapped around Nate's hard body, hands gripped in front, her helmeted head resting against his shoulder. I mean, how intimate could it get? Plus the Lycra had gone and now Nate looked human in regular, if expensive shorts and a shirt. In fact Belinda thought Nate Masterson looked very good indeed.

30.

It had been agreed that all the Misfits should meet at nine o'clock in the courtyard for dinner, when they would discuss the day's events. Meanwhile, Mac waited in the hall for Belinda to return, which she did a half hour later, squealing with laughter as Nate swung the bright yellow motorcycle to a stop in front of the glass doors.

"Hi there," she called, spotting Mac, and reluctantly letting go of Nate's body, sliding elegantly off the back of the Ducati with a great show of long brown legs. Then she and Nate strolled arm in arm up the steps.

Belinda noticed Mac's solemn face. "What's happened?"

"Let's go to the bar, I'll buy you a drink," he said.

Belinda and Nate glanced mystified at each other as they followed him. Belinda ordered a Cosmopolitan and Nate said he had never tried one, and nor had Mac, so it was three Cosmos.

They looked expectantly at Mac as the ice was crushed and the bartender added a couple of measures of Grey Goose vodka, a hit of Cointreau, and a measure of cranberry juice, shaken, then poured into chilled martini glasses. A squeeze of lime and the Cosmos were ready.

Belinda was the first to taste. She gave the bartender, whose name was Louis, a thumbs-up. "Very good. In fact almost as good as my own. I'm by way of being a martini expert," she told the others. "You know, the shaken-not-stirred kind, a hint of vermouth, ice-cold gin and salty olives."

"I've gotten through a few of those in my time," Mac agreed.

"Not me." Nate tasted his Cosmo critically. "The lime cuts the sweetness. It's good, though I'm more of a bourbon drinker myself. Only when under stress of course."

"Which in your job was most of the time," Mac guessed.

"Yours too."

Nate's answer was more of a question than a statement but Mac merely shrugged.

Belinda settled back on her red leather bar chair. "So, exactly why are we here, enjoying this delightful drink?"

"It's to do with the husband," Mac said.

Her eyes widened in surprise. "He's shown up?"

"No, but I believe two of his henchmen did. Sara was driving your Bentley. She'd noticed them at the Carlton in Cannes. They followed her in a Mercedes 600, cornered her in a rest area, came at her with guns—"

Belinda's horrified shriek turned the barman's head and he came over to ask if the drink was okay.

"Fine, it's just fine, great . . . thank you . . ." Belinda's anguished eyes met Mac's.

"She's okay," he said. "Badly shaken up, of course. Fortunately Billy spotted her in town. He said she was driving like a madwoman, almost ran him down she was crying so hard. He rescued her, drove round till she calmed down, revived her with brandy and got the story out of her."

"Where is she now?" Belinda was already on her feet.

"In your room, lying down. It's okay, Sunny's with her."

Belinda flopped back into the chair. "Obviously they thought it was me driving the Bentley . . ."

"No, but they certainly thought they could find out from Sara where you were, since she was driving your car."

"God, oh God . . . *Sara,* of all people."

"Belinda, what does the husband look like?"

"Jasper Lord—or Mikel Markovich is a more fitting name, the one he was given at birth by his mother in Belorussia fifty-five years ago." She took another sip of the Cosmo. "Mikel is right out of a James Bond movie, tailor-made by central casting to play the villain . . . massive like a bear, bald head like a fire hydrant, dark Ray-Bans, Italian suit, diamond pinky ring, the gold and diamond Rolex—he even wears a black South Sea pearl stickpin in his tie!" She threw them a dark glance from under lowered lids. "Trust me, you couldn't miss him if you tried."

"And *you* didn't try," Nate said.

Belinda lowered her eyes. "I had my reasons."

Mac didn't know what was going down with Nate but this certainly wasn't the time to be getting at Belinda for marrying a Russian mobster, because that was certainly what Mikel/Jasper Lord was. There were dozens of them here on the Riviera, spending lavishly and most with a glamorous woman, often a beautiful Russian, on their arm.

"I didn't know what he was when I met him," Belinda said suddenly. "I was . . . different then, naïve."

It was difficult to imagine Belinda ever being naïve but Mac knew everybody had their story. He said, "We're all meeting for dinner tonight, nine o'clock in the courtyard. They're preparing a quiet table for us near the fountain so our conversation can be private."

Belinda gave him that long glance from beneath half-lowered lids again. "You think of everything, don't you Mac Reilly, even about not being overheard, though surely there's no one here who could have any interest in us. Or in Mikel?"

"Or in Chez La Violette," Nate added.

Mac had noticed Nate was looking different, smart almost, in a casual sort of way. He said, "Chez La Violette is on our agenda too."

Nate groaned as he finished his drink. "Jesus, a business meeting. I thought I'd left all that behind."

Mac shrugged. "You can leave it behind if you like. There's no need to attend if you don't want to, but if you're interested in getting your money back, or in what happens to Belinda, then I advise you to be there."

Nate glanced at Belinda and said, "I'll be there. Want me to see you to your room?"

"Thanks." Belinda drained the glass then got ready to leave. "And thanks to *you*, Mac. God only knows what might have happened to Sara."

"Don't thank me. Sara got herself out of trouble and it was Billy who took care of her."

"Then I'll thank Billy later," Belinda said, with a farewell wave.

Mac noticed that Nate took her arm as they walked away, bending his head to her to catch what she said. Well, well, so Masterson was smitten with Belinda now, was he? At least he'd switched his attention from Sunny.

Back in their room, Sunny was waiting. Both dogs were on the bed with her, Pirate at the bottom, head on his paws, his one eye warily on the Chihuahua, who was curled into a tight ball on the pillow with Sunny fitting in between them any way she could.

"How's Sara?" Mac asked.

"Calmed down, no more tears, but now she's worried Belinda will blame herself for what happened."

"And she's right, Belinda does. Or if she doesn't, I do. Sara should never have gone to Cannes in that car." Mac shrugged regretfully. "Nothing she can do about it now. Those guys are on the lookout and Belinda is a wanted woman."

"What if they catch up to her?"

"Exactly." Mac's worried frown was not lost on Sunny. "Roddy called earlier," he said. "He told me the villa is still owned by Joel Krendler. He also owns a private plane. A Citation. I'm gonna call Alain Hassain at Interpol, tell him what's going on, ask if he can help."

Sunny sat up and took notice. Inspector Hassain had appeared on Mac's TV show several times in connection with international crimes. Now Mac gave him the Krendler/scam information, then said there was another problem, this one to do with Jasper Lord a.k.a. Mikel Markovich. He told Hassain that Lord's wife had left him and it looked as though he was ready to kill her if she didn't go back. "And maybe he'll kill her if she does," he added grimly. Then he said Lord was probably a mobster in his early days and he needed to know exactly what he was involved in now.

When Mac got off the phone Sunny was sitting on the edge of the bed, looking at him.

"I don't trust Krendler," he told her. "Ron Perrin told me not a lot is known about his personal life, though he's rumored to have been an actor in his youth."

"Hey, remember the theatrical makeup?" Sunny said. "The eye shadow that made him look like Camille in what's no doubt one of his favorite operas? I think our Krendler's a bit of a fake."

"He's not faking his money. The guy is seriously wealthy, though Perrin told me he's sure he must be hiding a lot of it, probably in Switzerland where, by the way, he flies quite often. To Zurich, a financial capital of the world. Perrin says he believes he owns a chalet in one of the cantons, on the far side of a mountain, which he very likely also owns."

"So, what does this have to do with our rental scam?"

Sunny was baffled and so was Mac. "I wish I knew," he said.

He took Reynaud's guest list from the nightstand. There were many famous names, French movie actors, American singers, international socialites. And amongst them was the name Gianni Valenti.

"Our new friend Valenti gets about." He folded up the list and replaced it on the table. "I wonder how he knows François Reynaud."

"They're both boat fanatics," Sunny said.

"True." Tired, he looked at her. She looked back at him.

"What say you and I go for a walk on the beach?"

"Just us?" She was already on her feet, smiling.

"And the dogs of course."

31.

It was nine o'clock and Belinda and Sara were waiting for the others at the courtyard table by the fountain. They were studying the night's menu.

Belinda had chosen to sit with her back to the wall, facing out so she could observe exactly who entered and left. She was wearing a sleeveless red silk jersey wrap dress with a ruffle down the front and silver sandals. She had not told Sara that it had crossed her mind, when she chose to wear red, that bloodstains from a possible bullet wound might not show.

Sara had not even wanted to come down but Belinda had insisted. She'd made up Sara's face for her, disguising the swollen eyelids with a taupe shadow and a thin stroke of brown eyeliner, though she could do nothing about the reddened eyes themselves. A rosy blusher and Belinda's favorite lipstick, Guerlain's Beige Sensuel, had transformed Sara from faded monochrome portrait to a charming color study. With her brown bangs and thick shoulder-length bob, wearing the peachy silk dress bought in St. Tropez, Belinda thought that, despite her trauma, Sara now looked part of "the real world."

"You realize you could go anywhere, looking like that?" she said.

Sara glanced up from the menu. "What? You mean? Like, *anywhere*?"

"Anywhere in the entire world. In fact I'd bet if your boss at the medical center saw you now, he wouldn't even recognize you. Who's that glamour girl, he'd say, looking very puzzled and quite pleased at the same time." Belinda was doing her best to cheer Sara up and she breathed a sigh of relief when she saw the younger woman smile. "Okay, so what are we going to eat tonight?" she asked, checking the menu.

"Perhaps I'll just have the fresh tomato basil soup." Sara's stomach was still in knots and she wasn't feeling too hungry.

"Okay, the soup." Belinda ran a finger down the list. "After that, I recommend the *noisettes* of Alpilles lamb, it's some of the best in the world. And perhaps a small green salad, then cheese—it'll be good, I already spoke to the chef and it comes fresh from the best supplier in Nice. Then we'll see about dessert." She beamed her big smile at Sara. "How does that sound?"

Sara put down her menu. "It sounds like a lot."

"Trust me, you'll enjoy it." Belinda had already summoned the waiter and was ordering two bottles of Château de Bellet rosé. "Make sure it's very cold, Gustave," she said. She knew the names of all the waiters and had already made friends with the chef, as well as with the hotel manager, the chambermaids and the gardeners. In fact Belinda knew everybody, and everybody certainly knew Belinda. It was just the way she was: charming, outgoing, friendly. And a great tipper.

"Tipping always pays off," she told Sara now. "Listen, I was once a hairstylist, right? I know from firsthand experience. You have to remember these people are working for their living and they look to you to augment their wages. It's expected, and it's necessary."

"Okay," Sara said. Personally, she always left the small change at Starbucks and was careful to leave exactly fifteen percent when she dined out locally. "The boyfriend never tipped," she volunteered. "He said it was unnecessary and that they'd already gotten paid."

"Bastard," Belinda said. "And quite in character. Ah, here come the others. With the man of the moment," she added, looking not at Nate, but at Mac.

Never in her life had Belinda been so glad to see a man. Well, perhaps that wasn't *quite* true, but in this case it was Mac Reilly she was glad to see, because, though she was keeping her cool for Sara's sake, inside Belinda was trembling. She knew the husband meant business.

"*Bonsoir*, Belinda, Sara." Holding the Chihuahua, Sunny greeted them with a smile, then edged round the table to kiss them, French-style. She took the chair next to Belinda, and with a brief good evening the three men sat opposite, facing the fountain. Pirate circled the table smiling his goofy hello then perched on the edge of the cool stone fountain, looking like a grizzled Bacchus.

Little Laureen was given the seat of honor at the end of the table, which suited her just fine because from there she had a direct view of the dining room and Bertrand. Bertrand had not arrived yet but the thought of their midnight rendezvous bubbled excitedly in her mind. She eyed Tesoro longingly, but Sunny was busy talking and did not offer to let her hold the dog.

The rosé was chilling in a silver bucket next to the table with its pretty coral-colored cloth and a bunch of iceberg roses in a pink bowl. A waiter hurried to light the hurricane lamps and fill their glasses. Badoit water was poured, and baskets of bread distributed along with little pots of tapenade, the typically Provençal spread made from olives and anchovies, which tasted, Sunny thought, like sunshine from the hills where the olive trees grew, sort of greenish and gold, a little tart, a little salty.

The waiter was a small compact man in a sailor-striped T-shirt with a red bandanna tied around his neck, *matelot*-style. His dark eyes twinkled into theirs as he glanced expectantly round.

"Mesdames, messieurs," he called for their attention. "Tonight our specialty is *daurade,* a sea bream caught fresh this morning. Also we have the John Dory, again line-caught today by our local fishermen. We have *gigot,* leg of lamb, roasted to pink perfection. We have the purple asparagus, grilled and finished with homemade hollandaise. There is a *tian* of our locally grown baby vegetables: eggplant, courgette blossoms, squash and tomatoes, roasted with herbs from our own garden, thyme and rosemary. The fish can be gilled or pan-roasted, as you prefer, and of course with a hint of garlic and herbs."

"Eh bien la petite," he said, starting with Laureen, holding court at the head of the table in her pink tutu. "What would you like?"

"Spaghetti Bolognaise, please."

"Little Laureen." Billy's voice had an exasperated edge. "Why not try the fresh fish?"

"No thank you." Laureen was polite but stubborn.

The waiter smiled. *"Bien sûr,* of course, *les spaghetti."* This was a family hotel and he was used to children.

The others mostly ordered the *daurade,* though Belinda chose the lamb and Sara, who was still feeling rocky, simply the *tian* of baby vegetables. She had never been a drinker but now she took a long sip of wine, looking tensely at Mac over the rim of her glass.

Mac lifted his own glass in a toast. "To all of you," he said, "who I have come to think of as my own bunch of International Waifs and Strays."

"To the Waifs and Strays," Belinda agreed.

"Or even the Misfits," Sunny added.

Billy's big laugh rang out. "What d'ya say, Little Laureen? You think we're misfits? Waifs and strays?"

Laureen's serious blue eyes met his. "Yes," she said.

"I know I am," Sara said.

"What about you, Nate?" Sunny thought he was looking smart tonight in white jeans and a very French cotton shirt in a pale blue and white check, sleeves rolled back showing tanned forearms. She'd bet Belinda had had something to do with that.

Nate lifted his shoulders in a dismissive shrug. "I've never thought of myself as a waif or stray, nor as a misfit."

"Then why are you here?"

Billy's question took Nate by surprise. He looked down at his plate where a crusty piece of baguette awaited.

"Well?" Sunny knew why he was here, but because everyone else had come clean in public about why they had rented Chez La Violette, she wanted Nate to speak up too.

Nate helped himself to tapenade. "The same reason as everybody else I guess," he said finally. "I'm here to find myself, find out what life has to offer. Real life, that is."

Just then the waiter interrupted with a salad of delicate mixed greens, the flavor enhanced with finely chopped fresh mint, lightly dressed with the best *niçoise* olive oil and a hint of lemon.

"Summer on a plate," Sunny said, but she noticed that worried little crease between Mac's brows again. He was obviously not thinking about the food and she knew where his mind was.

Looking round the table at them, Mac said, "So now we have not one, but *three* problems. The first is Chez La Violette, whose owner, Joel Krendler, denies all knowledge of the rental scam. I'm inclined to believe him, though there is something strange about him and I'm investigating further. Which leaves us with the same problem. Where is Madame Lariot?"

They ate their salads in silence, waiting for what might come next.

"The second is the husband, Jasper Lord, who as evidenced by Sara's nasty experience this afternoon, is on Belinda's trail and will stop at nothing to get her back."

A shiver ran down Sara's spine as she momentarily relived her terror. She took another gulp of wine.

"The third," Mac said, "concerns the art theft and murder that took place nearby on the night of the storm. The night you all arrived."

They looked up now, puzzled by the last addition.

"What does that have to do with us?" Billy asked.

Little Laureen gave him a condescending look. "*Daddee*, haven't you heard? There's a really big reward for the robbers' capture. Five hundred thousand euros."

Billy glanced astonished at his daughter. "And how do you know that, sweetheart?"

Laureen shrugged her shoulders looking down at her untouched salad. "I just know."

"To answer your question, Billy," Mac said, "it really doesn't connect with Chez La Violette. At least not yet." He had his own theories but he wasn't ready to explain right now. "Anyhow, our first priority is to protect Belinda. You"—he indicated Belinda with his glass—"must never go out alone. In fact it would be better if you didn't leave the hotel, at least for the next few days. The husband is very smart, he'll be on your tail before too long. Meanwhile we need to keep you safe, right here. And meanwhile, also, I have a contact at Interpol who's checking out Mikel Markovich a.k.a. Jasper Lord. The French are a tolerant race but they do not allow international crime on their turf, and you can bet the husband is up to no good."

Belinda's laugh sounded a touch bitter. "'Up to no good.' That's probably the understatement of the year."

"Did you never have even an inkling of what was going on? How and where the husband made all his money?"

"He told me real estate. That, and caviar and Russian vodka." Belinda sighed. "What did I know? I may look the role but I'm no good at reading people, I never even questioned him." She looked suddenly forlorn. "He was nice to me, you know, in the beginning. I liked him. My big Russian bear, I called him. He treated me like a lady, sent huge bouquets of flowers, and diamond earrings in a red leather box from Cartier, wrapped in newspaper like the fish and chips I'd ordered. He told me I was beautiful and he paid me the biggest compliment any man can give a woman. He asked me to marry him."

"And then he took you over."

Belinda ran her hands distractedly through her short blond crop. "Jasper controlled me. Everything from what I ate to what I wore, even to what I thought! I was going crazy. And when I rebelled Jasper got violent and I knew it was time to go."

Sunny patted her arm sympathetically. "He's a control freak. You were right to leave."

"It took a couple of black eyes before I got up the courage though."

"Jesus," Billy's shocked voice cut in. "The bastard," he added vehemently.

"*Daddeeeee . . .*" Laureen glared at him.

"Sorry, baby. Heat of the moment." He leaned across the table and patted Belinda's hand. "We're here now, sweetheart," he said kindly. "Don't you worry about a thing."

"Not only that," Mac said, "I'm arranging security for you. I'll know more tomorrow. Meanwhile, tell me, was the husband interested in art?"

Head to one side, Belinda considered. "He owned paintings, Russian mostly, there was a beautiful garden scene and a kind of scary nude. Oh, and a Botero bronze, you know the typical thing, a huge rotund figure, this one lying down, resting on one elbow, head propped on a hand."

"That's a famous piece," Nate said. "I've seen ones like it in the Museum of Modern Art."

"But you wouldn't say he was a collector? There were no auction catalogs lying around, information on art gallery openings, things like that?"

"He wasn't interested. I think he simply bought what you were supposed to buy, as long as it cost a lot. Everything Jasper did or has can be equated with money. By that I mean price. I guess he thought I had a price too, only it turned out to be too expensive for me. And now I'm trapped here in this hotel. I can't go anywhere."

"If you're gonna be trapped it might as well be at the Hôtel des Rêves. And from now on Belinda, one of us will always be with you," Billy reassured her. "Right, Nate?"

Nate was thinking of the good time he'd had with Belinda that day, and how things might suddenly turn out very differently. "Right," he said.

"We'll work out a roster," Billy said. "Then we'll always know exactly where Belinda is and who's with her."

They were discussing how to do this when Laureen spotted Bertrand on his way to his corner table by the window.

Sunny caught Laureen looking at him. She said, "Little Laureen, would you like to ask Bertrand to join us?"

Laureen's shocked eyes swiveled her way. "No. Oh no." Then, because her mother had taught her always to be polite, even when it was something you didn't want, and what she didn't want right now was to share Bertrand with the others, she added, "Thank you."

"Then there's the art theft," Mac said.

Nate raised his brows, remembering Mac's question to Belinda about the husband's art collection. "I see now where you're going."

"You think there's a connection with Jasper?" Belinda was surprised.

"Hey, right now, all I'm going on is gut feelings. I have no idea who's involved, or how. All I know is a young man is dead and Monsieur François Reynaud, the man whose artworks were stolen feels responsible, and I want to help him."

Laureen wasn't listening. Her quick sidelong glance took in the new woman, Renée from reception, walking toward Bertrand's table. She said something, then Bertrand got up quickly and followed her from the room. Laureen wondered what was going on.

A delicious aroma heralded the arrival of two waiters. Belinda checked out Laureen's spaghetti. "We call that spag bol where I come from," she said. "It's a staple in every English girl's diet, probably because it's cheap and the only thing any of us can cook. But yours looks wonderful."

"Would you like some?"

Belinda laughed and said no thanks, but Laureen's eyes were already back on Bertrand. He was walking into the dining room, head down, big hands dangling at his sides, like a puppet whose strings had been cut. *Something had happened.*

She wanted desperately to go to Bertrand, ask him what was wrong, but for the moment she could not escape. She had to sit there, moving the now-unwanted spaghetti round her plate with her fork, waiting for a reprieve.

Eventually, it came. They had finished eating and were sitting back, relaxed, pouring more wine, talking, talking, talking. All grown-ups ever did was *talk*. She said urgently, "Daddy, may I be excused?"

Billy looked at her, surprised. "Why? Where are you going?"

"I'm going to see my friend."

"Aah, Bertrand Olivier." Billy had remembered his name. "Okay, honeybunch. Just don't get lost en route, right?"

"Oh, Dad*deee*." Little Laureen's groan followed her as she half-ran from the courtyard and into the dining room.

Bertrand was sitting at his lonely table, staring down at his plate. Though he was normally pale, now his face had a transparent, almost alabaster cast to it as though all the blood had been drained from him. He did not even glance up when Laureen scraped a chair noisily across the tiles. The two sat side by side, not looking at each other, not speaking, yet lines of communication ran between them like electricity.

"Something bad's happened." Laureen wasn't prying, if Bertrand did not want to talk about it, that was okay, she simply wanted him to know that she understood.

Bertrand did not answer and they sat on in silence. He had not touched his roast lamb with the special *pommes Anna,* a crispy, buttery cake of potatoes, usually a favorite.

Laureen snitched a piece of potato from his plate.

"Maman just telephoned." Bertrand's voice was dead.

Laureen nodded and casually ate another piece of potato, as if what he was saying meant nothing to her, though she was guessing this meant Bertrand's mother was returning. Still, she did not ask, unwilling to break the invisible rules between them, like dark alleys they never crossed. Bertrand kept his emotions private and so did she.

Bertrand pushed back his chair. Hitching up his shorts, he said, in French, "I'm leaving."

Laureen jumped up. She followed him as he marched, head down, arms swinging stiff like a soldier, as though he was keeping himself together with a great physical effort.

"But Bertrand, what about our rendezvous?" She was whispering, afraid the other diners might hear. But Bertrand marched on.

He stopped at last by the glass front doors and turned to look at her. The ribbon of her ballet slipper had come undone and she went down on one knee, tying it quickly, looking anxiously up at him.

"Maman got married," he said, in an ice-cold voice that Laureen knew meant trouble. "I'm going to the beach."

He turned abruptly and stalked off. Laureen stood on the steps watching as he disappeared into the blue darkness. She wanted to go after him but knew she must not. Scared, she walked back to the courtyard where the adults were still sitting, talking and drinking wine, unaware that for Bertrand, like Chicken Little, the sky had just fallen down.

"Hey, sweetheart." Her father put his arm around her shoulders, and gave her an affectionate squeeze. Then Sunny put Tesoro on her lap and asked if she would look after the dog while she went to powder her nose. Sara and Belinda went with her and Laureen sat with the Chihuahua pressed so hard to her chest she knew it must be able to feel her heart pounding. Bertrand was in trouble and she didn't know what to do.

Presently the women came back, hair combed, lipstick freshened, talking about shoes, of all things. Why, Laureen wondered, did women always talk about shoes? All she needed were her ballet slippers and her flip-flops. Oh, and her cowboy boots.

Those boots had been specially made for her by a famous man in Laredo, Texas, and were of the softest leather in a pale golden color with pointy toes and almost-heels, and with a place for spurs, though of course she would never use spurs on a horse. Nor would she wear those boots for riding. They were copies of her mother's own. They were special. In fact the boots were upstairs sitting side by side in the bottom of the armoire where she had placed them when she'd unpacked and now she had a sudden urge to feel them on her feet, to feel at home and not far away in this strange new country.

She glanced at her Mickey Mouse watch, bought on a trip to Disneyland a few years ago because she'd liked the red strap and the fact that Mickey's yellow-gloved hands moved to point out the hours and the minutes. Shocked, she saw it was already eleven-thirty. Dinner started so late here in France and went on simply forever. Now Belinda and Sunny were eating dessert, perfumy wild strawberries that they said were called *fraises des bois,* with dollops of cream on top. Sunny asked if Laureen would like some but she shook her head and said no thank you and anyhow she was tired and was going to bed.

She put Tesoro carefully back on Sunny's lap. For a second their eyes met, then, shockingly, Sunny touched her lips to Laureen's brow in a kiss. Laureen flinched, eyes squinched as though she had been shot. *No one kissed her, except her father. No one else. Absolutely no one.*

"Good night, Little Laureen," Sunny said, puzzled by her reaction. "Sleep well."

Laureen walked stiff-legged back to her father. "I'll be sleeping by the time you go to bed, Daddy," she said. Like Bertrand she was holding her emotions together.

"Whatever you say, baby. But hey, I'll walk you back to your room, make sure everything's okay."

Telling the others he would be back, Billy took Laureen's hand and they threaded their way through the tables of late diners, who smiled as they watched the cowboy father and his odd, plump tutued little girl go by. It was late, they told each other indulgently, and the child was tired, probably had an exhausting day, swimming and running around in the sun . . .

But Billy knew better. "You okay, little sweetheart?" he asked, unlocking Laureen's door and switching on the lamp. "You're not getting sick or anything?"

"I'm just tired, that's all."

Laureen sat on the end of her bed and Billy came to kiss her good night. "Sleep well, my baby," he said tenderly. "Tomorrow is another day, and tell you what, you can choose exactly what you want to do. Parasailing, Jet Ski, the pirate boat, a visit to Monte Carlo to look at the yachts. You name it, kid."

"Thank you, Daddy."

He stopped at the door to look back at her, and suddenly glad for his reassuring, overbearing, presence, Laureen said softly, "I love you, Daddy."

"And I love you too, baby." And with a good-night wave, Billy was gone.

32.

Laureen took off the ballet slippers and pulled on the cowboy boots. She stood in front of the long mirror stuck inside the armoire door, turning this way and that, admiring them. She checked her watch again: 11:45. She climbed over the suitcases and the bed to get to the window and peeked down into the court-yard. They were still there, sitting around the table, talking, talking, talking. It was risky but if she were quick she could run down the stairs and slip out the door without them seeing her.

Climbing back over the suitcases, she opened the door and checked the corridor. Empty. She turned to look at her wand, lying on the bed. The silver star on top glittered in the lamplight and she hesitated. If Bertrand needed her help it would come in handy; but if they went exploring it would only be a nuisance, and anyway she was afraid she might lose it. No, no wand.

All the doors were closed on the corridor and the yellow cotton window curtains bellied in the breeze. At the bottom of the stairs she flattened herself against the wall, checking to see if anyone was watching. She was in luck. No one was around.

It was a moonless night but low lights were built into the side of the path, to the place where it met the beach. After that all was darkness.

She ran down the path and stood for a second, checking. Phosphorescence glimmered on the sea and languorous little waves hit the shore, sliding back with a slow shushing sound. *Cigales,* the Mediterranean crickets, chirruped in the umbrella pines and a breeze rustled through the long grasses at the edge of the small dunes, bringing with it the scent of night-blooming jasmine. The Beach Bar was closed and shuttered and no one was around.

It was hard to walk on sand in the cowboy boots and now she wished she'd put on flip-flops. She was half-afraid Bertrand wouldn't be there, that he'd gone somewhere else to be alone. But he was.

He glanced up when he heard her.

"Hi," she said, flopping down next to him.

Bertrand propped himself on one elbow, looking at her. His blond hair and white face gave him a ghostly look and his thick glasses hid his eyes. He spoke slowly, as though he'd been thinking about it for a long time. "My mother got married today, to the Italian. She told me she has three stepchildren now, two girls and a boy, my age. She said they don't have room for me."

Laureen's eyes widened; she was looking at a tragedy she understood.

"Maman said I'm 'difficult.' Her exact words. She said I can't come and live with them, and I'm to go to boarding school and finish my education. When I'm eighteen, then they will think about what to do with me."

Angry, Laureen sat up straight. *"Bitch."* She spat out the bad word. It came to her out of the blue, she'd probably heard the cowhands use it.

"Cow," Bertrand agreed, though Laureen thought *vache* sounded nicer in French.

She hardly dared ask what he intended to do, so she just sat there, looking at him, lying on his back again, staring at the sky as though hoping a great spaceship might come down and scoop him up and solve his problems all in one go.

"Bertrand, what shall we do?" she asked, automatically including herself in his life.

"Maman said I should stay here for the next few weeks. I should tell the hotel manager she will pay the bill as soon as she has a chance. He'll understand how it is, she told me, her getting married so suddenly, all the excitement."

"Not excitement for you." Laureen lay back too, watching the star-studded sky again, listening to the waves. "We'll just have to find the robbers then you can have the five hundred thousand euros and do whatever you want to do. You won't even need to ask her permission."

"Correct," Bertrand said solemnly. The two fell silent. Then, "I can't go spying tonight," he said.

"That's okay."

"Want to come and see my lair?"

"Where is it?"

"On a hill, not too far from here."

"Okay."

It seemed to Laureen to take a long time to get to Bertrand's lair, but even though her feet hurt in the pointy cowboy boots, it was worth it.

Bertrand had not brought his cape but they sat together on the sparse grass, propped against the rock that arched protectively over them. "Almost like a cave," Laureen said, half-expecting to see the stolen works of art, but there were only the curious lizards, woken from their rest, who came out to inspect them, then slithered quickly away.

The sea glimmered below and the stars glittered above but unlike the old saying, nothing in the heavens was right with *their* world. They were simply a pair of children, whose feeling of abandonment had caught up to them.

Tears streamed from under Bertrand's glasses as he cried silently. Laureen's own tears joined in, sliding down her face like hot rain, hurting and healing at the same time.

The first hint of gray lifted the sky when the two finally made for home. Laureen stumbled on the rocky outcrop in her boots and Bertrand took her hand.

At the hotel gates he said, "You go first. There'll be no one about at this time. There never is. Just keep close to the wall, and better take off the boots, they'll make too much noise."

Laureen tugged them off, then slid away into the still-dark dawn. Bertrand was right, there was no one about and she hurried, unnoticed, back to her room closing the door silently behind her.

Still in the tutu, now stained with grass, she flung herself on the bed. Quite suddenly, sleep came to her, closing her eyes in welcome forgetfulness.

For Bertrand it was not quite so easy. In his room, with the sound of "Riders on the Storm" playing softly, he sat at his table and began to write in his journal, about his "Secret Scientific Experiments." But it would never be the same. Real Life had caught up to him. He did not even know would become of him. Now he was truly Alone.

33.

Next morning, Mac and Sunny were enjoying a leisurely breakfast on their terrace. The coffee in a silver thermos was hot and strong and the basket of sweet rolls and breads tempting. Tesoro, of course, was snuggled on Sunny's lap, while Pirate balanced on a chair, inspecting French life taking place below, giving the occasional excited *wuff* whenever he spotted another dog.

"I'll gain at least five pounds," Sunny complained, helping herself to another small sugar-dotted gem.

"It's worth it." In his own habitat Mac was a blueberry-pancakes-breakfast kind of guy, but here, with a view of the calm blue sea, and with the scarlet geraniums fighting for supremacy over the climbing yellow-pink roses and the air heavy with their scent, the simple coffee and croissant filled his every need. He heaved a sigh of pleasure as he refilled his cup. "I'm a satisfied man."

Sunny gave him that upward mischievous glance through her lashes. "Glad to hear it."

"But . . ."

She groaned. "How did I know there had to be a *but*?"

Mac was reading the text message on his phone. "*But* . . . it seems I have business to take care of."

Sunny didn't want to ask "what business," but knew she must. "Okay," she sighed. "So tell me . . ."

"I have to make an appointment to see the *préfecture* of police in Nice." Mac was now rereading Raynaud's guest list. "I have a couple of questions for him."

"And why would the police chief want to answer *your* questions?"

"Because I represent François Reynaud, and Monsieur Reynaud is an important man in these parts. And also, on another matter, because my Interpol contact just informed me that Joel Krendler's plane has frequently landed at several small airports in the South of France. Despite what he told us about never coming back since the accident."

"Because of 'the jinx,'" Sunny said. "But what's Krendler got to do with Reynaud?"

"Probably nothing, but he's still a connection to our lost rental money."

Sunny threw him a skeptical glance. "Come on, Mac, this is getting farfetched even for you."

"So I'm wrong." Mac shrugged. "You know me, I always go on that gut feeling, and a connection, however intangible it may seem, is still a connection. Besides, where else am I to look for a link to Madame Lariot?"

"If that's even her name."

"I also want to get all the information from the police on the murder at Reynaud's place, and a list of exactly what was stolen. Plus any new insights on suspects."

Sunny was sitting back in a chair, coffee cup in both hands, gazing at him and Mac said, "Want to come along for the ride?"

"Actually"—Sunny put down the cup and leaned her elbows on the table, looking him in the eye—"*actually,* I have a little investigating of my own to take care of. So, yes, I'll 'come along for the ride,' Mac Reilly."

Grabbing her hands, he pulled her toward him so that their faces were almost touching. "What 'investigation'?"

"Oh, I'm curious that's all . . ."

Mac groaned. "For God's sake, tell me, woman."

"I'm curious about Violette. You know, who she was. What she was. When she built the villa. And why she left it."

"And why it's supposed to be haunted." He knew that was what she really wanted to know.

"Right."

"And where do you propose to do that, Miss Detective?"

"At the offices of the newspaper, *Nice-Matin.* I thought since she was local, they'd have something in their archives."

Mac's phone vibrated and he checked his messages. "Good," he said. "Lev Orenstein is on his way from New York. He'll be here tonight. I've put him in charge of Belinda's security."

Sunny's eyes widened. Lev had trained with the Israeli Special Forces, and was a triple black belt in karate. He owned and ran an international security company handling top people and with a strong antiterrorist commitment. Lev was quite simply the most experienced, and the best. It was Lev who had watched over Allie Ray when she was in trouble, and Belinda was lucky to have him on her side.

Mac was already dialing Belinda's cell phone.

"Who the hell is it at this time in the morning?" Belinda's weary voice answered.

"It's your very own detective, calling to tell you that by tonight you will have your very own security man, who also happens to be the very best in the business."

Belinda pushed the airline eye mask onto her head and sat up. *"Really?"*

"Really. His name is Lev Orenstein."

"How will I recognize him?"

Mac laughed. "You can't miss him, he's six-four, bald as a coot, usually wearing aviators, a Tommy Bahama flowered shirt, jeans and sneakers. And in good enough shape to take on all comers. Okay?"

Relief swept the tension out of Belinda's spine and she sagged back against the pillows. "Thanks, Mac. Really, thank you."

Mac knew how frightened Belinda was, despite the brave front she'd put on. "Better hope the husband doesn't cut off your bank account. Lev costs money."

"The husband can't do that. I had the foresight some months ago to transfer a great deal of money and a lot of expensive jewelry to the Bank of England that nobody can touch."

"Then that makes life easier. Okay, talk to you later."

Within half an hour, Mac and Sunny were downstairs waiting for the valet to bring round their car. Mac went off to deliver the dogs to the hotel kennel and Sunny waved to Caroline who was back behind the reception desk. Caroline called *bonjour* with her usual pleasant smile.

Sunny noticed she was wearing her emerald ring today, plus she had a very nice handbag. Chanel, white, quilted, and very expensive. She thought Caroline's boyfriend must have money and apparently he was treating her right.

"We missed you," Sunny said. "I hope you enjoyed your day off?"

"It was lovely, thank you. And you, Madame Alvarez, where are you going today? Somewhere pleasant for lunch, I hope?"

Sunny laughed. "I hope so too, though I'm eating so much I'm going to go back home twice the size." It occurred to her that since it was close by, perhaps Caroline knew the story of the villa. She said, "Caroline, I wonder, do you know anything about Chez La Violette?"

"*Moi?*" Caroline looked surprised by Sunny's question. She frowned. "*Mais rien, madame.* I know nothing. Only that the reputation of Chez La Violette is not pleasant. It's not a good place, everyone knows it has ghosts. That's why it never sells."

Sunny knew from Krendler that was not true but said nothing.

"You should be glad you didn't have to stay there," Caroline added. "You would *not* have liked it, especially at night."

"Just curious," Sunny said as Caroline returned to her computer.

"*Au 'voir, madame,*" she said, briskly, already busy with her work.

In no time Sunny and Mac were threading their way through the usual tangled St. Tropez traffic on their way to Nice.

"I thought we might have a nice dinner tonight," Mac said casually. "Then maybe take in the action at the casino in Monte Carlo."

Dismayed, Sunny glanced down at her sugar pink Lilly Pulitzer cotton minidress printed with a design of green palm trees. "Why didn't you *tell* me, Mac? I'm not dressed for it."

"I wanted to surprise you." He took her in, in a quick sideways glance. "Anyhow, you look great to me."

Sunny sighed. "Not great enough for a smart restaurant and the Casino."

"So, go shopping."

She laughed. Mac had the answer to everything.

He dropped her at the doors of the newspaper office and arranged to pick her up later, then took off for the police precinct.

Sunny pushed open the heavy glass doors, walked to the reception desk and told the woman what she wanted. She was led down into a basement that, it seemed to her, must run the entire length of the block, and pointed to the section marked "V."

It did not take long to find what she was looking for. In fact there were pages and pages of files on "The Extraordinary Chanteuse, La Violette."

Two hours later, Sunny had collected a great deal of information which she quickly photocopied on the machine provided, then tucked safely into her straw tote. Her brain was into overload and she was relieved to find Mac outside, propping up the wall, one leg crossed over the other, dark glasses on, and looking, she thought, exactly like a Private Eye.

"Have I got information for you," she said, after a quick preliminary kiss.

"More than I have then." Mac had drawn a blank with the cops. They had nothing new to tell, and all he'd come away with was the list of stolen artworks and the basic details of the crime scene. As with the previous art thefts, none of the paintings was recognizably famous, like for instance van Gogh's irises, or Monet's water lilies. All had been in private hands for years and only an expert, or a friend, would have known about them.

"I have a surprise for you," he said to Sunny. She stared warily at him, hoping it wasn't another murder he simply *had* to investigate. He said, "I thought we'd save the long drive home and stay overnight."

Sunny's spirits rose. "Where?"

"Where else but the best? The Hôtel de Paris in Monte Carlo. I've already booked it and made a reservation at Alain Ducasse's restaurant."

She'd heard of it. "The Louis Fifteenth."

"You can shop first for whatever you need, then a rest, a little late dinner, and then a little gambling . . ."

"I bet I'll win."

"You betcha, baby," Mac said.

34.

The Misfits were on the hotel beach, all in a row under blue canvas–swagged shade, sun-lotioned and lip-balmed, courtesy of Belinda who, though her tan was mostly spray-on, was ever careful of her skin and never left the house without such products. They were conveniently near the Beach Bar for those in need of sustenance, like for instance, Sara, who, Belinda observed, was already on her second glass of rosé and it was still only eleven o'clock.

Sitting up, she began to rub more lotion into her already glossy brown body, casting a shrewd look at Sara, who was sitting up, eyes hidden behind large sunglasses, mouth tense, fingers curled into tight fists.

"Better go easy on the booze," Belinda warned. "It's no way to steady your nerves. That takes 'resolve.' Trust me," she added. "As usual, I know from personal experience."

"You seem to have learned too much in your life, Belinda." Sara took another sip of wine. So what if it was only eleven? Anyway, it tasted better than a double decaf skinny latte.

Belinda leaned over and took the glass from her hand. "Listen to me, Sara Strange," she said sternly. "If you think I'm gonna sit here and let you drink yourself into oblivion because the husband's henchmen put the fear of God into you yesterday, you're mistaken. Get over it, girl. I promise it won't happen again. And by tonight we'll have our own security. You'll never have to worry again. Mac promised me."

Overhearing, Nate propped himself on one elbow. "Who is this security man?"

"He goes by the name of Lev and he's the best. He's flying in from the

States. He'll be with us tonight." Belinda scrambled to her feet. "I'm off for a swim. Anybody coming?"

Nate leapt up, brushing off the sand, and Sara followed reluctantly. Little Laureen remained on her mattress, still in the orange tutu, holding on to Tesoro who she'd discovered had been left in the kennel, and whom she had "rescued." She'd kind of hoped Bertrand would have found Pirate by now and rescued him too. Poor Pirate had stared so mournfully after her as she'd walked away.

Arms round her knees with the little dog tucked beneath, she thought about how to help Bertrand. She knew it was urgent because at the end of the summer vacation time in France, when everybody went back to work, Bertrand would be banished to boarding school and would probably never even see his wicked mother again. An image of Cruella De Vil in *101 Dalmatians* flashed into her mind. She thought Bertrand's mother must look exactly like that: sharp pointed face; big red mouth; pointy black eyebrows. The very picture of "wicked."

The others were already walking down to the water on the little straw paths laid over the sand to stop their feet from burning.

"You comin' for a walk, hon?" Billy said. "We could just wade. I'll bet that water'll be real cool," he added, noting her flushed cheeks.

But Laureen shook her head. "I can't leave Tesoro."

"Bring Tesoro along. Tell you what, let's take her for a walk along the water's edge. I'll bet you she'll like it."

Laureen thought the little dog looked hot so she said okay, and let her father take her hand and pull her up. She carried Tesoro until they got to where the sea surged quietly onto the sand, leaving it soft as silk, and bubbling slightly under her bare toes. She put the dog down. A tiny wave splashed close by and the Chihuahua leapt into the air. "Like a ballet dancer." Laureen laughed as Tesoro's lips curled back in a snarl, chasing the wave as it slid back, only to be hit by a second one.

Billy watched as his little daughter swept the Chihuahua up from the waves holding her aloft, paws waggling frantically. He couldn't recall the last time he'd heard Laureen laugh, but it was certainly before her mother died. It had taken a small dog to bring a modicum of joy back into her frozen heart, and to Billy that alone made the trip to France worthwhile. There were dogs on the ranch of course, working dogs mostly, or those belonging to the help, but as soon as they returned home he would take Laureen to choose one of her own, a Chihuahua if that was what she wanted.

"She's so cute, Daddy," Laureen said as they strolled down the beach.

Billy agreed, but he decided to keep the dog buying a surprise to cheer her up when they got back. He held her hand and with the little dog darting in front, they strolled silently on. Laureen seemed lost in her thoughts again, and Billy didn't try to force her to talk, though he was wishing she would at least let him buy her a bathing suit so she could be like the other kids on the beach, but Laureen seemed determined to stick to the tutu.

Bertrand had been on Laureen's mind since waking that morning and now, when she passed "their" rock where they had sat and talked and Bertrand had told her about his mother, she hung her head, unable to look because the memory was too painful. *Poor Bertrand. What would he do? Where would he go? Who would look after him?*

She glanced sideways at her father. He was wearing red surfer bathing shorts and whistling softly, his hat still jammed on his head. He never removed that ten-gallon Stetson no matter how hot he was. Suddenly, Laureen jumped up and snatched it off.

Billy looked down at her, astonished. "Now why'd you do that, honeybunch?"

"Because you're too hot. And Mommy would have said you'll have a stroke in this heat."

Billy nodded ruefully; he'd heard Betsy say that a million times. He ran his hands through his thick wavy hair, a surprising light ginger color that Betsy once said reminded her of fresh apricots.

"You must buy a straw hat, Daddy," Laureen said, looking after him now because her mother wasn't there to do it.

"Which reminds me," Billy said, "where did you get the straw hat you're wearing?"

Laureen blushed. "Ooh, I just found it . . . ."

Billy said sternly, "I hope you didn't find it before it got lost," and Laureen blushed some more. But just then Billy stopped.

He was looking up the incline from the beach over the grass-studded dunes to where the roof of a house peeked through the pine trees. A white house whose dull windows did not reflect the light and that, even on this sunny day, seemed steeped in shadow.

"Well, I'm darned," he said, "if that isn't Chez La Violette. I never realized it was so close. And it looks as though there's a path from the beach that leads right to it. Hey, maybe it wasn't so bad after all."

After a while, they turned and made their way back to where Belinda was just emerging from the sea, a graceful bronze naiad in a tiny white bikini. Sara followed her, stumbling through the waves, pink from the sun in her striped bikini, arms crossed protectively over her chest. Laureen didn't even notice. She was thinking about Bertrand and the urgency of finding the stolen artworks and getting the reward to save him.

Belinda saw them coming and stood, hands on her hips, a big grin on her face. Billy's carrot hair stood on end, matching the freckles on his square, ruddy face. There was a wide white stripe across his forehead where the hat had fit. Belinda laughed and said, "If it wasn't for Laureen and the dog, I swear I'd never have recognized you, Billy Bashford."

She went up to him and ran her finger across the white stripe near his hairline. "Soft as a baby's behind and untouched by sun or human hand." Billy's eyes were the color of raisins as he gazed silently back at her. She said, "You've been hiding your light under a bushel with that hat, my friend. But don't worry, I can help you, a little Clarins face tanner will take care of it."

Billy stared at Belinda, bemused. He'd never used a face cream—any cream—in his life. She linked her arm through his as they walked back to their shady mattresses. He could smell the sea on her skin, salty and sweetened with suntan lotion. It made his heart skip a beat.

And it made Nate quite jealous, though the truth was he was also still enamored of Sunny. He wondered where she was today.

35.

The Hôtel de Paris, in the Place du Casino in Monte Carlo, was sumptuous; a marble-pillared façade led into a lofty salon topped with a dome and a glorious Art Deco rose window. On every wall was a precious tapestry, a mural or a painting; antique tables held silk-shaded lamps and rich carpets muffled the sound of Sunny's heels as she and Mac made their way from the reception to the elevator.

The desk clerk had not raised an eyebrow when they'd said they had no luggage, he'd merely bowed respectfully and given the key to the bellman, who hitched their shopping bags onto a golden trolley and escorted them to their room, high enough to command a view of the great rock with the Grimaldi castle, flag flying, and of the harbor jammed with private yachts. Farther out, a cruise ship, an enormous floating white palace, blasted its siren as it sailed majestically off to the next port of call.

They stood watching the cruise ship depart until it became a mere speck on the horizon. Mac was thinking how different Monaco was from his home turf. Malibu was rawer, somehow, and more vigorous, with its surfers and showbiz folk, beach walkers and dogs, hamburgers and sushi and its great glass houses. Malibu was of today, while Monaco represented the past and hundreds of years of progress, ruled over by the Grimaldi family.

But the bathroom was definitely of today, if not tomorrow, all creamy marble with a huge tub, a double shower and elegant gold fittings. In fact the shower was just the right size for two, as they soon found out.

Later, looking at Sunny lying on the huge bed, her wet hair wrapped in a towel, reading glasses perched on her nose, a sheaf of papers in hand, Mac thought that maybe he did not have her full attention.

He plopped down next to her, running his fingers along the delicate sun-blonded hairs on her golden arm. "Violette is coming between us," he said.

But Sunny was still immersed in what she was reading.

"Listen to this, Mac," she said finally. "This headline says, 'La Violette Triumphs at Paris Opéra.'"

Remembering Krendler, Mac's ears pricked up.

"But Violette was no opera singer," Sunny added. "She was strictly French music hall, in the days when music hall ruled. You know, the follies and the big stages. It says she was 'A Cabaret Artiste, singer of sexy songs, glamorous, gorgeous, she brought a sense of intimacy to the stage so that every male in the audience believed she was singing just to him.'"

Sunny looked at Mac. "I'm quoting."

"You mean she was a sort of Piaf."

"Oh no. Piaf was Paris's 'Little Sparrow,' a tiny plain waiflike woman with a big voice. La Violette was tall with a soft sexy voice. Here I'll quote from this other review. 'La Belle Violette, tall, broad-shouldered, an Amazon in her liquid silver gown that slid over her breasts like a lover's hands.'"

"They said *that*—in *those* days?"

Sunny looked at the date. "This was in nineteen-thirty, when she was twenty-seven years old. And *gorgeous*."

She handed Mac a sepia-toned photograph, showing a woman with an oval face, a pert nose, a wide full-lipped mouth, innocent pansy eyes and a tumble of hair that fell over those alluring eyes and those white shoulders, half-hiding the famous breasts.

"She could play Caesars Palace, looking like that," Mac said.

Sunny handed him another picture, this one taken at a race meeting in Paris, of Violette in a chic spring suit that must surely be early Chanel, with little black kid booties that showed off her long slender legs. There was another of her sitting beside an English lord in a Lagonda sports car, and later ones of her on a terrace, in what in those days were called palazzo pajamas, soft and drapey, alongside the Prince of Wales and Mrs. Simpson.

Sunny peered at the photograph. "That's the terrace at Chez La Violette," she exclaimed. "I swear it." There were olive trees in the background and a glimpse of the mosaic-tiled pool in front, the pale flagstones, a tumble of bougainvillea and hibiscus, and the villa half-hidden behind rosemary bushes. A white-jacketed manservant stood respectfully to one side, guarding a cocktail trolley with martini shakers and a crystal ice bucket. The prince was smoking, and Mrs. Simpson stared unsmiling into the camera, severe in a narrow white high-necked dress with a thin black belt and pearls of a considerable size. But Violette herself was beaming from ear to ear. "May 1937—Riviera Hostess captures Royalty. The Couple of the Moment," the caption flared in heavy black print.

Sunny made some quick calculations. "Edward was still prince then," she said. "He didn't abdicate and marry Mrs. Simpson until nineteen thirty-eight. My oh my, that was some coup for La Violette. British royalty. It didn't get any heavier than that."

She rolled across the bed to look at Mac. "So you see, Chez La Violette must have been splendid once."

"Pity it wasn't splendid today." Mac had no pity for the missing rental scammer. And none for Joel Krendler, who had the money to fix up the place. As a self-proclaimed "patron of the arts," at least he could have made it a memorial to a once-famous French singing star known, so Sunny now told him, as "*La Violette, Chanteuse de Tout Paris.*" But Sunny was propped against the pillows once more, immersed in another news story.

She skimmed it quickly. She knew PR fluff when she read it and this definitely was not that. This was real. She threw Mac a you're-not-gonna-believe-this glance and then she began to read it to him.

Sunday Telegraph
Nice, September 1995

There's a small hill outside of St. Tropez. A green hill with a covering of Mediterranean pines that leave a lingering scent in the air, like that of well-aged wine casks. A long while ago, in the stillness of the evening, just before night fell, the sound of laughter and music would float up that hill from the festively lit yachts where champagne and rosé wine flowed, a preliminary to dinner onboard. Or perhaps, instead, to a meal ashore, in one of the simple bistros and cafés lining the small town that used to be, not so very long ago, a fishing village. It was a place that drew artists of all kinds: painters, writers, Paris designers in search of the simple life. Some lived in fishermen's cottages and crumbling villas; they ate fish fresh from the sea, with anise yellow Pernod or the thin local pink wine to wash it down.

"There's something about St. Tropez," they would say happily to each other. "Just something about St. Tropez."

And then La Violette arrived, fresh off her latest European
tour. She fell in love with St. Tropez, and with the green hill—
and probably also with the pianist who, in later years, accompanied her in her performances, and was said to be her true
love, a young blond German fellow whose name has been lost
to time. It doesn't matter, the beautiful Violette was notorious
for her habit of flitting from man to man. "Like a humming-
bird to a flower," she used to say with that wicked throaty
chuckle that promised much, and, those who knew said, always delivered.

Her Amazonian beauty and her singing career on the stages
of Europe had netted La Violette a small fortune, made even
larger by the jewels and houses lavished on her by her admirers, and lovers, several of whom were nobility, and at least
one of whom was a Royal. (The diamond tiara he gave Violette
sold twenty years ago at a major jewel auction in Geneva for
an enormous sum, even at today's prices.) They called it "Violette's trophy," but in truth there was more to it than that.
Violette had been fond of her Royal, even though she was rumored to have said he was not a good lover.

The house she built on her hill on the site of an old priory
overlooking the sea was plain, squarish, not unlike the fishermen's cottages that lined the harbor, but Chez La Violette had
arches and patios and pinkish tile roofs and a small tower at
the center. And of course it had extra-large windows because
Violette, who was rumored to have come from a poor background, an orphan brought up in some obscure provincial
asylum, though no one has ever proven this story; anyhow, Violette loved everything to be light and welcoming. There were
to be no shadows in her house.

Until passing time took its final toll there were still people
here in Nice, old of course, who when they cast their minds
back thought fondly of Chez La Violette, recalling long sunlit
days by the azure swimming pool, with lunch served by a
manservant, impeccable in a white jacket. And of drinks in
the late evening on the cool-tiled terrace with its view down

the slope to the sea, glinting crystal and pink in the sunset. They remembered delicious dinners served under the spreading branches of the olive trees where tiny birds perched, eyeing them and occasionally singing for their supper.

They recalled Coco Chanel stopping by to visit from her fisherman's cottage on the harbor, and Colette scribbling stories in a shady corner. They talked of the artist Paul Signac, who painted so evocatively the familiar views of the village and the piney landscape, and of the visits of the English prince and his woman, when everything had to be top-notch to suit such exalted guests, who were not used to "roughing it" in the casual way of the house.

They said Piaf had been there, and Chevalier, and Mistinguett and Josephine Baker, with all her many children of different races and colors. Presidents and Generals came too, all adoring friends—or perhaps lovers, but though Violette was a woman who could drop names with the best, she never told.

And then war came to Europe. Eventually it made its way as far as the Riviera. Violette fled to Paris, living there, but often retreating to her now lonely villa. She still went onstage, still sang, though this time it was for the Nazi occupiers of Paris, as several of her contemporaries also did. It was said that, like Coco Chanel, she had a new German lover, but if so, she never brought him to Chez La Violette. And no one visited her there anymore.

Then, at the end of the war, when the Allies liberated Paris, Violette was arrested, accused of being a collaborator. She hid her still-beautiful face from the photographers in shame. But quite suddenly, and without any fanfare, she was released. Her new "enemies," once her friends, said it was because Violette knew important people. That Violette had stories she could tell they would not want made public, and that this was how she gained her release. Was the beautiful Violette a collaborator A blackmailer? A woman who used her power for her own good?

No charges were ever brought, no proof ever offered, no vindication made, and Violette returned to her villa. The woman who had once had everything, including the world at her beautiful feet, lived alone but for a multitude of stray cats, whom she nourished and loved like the children she'd never had.

And then, on a day in early summer, she was no longer there. Violette simply disappeared, leaving behind nothing more than the villa she had built in her favorite place in the world, and her beloved cats, with a will stipulating that the last of her jewels be sold and the money used to pay a woman in the village to come in daily to feed and take care of them.

You see, the one thing Violette offered in such great abundance, all her life, was love. A love of friends, a love of all animals, a love of life itself. Perhaps Violette gave her love so freely because she'd had so little of it in her youth. And there were many who, remembering the way things used to be, were grateful for that love. But now it was only a memory.

Violette, Chanteuse de Tout Paris, would not recognize Chez La Violette today. Abandoned for decades, unloved and unlived in, it stands as a monument to the mystery of her disappearance so many years ago. And to the persistent rumor that it is haunted.

By whom? you well might ask. Why, by the woman herself, of course. La Violette.

36.

Sunny's tears dropped onto the copy of the newspaper article. She said in a wobbly voice, "Do you really think beautiful La Violette was a *collaborator?*"

"She had a Nazi lover and went onstage and sang for the Germans."

"But so did lots of artists, movie actors, ballet dancers, opera singers . . ."

"*Opera singers,*" Mac said. "Back to that again. Ironic, wouldn't you say, that Joel Krendler, the patron of the arts, lover of music, would not have made Chez La Violette into a memorial to its famous owner?"

"Its *once*-famous owner." Sunny wiped the tears away with a fist. She said, "Nobody remembers La Violette now. She never became the legend Piaf did."

"Violette died a long time ago," Mac said. "And her career ended long before that. After the war, life as she knew it was finished."

He lay back, hands behind his head, eyes fixed on the ceiling, thinking about it.

Sunny was caught up investigating a possible crime from the past, while he was investigating the present. Some vacation!

He said, "So now we have a fourth mystery. Did Violette really collaborate with the enemy? And if so, why was she arrested and then let go? And if she was innocent, why was she never publicly vindicated?"

Sunny's long lashes still held the dregs of her tears and Mac thought she looked like an exotic Tinkerbell, sparkled with fairy dust. He leaned over and kissed her tenderly. She was so caught up in Violette's story, he knew he had to help her.

"Where did she disappear to?" Sunny said. "Did she kill herself? Or did she run away, start a new life, somewhere else, in a country where no one knew her?"

"Like Argentina."

South America was where many escaping Nazis and collaborators had run before they could be captured and brought to trial. "Maybe," Sunny said, doubtfully.

Mac knew she was doubtful because in the final paragraph in the article, the writer had questioned whether the house was haunted, and if so, was it by Violette herself. Which meant he believed Violette had died there. He took the photocopied newspaper story from Sunny's hand and checked the byline again. The writer was a Mr. Craig Henley-Forsythe.

"About as English a name as you could get," he commented. Then, on an impulse, he went to his laptop and Googled Craig Henley-Forsythe. To his surprise, the information flashed immediately onto the screen. Apparently, Mr. Forsythe was by way of being quite famous himself.

Craig Henley-Forsythe, journalist. Younger son of Sir Robert Forsythe of Henley-on-Thames, Berkshire, England. Born 1929. Honoured with an OBE by Queen Elizabeth II in 1980 for his pioneering work in journalism and the arts. Known for his critical and informative reviews of ballet and opera, but also for his investigative story pieces on artistic legends of the past and present, Dame Margot Fonteyn and Rudolf Nureyev, Maria Callas and Luciano Pavarotti, as well as many other well-known artists of stage and screen. Mr. Forsythe counted among his friends such disparate luminaries as Fred Astaire and Marilyn Monroe. Now retired, Mr. Forsythe lives in a thatched cottage in a Berkshire village, not far from where he grew up.

Astonished, Mac said, "This reads like an obit. I swear the guy must have written it himself."

"Perhaps he did, and perhaps it is. Maybe he died."

"If he did it would say so here. I think Mr. Henley-Forsythe, younger son of Sir Robert and opera critic supreme, is very much alive. And judging from his story about Violette, he's very good at what he does."

Whether Forsythe's phone number would be listed was a long shot, but Mac got onto inquiries immediately. Two minutes later he was listening to the phone ring in a thatched English cottage, and then the answering voice saying "Yes?"

"Mr. Forsythe," he replied, "you don't know me but my name is Mac Reilly."

There was a long pause. Forsythe was probably wondering whether or not to talk to a stranger. He surprised Mac, though.

"I know who you are," Forsythe said. His voice was thin but firm. He was obviously an old man but still in control. "We get your show here in England, you know. I congratulate you, sir. I find it fascinating."

"Thank you." For once Mac was stuck for words, but he needn't have worried, Forsythe simply continued.

"I can't think of any reason in the world you might be calling me but, advanced in years though I am, I confess I'm secretly hoping you're about to ask me to assist you in solving some incredible crime. And hopefully it's out there in Malibu, where life seems always to be lived to the hilt by the young and glamorous, or coming to a bad end by the slightly older and less glamorous. What do you say, Mr. Reilly?"

Mac heard him chuckling down the phone and instantly liked him. "Actually, sir, I *was* about to ask for your assistance. But I'm not in Malibu, I'm in the South of France. St. Tropez, to be exact."

"St. Trop, they used to call it when I was young. Meaning, Reilly, as you probably know, 'Too much.' Though I never found it that way myself. I always had an eye for a pretty woman and there were always plenty of them there."

"Still are, sir. And I'm sure they would still be interested to meet you."

Forsythe's laugh boomed unexpectedly down the phone. "Reilly, there's no need to flatter an old man. Now, tell me the real reason you're calling me, on a Saturday night when I've just settled in front of the TV with a glass of good claret and a handful of cheese straws. Made 'em myself of course. I always prefer homemade."

"Sorry to interrupt, sir. I'll tell you quickly why I'm calling."

Mac filled him in on the Chez La Violette rental scam and the connection with Joel Krendler.

Forsythe sounded thoughtful as he said yes, he had heard of Krendler, though he did not know him personally. "But, now I come to think of it, no one does," he added. "The man is known to be aloof, keeps himself to himself. Especially after the accident. I believe he's now in a wheelchair?"

"Correct," Mac said. "I wonder, sir, do you remember that accident? Where it took place, and when?"

"Oddly, I do. I happened to be in the South of France at the time, doing a story on the Cannes Film Festival. It was May of 1988. Mr. Krendler fell off a boat, got caught between that and the dock. It didn't make the newspapers because he wasn't that important then, and at the time Cannes was filled with superstars."

Mac said, "Sir, I know you never met Violette, but reading your article it's almost as if you knew her."

"Indeed, I felt I did. Violette was the kind of woman who got under a man's skin. A woman who, when she loved, did so with all the passion of her being. I believe she was quite a woman, Mr. Reilly."

"And do you also believe she was a Nazi collaborator?"

Forsythe hesitated. "I believe Violette did what she felt she had to do."

"You mean she was in the Resistance?"

"No, I don't think so. Not officially anyway. Had she been, they would certainly have come to her defense when she was accused and put in jail. No, what I mean is I believe Violette did what she could to help her friends, working on her own." He stopped and thought for a while, then added, "And for her lovers, of course. There was a young German piano player, you know, handsome, blond. He accompanied her on her tours. I always wondered about that."

And now Mac did too. He said, "Tell me, sir, was Violette that gorgeous?"

"That's what they said. And judging from the old photos, how could she not have been? With that mass of long red hair, the sheer height of her, the long legs, the impeccable breasts." Forsythe heaved a long sigh. "It makes a fellow quite nostalgic, just thinking about it," he said, with a smile in his voice. "And now, if you don't mind, Mr. Reilly, since you are not about to offer me employment as your assistant, I'll get back to my claret and my television program. I still like to watch ballet, you know, and the opera."

"What's your favorite, sir?"

"My favorite? That would be Callas in the early days, in *Norma*. But, today, Renée Fleming in just about anything. If you're going to have a voice like that you should have a face to match is what I say."

Mac thanked him and still chuckling, Forsythe said goodbye.

Mac looked at Sunny. "Violette may have been in love with the German piano player. And Joel Krendler lied about the date of his accident. It was in 1988, right here in the South of France. He fell off a boat and got his leg trapped. He wasn't so well-known then so it didn't make the international news, though we can check the archives in Nice again. Anyhow, that was more than twenty years ago, and not the ten he claimed. Which is also the date he said he bought the house."

"But why would he lie?"

Mac smoothed the puzzled frown from between Sunny's brows with his finger. "That, my beautiful Sunny, is what we have to find out."

Her eyes said a mute thank-you and he kissed her again, holding her close.

After a while he said, "Sunny?"

She pushed away from him, alarmed. "What?"

"You know I'm an all-American guy?"

"Right?" She was suspicious now.

"Truth is—I feel like a steak tonight."

Sunny punched him on the shoulder. "*What?* You mean no Louis Fifteenth? No supreme-Michelin-starred South of France cooking? *Here? In* the South of France?"

"Well . . . if you insist." He still sounded reluctant and Sunny laughed. "There's another restaurant in the hotel, Le Grill. Now, I'd say a place with a name like that would have a steak, wouldn't you?" Then, remembering her Paris days and the thin, blue, barely cooked beef the French called a steak, she added, "Though you might have to beg them for it, *and* explain exactly how you want it cooked. And then it'll probably still come with roasted artichokes and braised fennel or something, though I'll bet if *I* ask *very* nicely"— she tilted her head, smiling and fluttering her eyelashes, demonstrating—"I could even get them to cook some french fries in duck fat."

Mac rolled his eyes, already in steak heaven. "They call 'em french fries here?"

"Pommes frites."

He snuggled her closer. "Now I know what to ask for."

Mac's phone rang. Sunny heaved a sigh. Didn't it always?

Mac said, "Hi, Lev."

"Just landed. On my way to St. Trop. Thought I'd let you know. And I already have my guys on round the clock."

"Never one to lose a moment, huh!" Mac laughed. "See you there tomorrow, my friend."

37.

Lev Orenstein deplaned at Nice airport and made his way quickly through immigration and customs. He had only one carry-on bag and had nothing to declare. He knew the Riviera, having been partly brought up there. He spoke perfect French and many of his own men worked full-time there, guarding the very rich, and sometimes the controversial.

He strode through the Salle d'Arrivées, a tall, commanding figure who could have body-doubled for some of the movie stars he kept guard over. Six-four, with a shaven head and deep dark eyes that missed nothing, he had a charming smile that he used to good effect, and he also had a surprisingly soft heart.

The man waiting to greet him by the door at Arrivals was short and stocky, with the shoulders of a bull and a face to match. He wore sunglasses, but then so did everyone else on the Mediterranean. He had on a discreet gray shirt and white shorts. He could have been anybody, anyone at all, except he was one of the best bodyguards on the Riviera, and beneath that shirt he packed a Walther P99 Compact, for which, as a licensed bodyguard, he had a permit. He also had a Taser gun in his pocket, next to the can of Altoids which he chewed on a permanent basis. His name was Federico Manini and he had the best breath of any guard on the Côte d'Azur.

"How're ya doin'?" Lev and he greeted each other with hugs and shoulder punches. They had been in business together for over twenty years, and friends for longer than that. Lev had once gotten Federico out of a serious situation and Federico would never forget it.

They walked together to the parking lot and Federico's Lancia, which was compact and businesslike, but with a hot engine that could reach well over the max on any autoroute, and often did. Federico preferred his cars small but Lev was a big guy. The car Federico had picked for him was specifically fitted for speed, safety, cornering, overall handling and acceleration, a silver-gray Alfa Romeo 159, sleek and as fast as if not faster than his own. They both got in the Alfa and Lev pushed buttons and adjusted mirrors, checking out the car while they talked.

Federico said, "I had my boys go over it, they said you'd never be caught in traffic in this. The way they fixed it, it can turn on a dime and weave its way through a friggin' maze."

"I'll bet it can." Lev was smiling. Federico's hometown was Nice which, next to Naples, was probably the best place to get anything you wanted fixed, on the quiet. Besides that, Federico knew everybody there was to know in the substrata world of the Riviera.

Federico said, "I have two guys doubling up, staking out the Hôtel des Rêves round the clock, and one following Jasper Lord around. He's still in that kind of palace he bought in San Remo, Italy, but two of his thugs are at the Carlton, in Cannes. They've tried to gentrify themselves a bit but a thug still looks like a thug even in a designer jacket."

Lev looked at Federico and laughed. "Same goes for all of us, I guess."

"Waddaya mean?" Federico grinned back. "Anyhow, the thugs are still not onto the Hôtel des Rêves, a bit off the beaten track for them. And for Mrs. Jasper Lord."

"Belinda," Lev said.

"Correct. Belinda Lord. Tall, blond, good-looking. Here's a current picture, taken yesterday by my guy, on the beach."

Lev studied it. "Pretty good," he said. "Mac Reilly told me she's okay, and also about who she's currently keeping company with. 'The International Misfits' he called them. Good thing is, so far Belinda has not been alone and running around St. Tropez too much, which makes it harder for Lord to access her."

"You mean when he finds her."

Lev gave him a keen look. "*If* he finds her. Our job is to make sure he does not."

"Right."

Federico clicked open the glove compartment and took out a smallish parcel, wrapped in a black flannel cloth. He handed it to Lev. "A Glock 29. A bit girly for you, but it's small and fast and easier to conceal when all you're wearing is a pair of bathing shorts and a beach shirt. And here's the permit to go with it. In your name of course."

Lev hefted the automatic pistol from hand to hand, liking the light weight and overall feel. Federico gave him the box of 9mm ammunition and a shoulder holster, custom-made to fit beneath his shirt, the way Lev preferred.

"So, man." Lev smiled at his old friend. "I'll be on my way. I remember the St. Tropez traffic is hell in the summertime."

While he was dodging that traffic on the autoroute heading east, Lev's own words came back to haunt him in the form of a song. "In the summertime . . . In the summertime . . ." No that's not quite right . . . He hummed it to himself, but for the life of him he couldn't remember who sang it, or who had written it. It was just stuck in his mind, alongside the image of Belinda Lord in a white bikini. A woman whom he had pledged to protect with his own life if necessary.

38.

Night had fallen by the time Lev swung the Alfa Romeo through the gates of the Hôtel des Rêves. A half-moon hung in the jeweled dark blue sky and the noise of the crickets in the pine trees stopped the minute his headlights hit them.

A young man, whose name, Marco, was on the badge pinned to his white shirt hurried to help, but Lev told him he preferred to park the car himself, and was instructed to leave it round the back where there was plenty of room.

Mac had primed the manager to Lev's arrival and his job. Now he checked in with a Mademoiselle Renée Cassini, a charming redhead who gave him a welcoming smile that made Lev wonder if all the other guests got the same smile or if she meant it specially for him. Smiling appreciatively back, he hefted his bag himself and followed Marco up the stairs to a small room, directly over the front portico.

"You were lucky to get it, *monsieur*," Marco said, showing him the facilities and the air-conditioning and thanking him for his tip. Generous, of course. Lev never stiffed the help. "Usually, this time of year, the hotel is full, but we've had a couple of cancellations recently that left this room free."

"Then I count myself a lucky man."

When the bellhop had left, Lev switched off the lights, pushed open the green wooden shutters and stood on the balcony in the dark. The clatter of a cocktail shaker came from the direction of the bar, and the high-pitched whine of a tired child from somewhere along the corridor. Not too far away the sea glimmered restlessly, dotted with tiny specks of light, the fishing boats already at work. In the far distance, a cone of yellow light beamed from a lighthouse, and in the garden below the gentle wind rustled playfully in the trees.

Paradise, Lev thought. But as anybody who read the Bible knew, Paradise hid a serpent in its midst.

Ten minutes later, showered and correctly dressed for the Côte d'Azur in white pants and his favorite Tommy Bahama flowered shirt, the Glock, armed and strapped invisibly under his shoulder, he made his way downstairs to the bar. He introduced himself to the bartender, whose name was Louis, and ordered a Coke and lemon. Lev never drank while on duty. There were still a few people around, but most had already made their way to the dining room or were heading into town. Lev had been given a full description of all the "Misfits" and knew they would be dining in the hotel. He finished his drink, chatted to the bartender in perfect French, then said *ciao* and went in search of them.

Belinda Lord was hard to miss: tall and sexy in a floaty white dress that dangled from her bronzed shoulders by two of the skinniest straps ever invented by a designer. Multistrands of translucent Lalique-looking stones were wrapped around her long neck and a thick bangle of what looked to Lev like plastic, but more likely was something far more expensive, surrounded her right wrist.

A good-looking guy, no doubt Nate Masterson, sat next to her, attentive to her every word. Next to Nate was another young woman, her skin pink from the day's sun, heavy brown hair falling over her eyes in a thick fringe that successfully hid her face, wearing a plain white T-shirt and a thin gold chain necklace. This had to be Sara Strange. And the rugged guy with the look of an outdoorsman, sandy-haired, freckled, was Billy Bashford. With him was his young daughter, known to everyone as Little Laureen. She was holding a Chihuahua that Lev thought looked remarkably like Sunny's little fiend, Tesoro, now looking as though butter wouldn't melt in its snappy little mouth. The tutu threw him a bit though, Mac hadn't told him about that when he'd filled him in on the Misfits.

Sara Strange must have felt his gaze because she looked up suddenly. A blush turned her face even pinker and she said something to Belinda, who lifted her head and met Lev's eyes straight on.

She eyed him up and down. "Well, if it isn't a god in our midst," she said appreciatively. "Welcome to the South of France, Lev. It is you, isn't it?"

Lev went round the table shaking hands, including Little Laureen's. The dog on Laureen's lap raised its head, lip curled.

"Oh, Tesoro," Laureen said, hugging the dog closer.

Lev grinned. He knew Tesoro's habits from old.

Belinda patted the chair next to her. "Come, take a seat by me, Lev, then we can talk."

"Ma'am, the only thing we need to talk about is your security. That's why I'm here, and that's my priority."

Belinda's mouth turned down comically at the corners. "That put me in my place and no mistake."

"I didn't mean to be rude. And of course I'm including everyone around this table in whatever we say. Mac told me they've been deputizing as your guards, but now I have two men on round-the-clock patrol and I personally will oversee your safety."

"You mean you'll make sure the husband can't find me?"

"That would be our aim, ma'am."

"Oh for God's sake, stop calling me ma'am. It makes me feel about a hundred years old." Belinda gave him an assessing glance. "And I'll bet I'm not much older than you."

Lev knew exactly how old Belinda was. He had made it his business to know everything about her. And she was right, she was two years older than he was. "Probably" was all he said though.

Belinda suddenly perked up, scanning the table with a big grin on her face. "Tell you what, guys, now Lev is here to protect us, I vote we all head directly for Les Caves du Roy."

"What's Les Caves du Roy?" Sara spoke up, suddenly shaken out of the comatose state she'd fallen into since first setting eyes on Lev.

"Only the best nightclub in St. Trop, full of the hippest, hottest and the cutest. *And* they'll be dancing on the tables."

Sara shrank back in her chair again; she didn't go for the dancing on the tables bit.

But Belinda was revved up now. "Or perhaps we should go to Le VIP Room, it's a little more techno, if you like that kind of thing?" She beamed her question at Lev.

He shook his head. "Ma'am, Belinda, I'm sorry but nightclubs are out. In fact, right now St. Tropez town is a no. We need to keep you tucked away here at the hotel, out of sight."

"Jesus! You mean I'm still *trapped* here? I can't go out? Even with round-the-clock guards?"

"I'm sorry, ma'am, but that's just the way it is. For now."

She glared at him. "Oh for God's sake, I asked you not to call me ma'am."

Lev grinned, remembering the reason and got a reluctant smile in return.

"Listen, all of you," he said. "Jasper Lord's thugs are still in Cannes, still looking for Belinda. I am determined they will not find her. As you know, Mac is investigating Mr. Lord. Once he finds out what he's up to, we'll take care of him. And we're sure he's up to something, especially since he opted not to come to the South of France himself, and remained behind in Italy."

"In that friggin' pink palazzo that's cold as hell even on summer nights." Belinda shivered, remembering those nights when the husband had used violence to make sure she knew he was boss in his own palazzo, and to prevent her from ever escaping.

Lev guessed what she had gone through and respected her for keeping a brave face. He had a particular hatred for men who mistreated women. To him, they were nothing but scum and the world would be better rid of them. But that was not his job; Belinda Lord's safety was. And indirectly, because of Belinda, the safety also of the other people sitting around the table.

He said, "This involves all of you. I won't be keeping you company but I'll always be around. It's my job to stay in the background, but trust me, I'll be there when you need me."

Belinda stared silently into the cup of rapidly cooling espresso in front of her. "Seems to me I'd be better off taking a sleeping pill than jazzing myself up on espresso," she said with a sigh and a heavy glance directed at Lev.

Sara took her hand and squeezed it comfortingly. "I'm sure Mr. Orenstein knows what's best, Belinda. And it's so lovely here, we can't complain now, can we?"

Lev thought she sounded like a kindergarten teacher consoling an unhappy three-year-old. He took another look at her: at the drooping shoulders of a woman who'd probably been hiding the fact that she had breasts since adolescence; at the neat profile, pure like a Madonna's; at the worried frown that was probably permanent; and the swing of brown hair that shone like well-polished boots under the white fairy lights threaded through the trees. Sara's gaze left Belinda and her large brown eyes focused on him again.

She said, "Thank you, Mr. Orenstein—"

"Oh, it's *Lev*, for God's sake!" Belinda told her, impatient as ever.

Sara started again. "Thank you, *Lev*. I know you only have Belinda's best interests at heart. We all do, don't we?" She looked at Billy and Nate, who said of course and that they understood their roles in Belinda's safety.

"We'll make sure one of us is always with her, always on the alert," Nate said.

Lev handed Belinda a small electronic device that he told her connected directly with him. If she was afraid, worried, unsure, she was simply to press the button and he would be there. If she went to the beach, he or his man would be there.

It was getting late and most everyone had left the courtyard. Waiters dusted up crumbs, put on fresh tablecloths and blew out candles.

"So now, if you're ready, I'll escort you to your room," he said to Belinda.

She looked up at him, surprised. "That's okay, Sara sleeps with me." She thought about what she'd said, then added with a grin, "I mean Sara and I room together, so I'm not alone."

"Nevertheless." Lev waited while Belinda and Sara collected their bags and Billy collected his daughter and the dog, who was quiet now. As they walked through the dining room he spotted a boy sitting alone at a corner table. Laureen had also seen him. She said something to her father then skipped across the dining room to speak to him.

"She just wants to say good night. Bertrand Olivier is her new friend," Billy explained, but Lev indicated that he would wait for her.

Talking to Bertrand, Laureen glanced impatiently over her shoulder at them, said something to the boy, then bent to pat Pirate who'd emerged suddenly from under the table. In a flash Tesoro jumped on the dog and there was an almighty scuffle with Little Laureen yelling and Bertrand Olivier bravely plunging in to separate them.

Lev and Billy rushed to lend a hand. "I might have known it," Lev said, prizing Pirate's ear from Tesoro's jaws. "That Chihuahua is a bundle of trouble."

Kneeling on the floor with Tesoro's lead clutched in her hand, Little Laureen gave Lev a cold stare. She said a quick good night to Bertrand then trotted off, flat-footed in the ballet slippers, orange tutu wagging like Pirate's tail.

The Misfits dispersed to their various rooms and Lev made a note of the numbers. Later, he would go outside and check their positions and access.

When they got to Belinda's room, Lev went in to inspect it. There wasn't much to see, it was simple, and like most women's rooms, awash in clothes and shoes. There was a largish bathroom and a spacious balcony that faced the garden with a path beneath that led, he guessed to the pool and then to the beach. He would check that out later.

He said good night to Belinda who gave him a cool hand to shake, though he thought she would have enjoyed it more had he kissed it. Sara's hand was as warm as the pink glow on her Madonna face and she pulled it back hurriedly, as though afraid of the contact. Still, she did give him a smile as she closed the door.

Downstairs, the beauteous Renée was no longer on duty. A man had taken her place as night concierge. He had already been primed by the manager as to what Lev's job was and Lev knew from the picture he'd been shown earlier that the night concierge was who he claimed to be.

He walked down the steps and round the corner to the back of the hotel, the parking lot and the staff entrance. A car was parked just inside the low double gates he knew were kept unlocked. He went and checked. It was his man on duty.

Circling the hotel he walked the length of the façade, checking the location of Belinda's room. Mac's was the corner one on the left, and Belinda's was next to it. Balconies jutted out forming a shady walkway beneath, lined with the French doors that led to the bar and the main hall. The doors had been closed for the night. All the balconies adjoined each other, separated by barriers over which bougainvillea grew on a wooden trellis, giving each privacy, though of course conversations could still be overheard.

Lev knew it would be comparatively easy to access any room via those balconies, if you were agile and cunning enough. He decided to check with the night concierge who the guests were in the neighboring rooms, and if they were well-known at the hotel.

He was walking along the path to the beach when he heard something. He stepped into the deeper shadows of the covered walkway, every sense alerted, eyes scanning the gloom.

Little Laureen, still with Tesoro clutched to her chest, came into view. Lev knew she wasn't just taking the dog for a pre-bedtime walk, certainly not at this time of night and without her father around.

Lev's hand on her shoulder sent Laureen skyrocketing upward. She dropped the dog, who howled, then bit Lev's foot.

Lev removed the dog's teeth from his shoe and said, "Hey, kid, where're you goin'?"

Laureen struggled for an explanation. "Just for a walk. With Tesoro."

Lev didn't have to ask if her father knew about the walk, he already knew the answer. "It's midnight, kid. What d'you think your dad would say about you going 'walking' alone at this hour of the night?"

Laureen shrugged and said she didn't know. But of course Lev knew she did.

"Who were you meeting?"

Laureen's head shot up. She sensed there was no way out but still she tried to keep her secret. "No one. Really, no one." She desperately did not want to expose her rendezvous with Bertrand.

"My guess is it's Bertrand Olivier." It wasn't hard. Lev had seen them whispering to each other before Tesoro got his teeth into Pirate.

"Tell you what, I'll take you back to your room and I promise I won't tell your dad. Then I'll come and tell Bertrand you can't make the midnight rendezvous." He tipped her chin up with his finger, so she was forced to look at him. "No way. Get it, Laureen."

He spoke sternly. He did not approve of children sneaking out alone after hours. Anything might happen to them, especially now.

Laureen wondered silently what would happen to Bertrand. "Yes, sir," she said.

Lev took her hand and with Tesoro on the lead, walked her back into the hotel and up the stairs to her room.

She stood uncertainly outside the door for a second before she unlocked it. Then she said a quick good night and went in.

Lev waited until the door closed. He heard the bolt slide shut, then he walked back downstairs and out to the beach.

As he expected, he found Bertrand farther along in the shadow of a small rock. As the thin beam of Lev's flashlight caught him, the boy jumped up putting his hands protectively over his clumsy glasses.

"Go back to your room, son," Lev said kindly. "Laureen cannot meet you, and besides, it's dangerous the two of you being out here alone at night."

He moved the beam off Bertrand's face onto the sand and the oilskin camouflage cape and the ancient pair of binoculars. He shook his head. Kids, he thought, watching Bertrand hurriedly collect his stuff.

"Come on, son, I'll take you back to the hotel," Lev said. "And next time, arrange your rendezvous in daylight hours. Okay?"

"Okay, sir."

Bertrand did not speak another word until they reached his room, then like Little Laureen, he said good night quickly, opened the door and hurried inside.

Lev heard the bolt slide shut. He sighed. Sorting out a couple of kids' misdeeds was not exactly what he'd expected to be doing tonight. Still, he was glad that was all it was. For now.

39.

Mac and Sunny lingered over dinner in the rooftop Le Grill, where the ceiling slid open to reveal the stars and the tall windows were draped in silk, roped back to reveal on one side the view of the harbor, and on the other the turreted Casino. The room was grand but soft and elegant, the service impeccable and the food a wonder.

One of the Grill's specialties was the famous Charolais beef and of course Mac ordered his "special" steak as well as the *pommes frites* cooked in duck fat that he swore could possibly be the best thing he ever tasted, and Sunny had a beautiful turbot, with a salad so simple she wondered how it could taste so good.

She looked out of the window at the twinkling panorama and then up at the stars twinkling overhead. "Tell me," she said. "Why does this seem a million miles away from the fish shack on Pacific Coast Highway, where you sit at those scarred wooden tables, up two or three flights of wooden steps, and gaze out at the view of the Pacific from behind the plastic curtain that's supposed to shelter you from the wind?"

"Each has its own charm," Mac said. He was very fond of that fish place. Then he said, "You look wonderful tonight."

Sunny smiled. "Eric Clapton. He wrote that song to his wife."

Mac said, "Maybe I can't write songs like Clapton, but at least I can quote him." He smiled at her. He was so in love with her, and so in love with the way she looked tonight, he wanted his eyes to tell her that.

They had gone shopping that afternoon, not a major shopping, just something for Sunny to wear instead of the pink cotton with the palm tree print. Now she had on a slim slip of a dress with a round neck and bare shoulders. The delicate chiffon fabric fell in soft flat pleats, sashed at the waist with narrow black satin. At the back, the dress was open from neck to waist, fastened only by three tiny delicate cristal buttons, like sparkling dewdrops. With it, she wore high black suede Manolos and diamond earrings. Simple. Perfect.

Mac said, "It's worth taking you shopping, y'know that?"

She flashed him a glance from under those fabulous lashes that sent his "amour" into overdrive. "Thank you, sir."

Their eyes linked. Mac said, "I don't know if I want dessert now."

Sunny grinned. "Too bad because I intend to eat everything they put in front of me."

And she did. And they both drank a glass of a delicious white wine from the Graves area, south of Bordeaux, "mined" from the six hundred thousand bottles in the wine cellar carved from the rock beneath the hotel.

After that, they sipped espresso and tasted delicious *petites gourmandises,* tiny sweet bites that only made them want more. But Sunny's eyes had taken on a faraway look.

"Violette's back," Mac guessed.

"I feel as though now I know her," she admitted. "Tomorrow, I'll investigate some more, try to figure out what happened in Paris."

"Not tonight, though. Please, no more Violette."

"I promise." Her smile sealed it.

They said goodbye to the waiters who had looked after them so well, thanked the captain and the maître d' and hand in hand, strolled across the plaza to the Casino, a gilded rococo pleasure palace. They made for the plush private salons, where the betting on chemin de fer, roulette and blackjack was for higher stakes and there were no noisy slots to distract serious gamblers.

Mac stood behind Sunny while she lost money at roulette, scanning the room as he always did. His attention was caught by a woman in the next salon. Her back was toward him but there was something familiar about her. She wore a short blue silk dress and her long blond hair fell smoothly past her shoulders. She looked expensive in an overt way and she was certainly not discreet; Mac could hear her loud laugh from where he stood. She was playing craps and obviously for big stakes because there was an admiring a crowd around her.

In between keeping an eye on Sunny's rapidly mounting losses Mac kept an eye on the woman. He *knew* he knew her from somewhere. Then he saw Gianni Valenti cross the room and tap her on the shoulder. The woman turned her head and gave him a big smile.

"Jesus," Mac said, surprised.

Sunny glared indignantly at him over her shoulder. "I haven't lost *that* much."

"It's Gianni Valenti," Mac said, indicating with his head where to look.

Sunny looked. "Oh. The sailboat guy from the hotel."

"And guess who's with him."

Sunny looked again. She sat up straight. "That's *our* girl. Caroline Cavalaire."

"Our sweet receptionist from the hotel."

"Looking *dazzling. And* expensive." She looked closer. "Who knew she had all that hair, it's always tucked up in that businesslike chignon. *And* she's wearing a diamond clip in it instead of a pink carnation."

"Either she's come into money or someone is taking *very* good care of her."

Sunny remembered the emerald ring and the Chanel bag, and now she recognized that the dress Caroline wore was a designer label, and that her gold sandals had the distinctive red soles that gave them away as Christian Louboutin.

She said, "I'll bet it's our Mr. Valenti." She recalled Caroline following him into the dining room, radiating smiles. She shrugged. "Hey, why not? She's young, attractive. If I were a guy I'd probably want to date her, looking like that."

"The thing is we've never seen her looking 'like that' before. And if Valenti is so hot for her that he's keeping her in a style to which she's happy to become accustomed, why is she still working as a receptionist at a small family hotel?"

Sunny groaned. "Mac, oh, *Mac*! Don't do this to me, I beg you. *Please* . . . let's not invent another mystery to solve."

"I don't 'invent' mysteries. Mysteries just happen, and usually because something 'mysterious' is going on."

Sunny placed the last of her chips on black. She watched the wheel spin and come up red. "See, you put me off," she complained, slipping her arm through Mac's and walking away from the table.

"You were losing before I distracted you."

But Sunny was checking out Valenti and Caroline. They had stepped back from the craps table and were drinking martinis. Head lowered, Valenti was talking to Caroline, almost into her ear as though he wanted no one else to hear what he had to say. Caorline tossed back her long blond hair and looked Valenti in the eyes. Whatever she said to him there was an angry look on her face.

"What d'you think?" Mac said. "Do we go over and say hello?"

"Not on your life. It looks like a lovers' quarrel to me. Maybe it's a good thing she kept the day job after all."

Mac laughed as Sunny tugged him away. "Where are we going?" he asked, putting Caroline Cavalaire out of his mind.

"Bed, baby," she replied with that impish smile that always got his "amour" going.

"Why 'bed'?" he asked. "There are so many other locations."

"Like where?"

"Did you ever make love in the back of a car?"

"Yes."

He stopped and looked at her. He hadn't expected that answer. "Who with?"

"With whom." She corrected him. "And it's none of your business."

Mac thought about it. He guessed she was right. "I wish I'd never asked," he said gloomily.

"So do I."

They were in the elevator. Sunny put her hands behind her back and unhooked the three little cristal buttons that held her black chiffon dress together. She slid it off her shoulders. Her breasts were high and round and pink-nippled. The nipples were erect.

"You ever make love in an elevator?" she asked, smiling.

"Oh my God." Panicked, Mac hauled her dress up again. Just in time. The elevator pinged and the doors slid open. The waiting couple eyed them suspiciously before they got in and Mac wondered guiltily if they could possibly know.

The elevator stopped at their floor, and with a serene smile, Sunny said *bonsoir* to the couple and stepped past them.

Her dress in back was open to the waist. He heard her laughing as she ran down the corridor. He flung a quick glance at the couple as the elevator doors closed on them. He would never forget the look of astonishment on their faces.

"Naughty," he said, catching up to Sunny.

"Yeah. Isn't it fun?" she said. And grabbing his hand, she ran with him back to their room.

Mac heaved a happy sigh. What more could any guy want? It was the perfect end to a perfect night. Tomorrow, this vacation would be all business again. But tonight was his and Sunny's.

40.

The next day when they got back to the Hôtel des Rêves around elevenish, Mac was surprised to find Gianni Valenti at the Beach Bar, enjoying a beer. He was alone.

Mac already knew that Caroline was not on duty because he'd just passed Renée at the desk. Now he wondered what had happened the previous night. Had love's young dream fallen through for Caroline? She wouldn't be the first woman to come to grief over a man, as two of his own little band of misfits could prove.

"How about a drink on the *Blue Picasso* this evening?" Valenti called to him. "I make a great martini and we can watch the sunset." He grinned as he added, "Of course, that's only an excuse. What I really want to do is show off my boat. And please bring Sunny with you." His dark eyes swept the beach and came to rest on Belinda, bikinied and supine, as were the other Misfits, under the *ombrelles*. "And bring your other friends. It'll be quite a party."

Curious about him, Mac agreed. "How about six o'clock?"

"I'll be at the jetty with the dinghy at six, and remember the more the merrier."

From the way Valenti was eyeing Belinda, it looked as though Caroline was definitely out of the picture. Mac felt sure she would not be included in tonight's invitation.

He checked his watch. He had some information for Lev and they had an appointment in fifteen minutes at Le Café, in the place des Lices. Lev had told him it would be quieter there than at the Sénéquier. "More discreet" was what he'd said. Apparently he had forgotten it was market day.

By the time Mac had found a parking spot it was eleven-fifteen and the place des Lices was awash in women tourists in shorts and sunglasses picking over the linen skirts in search of a chic St. Tropez bargain, while local women wearing head scarves and carrying net bags picked over the fruit and veggies in search of perfection.

The delicious smell of chicken sizzling on the open spit came from the nearby rotisserie stand. Mac sniffed it longingly, watching the proprietor shoveling potatoes and slices of onions and red peppers into the vat beneath, where the juices had accumulated. The glistening vegetables crisped gently as the spit turned, browning the chickens. Dinner would not be a problem for many people here tonight.

He spotted Lev from across the street, under the awning on the café terrace, his six-four frame folded into a small cane chair at an even smaller table, keeping his elbows to himself so as not to infringe on his neighbors' territory. His sunglasses were pushed up onto his bald tanned head and a tiny cup of coffee was on the table in front of him.

Amused, Mac thought he had never seen a man more uncomfortable than Lev right now.

Lev saw him coming, nodded, waved down a waiter and ordered Mac a *crème*. The two did not go unnoticed by the vacationing St. Tropez women, who eyed them with charming come-on smiles.

Mac smiled back as he squeezed into the chair. Both men sat facing the street, as did everyone else. On a French café terrace nobody ever looked at each other, they were too busy checking out the passing "show." People watching was one of the great pleasures of St. Tropez.

"Thanks," Mac said, tasting the *crème*. As usual in France, the coffee was good. "So?" He glanced at Lev.

"Belinda's covered. No problem. And the husband is sticking to his Italian palazzo, hasn't moved out of there in days."

"He knows he wouldn't be welcome here," Mac said. "Not just by his wife, but officially."

Lev raised his brows in a question.

"I spoke with my contact at Interpol," Mac said. "Jasper Lord is thought to be trading Russian arms. To Iran."

"Hmmm." Lev thought about it. "Possible terrorist connections?"

"Not proven, but enough that if he showed his face here they'd keep a pretty strict eye on him. Not that he's dumb enough to make a move personally. A mobster always hands that off to underlings. By the way, do you know if he's an art collector?"

"The only thing that guy collects is women."

"What's his mode of transportation?"

"Bulletproof Mercedes Maybach 62S, plus a golf cart that he uses on the grounds of the palazzo—looks like a mini open-air version of the Merc though obviously it's not bulletproof. I guess he just takes his chances on the local golf course, and anyhow he's always surrounded by his guys. Besides, it's a private club and he's richer than everybody else. They make sure he's looked after and no doubt he feels safe. Plus of course he owns the usual billionaire's plane, a Citation, seats ten. And his favorite, a Bell 429 helicopter that he pilots himself. It's a single-pilot design. It just shows what an asshole he is, he ordered it in bright red. You can see it coming a mile away. Anyone who wanted could identify it and shoot him out of the sky, easy."

"Pure ego," Mac said. "So? Why no yacht?"

"Too much officialdom in ports. Besides, he comes from a landlocked country, hates the sea. His palazzo is way up in the hills. He's an urban guy at heart though, more usually to be found in cities. He owns apartments in Manhattan's Upper East Side and London's Belgravia. The palazzo is rented by the way."

"If he's hanging out in San Remo there has to be a reason."

"It's not a woman. In fact rumor has it Belinda was really the one he liked most, her looks, her feistiness, her willingness to stand up to him."

"Until his control and violence got too much for her," Mac said. "No amount of Dior dresses and Cartier necklaces is worth it. And now he wants her back. A man like that, driven by his ego and his mercenary head and never by emotion, he'll find a way to get her."

"Even," Lev said quietly, "if he has to kill her."

41.

At the Hôtel des Rêves, Pirate slunk down the stairs and into the hall behind Sunny. His woebegone brown eyes indicated that he was not a happy dog. Sunny carried Tesoro, who never seemed to walk anywhere much on those short legs, but now she bent to pet Pirate.

"Poor baby," she murmured, seeing one ear lift in response. "Poor darling, Daddy's neglecting you, isn't he? He left you yesterday, and again this morning? Well, I'll tell you what, my sweet boy, you and I are going off on a little adventure together."

Pirate's other ear perked up, obviously wondering if this meant a walk.

"We'll leave Tesoro with Little Laureen, and it'll be just you and me. How about that, Pirate, baby?"

The dog wagged his tail hopefully.

"First, though, I have to ask Caroline a question." Sunny checked the reception desk and saw that Renée was on duty, not Caroline. She wondered about last night and what had happened with Gianni Valenti.

The dog waited patiently while she asked Renée her question, which was were there any bicycles for rent.

"Mais bien sûr, madame. But not for rent, they are free. We have a few outside in the parking lot for those who would like to use them." Renée gave Sunny her big smile and said, "We are a family hotel, *madame,* we think of everything."

Next, Sunny headed for the beach where she found the Misfits lazily contemplating lunch at one of the umbrellaed tables at the Beach Bar. They asked her to join them.

"Not for me, thanks," she replied. "Pirate and I have some exploring of our own to do. I was wondering, Little Laureen, if you would look after Tesoro for me."

"Of course." Laureen's face actually lit up. She had not seen or heard from Bertrand since Lev had sent them both packing. She had left a note under his door, but Bertrand had not responded and now she was worried. She wondered if he was at his lair, and how she could escape her father and go find him. It would not be easy, even with the pretext of taking Tesoro for a walk.

Sunny waved goodbye and with Pirate on the leash, wobbled on her borrowed bicycle out of the parking lot then onto the road that ran in front of the hotel. She made a right with Pirate limping along next to her, tongue lolling, ears flopping, smiling his goofy "smile."

The villa was closer than Sunny remembered from that stormy nightmare drive, though she did cast a wary glance into the bushes at the side of the road where she'd thought she'd seen a man. Of course he'd only been the product of her overworked imagination, as was her impression that Chez La Violette was a house that had kept its secrets, and that perhaps Violette herself had never quite let go of it. And yet when she'd returned there with Mac she had gotten that same uneasy feeling. Then of course there was the question of the lamp that went on by itself in Violette's boudoir, and the overwhelming scent of flowers that she'd bet were violets. *And* that mysteriously open piano lid.

Dismounting, she propped the bike against the wall next to the blue and yellow tile with the curlicued name *Chez La Violette*. This time the gates opened easily. She let Pirate off the lead and he trotted in wide circles, snuffling in the long grass, following her to the front door.

Nervous again, Sunny dithered on the steps: she was doing exactly what Mac had always warned her against, going into an unknown situation, alone. But this wasn't François Reynaud's house, where a murder had been committed. This was just Violette's place.

Still, when she opened the door, she noticed that, like last time when she'd come here with Mac, Pirate did not bound ahead. Instead, he stuck right there, at her heels.

She stepped across the threshold. Silence surrounded her like an invisible wall, locking out the song of the birds and the cheerful chirrup of crickets. It was as though she had entered another world.

Glancing apprehensively behind, she decided to leave the door open for a quick exit, while at the same time telling herself that of course she didn't need one. There was no Nate Masterson brandishing a sword today, and no ghosts either. Still, she was glad to feel the reassuring shape of her cell phone in her shorts pocket just in case she needed to call for help, though *of course* she would not.

All the shutters in the house were closed on the inside. The only light came from the open front door. *Something moved behind her.* Sunny jumped round just in time to see a rabbit take off with Pirate after him. Smiling, she told herself again how silly she was.

When the dog came panting back she put him on the lead and walked across the hall to Violette's room. This time when she ran her hand down the wall to find the light switch, the lamp did not go on by itself. Only the twin chandeliers lit up, but so many of the bulbs were out the room was still in semidarkness. Dragging a reluctant Pirate with her, Sunny unlatched the shutters and threw open the French door.

Feeling as though she had undergone some sort of ordeal, she stood for a while, breathing the fresh clean air. The view was beautiful, of a turquoise creek and the mingled aquamarine and crystal sea lapping the shore. A breeze fluttered the thin voile curtains, bringing with it that haunting scent of flowers. Yet when Sunny looked she saw there were none around, only heavy bushes of hot pink bougainvillea, long neglected so now they draped across the flagstones. A waist-deep lawn of chamomile ran down the slope, bending under the breeze like a silver green sea, and tall poplars fluttered delicate leaves with a faint tinkling sound.

A filigree white wrought-iron table and a pair of matching chairs, chipped and blackened, stood on the terrace, and Sunny imagined the beautiful Violette in a chiffon peignoir, her long red hair tied back with a satin ribbon, sipping her morning coffee from one of those wide, handleless bowls the French used, perhaps planning a party for her guests. Maybe the beautiful young German lover had been with her, discussing the music for her next concert?

Not knowing exactly what she was expecting to find but hoping for more insight on Violette, she went back inside. Underneath the decades of dust and the grime, the dove gray paneled room had undeniable appeal, a kind of eccentric charm as unique as the woman herself. Sunny poked around, checking empty desk drawers, running her hand along dusty bookshelves, opening a door that revealed only an empty closet and a large mirror. Sighing, she gave up.

The enormous bed with its crumbling silvery silk drapes drew her and she climbed the four wooden steps and flung herself onto it. Arms crossed over her chest she gazed up at the pleated canopy. Dust motes flitted through a beam of sunlight and all was silence.

"Where, oh where," she asked out loud, "would a woman keep her most secret papers? Her journal? Her treasured photographs, her mementos?"

The answer flew into her mind as though sent by messenger. Why, under the mattress of course! That classic hiding place where throughout time women had stashed their treasures, their savings, their illicit love letters.

Forgetting the steps, she tripped and almost broke her ankle as she leapt from the bed and pulled back the coverlet. She stared at the mattress. This was not one of your modern-day supersprings; it was a relic from another era with a striped ticking cover and a Paris label proclaiming it to be stuffed with "pure horsehair." Dismayed, Sunny knew it must weigh a ton.

She managed to get her hands underneath, but when she attempted to lift, the mattress didn't move. She shifted her position, lowered her shoulders, hefted again. Only an inch. Frowning, she glared at the mattress. It would take four people to turn this lump. She managed to lift it just enough though to get her hand underneath. She felt around and her fingers closed on a small square object. She pulled it back and looked at it. A dark blue velvet box.

"Oh . . . my . . . God," she exclaimed loudly.

It opened as easily as if it had been used yesterday. And inside was a ring. Not one of Violette's serious jewels, just a small gold signet ring. A crest was engraved on it: an eagle and fox facing each other on a checkerboard shield. The elaborate letter *M* swirled over the center, with a *V* to the left and a *K* to the right. The *V* was for Violette, of course, but Sunny had no idea who the initials *M* and *K* could be for.

Nervous, she slid the ring on her finger, half-expecting to hear a clap of thunder, but all that happened was that it was too big and even on her middle finger it slid around.

Wondering what else might be hidden under the mattress, she had another go at it, but it was impossible to lift. Violette would have had a problem hiding much under there.

Sunny smoothed the fraying silvery coverlet back into place, then on an impulse climbed up and lay on the bed again. She stared up at the canopy that had sheltered the famous chanteuse for so many years, telling herself that Violette had lain here just like this; that Violette had asked herself the same questions women always ask of themselves, when things go right, and when they go wrong.

Closing her eyes Sunny tried to imagine what life was like for the beautiful singer when she was young and in love and all the world was at her feet. Sunlight pressed against her closed eyelids sending strange patterns, reds and golds . . . She was drifting backward in time, into a kind of sleep . . . The scent of flowers hung on the air like a drug, that same lovely violet scent. The bed draperies rustled delicately.

Sunny jolted upright. It was as though she had returned from another world. She leapt off the bed, grabbed Pirate's lead and ran for the door. Then she remembered—she had left all shutters open. *She had to go back in there.* Telling herself not to be so ridiculous and that the flowery scent must be coming from the garden, she ran back inside, slammed the French door shut, turned the key in the lock and latched the shutters across it.

Now the only light came from the misty chandeliers. A bulb flickered, then died. The scent of flowers drifted on the air, heavy, seductive . . .

Sunny didn't know whether she dragged Pirate or Pirate dragged her but they were out of there in a flash, into the hall and through the front door, pausing only long enough to lock it.

Then they were running down the gravel drive. She leapt on the old bicycle and pedaled like mad, back to the everyday world of the Hôtel des Rêves.

42.

"*Why* are we going on Valenti's boat?"

Sunny and Mac were in their room and she was tugging on a pair of white shorts. She stood to button them, then slid her feet into navy canvas boat shoes. She had hoped for another night with just the two of them alone, but somehow this vacation had become a communal effort.

"We're going on Valenti's boat because he invited us. And because I'm curious about him."

Worried, Sunny stopped in the middle of pulling a navy-and-white-striped tee over her head. "Uh-uh, don't tell me . . . not another mystery."

"The only thing mysterious about Valenti so far is his relationship with the fair Caroline. And the fact that he has a very expensive sailboat out there. Quite beautiful."

"Caroline or the sailboat?"

This time Mac laughed. "Which would make you most jealous?"

"Definitely the boat. I know how crazy men can get about things like that. Nothing's too good for it, no expense spared. And a boat's better than a mistress because it doesn't talk back at you and take you shopping."

She smoothed the T-shirt then gathered her long hair into a ponytail and secured it with a rubber band. She pirouetted in front of Mac, pointing a finger at her chest. "See. Low maintenance." Then she collapsed on his lap in a fit of laughter. "Do we *really* have to go? I mean, can't we just sneak away? Send the others on their own?"

"Belinda's going. I need to be there."

Sunny sat up straight. "What about Lev? I thought that was his job."

"Normally it would be, but this time I'm in charge. Besides, it's a fairly safe environment, on a boat moored just offshore."

"Unless the husband gets wind of it and shows up in his red helicopter to gun us all down. And by the way, doesn't everyone we've come in contact with on this vacation own his own plane?"

Mac kissed her. "Yes. But did I ever tell you, you have too active an imagination."

"Probably. I mean, yes you did. But *this* isn't a product of my imagination." Sunny went to the dresser and came back with the gold signet ring.

Mac ran his finger over the crest. "Where did you get it?"

"Where else? Chez La Violette." She slid it onto Mac's left pinky. It fit perfectly. "There, you see," she cried triumphantly. "It's a *man's* ring. I bet Violette gave it to the young German lover."

"Wait, wait." Mac put up both hands in protest. "Begin at the beginning."

Sunny told him the story of her afternoon adventure at Chez La Violette.

"And I still believe it's haunted," she finished, shivering as she remembered the flowery scent and the way the sun had seemed to press her eyes shut, the drugged feeling and her sudden frightened leap back into the present day and reality.

Mac knew Sunny was no scaredy-cat, but she was also definitely into this Violette thing and it wasn't good for her. His Sunny was brave and capricious and funny, and he had only seen her seriously scared a couple of times, both of which had involved bodies and murder. She did not scare easily. A good thing too, hanging around him, where danger always lurked.

"I don't want you going there alone again. Okay?"

"Okay," she said in a small voice.

He took off the ring, checking the initials. "We don't even know Violette's full name," he said. "She only ever seems to have been known as Violette."

"I'll go back to the newspaper archives," Sunny said. "There must be some true-life details somewhere there, about who she really was."

Mac said, "Who she *really was*, was 'the star.' I think she left that other orphaned girl behind and changed herself into the fantasy woman all men adored. La Violette must have soaked up love the way a sponge does water."

"Like me." Sunny snuggled on his lap, kissing the ear closest to her lips. "Do we have to go?" she whispered again. But Mac said they did and sighing, she followed him out the door.

"By the way," he said, "I checked on who was paying for the utilities to be permanently turned on at Chez La Violette."

Sunny shrugged and looked at him, brows raised.

"It's Krendler, of course. The man who claims he never visits the villa. Or the South of France."

Sunny looked astonished. "You think he's the rental scammer?"

"Not that. But I'm willing to bet he's up to something."

43.

"You can't wear that." Belinda shook her head at Sara, who had just zipped up the Cavalli dress and was in the process of tying the green snakeskin sandals.

Sara looked up at her, dismayed. "But you told me this is the perfect outfit."

"Not for drinks on a sailboat it isn't. Any sailor would kill you if you walked on his deck in those heels. Besides, it's casual, just a sunset drink. Put on the shorts, baby, and the flip-flops, and you're set."

Sara shook her head. She simply didn't get it. Now Belinda was telling her to dress the way she had dressed before they met, which was the way she'd told her she shouldn't. And anyhow, what was so special about the deck of a boat? It was probably only made of plastic these days. Still, Belinda was wearing shorts and rope-soled espadrilles, and Sara pulled on a pair of denim cutoffs and a T-shirt with sparkly writing across the chest. She would never get the hang of this clothes business. Still, now she was ready and the two walked downstairs to the hall.

"Hi there." Billy announced his arrival loudly from the stairs, waving a big hello, and clutching Little Laureen by the hand.

Belinda grinned at him. He was not wearing the hat. Little Laureen was in the inevitable tutu, but with the boots this time. Belinda sighed and whispered to Sunny, "Whatever are we going to do about that child?"

Sunny shook her head. "I think we just have to wait and see what happens."

Mac had already gone to deposit the two dogs in the kennel: claws were as forbidden as heels on a boat.

"Sweetie." Belinda drew Laureen to one side. "I think the cowboy boots have to be left behind, for now. Sailors don't like hard shoes on their smooth decks."

There was that familiar faraway look on Laureen's face, as though she inhabited some other planet. "Why not?"

"They leave marks." Belinda gave her a nudge and a quick wink. "It's one of those guy things, y'know what I mean."

Laureen did not know, and anyhow she didn't want to be here. She wanted to be with Bertrand. There had been no sign of him all day and when she'd knocked on his door he had not answered. She'd stood there wondering where he had gone, then she'd left another note, asking him to meet her at the beach at ten P.M. and warning him to be on the lookout for the new guards. She hoped he would make it and that this time they wouldn't be caught.

She slipped off the boots and handed them to Belinda who left them with Renée at the desk as they left.

Gianni Valenti was already at the jetty, looking South of France casual in expensive shorts and a rock-and-roll T-shirt, dark hair still wet from the shower, dark eyes hidden behind dark glasses. He waved hello, holding out a helping hand to the women as they jumped into the large black dinghy, big enough to seat them all. They sped across to the *Blue Picasso,* a spray of crystal foam flaring behind from the superpowerful motors.

"You see, my sailboat is blue," Valenti called over the din of the motor as they approached. He was looking at Belinda who was shaking spray from her hair. She had been unfortunate enough to be the one nearest the stern, and not only was her hair wet so was her T-shirt, which now clung becomingly to every curve.

"I wonder if Valenti sat her there on purpose," Sunny whispered to Mac as the dinghy circled so they could admire the sailboat from every angle. "And didn't I tell you men like boats more than mistresses?"

"Not this one." Mac hugged her. Nevertheless, he had to admit Valenti's boat was beautiful, its dark carbon blue hull sleek as a shark, black sails folded into themselves against the three masts, every white rope neatly coiled, every steel fitment agleam.

Even Sara now saw what Belinda had meant; you'd be afraid to go barefoot on this example of maritime perfection.

Valenti swung the dinghy gently alongside, then leapt out and held out his hand to help them as he had before.

"Valenti, she's a beauty." Mac stood next to him at the rail. "But she's so big, how can you manage her by yourself?"

Valenti shrugged. "I prefer to be alone but with seventy feet it's necessary to have an assistant. He's here tonight to help out. If you wish, we could go for a sail later, before it gets dark."

"Terrific." Sunny beamed. She had decided she liked boats, anyhow, ones like this.

Valenti gave them a tour, showing how the sails worked electronically, explaining the powerful motors that supplemented the sails when the wind let him down.

"That's part of the allure of sailing," he said. "It's like a woman, when she lets you down you need another in the wings to fall back on."

Not exactly the sentiments of a gentleman, Mac thought as Valenti showed them into the main saloon. It was smaller than Mac had expected, and deeply paneled in rich glowing wood, with comfortable sofas and chairs and a bar in one corner, gleaming with crystal glasses that, like the lamps, were battened down to accommodate heavy weather.

But it wasn't the bar that took Mac's eye. It was the large Picasso hanging in the space between two portholes, fitted into a recess that had obviously been tailor-made for it.

"I see you're admiring my Picasso." Valenti patted it lovingly. "Not the Blue Period, you see, though of course the boat was named for it. It's a portrait of his second wife, Jacqueline."

Mac knew it was a masterpiece but somehow he couldn't get his head around it. He said, "I hate to think what insurance must cost you."

Valenti laughed. "*Nothing*, my friend. That's *exactly* what it costs me. Let me tell you the story of my beautiful Picasso. Years ago, I used to sail the waters off the Balearic Islands. I'd put in at Mallorca and was hanging out at a waterfront bar in Palma when I got talking to a man who claimed to be an artist. Later, he took me back to his place to show me his paintings. Of course he wanted to sell me one, and of course he was drunk, and of course I knew immediately what his true vocation was. The man was an expert forger; he could do anything, any artist, any period. He was the Rembrandt of forgers. I told him I was on to him but I would keep his secret if he would paint only one canvas for me."

He waved his hand at the painting in back of him, an outline of a woman's head, the hair mere streaks of blue, the aquiline profile with the eye set, classically Picasso, full-on. "I'm an ardent admirer." He shrugged. "Of course it's impossible now to afford a Picasso, should one even come onto the market, which is rare."

"But were the forgeries good enough to fool the experts?"

"Every one of them. And believe me, there were many in the art world who felt like fools when the truth came out. Later, of course, restitution had to be made by those experts who'd authenticated them and the galleries and auction houses who'd sold them on. In fact there are probably collectors today who own the forgeries and still believe they're the real thing."

Nate wasn't a Picasso fan either, but he knew about the astonishing prices on the art market. "What happened to the forger?"

"He got caught, slammed into jail for passing off his forgeries on the art market as the real thing."

Billy peered more closely at the work of art. He preferred western paintings himself and those rousing life-size bronze sculptures of men on horseback. Picasso was definitely not his line. "I wouldn't know the difference between the real thing and the fake," he said.

"Nor would any layman. Only those who have studied Picasso's work, who know it better than their own faces, could tell the difference."

"Then why does it matter?" Laureen got right to the truth, as she always did. Looking at the painting she guessed she could do a Picasso too, with her new Crayola chalk pens.

She slumped onto the sofa next to Sara, legs sticking out, bare toes wiggling, raspberry tutu akimbo. The boat was okay but she wished Bertrand was there.

"I guess you're right and whether it's authentic or not doesn't really matter," Mac answered Laureen. "And certainly it saved Mr. Valenti a lot of money."

"Please—it's Gianni." Valenti corrected Mac with a smile.

Laureen eyed him suspiciously. He seemed a very smiley person.

"Come see the staterooms." Valenti was proud of his boat as well as his fake Picasso. There were three cabins, compact, well-fitted, comfortable, and like the saloon all paneled in that rich wood that glowed, Sunny thought even more beautifully than his painting.

Back on deck, Valenti's assistant, a swarthy young Neapolitan, was ready with hors d'oeuvres and the martini fixings, though Valenti made the drinks personally.

"You shake that like a professional," Belinda teased, watching as he poured the mixture—gin with a hint of dry vermouth James Bond style—into a frosty glass, added a couple of olives and handed it to her.

Valenti's dark glance met hers across the glass. "It's only one of my many accomplishments," he promised, causing Belinda's eyebrows to raise.

Sara was sitting alone on the ink blue canvas bench that lined the rail.

She was glad she was wearing flip-flops because there was not a single scratch on the fabulously polished teak floors. At least she assumed they were teak. Wasn't that what you usually saw on ships? With a pang, she remembered the ruined cruise and the boyfriend, but then she shrugged it off. After all, look where she was now, sitting on a million-dollar boat sipping martinis with glamorous people she never would have met back in small-town Kansas. Her glance lingered longingly on the shore where the lights of the hotel gleamed into the evening blueness. She wondered where Lev was.

"Mac?" Sunny said. The martini glass was practically freezing her hand off and she took a quick sip.

"Yeah?" Mac wasn't drinking, but he did accept a skewer of lobster, which was in fact excellent.

"Tell me, how can Valenti afford all this? I mean, who exactly is he?"

Mac glanced skeptically at her. "You creating another mystery for me to solve?"

She put a hand to her mouth in pretend shock. "Forget I even mentioned it. And will you just look at Billy Bashford, right up there with Belinda. Do you get the feeling he doesn't want Mr. Show-off Valenti to get close to her?"

Billy was leaning on the rail like a third wheel while Valenti monopolized Belinda's attention. Mac wondered if Sunny was right and Billy was starting to like Belinda in more ways than one.

Meanwhile, Nate, ever the loner, had wandered to the stern and stood, gazing out to sea, his face unreadable. Was he also keen on beautiful sexy Belinda?

"That woman is a catalyst," Sunny whispered. "You watch her, she changes every man she meets. You'll see, soon Gianni Valenti will be giving up expensive boats."

"And taking on an expensive mistress," Mac said, making her laugh.

Little Laureen had found a pair of binoculars and was scanning the shore, mouth pursed, a frown between her eyes. As she looked at the big villas, each with its own boat moored at private docks, something had just occurred to her.

"You looking for Tesoro?" Sunny called.

Laureen lowered the binoculars. "I was hoping to see Bertrand," she answered honestly.

"He's probably getting changed for dinner." Too late Sunny realized what a ridiculous statement that was. "Come sit here." She sat down and patted the bench next to her. "I'm glad Bertrand has become your friend," she said.

Laureen nodded. Then, surprising herself, she blurted, "His mother got married."

Sunny instantly recognized this as a great confidence. She held back her astonishment since, as far as she knew, Bertrand had never even left the hotel and his mother had yet to put in an appearance. "She did?" she replied quietly.

"She doesn't want Bertrand anymore," Laureen said.

Sunny's heart lurched. *Oh my God,* she said to herself, *oh my God . . . poor child.* But to Laureen she said only "I'm sure that's temporary, you know, just for now, until she works things out, her new husband, a new home . . ."

"No," Laureen said flatly. "It's for good. She has other children now. New ones. She doesn't want Bertrand. He's being sent away to school until he's eighteen, then she'll think about what to do with him." She looked anxiously at Sunny. "Bertrand hasn't told anyone else, just me. I don't know why I told you, it just came out that's all."

"It's because you're worried about your friend," Sunny reassured her. "But I promise I won't tell anyone."

"You'll tell Mac." Laureen already knew the ways of women.

Sunny bit her lip. "Okay, but *only* Mac."

"I promised to help Bertrand," Laureen said. "I have a plan."

Sunny waited for her to tell, but this time Laureen was silent.

Then, "It will all work out for the best," Laureen said, sounding too grown-up for an eight-year-old. She added, "My mommy used to say that when I was upset about something."

"And you know what, Little Laureen," Sunny said. "I believe your mommy was right." In her heart though, she wasn't so sure and, judging from her bleak expression, nor was Laureen.

Mac strolled over to where Valenti stood at the rail, chatting up Belinda. He took a closer look at his man. He was older than he'd first appeared, with his youthfully brushed back dark hair curling into the nape of his neck. Now Mac saw the deep lines etched around his dark eyes, sailor's eyes with that penetrating gaze earned, no doubt, from eternally scanning the horizon. The same lines ran from nose to mouth, offset by a deep tan, gained, Mac was certain, more from the tug of the wind at sea than from sunbathing on a Riviera beach. Valenti was tall and he was certainly in good shape, not an ounce of body fat, yet Mac estimated him to be in his late fifties. In fact Valenti looked the epitome of the rich Riviera bachelor on the make. Which brought Mac's train of thought immediately back to Caroline.

He went and stood at the rail next to Valenti—somehow he could not bring himself to call him Gianni—gazing at the shoreline. "The Hôtel des Rêves is quite a find," he said casually.

Valenti agreed. "I've been using it for years as a sort of in port pied-à-terre. It's convenient."

Mac said, "It was surely convenient for all of us when we found out, too late, that we had all rented the villa Chez La Violette in a very simple but effective scam."

Valenti's sharp gaze shifted from the shore to Mac. "Of course you found out who did it?"

"In fact, no. Not yet, though I have my own ideas about that."

Valenti frowned. Surprised, Mac thought he seemed overly concerned about the scamming of people who, after all, were merely passing strangers.

He said, "We were saved from having to sleep on the beach by Caroline Cavalaire, the receptionist at the hotel. By some miracle she found us all rooms."

Valenti continued to stare at the twinkling lights of the hotel as dusk began to settle.

"You know Caroline?" Mac asked.

"I've seen her at the hotel. I don't know her well but she seems a pleasant young woman."

"Yes," Mac replied thoughtfully as Valenti turned away. "Caroline certainly is that."

There was a sudden flurry of activity as Valenti took the helm and the Neapolitan manhandled the sails, which unfurled in an electronic sequence, huge rectangles of black canvas.

"Like a pirate boat," Laureen breathed, awed as the black sails soared into the dark blue sky.

Watching Valenti at work, master of his boat, and owner of his Picasso, Mac knew the man was a liar. He wondered what exactly it was that he was concealing.

44.

Valenti herded them to the front of the boat as it parted the waters, speeding arrowlike, parallel to the coast. The bow lifted and the black sails clattered and the wind sang in the halyards. Face to the wind, Sunny clasped Mac's hand. Her breath was snatched away and she laughed, exhilarated.

Nate stood alone, balanced, feet apart, arms crossed over his chest, scanning the horizon as it blurred into focus then out again. Belinda, head thrown back, laughed joyously, and even Sara joined in, while Billy held Little Laureen in front of him, stretching her arms wide, *Titanic*-style.

Laureen closed her eyes then turned her face up to the heavens. Her tutu fluttered and her breath seemed caught in her chest. "Mommy would have liked sailing," she said to Billy, but her voice was snatched away and flung to the empty sky.

Mac watched Valenti at the helm. His face tight, alert eyes leveled at the sea in front of him, he was a man in perfect control of his boat, a man who loved sailing more than women.

There was no guttural engine noise to spoil the moment, no fumes, nothing but the sound of wind and water, then the flapping of the sails as the boat began to slow. The Neapolitan needed no instruction, he was ready when Valenti pressed buttons and the sails began to furl, and the boat tacked slowly back to shore.

Belinda swung round, eyes sparkling. She said, "That was wonderful. Thank you."

The others chorused their thanks, running hands through windblown hair, laughing, exhilarated. Sunny turned to look at Valenti, still in control. His

intense face had relaxed, though he was not smiling. Oddly, Sunny thought
he looked like a man who had just made love. She glanced at Mac to see if
he had noticed.

"What did I tell you about boats and mistresses?" she said, quietly so
no one else could hear.

But Mac was looking at the sparkling lights onshore. They were heading
into St. Tropez port. Or at least as close as Valenti could get without a berth.

"Where are you heading?" he called.

"Thought we would go into town, have dinner." Valenti gave him his thin
smile. "On me, of course," he added. "You are all my guests."

Belinda gave a cheer, jumping up and down like a child. "Oh, thank
God," she cried. "I'm going stir-crazy. I thought I'd never be allowed out
again."

"You won't," Mac said sternly, but Belinda turned big pleading blue
eyes on him.

She said stubbornly, "I'm going." It was her decision and Mac knew he
had no choice.

The sails were furled now and the motor fluttered gently as they glided
closer to shore. Mac got on his phone and called Lev. He got no answer and left
a message that they were on the *Blue Picasso* coming into St. Tropez and that
Belinda was determined to make a night of it. He said he did not yet know
where they were going, but at least he wanted Lev on alert. It was all he could
do. That, and stick like glue to Belinda.

It wasn't that easy. After Valenti had thrown out the anchor, they boarded
the dinghy and minutes later stepped out at the Old Port.

Valenti took Belinda's arm and guided her through the crowded streets.

"Where are we going?" Belinda turned a beaming face to him.

"I thought we'd start at the Byblos, have dinner there, then go on to the
Caves du Roy for some dancing."

"On the tables!" she exclaimed, laughing.

The two walked through the crowd that, Sunny thought amused, parted
before them like the Red Sea for Moses. Not surprising since Belinda looked
every inch the celebrity, soaking wet and blond gorgeous in her T-shirt,
long-legged in high wedge espadrilles and with a wicked grin on her face.

"You have to admit they make a spectacular couple," Sunny said to Billy,
who was walking next to her, holding his daughter's hand. "But heaven knows
how they're going to let us into a nightclub looking like this."

"She looks great," Billy said.

He sounded gloomy and Sunny glanced anxiously at him. Was he really smitten with Belinda, who flirted with any man within range? The night did not bode well for Billy.

Nor for Sara, who was worrying about showing up somewhere smart for dinner and then on to a nightclub in her old cutoffs and the T-shirt that said GLAMOUR PUSS across her breasts in pink curly writing. She'd known the minute she bought it that T-shirt was a mistake, but she'd thought the boyfriend would think it sexy. She'd worn it tonight, hoping for the same response. Now she knew it was wrong.

Nate was talking to Mac. "What about security?" he asked in a low voice, so Valenti would not hear. "I thought Belinda wasn't allowed out."

"She's not. I had no choice."

Nate shrugged. "Well, I guess she's a big grown-up girl."

"Not grown-up enough to face a couple of thugs and a violent billionaire husband on the warpath," Mac said. He had yet to hear from Lev and he tried his phone again. This time Lev answered.

"Couldn't hear you clearly before, and couldn't reach you," Lev said.

Mac explained quickly that they had been out at sea. He told Lev what had happened, who they were with, and where they were heading.

"There's no stopping Belinda now," he said. "This girl's hittin' the town."

"I'll be right behind her," Lev said.

45.

Windswept and glowing, they were welcomed at Le Byblos as though they were extraterrestrials visiting for the night. Nothing fazed this management, they had seen it all before. Beautiful and eccentric people were always welcome, they added class and drew customers. Not that they needed any tonight, the place was full. Still, a table was rolled out, a cloth thrown on top, chairs arranged, flowers, candles, a phalanx of glasses. Water was brought, drinks ordered, menus presented.

Within ten minutes they were relaxing by the blue pool, palm trees swaying in the breeze, sipping wine and picking out celebrity faces—*hollywoodiens,* as they called them in St. Tropez.

But Mac's eyes were searching for something else. He saw Lev at the bar. That made him feel slightly better. He was nervous though and wished he had never gotten roped into this thing. Still Belinda was having a good time, making them laugh, patting first Valenti on the knee, then Billy, and flirting across the table with Nate, casting complicit looks at Sunny and Sara, including them in her little charade. Because charade was what Mac believed it was. He did not think Belinda was seriously attracted to Valenti. He thought there was more to Belinda than that, more than she was letting them see. He believed Billy had seen that other side of her too, or he had sensed it, and that was why Billy did not like Valenti. He did not think the man was worthy of her.

Mac didn't like Valenti either. The man made him uneasy. He knew he'd lied about Caroline, and now he wondered if he'd lied about the Picasso. The story had sounded authentic enough, about the Rembrandt of art forgers, but Mac had heard that story somewhere before. Years before in fact. Sipping a glass of steely white wine, a Montrachet, he kept an eye on Belinda.

Sunny noticed Mac was disturbed and although she wished it hadn't happened quite the way it had, in this fun, elegant, outdoor atmosphere it was difficult to believe Belinda was in any real danger, and she was enjoying herself. Le Byblos was enchanting, like a Hollywood movie set of a Riviera hotel, pastel-colored and palm-treed, complete with turquoise pool and dotted with famous faces and exotically dressed women. Surprisingly, she didn't feel out of place in her shorts and striped tee; after all this was the South of France and she had just come off a boat. The wind had wrecked her hair and burned her nose but she didn't give a damn.

She squeezed Mac's knee under the tablecloth and whispered, "It's okay, babe, Lev is here."

He nodded. "Sorry, I didn't mean to ignore you." He turned to look at her, his golden glowing Latina lover, love of his life. He wished with all his heart they were alone as they had planned. "How the hell did we get into this?" he asked.

Sunny shook her head. "All we can do is enjoy it." She consulted the menu. "I am going to have the *gigotin de lotte clouté aux anchois*."

Mac stared at her, surprised. "What's that?"

"I have no idea but it sounds fantastic."

Sunny asked Little Laureen sitting across the table, what she had chosen.

"Spaghetti Bolognaise," Laureen said shyly.

"Your favorite." Belinda remembered how she had chosen it at the hotel.

"Her mother used to make it for her all the time," Billy said. "Spaghetti Bolognaise."

He smiled and attempted to smooth Laureen's windblown hair, but it resisted, straggling in knots over her shoulders.

Belinda got quickly to her feet. "Come on, girls," she said, glancing round the table. "Let's take Little Laureen and tidy ourselves up."

Taking Laureen's hand, she wound her way through the tables, followed by amused glances as the other diners took in plump Little Laureen in her tutu and bare feet, with Belinda and Sunny, gorgeous and long-legged, following, and pink Sara bringing up the rear.

They were passing the bar when Sara spotted Lev. "Oh," she said, turning even pinker. Lev looked very handsome in a dark blue shirt and jeans, all tanned and lean, the way the men she met in Kansas never looked. Lev was just about the most attractive man she had ever seen, and that included Mac *and* Gianni Valenti, who was quite a European dish if you liked that kind of thing. Which Belinda obviously did.

She lifted her hand in a wave but to her surprise Lev turned his back. He had cut her dead. Sara's cheeks burned again.

In the ladies' room Belinda said, "Did you see Lev Orenstein sitting there looking like Buddha with his bald head and dark glasses?"

"I thought he looked great," Sara blurted before she could stop herself.

Sunny and Belinda stared at her and she blushed again. "He ignored me," she said.

"Of course he did," Sunny said kindly, seeing that Sara had felt slighted. "Lev's on duty. He doesn't want to draw attention to himself and he can't be seen to be talking to us. Lev is Belinda's security man, Sara."

Belinda had taken a comb from the small blue snakeskin Dior bag slung across her chest and was pulling it gently through Little Laureen's knotted hair. The child closed her eyes and tilted back her head, relaxed for once.

"You know, you have pretty hair, Laureen," Belinda said. "I used to be a hairstylist so I know about these things. All it needs is a good trim. You know, snip, snip along the ends to give it a nice even edge, then it'll swing beautifully, just like Sara's."

Laureen opened her eyes and inspected Sara's hair. "Mine will never be as pretty as that."

"You bet it will when I've finished with it." Belinda looked at Sunny. "You got another of those rubber bands?"

"Sure." Sunny fished in her bag and gave one to Belinda, who smoothed Laureen's hair back and fixed it in a ponytail.

"There, look how pretty you are." She turned Laureen to the mirror.

Laureen looked at herself, surprised. Usually her hair hung around her face, all messy. Nobody ever told her off about it, and she'd seen no reason to do anything with it. Now though, her face somehow looked okay.

"And now you look like a real ballerina," Sunny said, and Laureen threw her a grateful glance and said thank you.

Then everybody rushed to wash their hands and comb their own hair and, girls together, made their way back to the table.

This time Sara did not so much as look in Lev's direction, though every hair on her body seemed to stand up as she walked quickly by. Once past though, she sneaked a look. He was sitting with his back to the bar, propped on one elbow, half in shadow. She doubted he'd even noticed her.

Back at the table, Sunny's dish turned out to be monkfish studded with anchovies that had almost melted and was the best thing she had ever eaten. Well, at least since the previous night. And then again, there was always to-morrow. She wished she were not such a foodie. Did extra pounds lurk in the offing? Oh the hell with it, she was on vacation with Mac. Or was she? Didn't Mac seem more involved with Belinda right now, than being on holiday with her? Everybody was having a good time, including Valenti, who she saw never took his eyes off Belinda, which meant he ate very little while Belinda downed his food as well as her own and quite a bit of Billy's. In fact Billy was the only one who seemed not to be having a good time. For once his smile was missing.

And Sara was wrong. Lev noticed everybody and everything. The hands on his watch crept round to eleven-thirty, then twelve. More people were arriving . . . St. Tropez was a late town . . .

At twelve-fifteen they finally made a move, though not far, just across to the Caves du Roy. All except Billy and Little Laureen, who anyway was too young to be admitted, and who looked pleased when Billy said he was taking her home in a taxi. It was late but she hoped Bertrand would still be waiting. And since Lev was here in St. Tropez, they would not be caught. Tonight, she and Bertrand would put her plan into action. Billy waved goodbye and they were gone.

46.

The nightclub glimmered darkly; techno music resounded from the walls and bounced off the ceiling; they were encased in sound, borne along on a beat that swept Belinda instantly onto the crowded dance floor, gyrating like a wind-spirit found on Valenti's sailboat. Valenti was right there with her, and, unable to resist the pull of the music, Sunny joined them, then Nate dragged Sara onto the jammed floor, protesting all the way. Mac watched for a minute but he was aware of Lev in the background and aware of everything that was going on, checking faces beaded with sweat and flickering color and real jewels under the shimmer of black light.

Mac saw a face he knew. Caroline was alone at a small table near the back. This was not the hotel receptionist Caroline, it was the Caroline from the Casino, in a chiffon dress, diamond chandelier earrings, pale blond hair hanging in a sleek fall over her eyes. Even though her face was half-hidden, Mac knew it was her; there was just something about this version of Caroline, the way she sat with her head tossed arrogantly, one arm resting along the back of the chair next to her, one foot tapping impatiently, that was unmistakable.

Two martini glasses were on the table in front of her, both empty. Mac checked Valenti, but his attention was on Belinda and Mac doubted he'd even noticed Caroline.

He threaded his way to where she was sitting. Coming from behind her, he said, "Caroline?"

She jumped, then swung round, looking at him. Watching the changing expressions flit across her face, for a minute Mac thought she was going to deny it was her.

Then, "Oh, Monsieur Reilly," she said. She glanced away, flustered. "I didn't expect to see you here."

"Nor I you." Mac indicated the empty chair. "May I?"

"But of course." Caroline ran her hands distractedly through her hair.

"You look lovely tonight," Mac said, taking in the earrings, which he'd bet were the real thing, though Sunny would know for sure.

"Thank you, Monsieur Reilly."

"Please, call me Mac. After all, I feel I know you." This was totally untrue but it opened the conversation. "At least I know the you from the hotel. I must admit *this* Caroline is a surprise."

This time Caroline smiled. "I think you are a very nice man, Monsieur Reilly. Mac, I mean."

"And I think *you* are a very nice woman. Or maybe *two* different women." He was pursuing his theme. "Are you expecting someone?" He indicated the glasses.

She shrugged, that expressive little shrug French women do so well. "My girlfriend just left. Now I'm waiting to see if my boyfriend shows up."

Mac raised a brow. "And why is that in question?"

Caroline laughed. "Because, Mac Reilly, we had a fight last night. So now I don't know where I am with him."

Mac could have told her but thought he'd better not. Instead he offered to buy her a drink. He checked Lev, standing in the shadows. Everything was still okay on that end.

Caroline sipped her martini, eyeing him over the rim of the glass. "So, Mac, what have *you* been up to?"

"Well now, let me see . . ." Mac rolled up his eyes, pretending to think, making her smile. "Yes, of course. Last night Sunny and I went to the Casino in Monte Carlo and Sunny lost a great deal of money at roulette."

He waited for Caroline to say that she was also at the Casino, but she did not. He said, "And then tonight we went for a sail on a boat called the *Blue Picasso*."

This time he got the reaction he'd expected. Caroline slammed her glass on the table, spilling some of the drink. Mac took a napkin and mopped it up.

"Yes, a wonderful boat." He talked on, his eyes on Caroline's face, waiting for her to say she knew Valenti, that in fact he was her boyfriend. He knew something was going on, something more than just a relationship on the rocks.

Caroline was silent. Then she gave him a long full-on stare. There was a look in her eyes that made Mac uneasy. Was it anger? Hatred? Fear?

She leaned closer. "I know about your TV show, Mac. I know you are a detective, I know you have a good reputation, that you are clever . . . I need to talk to you."

"Anytime. Like now, for instance?"

She cast a glance at Valenti. "No. I must leave now. Please, give me your phone number. Tomorrow, I will call you. I'll tell you what time I will be free." She hesitated, then took a card from a small black bag that had, Mac noticed, the expensive triangular gold Prada insignia. She handed the card to him. "This is my address. We can meet there, later in the day."

"Just let me know." He caught the glance she swung at Valenti and then she was on her feet. "And Caroline?"

"Yes?" She stood, poised as if ready to run.

"It'll be okay, I promise."

Caroline gave him a long steady look. "I'm not sure it will. Not after you hear what I have to tell you."

Then, with a whisk of short chiffon skirts, she quickly blended into the crowd and was gone.

When Mac returned to his table Sunny and Sara were draped over their chairs, exhausted.

"This is the wildest crowd ever," Sunny exclaimed, eyeing a couple of stoned young things in mini Versaces and five-inch gold stilettos prancing on a table, long hair flinging back and forth, sweat trickling between their breasts, excitement building. The floor heaved with bodies and Mac felt glad he had not had to participate. Dancing was not his forte; he was old-school, the kind that liked to hold a woman in his arms when he danced. And that was exactly what he did now, pulling the protesting Sunny back onto the floor and slow-dancing, cheek to cheek.

"Like Fred and Ginger," she said into his ear.

"Only better," he agreed. But out of the corner of his eye he'd spotted Lev making a move. Mac's eyes swiveled to the door. Two men were standing there: white jackets, shades, black shirts; big, bulky, expensive and flash. They looked like what they were.

Mac saw Lev signal across the room then two of his men circled the floor heading their way. Only Mac would have known that all were packing guns. He glanced round for Belinda, hoping the thugs might not yet have had time to see her. But Belinda was the star of the show tonight, dancing, laughing, having fun, totally unaware of any danger.

"Sunny," Mac said. "Get Belinda and go quickly to the ladies' room. And go directly across the dance floor, not round it. Stay there until Lev comes to get you."

Sunny didn't ask for explanations, she knew the sound of trouble when she heard it. Mac covered her as she tapped Belinda on the shoulder, then taking her by the hand, led her into the crowd. He breathed again. Crowds were good. Even these thugs would think twice about abduction and gunfire in a busy South of France club.

He turned and walked over to where Lev's men now stood in back of the two Russians. Mac stopped in front of them. They shifted their eyes from the dance floor, lifted their solid chins and glared at him, hands automatically heading inside their jackets.

"Gentlemen." Mac smiled easily at them. "I do not think the management here would be thrilled about a pair of tough guys like you packing heat in their club. In fact I'm willing to bet that right now, you are about to be asked to leave."

Mac's eyes shifted to the right. Their eyes followed. A pair of burly bouncers flanked the door, watching. The Russians swung round, only to come face-to-face with Lev's two bodyguards.

Shrugging nonchalantly, as if to say what the hell? the Russians walked back and out the door they had just entered.

Mac followed them, watching. "Gentlemen?" he called after them. They did not turn round. "Better tell your boss that thugs packing guns do not go down well with the *flics* in St. Tropez. Nor anywhere else on the Riviera."

He turned to Lev, who had kept deliberately out of the scene, not wanting to be identified. "Belinda's in the ladies' with Sunny," he said. "Get her out of here, any way you can without her being followed."

"They saw her, y'know," Lev said.

Mac heaved a giant sigh. "Shit. I know they did. So now what?"

"Only thing I can think of is you take her home to Malibu."

Mac gave him a look. "And what would Sunny say to that?"

"That's your problem," Lev said, already en route to rescue Belinda.

Mac took care of Valenti, telling him Belinda had felt unwell and had returned home. He thanked him for the evening and said good night. He knew Lev would already have alerted the local police. The thugs would not be back, but others would certainly take their place. There would be trouble to come.

47.

The following day, Mac and Sunny had escaped their Misfits and were strolling the narrow streets of St. Tropez, window-shopping, stopping for one of those delicious *tartes tropeziennes,* or a *framboise,* with raspberries layered in cream and custard that melted in the mouth; pausing in cafés for an espresso here, an iced drink there, resting their feet, people-watching. In fact for once they were behaving like regular holidaymakers. Except that Mac had two other women on his mind besides Sunny.

Belinda, of course, who, much chastened, had promised not to move out of the hotel and who Mac knew was currently safely ensconced under a beach cabana, along with Little Laureen and Billy and the Chihuahua.

Sunny said she believed the dog was switching her allegiance to the little girl. "Not a chance," Mac replied, thinking fleetingly of the way their lives might be without feisty Tesoro's interfering little teeth. Still, he told Sunny not to worry, Tesoro's heart belonged to her, that she was just escaping the hot sun and doing what any lazy dog wanted, that is, resting in the shade in the company of an adoring female.

Lev had informed him that the pair of Russian thugs had checked out from the Carlton and driven back to San Remo. For now, they were out of the way. But not for long, Mac was sure of that. What he wasn't sure of was what to do about it. It was that old familiar situation known to anyone in family or divorce courts: the cops couldn't arrest the husband because he hadn't yet done anything; and if they waited until he did something, it would probably be too late for Belinda. The husband would have to make a move before Mac could have him arrested, and with a man as powerful as that, it would not be easy. Still, Interpol was following up the arms-trading link and he would see what came of that.

The other woman on his mind was Caroline Cavalaire, who had not yet called him. It was already three-thirty. He'd felt sure she would have been in touch before now.

Sunny stopped to look in a musty little shop on a narrow backstreet, whose window was filled with antiquey bits and pieces; freaky stuff like old powdered wigs and tortoiseshell hair combs, lace mantillas and faux Maltese crosses; costume jewelry left over from the sixties and silk shawls from the eighteen hundreds. Fishermen's nets with heavy round weights draped the window, and gilded coffee tables were squeezed next to frayed silk chairs. The shop was a mishmash of junk with "possibilities" that immediately captured Sunny's romantic heart.

She went inside and began to delve through what might, or might not, turn out to be a treasure trove while Mac took the card Caroline had given him and called her number. No reply. He checked the address. Stopping a passing stranger who looked as though he might be a local, he asked if he knew where it was. The man told him it wasn't far, right in the center of St. Tropez in fact, and within a few minutes' walk.

Mac stepped into the musty little shop, dodging draped fishing nets and old velvet curtains and dangling beads. A cloud of dust seemed to hover in the air making him sneeze. The long narrow shop was dimly lit but Sunny's smile was a thousand watts.

"You must have read my mind!" she exclaimed. "I was just about to come and get you. Take a look at this."

She held up an oil painting, an unframed canvas maybe two feet by three. It was a typical Mediterranean scene: sea and sky, cypresses and umbrella pines, a terrace where a child played by the pool while a woman lazed in a chair beneath an olive tree. Behind her a group of people sipped drinks from tall glasses and took their ease.

"It's her," Sunny said dramatically.

Mac didn't have to ask who. "Aw, come on, hon," he protested. "It's just one of those tourist paintings people buy to hang on the wall back home to remember their vacation by."

"*Maaaac!* No it is *not. This is Chez La Violette. This* is the terrace. And *this* is Violette herself. Look at the red hair."

Varnish had darkened the old canvas, nevertheless the woman's hair was undoubtedly red, and it flowed over her shoulders, almost to her waist. Her features were indistinct, but it certainly looked like the villa's terrace.

"Maybe you're right," he admitted, surprised.

"It's serendipity." Sunny was excited. "I mean, why would I just happen to walk along this street today, and just happen to notice this little shop, and just happen to come in for a mooch around? Don't you see? I was meant to find it."

Mac gave her that sigh that meant "aw come on Sun, baby, this is carrying it too far," and she gave him an indignant glare back.

"Mac Reilly, this painting was meant for me. I don't know why or how I came to find it. Perhaps there's a message in it, something that will unlock the mystery of Chez La Violette."

"Sun," he protested. "It's just a woman taking her ease, looking after the kid playing in the pool. It could be any villa, any terrace."

"I know it's Violette," Sunny said stubbornly, and went to find the owner in his cramped little office at the back. He was sitting on one of his frayed silk chairs with a red price tag attached to it, at a cluttered desk, also with a red price sticker.

"Oh, that," he said, adjusting his glasses and looking at the painting. He ran a hand through his sparse gray hair. "A woman brought that in a few weeks ago. I gave her more for it than I should have, but it was attractive and I thought someone would find it and want it one day. That day has come sooner than I thought, though."

He quoted Sunny a too-high price but she did not bother to bargain. The painting was hers, whatever it cost. The shop owner wrapped the canvas in brown paper, taped it up and wished Sunny *bonne chance*.

She went outside to join Mac, who was on the phone again trying to get ahold of Caroline. It was already five-thirty.

He took the brown paper parcel from Sunny, tucked it under his arm and said, "Come on, hon, we're off to see Caroline Cavalaire."

"Why?" Sunny strode along beside him, thankful she had put on espadrilles because the cobbled street was a minefield for a woman in heels.

"Because, my love, Caroline has something urgent to tell me, something she said I'm not going to be too happy with. And also because I think Caroline needs help and I'm worried because she hasn't called me as she promised."

The address Caroline had given turned out to be an apartment over a small handmade chocolate shop on one of St. Tropez's more charming little squares, next door to some pricey boutiques and a little café with chairs and tables set beneath old plane trees. Mac left Sunny there with her painting, ordered her a *citron pressé*, said he wouldn't be long and walked to the door at the side of the chocolate shop. A single bell with a brass sign said CAVALAIRE.

Mac pressed it and waited. No response. The smell from the chocolate shop was intoxicating and he could see mouthwatering mounds of chocolates with exotic flavors like pink peppercorn and Arabian spice in beautifully beribboned boxes.

Still Caroline did not answer her doorbell.

He pressed the bell one more time and also he called her number. Listening to the phone ring, he watched Sunny at the café, sipping her cold fresh lemonade and glancing possessively every now and then at the painting in the brown paper wrapper on the chair next to her. He shook his head. When Sunny got on to something she was like Tesoro: she didn't let go.

Meanwhile, Caroline was nowhere to be found and he had to give up. He collected Sunny and suggested they go out to the beach and watch the sunset.

"You mean on our own?" she asked, wide-eyed with surprise.

"Darn right, babe," he said. Right now, he'd had enough of the Carolines and Belindas of this world.

48.

They were walking back down the street when Mac's phone finally rang. "Yeah?"

"Mr. Reilly, this is François Reynaud."

"What can I do for you, sir?"

"One of my paintings, a Seurat known as *Les Pins d'Antibes,* has been spotted in Zurich. It was being offered for sale, very quietly, to a well-known collector. Now this painting has not been seen in public in the forty years I've owned it, but the collector knew his stuff. He didn't fall for the anonymous-seller routine. He's a man of integrity; he called various art dealers, came up with my name and called me."

"And the Seurat is from your collection?"

"Unless it's a fake, I believe it is."

Mac thought about Valenti's Picasso. "Tell me, sir, if the fake were good enough, would a dealer be able to discern the difference?"

"Possibly not, but anyway he would have it authenticated by an expert."

"And it's possible that even an 'expert' might be fooled, if the fake were good enough."

"Possible, but rare. But then, as I'm sure you're aware, experts are not infallible. It's a question of familiarity with the work of a certain artist, a discerning eye. No man is capable of always being right."

"Do we know who was offering the painting for sale?"

"A woman by the name of Suzanne Lariot."

"*Jesus.*" Mac looked astonished at Sunny.

She stared back at him, brows raised. "What?" she mouthed.

Reynaud said, "You know this woman?"

"Not exactly. I rented a villa from her over the Internet, along with several other 'innocents abroad.' The house turned out to be a wreck and Madame Lariot was nowhere to be found. In fact she'd taken our money and run. And now she turns up in Switzerland trying to sell your artwork."

Reynaud said, "This must be more than a coincidence."

"I take it you're in touch with the Swiss police?"

"I am, and with the local police."

"Do we have a description?"

"Dowdy, middle-aged, glasses, brown hair. She was cheaply dressed which instantly aroused the collector's suspicions. As you might know, Mr. Reilly, people in the art world may be dressed in expensive business suits, or in torn jeans and T-shirts, but you'll never find them looking, as my contact said, as though they shopped at a low-end department store."

"I understand. I'd appreciate it if you'd keep me informed, Monsieur Reynaud."

Mac looked at Sunny. "Our Madame Lariot has surfaced in Zurich attempting to sell a Seurat stolen from François Reynaud. She didn't look like a regular art dealer and the collector she tried to sell it to had no idea who she was. He became suspicious and informed the police."

"*Our* Madame Lariot?"

"The very same."

Sunny took the oil painting in its brown paper wrapper from under Mac's arm and clutched it to her breast, as though suddenly afraid it might also disappear and be sold to a Zurich art dealer. "What now?"

Mac grinned. "Baby, right now you and I are going to find some little bistro where they serve pizza and beer and local red wine. We're gonna watch that sunset and forget all about Madame Lariot, at least for a few hours."

"But *who* is she?"

"My guess is she's a local woman. The cops have a description from Zurich, but since our Misfits voted against going to them, there's nothing I can do. Unless I can persuade them to change their minds, of course."

As they lingered over simple pizza and a beer, Sunny was privately hoping they would not. All she needed was the local cops muscling in on her vacation.

49.

Bertrand had been disappointed when Laureen had not shown up the previous night. He'd guessed she was with her father and the Riders on the Storm, as he still thought of the group from Chez La Violette. After waiting a long time he'd finally given up and gone to his lair, his safe place where no one would ever find him. Not that anyone would come looking anyway.

He'd slept there, flat on his back, his myopic eyes turned to the stars in a heaven so vast it promised a whole new world, one that featured only in his dreams. Hunger finally drove him back the next morning, disheveled and with his tummy rumbling so loud he'd felt sure Caroline would hear it and catch him on his way to the stairs. However, it was not Caroline at the reception desk, and Renée was too busy with new guests to notice.

He found the note Laureen had pushed under his door and was surprised to find he was smiling. She wanted to meet at eleven that night. It was something to look forward to.

He showered and put on his old but clean polo shirt, hitched up his shorts with his dad's tie and ran back downstairs where, to the waiter's surprise, he ate a hearty breakfast. Then he went back upstairs to play his Doors CDs and write up his Scientific Experiment Journal, and finally fell asleep, waiting for night to come.

Like Mac and Sunny, Laureen and Billy also had pizza, at a little waterfront joint they found simply by almost falling over it. Billy had driven out of St. Tropez along the coast road, veering off at a roundabout that said Théoule.

He'd found himself on a small *quai*, with old row houses on one side, and on the other, cafés built on shady platforms jutting out over the calm bay, one of which had a PIZZA sign in giant red letters. With thoughts of a cold Bud and pepperoni, Billy had parked and now there they were.

Little Laureen chewed thoughtfully and silently on a single slice of pizza margarita that seemed to have lasted her a long time. In fact, it was all she had eaten in half an hour, along with an Orangina, the fizzy French orange drink to which she had taken a liking.

"You okay, Little Laureen, baby?" Billy asked, concerned.

"Yes, Daddy."

Billy took another slice of the pepperoni pizza, his third. "You happy here?"

Laureen looked at him over the top of the crust of pizza, nibbling on the cheesy bit. She didn't like crusts. "Daddy?"

"Yes?"

"Do you think Mommy would have liked sitting here in France eating pizza with us?"

Billy stopped chewing. Laureen almost never mentioned her mother.

"I think Mom would have enjoyed it. You know she always liked being by the sea."

"The Mediterranean. And she specially liked the color blue."

"It is pretty special," Billy agreed.

Laureen nibbled right to where the cheese stopped, then she put the crust carefully on her plate. Looking at Billy, she sipped Orangina through a yellow straw. "Daddy?"

"Yes, hon?"

"Do you think Mommy can see us right now? Sitting here eating pizza and looking at the blue Mediterranean."

Billy's heart wrenched with an almost physical pain. He had come to terms with his wife's death, memorializing her in the endowment fund for Texan schoolchildren, but he missed her, especially at moments like this, when his small daughter wanted answers and there were none.

Laureen's restless fingers pleated the tulle of her pink tutu, leaving cheesy smudges. "You don't know, do you, Daddy?"

Billy sighed. He reached across the table and took her hand, smoothing out those fingers. "It's like this, darlin'," he said gently. "No one really knows. There is no way, you see. It's like a giant secret, and all we can do is believe."

Laureen gripped his hand tightly. "I believe," she said in a small voice.

"And it's good that you do." Billy pushed back his hat, smiling at her. "And just remember, Laureen, Mommy loved you."

"I will," Laureen said solemnly. Then with a complete change, she glanced anxiously at her Mickey watch. It was nine o'clock. They had eaten early for France, most people were only just showing up for dinner. Her rendezvous with Bertrand was at eleven and they still had to drive all the way back to St. Tropez.

"We're going to be late," she said.

Billy's brows rose. "For what?"

"Oooh, y'know, just . . . late."

"Anxious to get back to the Hotel of Dreams, huh? And that kid Bertrand, I'll bet."

Laureen batted her eyelashes but said nothing. She wasn't telling anything about Bertrand.

Billy paid the bill and soon they were on their way.

It was late when they got back to the hotel. Billy took Laureen to her room, kissed her good night, and told her he was going back down to the courtyard to see if any of the Misfits were dining there.

Bursting with anxiety because she was late again, Laureen forced herself to wait five minutes, timing it on her watch. Then she peeked along the corridor. All clear. The heels of her cowboy boots clattered as she ran and she wished she had thought to change them. Too late now, and she couldn't just stop and take them off. In seconds she was downstairs and hovering in the hall. People were still at dinner and it was empty. Even the night concierge was not at his desk. Nor was the barman.

She flitted through on tiptoe. Something on the bar caught her eye and she stopped to look: it was a glass cocktail shaker filled with a pink liquid. She had heard the grown-ups talking about Cosmos. They were this exact pink.

She darted across, snatched up the shaker, realized she had nowhere to hide it, so held it against her side, arm stiff to grip it, edged away and ran full tilt for the open doors. The shaker was slipping and she grabbed it with both hands. Clomping along, short tutu bobbing, she hurried down the path to the beach.

Bertrand heard her coming and turned to look as she slid down the small sandy dune.

"Look what I brought." She held up the cocktail shaker.

"What is it?"

"It's pink," she said helpfully. "Grown-ups drink it."

"Booze, you mean?"

Laureen shrugged. "Why don't you taste it?"

Bertrand took the shaker and removed the cap. He sniffed suspiciously. "Smells fruity."

"It's like juice, only with vodka and some other booze."

Bertrand then lifted the shaker to his mouth and took a long slug. He handed it back and leaned against the rock, eyes suddenly slitted behind his glasses.

Laureen inspected him for any ill effects, then she too took a long drink. Sputtering, she pulled a face. "Is this supposed to taste *good*?"

Bertrand took the shaker and held it up to see how much was left. "Another mouthful," he said, having first go.

Laureen copied him. "Uh-uh," she said. "Now it's all gone. What do we do with the cocktail shaker? I can't take it back to the bar, someone might see me."

"Leave it at the Beach Bar," Bertrand said, surprising himself with his quick thinking.

Laureen unraveled herself and got to her feet. She was surprised too, but this was because her knees were buckling. "Uh-uh," she said, sitting abruptly back down. "Do you feel okay?"

Bertrand starred dreamily at his own feet, which suddenly looked the size of dinner plates. "I never feel okay."

He slid along the rock face until he lay faceup on the sand. Laureen slid down to join him. Spread-eagled they stared up at the inky sky scattered with about a billion points of light. A shooting star flickered fast and bright across the heavens, as though putting on a show specially for them.

After a while, Laureen had no idea how long, she said, "Do you think we're drunk?"

"Yes." Bertrand's voice was slower than usual, then it trailed off altogether.

After another while, Laureen asked, "Do you feel sick?"

"No."

"I do," she volunteered. "I don't know why grown-ups drink this stuff, it must be poison to make you feel like this. Oooh." She held her breath for a minute. "I really don't feel good."

"Serves you right for stealing," Bertrand said.

"I *didn't* steal." She was indignant. "It was just sitting there so I took it."

"Like the sunhat."

"Oh, that . . ." She was defensive.

"What do you think your mother would say about that?"

Laureen drew in a sharp breath. Her head was spinning and her stomach churned but what Bertrand had said was so shocking she forgot about it. She moved sideways so she could see him. "And what do you think your mother would say if she knew you'd drunk liquor?"

Bertrand grabbed the cocktail shaker and struggled to his feet. He took her hand and pulled her up. They clutched each other, swaying slightly, then together they stumbled to the Beach Bar and left the shaker on the shelf for the staff to find the next morning.

They stood, holding hands, staring at the sea shushing softly toward them in a never-ending game of catch-up. Laureen wished she had never stolen the Cosmos, but then if she hadn't Bertrand would not have been able to talk about his mother. And hers.

Bertrand turned and looked back at their rock. He had forgotten all about his cape and the binoculars. Letting go of Laureen and tripping over his own feet, he went back and retrieved them. When he returned he wrapped the cape carefully around her.

"Why?" she asked, smiling giddily because her tutu made the cape stick out and she looked twice her normal size.

Bertrand strung the binoculars around his neck then took her hand again. "We need to cover up that pink ballet dress," he told her solemnly. "So no one will see you."

"Why?" Laureen asked again. Her stomach had stopped heaving and she could feel a silly grin on her face.

"Because we're off to Chez La Violette," Bertrand said importantly. "The new headquarters of the Scientific Experiment of the International Duo, Seekers of Stolen Art and Winners of a Fortune in Euros."

"What's a 'duo'?" Little Laureen asked.

50.

Still holding hands, they walked down the beach. Laureen just knew she was going to throw up.

"Bertrand?" she said.

"*Oui?*" He was speaking French tonight.

"Are you sure you don't feel sick?"

Bertrand did but he wasn't about to admit it to a girl. Instead he gave a little Gallic shrug that indicated he was cool. His stomach heaved and he wondered what to do.

"Bertrand."

Laureen's voice had become smaller. Bertrand knew the situation had become urgent and he dragged her quickly to a garbage can at the side of the beach, turning his back discreetly as she heaved up the booze. Hearing her set him off too though. He made it just in time.

Trembling, they looked at each other. "So, okay," Laureen said. "I'll never drink again."

"Me either." Bertrand looked at her, messy and distraught, still wrapped in his camouflage cape. "Come on," he said and marched off toward the sea.

Laureen watched him for a minute, wondering what he was going to do. She saw him put his binoculars carefully on the dry part of the sand then walk into the water.

"Bertrand," she cried, panicked. He turned and looked at her.

"Come on," he called. "It'll make you feel better."

She cast off the cape and ran toward him. The waves were already lapping at her feet when she remembered her precious pink tutu. She unzipped it quickly and stepped out of it. Looking at it, lying there on the sand, she thought it looked like a fluffy pink bird. Then, in her underpants and T-shirt, she followed Bertrand into the water.

He was floating on his back, arms spread, exactly the way he had lain on the beach. Laureen hurled herself in, tasting salt, flinging herself toward him in a wild crawl, kicking like mad so she wouldn't sink. She had learned to swim at an early age because her parents were afraid she might fall in their pool and drown, but she had never been really good at it. Now, for the first time, swimming in the dark whispering Mediterranean, she felt the sheer exhilaration of being one with the elements, just her and the sea and the starry sky.

"Look at me, Mommy," she yelled, spitting out a mouthful of water. "Just look at me now."

After a few minutes though the water began to feel chilly and they swam silently back, wading the last few feet until they were once more on dry land.

"Better get out of those wet things," Bertrand said wisely. "Put your tutu back on then I'll lend you my cape again."

Laureen quickly did as she was told, though her teeth chattered quite a bit and the tutu felt scratchy without underwear. "What about you? You're wet too."

He plucked at his wet shorts. He had been as wet as this on the night of the big storm. "I'll soon dry off." He arranged the cape around her plump shoulders. "Do you feel better now?"

Laureen did. In fact she felt great. "I'm okay. When are we going to Chez La Violette though?"

"Right now."

"Bertrand?"

"*Oui?*"

"I saw all the big villas have their own docks. It would be easy to steal stuff and get it away on a boat."

"I'll bet you're right," he said, amazed at how clever she was.

A half-moon glimmered low in the sky, giving just enough light for them to make out the path leading up from the beach to the lane. It was darker there, where the trees crowded close, and also because Bertrand with his nighttime experience, insisted they keep to the side of the road where no one could see them.

"But no one will see us, there's no one here," Laureen objected. She'd stuffed her wet things into her boots and she plodded barefoot behind Bertrand, a boot in each hand, cape trailing behind her.

"You never know," Bertrand replied, with memories of the headlights flashing in back of him on the night of the storm.

Laureen's legs were prickled by bushes and she was afraid maybe a snake might jump out and bite her, but she didn't tell Bertrand that. After all he'd included her on his nighttime Scientific Experiment and she didn't want him to think she was just some silly girl.

"Bertrand?"

"Yes."

"How do you know how to get there?"

"I've been there many times, even though it's haunted. I know Chez La Violette inside and out." He was bragging now, though in fact the only time he'd been there at night was when the Riders on the Storm had arrived.

"Haunted?" Laureen's voice was a frightened squeak. "You mean you saw *a ghost?*"

Bertrand gave that shrug again that implied maybe he did maybe he didn't, but then he caught sight of her frightened face. He took one of the boots from her and clasped her hand again. "There are no ghosts," he said. "I've been there many times. I found the binoculars there, remember?"

"*Stole* not *found*," she corrected him.

"Anyhow, it's a good place for our new Secret Society," he said, pulling her on down the lane. "In fact, if I were a robber I'd use it as my secret hideaway. No one ever goes there."

"Except us," Laureen muttered. The lane was rutted with hard mud and she wished she'd put on the boots. Besides, the tulle tutu was very scratchy.

"Anyway the ghost is only supposed to be of the old singer, Violette. She built the villa but I'll bet if she saw it now she wouldn't bother to come back and haunt it."

They were walking alongside a wall. Bushes of night-blooming jasmine grew over it and Laureen stopped to sniff. Maybe Chez La Violette wasn't so bad after all.

Bertrand grabbed her hand again and pulled her onto a narrow path that led through the bushes. A wooden gate, half-open, was in front of them. They edged through and stood looking round.

The swans'-head fountain was silhouetted against the pale bulk of the villa and somewhere a startled bird cried out.

"It's the kitchen garden," Bertrand whispered, thrilling to the sound of his own voice in the dense silence.

"Bertrand?" Laureen was also whispering.

"Yes?"

"What do we do now?"

To tell the truth, Bertrand didn't know. The house looked dark and intimidating and the stories of the ghost haunted his mind as the ghost was supposed to haunt the house. But of course he couldn't let Laureen know he was scared.

"We'll go inside," he whispered back, and with a quick "Follow me," he led the way. He stopped at the kitchen door. Laureen was right behind him, practically stepping on his heels.

Bertrand felt around in the pot of geraniums for the key he knew the janitor usually left. It wasn't there. He took off his glasses, polished them on his wet T-shirt and put them back on again. The empty house looked as intimidating as before.

"Bertrand?"

He sighed exaggeratedly. "Yes?"

"I'm scared."

He managed a laugh, a muffled sound that caught in his tight throat. He was scared too. "Silly," he said, gripping her hand tighter. "Come on, I know how to get in."

"Bertrand?" Laureen trotted reluctantly behind him.

He sighed again, as though girls were tiresome beings who didn't belong on such an adventure. "Yes?"

"I don't think I want to go inside."

They rounded the corner to the rear terrace. He said, "The lock on the French door is broken, we can get in there."

"Bertrand?"

This time he groaned.

"I want to go home."

"Hummph," he said scornfully. "What are you? Some *girl*?"

"Oooh. No. No, of course not." Laureen wasn't going to be called a wimpy girl and she tiptoed, still barefoot, after him, a boot in one hand—Bertrand was still carrying the other.

She saw it first. Through the window. A flicker of light. Just a flicker, moving in the darkness. Then it was gone.

"Bertrand!"

"Shhhh." He crept toward the paned glass door. Then he saw it too. A light. Moving across the room. The hair on his neck stood on end. He took a step back, heard Little Laureen's *"Oooh, Bertrand."* And then she screamed.

He clamped a hand across her mouth. *"Taissez vouz,"* he hissed, then he

grabbed her and together they ran back round the corner to the kitchen garden, down the path and through the wooden gate onto the road.

Bertrand could hear Laureen gasping for breath and her hand gripped
his as though she would never let go.

"It was the ghost," she wailed between gasps, as they fled down the leafy
path that led onto the beach.

They stopped to catch their breath, leaning against the trunk of an umbrella pine, hidden deep in its shade. Looking back Bertrand saw no one.
He looked out to sea. The lights of the fishing boats promised a security that
land did not at this moment. Closer in, he saw the outline of another boat,
dark on dark against the sea, low in the water and sleek as a fish. There were
no lights on it.

Laureen stumbled silently alongside him as they walked back down the
beach.

"Was it the ghost?" she asked finally.

"Of course not." Bertrand didn't want her to be scared anymore. "Lots of
people go there. You know, like lovers and things."

"You mean like boyfriend and girlfriend stuff?"

He nodded. "Yes. And other people. I know because I've seen their beer
bottles, and their footprints all over the house." He was exaggerating. He had
once seen a beer bottle, but that was in broad daylight and he'd guessed the
janitor had left it there. "And things were moved," he added. That was also
true, but again he blamed the janitor.

"I'll bet it was the ghost," Laureen said.

"Ghosts don't drink beer."

She guessed that was true.

"Bertrand?"

"Yes." He strode on.

"What about our Secret Society of the Euro Duo?" She couldn't remember the exact title.

"Our new headquarters will be at my lair."

Laureen breathed a sigh of relief. She definitely did not want to see any
more ghosts.

"Bertrand?"

He stopped and looked at her. He was sorry she had been scared, and
sorry he had been too. He didn't want to see any more ghosts either.

She said, "Maybe we shouldn't have drunk the Cosmos."

"You're right."

"Serves me right for stealing them."

He nodded.

"I promise I won't steal anything ever again."

"Okay."

They were near the Beach Bar now. Bertrand checked to see if anyone was there. Laureen looked too, especially for Lev's secret agents who might be anywhere. "Coast clear," Bertrand whispered.

He gave her back her boot and she gave him back his cape.

"Go on, run," he said. "And remember, keep to the bushes, don't let anyone see you."

He watched her tutu bobbing out of sight, straining his ears for any cries of alarm. Nothing. With a sigh of relief, he set off for his lair. Though he would never have admitted it to Laureen, he believed he had seen a ghost. This had been one of the most frightening nights of his life.

51.

Mac was up early to walk the dogs. Leaving Sunny still sleeping, he pulled on a bathing suit and beach sandals, planning on a swim on the way back.

On his way out he spotted something lying in the hallway; one of Little Laureen's cowboy boots. She must have dropped it last night. He picked it up and saw something stuffed inside. His eyebrows rose. It looked like wet underwear to him. Mac grinned. He'd bet Billy didn't know his daughter had been midnight skinny-dipping, and probably with the weird young French kid. He left the boot outside Laureen's door and, dogs in tow, ran down the stairs.

He was surprised to see Caroline Cavalaire at the reception desk, busy checking out a group of guests. She glanced up and her eyes met his. She nodded a quick *bonjour* and returned to her work.

Mac walked over to her. "Sorry I didn't hear from you yesterday, Caroline," he said.

"Aah, *oui. Mais monsieur,* I was so busy all day. And I'm busy now. Besides, it was really not that important."

"Glad to hear it, though it would have been better if you had called and told me."

He saw the color rise in Caroline's cheeks. She said of course, but she simply had not had the time. "*Je suis désolée, monsieur,* I'm sorry," she said, returning to the guests.

So much for that, Mac told himself, but he still had that uneasy feeling she was hiding something.

Outside, Tesoro trotted docilely next to him, while Pirate, let off the lead, galloped joyfully ahead. Mac realized his footsteps were taking him in the direction of Chez La Violette. When they reached the long wall he pushed open the gates and walked up the gravel drive. He stood looking at the villa. It was, he thought, like the actress herself: once beautiful then old and broken down. And yet there was still an elusive air of magic about it, an aura of times past when in the prime of its beauty, the villa played host to the fashionable people of the world.

The front door was locked and he did not have the key. Carrying Tesoro, and with Pirate now sticking close, he tried the kitchen door. Locked too. Odd, he could swear he had left that open earlier. Still, the janitor had probably been round, checking on things; perhaps he'd locked it.

Shrugging it off, he walked back through the kitchen garden and out the green wooden gate, then across the lane onto the path that led to the beach. Hitching both dogs to a tree, he ran into the water, feeling little flickers of pleasure in every nerve as he swam. *This* was what the Mediterranean was all about: cool, salty, smooth on the skin. It was like the swimming equivalent of drinking the local rosé wine.

Exhilarated, he collected the dogs and walked along the shoreline, stopping at the Beach Bar for an early espresso. Back in the hotel he was surprised to find Caroline no longer there. Renée had taken her place. He called *bonjour* and asked what happened.

"Caroline had a phone call. Her mother is sick and she had to go to Avignon. She asked if I would take her place and of course, I said yes."

Upstairs in their room, Sunny was sitting on the terrace, long golden legs propped on the rail, sipping coffee. Tesoro bounded onto her lap and she bent to kiss her, then turned to look at Mac.

He bent to kiss Sunny too. "Hi, honey."

She said, "There's a red helicopter out there."

Mac took a look, then got Lev on the phone.

"Looks like maybe Jasper Lord is scouting the beaches for his lost wife."

"I told you you should have taken her back to Malibu," Lev said.

"What? You think he wouldn't find her there? Belinda would be hitting all the high spots."

"They're not too big on helicopters landing in St. Tropez," Lev said. "It disturbs the posh locals."

"François Reynaud has one."

"He's one of the posh locals."

Mac laughed.

Lev said, "Belinda hasn't emerged, she's probably sleeping late. Best thing she could do, considering. Anyhow, I'll check where the copter lands, and who the pilot is. Meanwhile, keep Belinda indoors. I'll get back to you."

"Perhaps I should take Belinda with me," Sunny said.

"Why? Where are you going?"

"Just thought I'd go back to the newspaper offices in Nice, see what else I can dig up on La Violette and that ring with the crest. Nobody would ever find Belinda down in those dungeons."

She stretched, arms over her head, long black hair swishing around her shoulders. Mac thought she looked like something between a Playboy Bunny and a Botticelli angel.

The phone rang. It was his friend Alain Hassain of Interpol, saying that Joel Krendler's plane had been tracked, via flight plans, to various small airports in France. The closest and most recent was Toulon. "Between Marseilles and where you are," he said. "And that was two days ago."

Mac asked if Krendler ever flew to Zurich.

"He does frequently, for 'business reasons.' Remember he's an international businessman, as well as an opera buff. In fact, in season, he often flies to Milan, where he's a patron of La Scala opera house. Just thought you'd like to know."

Mac ended the call and said to Sunny, "This gets more interesting. Now why would Krendler, who claims not to have visited the South of France in a decade, fly into Toulon?"

Sunny shrugged and shook her head. "There's no international opera house there that I've heard of."

"Exactly. There's more to Monsieur Krendler than just opera, and I'm beginning to think it might be art."

Sunny's brows raised in a question.

"Art with a capital *A*," Mac said.

"As in *stolen* Art?"

"Could be."

"Oh, come on, Mac, that's a bit far-fetched."

"Far-fetched is always good, leads the mind to better things. Bigger things."

"Like rental scams."

Mac laughed. "That's a different problem. I seem to have come to a dead end on Madame Lariot."

"You mean she's gotten away with all our money?"

"Looks like it, babe."

He went and sat next to her on the terrace. He put an arm round her shoulders. "Sure you want to go and spend the day in those newspaper dungeons?"

She gave him that upward long-lashed glance. "What else do you have I mind?"

"We could hang out here, spend time together, hold hands . . ."

"In the moonlight, you mean? Not a chance, Mac Reilly. Anyway, you've got some detecting to do."

Mac sighed. He had failed on the Lariot scam and now he was involved in investigating the affairs of a man he had met only once and knew very little about.

"Why do I do this?" he complained.

"Because, my love"—Sunny deposited a kiss on his lips in between words—"you can't help yourself. I've become accustomed to it and I thought you might by now."

Mac grinned and pulled her closer. "Now I know why I love you," he said, running his hands down her lovely rib cage. That is until Tesoro gave him a quick little nip, putting a stop to that.

52.

Lying on the beach in his faux-Hawaiian surfer shorts, Nate felt like a fraud. He was no surfer and had never been to Hawaii. And no matter how Belinda dressed him up, he wasn't like these people, the hedonistic sunbathers, the women sun-bronzed and half-naked, the men keeping an eye on their children, running with them into the sea, kids screaming with joy. He envied those men returning to the pretty young wife, dropping sly kisses on her neck as she wrapped a child in a beach towel to dry him off. He envied them when the pretty young wife turned her face up for that extra lingering kiss, a hand on the bare brown shoulder still glistening with seawater. He almost envied them their kids, squirming little bundles of trouble, eager for the next adventure.

Of course this was simply their vacation and Nate knew from experience nobody's life was perfect. But for them, moments like these made up for it.

For Nate, despite the Riviera vacation, despite the new French clothes, despite the fresh grilled fish and the rosé wine, it was still the same, this disassociation from what he guessed was "real life." He still woke every morning thinking he should leap out of bed and get to the office as fast as possible: be first there, beat out the others in the numbers game. He should be thinking about making money, not about Sunny Alvarez, or Belinda Lord. Other men's wives.

Impatient with himself, angry that he couldn't shrug off the "mortal coil" of making money, he went to his room, showered, put on the new shorts Belinda had talked him into, a Hanes white tee and sneakers. He grabbed his helmet, went downstairs, collected the Ducati from the parking lot and set off on the road out of St. Tropez. He didn't know where he was heading but he guessed it was for the hills.

Three hours later he stopped the bike. He was somewhere in Provence, in a walled hilltop village that clung desperately to a rock face so steep and so sheer he marveled they had ever built a road up it. He hadn't even checked the signs, and did not know where he was; he'd just roared away, wanting to escape himself and his life, yet not knowing how to achieve that escape. Now he took a look around.

He was in a place called Gordes, in a wide cobbled square surrounded by narrow stone houses and tiny shops selling all kinds of goods from lavender bags to olive wood bowls and those gaily patterned yellow and blue tablecloths. The Café Renaissance took up one corner, spilling into the square. It was doing good business; people were packed under the umbrellas, sipping cold drinks, taking their ease. Looking at them, Nate marveled that no one but he seemed to have this urge to move on, to always be somewhere else, to be doing something.

He realized that wasn't quite true. What he meant was "to be doing what he always did." Even as he stood admiring the view of the valley stretching into infinity under a haze of heat, hearing the snatches of laughter from the café, watching local women pushing babies in strollers, buying oranges and cucumbers and grapes, and fish from the refrigerated van that had parked in the square, planning their dinners, living their lives, Nate felt out of it.

He climbed back on the Ducati and roared off through the village, the bright yellow bike turning heads as he passed. He drove along a leafy road where the grass grew in great clumps from the rock face and the bleat of goats and the tinkle of their bells could be heard from the rocky landscape known as the *garrigue*. The thrum of the powerful motor beneath him, the sky above, blue and cloudless, the heat of the sun, the sudden stillness in the air, combined to make him feel as though he were the only person left in the world. He was completely alone and quite suddenly he found himself smiling. For a fleeting moment, a stranger in an unknown place, he felt free.

A sign in front said he was coming to the village of Bonnieux. He slowed, wondering whether in fact he wanted to go into another village, whether he wanted to become part of the "real world" again, a world in which he did not belong. He reminded himself that *his* New York was the real world: Nate Masterson and Wall Street went together like coffee and cream, like Scotch and soda, like women and men. He smiled as he idled into the village, canceling that last thought. There had been too many women in Nate's life but none for any long period of time. And none with whom he had been able to contemplate living. Face it, he told himself, parking in a lot on the village outskirts, you are meant to be alone.

He found himself in another small medieval fortified stone village that clung to the top of a rock by some miracle of construction, to which the olden-days builders had obviously had the secret. Narrow cobbled streets; tall thin buildings leaning into each other; paned windows deep-set; stone the color of the rocky earth. A butcher, a baker, a greengrocer, cafés and small boutiques, a cherry-laden tree in the garden of a small hotel; a church that looked as though it had been there for all time, ever since people believed in God. An ironmongers called a *quincaillerie;* a sign outside a row house that said a famous artist had once lived there; the smell of something good floating from a tiny kitchen window. Suddenly hungry, Nate closed his eyes, sniffing, trying to identify it.

"*Daube de bœuf,*" a man's voice came from behind him.

Nate swung round.

"A kind of a beef stew," the man said in English. "Beef and vegetables, always in a rich sauce, no doubt made with an entire bottle of good red. A bit heavy for a hot day like this but I suppose when the man of the house returns home tonight he'll be hungry."

For a second Nate found himself envying that unknown "man of the house." His own kitchen in his supersmart steel and concrete loft had never been used.

"Thanks for the information," he said with a smile. "He's a lucky man."

"That he is. But if you're hungry I can recommend a little place down the hill a-way. Le Moulin de Hubert. Used to be an old olive mill before the new civilization here in the Luberon caught up to it. Now it's run as a small restaurant by a couple of English folk." He grinned at Nate and offered his hand. "One of whom is myself. So you see, I'm not entirely impartial."

Nate laughed as he shook his hand. "At least you're honest."

He was looking at a slightly built man in his sixties, balding, gray, tanned, short and with a raspy-looking gray beard.

"Malcolm Finney," the man said. "Pleased to meet you."

"Nate Masterson. And good to meet you too." Nate eyed him curiously from behind his dark glasses. "A silly question I know, but do you live here?"

"I do. And have for twenty years. Wouldn't live anywhere else."

"And why is that?" Nate wanted an answer so he could understand what the holy grail was everyone but him was looking for.

But Malcolm Finney shook his head. "Young man, if you can stand here and ask that question then you obviously don't understand." He hesitated, eyeing Nate, then he said, "Look, why not come and have a bite of lunch? My partner, Roger, cooks other stuff besides *daube de boeuf*. Come with me and I'll tell you all about it. Or better, I'll show you." He grinned, showing large horsey-looking teeth. "My treat," he said. "Just to prove I wasn't trying to sell you on my restaurant for lunch."

Nate found himself laughing as they shook hands again. "Agreed, but I buy the wine."

He followed Malcolm Finney's ancient Land Rover down a bumpy side road that ended in a low wooded area and an old stone mill house on a small rushing stream, complete with the original mill wheel. Tall, for a Provençal house, and built of rugged grayish stone, it had obviously once worked for its living, grinding whatever could be eked from the rocky valley. Now though, an awninged loggia had been built out over the millpond with a view of its busy little weir. Tables set with green-and-white-checkered oilcloth and white paper napkins, were dotted with lazy lunchgoers, who, Nate thought amazed, sipped their wine the way everybody did here, as though time were never of the essence, and anyway who cared, there was always tomorrow.

In the rear of the loggia, large sliding windows had been pushed back to reveal a low-beamed dining room crammed with copper pots and dominated by a large fireplace. It was, Nate thought, a place where a man could seek refuge on a cold winter night, settled near the flames with a glass of Scotch and a *daube* of beef to keep him warm.

That old feeling of envy crept over him again as Malcolm Finney showed him to a corner table under the awning, then waved down the waitress, a pleasant woman in a blue overall with a matching kerchief tied over her dark hair, and asked her to bring Badoit water and a bottle of the Vieux Télégraphe.

"Since you're buying, thought we'd try the good stuff," he told Nate with a cheeky grin. "And trust me, it doesn't come better around here than the Télégraphe. It's one of the best Côtes du Rhônes you'll ever taste."

He went off to find his partner, who, he said, was in the kitchen doing the cooking. "Or most of it anyway."

He came back with a tall dark guy in a chef's white jacket and red shorts, wide-built, mustached and Mediterranean-looking. Turned out he was Welsh and the two had been together for twenty-five years.

"Don't know how we've lasted," Roger said, shaking hands and accepting a glass of the Télégraphe.

"Truth is we wouldn't if we hadn't come here on vacation and found this place," Malcolm added.

Roger lifted his glass to him with a smile. "Our lifesaver."

Malcolm turned to Nate. "It got us out of the rut, that thing some folks call 'living.' We were in catering. That posh dinner-party circuit, all fancy hors d'oeuvres and small exquisite portions on smart plates and it like hell better not be the same as anybody else's party they'd been to."

"After a while you begin to run out of ideas," Roger said. Then added, "My God this wine is good."

The dense fruity wine tasted simple at first on Nate's palate, then became flavors he knew would have wine writers going on about spice and varietals and overtones of this and that. Godammit, all it tasted to him was good. Great, in fact.

"That your Ducati?" Roger nodded at the bike, propped up in the shade of the massive trees.

"Just bought it," Nate confessed. "I live in New York, in the city. Not much need for a car there."

"So what d'you do?"

"Wall Street," Nate replied, not wanting to go into it. He was having too good a time.

Roger had asked the waitress to bring out the hors d'oeuvres, a dozen baskets of good things. Then there was roast chicken with tiny potatoes and baby vegetables plucked from the garden, sautéed in butter and with a gray sea salt that came from the Camargue to sprinkle on top, and a green salad dotted with orange nasturtiums and fresh lavender.

It was a first for Nate: vegetables and herbs fresh-picked from the garden, flowers in his food, and a wine that tempted him to have more, though he would not. A guy in charge of a powerful Ducati had to know exactly what he was doing. Instead he drank the Badoit water.

Roger had gone back to his kitchen and, surprising himself, Nate said to Malcolm, "I envy you."

"Oh? And why is that?"

"Because I'm looking at a man who found exactly what he wanted in life. A man who found freedom."

Malcolm smiled. "You know well enough none of us are ever free. That's just the way life is. Responsibility of some sort always claims us, whether it's a woman, a partner, a business. Or even a Ducati." He eyed Nate levelly. "A Ducati costs money. And that kind of money has to be earned by your soul."

"Then my soul's a slave to that fuckin' Ducati. I paid cash for it. But I envy you this." Nate waved an arm, taking in the old mill, the shady loggia, the wine-drinking summer-lazy diners, even the little tribe of ducks that suddenly waddled across the yard making for the pond set amid the trees.

"Too Disney for words, isn't it?" Malcolm said. "But this isn't for you."

"No? And why not?"

"You're a bachelor. Busy man. This place needs constant upkeep. We've made a go of it here but it's hard work, even though it looks like one long lovely day of pleasure. Still, I do think I know exactly what would be right for you."

"What do you mean?"

Malcolm looked at him. "I must warn you, I'm in real estate."

Nate nodded, seeing what was coming. "Okay."

"It's in Bonnieux," Malcolm said. "A village house. Front door leads right off the street. Five floors with a room on each floor, small courtyard out back overlooking the entire valley. Currently owned by a German guy who's getting a divorce. Fully restored, fully furnished, very old outside, very modern inside. It's the perfect bachelor pad."

"For a bachelor who lives in Manhattan?"

Malcolm shrugged. "It's a better bet than a Ducati for keeping your soul warm on those cold lonely winter nights."

Nate took a deep breath. Malcolm had somehow gotten to the essence of where he was at. He took a last swallow of the Vieux Télégraphe. He would remember that taste forever. "Let's go take a look," he said.

53.

Sunny was on her way to Nice and the newspaper archives. She had left with Belinda and Sara, via the kitchen door, with Belinda disguised in long baggy linen pants and a pink gingham shirt with a matching bandanna tied over her short blond hair. With the de rigueur large dark glasses, she now looked like Bardot in the fifties.

"Cute," Belinda decided, inspecting herself in the car mirror. "This may be my new look."

"I like it more than the old one," Sara said.

Sunny was driving the silver rental Peugeot with Sara beside her, holding Tesoro. Belinda was in the backseat and grumbling about it, saying her legs were too long.

"Suffer in silence," Sunny warned. "At least I got you out of the hotel, or you'd be sitting in your room watching French television and wishing you'd never left San Remo."

"Wishing I'd never left the husband? Hah! I don't think so."

Belinda turned to look out the back window. Lev was right behind them. "That Lev sure knows what he's doing, I've never felt so safe in my life."

"Is Lev there?" Sara craned her neck.

"Why? You interested in him?"

Sara blushed. "Of course not, he's just . . . well, nice, that's all."

"And cute!" Belinda was laughing at her, but in a nice way.

"Anyhow, I think he likes you," Sunny said, negotiating the roundabout and heading out on the road that led to the autoroute. "He always has that special smile for you."

"You think so?" Sara's blushes were mixed with a smile now. "You know that song he's always kind of humming"—she hummed a few bars—"he said he doesn't know what it is but it's stuck in his head. Well, *I* know."

"Is that right?" Belinda's eyes met Sunny's in the rearview mirror. "And what is it, Sara?"

Sara shook her head. "I'm going to tell Lev next time I see him." Then she said, "Oooh," with a frightened glance past Sunny, out of the driver's window. "Oooh, that's where it happened, that's where they almost got me—"

"Okay, okay, it's all right now, just don't let yourself dwell on it, don't go back there." Belinda leaned forward and patted the back of Sara's head sympathetically. "Gosh, Sara," she said, quickly changing the subject. "You know you have the most wonderful hair. You really should let me cut it for you, get rid of all that weight hanging around your face. We can hardly see you as it is."

Sunny took a quick look at Sara. "She's right, y'know, you could do to show your pretty face more."

"Hardly 'pretty.'"

"Are you mad, girl?" Belinda laughed. "You're downright gorgeous, or you could be if you'd let me get my scissors onto you."

"I'll think about it." Sara wasn't about to be parted from her face-sheltering hair so fast. It was like the arms she folded over her chest; it protected her.

"Anyway," Sunny changed the subject. "This is the reason we're going to the newspaper archives." She took the gold signet ring from her pocket and handed it to Sara, who inspected it closely.

"It's a checkerboard shield with an eagle and a fox and a monogram." She tried it on. "It's too big."

Belinda took it from her. "It had to have belonged to a man. It's kind of an upper thing, you know, aristocrats, they always wear them on the pinky. Prince Charles wears one."

"So you think this belonged to an aristocrat?"

"I'd be willing to bet on it. You can check the heraldry, they can find out whose crest it is. But anyhow I don't think it's English."

Sunny said, "I'll bet it must have belonged to Violette's German lover."

"She had a lover?"

"She did, and half her age."

"Lucky her," Belinda said. "So that's what we're researching at the newspaper archive?"

"I want anything I can find on her, and him. But first we need to know his name."

"Violette will tell you. If he's her lover she will have written to him and saved his letters to her," Sara said. Sometimes she seemed wise beyond her years.

An hour later they were inspecting microfilm and dusty papers, deep beneath the streets of Nice. There were old playbills from the Casino announcing personal appearances by La Violette, with pictures of her gorgeously gowned by Schiaparelli and Lanvin, and always holding a bunch of violets to her face.

"Parma violets," Sara said. "White ones. She always carried them or wore them pinned to her suit because of her name."

"How do you know that?" They looked at her amazed.

"It says so right here."

They hung over her shoulder and read the newspaper story.

"La Violette resembles her namesake flowers," it said. "With her wide violet-color eyes and the scent that always surrounds her, made from the precious and most costly white violets from Parma, a scent that is made only for her. It precedes her into a room, soft and delicate as the woman is tall and beautiful, in her silvery dresses and fabulous jewels, gifts from her many admirers."

Sunny shivered, remembering that elusive scent in Violette's room. "They mean lovers," Belinda said. "Guys don't just give you jewels because they admire you."

"They did in those days," Sunny said. "Stage-door Johnnies, they called them. They showered stage stars with pricey gifts to show how much they admired them."

"Fancied them, you mean," Belinda said and they laughed.

"I know what her perfume smells like," Sunny said. "I could smell it in her room."

"Sometimes perfume can linger." Sara sounded doubtful.

"All these years?" Sunny shook her head. "I don't think so. I believe Violette is still there."

"You mean you think she *haunts* the place?" Belinda said, astonished. "Aw, come on, Sunny, that's crazy."

But just then Sara gave an excited cry. "Look what I found," she said. "The name of the lover. And there's a picture."

They crowded round, looking at the blurred photograph of a blond young man whose hard pale eyes stared intimidatingly into the camera. His name was Kurt Von Müller. And he was wearing a Nazi uniform.

"Oh, my, God," Sunny said. "Then it's true. Violette was having an affair with a Nazi."

Disturbed, she finally closed up the files. They straggled back out onto the street, surprised to find the sun still shining. Lev was there, casually glancing through newspapers, cigarette in hand, looking like every other passerby. They felt better knowing he was around.

They found a cute little brasserie on a backstreet and ordered omelets and salads and glasses of wine.

"Now all I have to do is check Herr Kurt von Müller in the *Almanach de Gotha*," Sunny said.

"What's that?" Sara was eating her ham and cheese omelet while keeping a hopeful eye on Lev a few tables away.

"It's the *Who's Who* of Germany, tells your birthright and how far up the aristocracy ladder you go." Belinda knew all about such things. "We'll find it on the Internet," she added, ordering a second glass of the light pink wine that came from the hills just behind where they were sitting.

Sara leaned back in her chair, a contented look on her face. "You know, I like it here," she said.

"That's good."

"I have to leave next week."

They looked up, concerned. "So soon?" Belinda said. "Sara, whatever will I do without you?"

"Oh, you'll manage. People can always manage without me."

"*Sara!*" Belinda banged her fist on the table sending glasses rattling. Sara caught hers just before it fell. "When are you gonna stop this 'poor me' stuff? What the fuck is wrong with you anyway?"

Sara frowned at the F-word. "But it's true," she said.

"It's only true if you allow it to be. Look at me, Sara." Belinda poked a finger into her own chest. "I am what I made myself. Right?" She appealed to Sunny for support and Sunny nodded in agreement.

"That's it," Belinda announced. "I'm cutting the hair. If you have to go home then you're going a new woman. Right?" She held up her hand and Sara meekly high-fived her.

"If you say so," she agreed and Belinda groaned again.

"Not if I say so. *If you want it. Get it,* Sara." She was determined to stiffen Sara's backbone, she couldn't let her go back to Kansas to be walked on all over again by some opportunistic new guy.

She said to Sunny, "Can we go by the airport on the way home? I need to pick up some English magazines, *Tatler* and *Harper's and Queen*. I know it's en route."

They were walking through the airport Departures Hall, which was where they sold magazines, when Sunny saw him. Her head swiveled. She took a second look.

His back was toward her and he was striding along, a tall rugged man in an impeccable beige linen suit. He was carrying a leather briefcase and his thick silvery hair was swept back like a lion's mane. And he had a small brindle greyhound on a lead.

Stunned, she said, "It can't be him."

"Who?" they asked, turning to look.

She shook her head, still not believing. *"Joel Krendler. But where's the wheelchair?"*

Wild-eyed, Sunny spun round, searching for Lev. And then all hell broke loose.

54.

A paparazzo with a camera leapt at Belinda. Belinda screamed. Flashes went off. Lev leapt on the man, dragging him away by the scruff of his neck and throwing his camera to the ground.

He grabbed Belinda by the arm, yelled at the others to follow and hustled them out to the parking lot in less than a minute.

"But Lev," Sunny cried, dragging Sara obediently after her as they ran for the cars. "Lev, it's him. *I saw Joel Krendler . . . Lev . . .*"

Lev shoved Belinda into the back of a compact Lancia, slammed the door, said something to the driver who took off immediately. Lev swung round, scanning the area. Sunny heard Sara's half gulp, half scream as she saw the gun in his hand.

"Oh my God, oh my God, like, like Lev's got *a gun,*" she said in a strangled voice. "And where's Belinda gone with that stranger?"

"Lev, *please,*" Sunny implored. Finally he turned to look at her. "Sorry," he said, smiling his cool smile. "Just had to take care of business. All's clear now."

Bug-eyed, Sara watched Lev slide the gun into the invisible holster under his arm. Her teeth were chattering with fear. Suddenly her handsome Lev with his warm smile was different from the man she'd thought he was. *"Oh my God, oh my God,"* she said again, panicking. *"That paparazzo might have been a killer . . ."*

Sunny knew it was too late to catch Krendler. If it had really been him, that is, which she was now beginning to doubt. Quickly, she told Lev her story.

"Krendler had an accident years ago, he's crippled, permanently in a wheelchair. How could it be him? Striding through Nice airport like it was normal?"

"Let's find out," Lev said, getting Mac on the phone.

First Lev told Mac the paparazzo story. He said, "I have a guy in there taking care of him. He might or might not have been legit. We'll soon find out, but I wasn't prepared to give him the benefit of the doubt. A gun could go off just as easily as a camera flash. Meanwhile paparazzi are discouraged in this country, I'm not the first to smash a camera. I knew I'd get away with it and anyhow my concern was to get Belinda out of there."

"And also not to have her picture in the papers," Mac agreed.

Lev put Sunny on the phone and she told Mac what she had seen. "Krendler walking," she said. "Like a man risen from the dead."

"Not quite," Mac said. "Meanwhile Krendler's plane is in Toulon. He could have caught a shuttle to Nice, easy."

"Mac?"

"Yeah?"

"He had a greyhound. A brindle. On a leash."

Lev tapped her on the shoulder. "We have to get out of here."

Sunny nodded. Sara was already in the backseat, quivering with nerves. Sunny climbed into the driver's seat and Lev shut the door. "Talk to you later," he said through the window. "Meanwhile I'll get my guys onto Krendler."

As she drove off Sunny was surprised to find she was trembling. She had never seen Lev in action before and the speed and efficiency with which he had taken charge impressed her. Who knew—maybe he'd even saved Belinda's life. Whatever, it was surely comforting to have him around, and now she couldn't wait to get back to Mac and go over what had happened. Could it really have been Joel Krendler? It had happened so fast, she was no longer sure. After all, it could have just been a look-alike.

But then there was the greyhound, looking exactly like the bronze one in front of Krendler's green marble fireplace. Now that was a fact.

55.

Mac got Ron Perrin on the phone.

"How's the vacation going?" Perrin boomed.

"What vacation? I'm following up one murder, one art theft, one missing woman involved in a rental scam, one attempted abduction and one seriously disabled wheelchair-bound fuckin' billionaire who might or might not have just been spotted walking though Nice airport."

"Sounds like fun," Perrin agreed.

Mac heard the grin in his voice and the sound of music in the background. There was a slurping noise and he said suspiciously, "What are you eating?"

"Figs," Perrin said. "Ripe and just picked from our own tree. The juice is running down my chin."

It was not an image Mac cared to think about.

"Krendler's the cripple, right?" Perrin did not bother with political correctness.

Mac sighed. "Right."

"I think I might know somebody, who might know somebody, who knows him. She's an opera singer that my connection's connection happens to be having an affair with."

"Convoluted," Mac said doubtfully.

"Pillow talk. Nothing beats that after-sex moment for getting to the truth."

"I hope you're right. Meanwhile I feel I'm chasing someone who's risen from the dead."

"Or at least from his couch."

"A ghost," Mac said, thinking of Violette and Sunny. "Too many ghosts here in the South of France," he added and heard Perrin laugh.

"Why don't you just drop the whole thing, get your ass up here to the Dordogne? Nothing but peace and quiet round here."

"I seem to remember differently." Mac had memories of the mayhem a couple of years ago when Perrin's movie-star wife had been in danger of losing her life.

"Yeah, well, that's all over with. And remember you and your gorgeous sidekick are always welcome."

"Thanks, but Sunny wouldn't appreciate being called a sidekick."

Perrin chuckled. "I'll get onto the Krendler thing," he said. "Wish you could taste these figs. Be back to you soon."

Mac waited in the parking lot behind the hotel looking out for the Lancia. When it drove in, fast, he opened the door, helped Belinda out, said a quick thanks to the driver and hurried her in through the kitchen.

"Shit," Belinda said. "I was having such a good time. All I wanted was my Brit magazines from the airport newsstand."

"Foolish," Mac said, tight-lipped. "Don't you get it, Belinda? Jasper Lord is circling St. Tropez in his helicopter, he has thugs everywhere, maybe even in the airport."

"You think so?" Belinda was scared now, as Mac took her up the back stairs to her room. "What am I going to do?" Her blue eyes beseeched and Mac got over his anger at her recklessness, part of which Sunny was responsible for anyway, for agreeing to take her to the airport.

"We'll figure something out," he promised, remembering Ron Perrin in the Dordogne.

He put Belinda in her room, told her to stay there, Sara would keep her company when she got back and they could order room service.

"Shit," Belinda said gloomily again.

"Serves you right. I told you to stick around here and lay low, but you're like a cork in water, always popping to the surface. Please, just stay put until I work something out."

There was a defeated look in her eyes. "It's all my fault. I should have stayed with the husband, taken my punishment like a good girl."

"You didn't trade in your self-respect when you married him," Mac reminded her.

"Right now I'm not so sure."

Mac watched uncertainly by the door as Belinda flung off her shoes then threw herself onto the bed, the one nearest the window she'd claimed first

dibs on from Sara. He felt sorry for her, a woman who had had everything—
and nothing.

"Tell you what, I'll get you a martini. Cheer you up, steady the nerves . . ."

"You turning me into a lush?"

The mischievous twinkle was suddenly back in Belinda's eyes. Mac
thought you couldn't keep her down for long. Not unless it was in a coffin
you couldn't.

He was laughing as he closed the door. "Back in a minute," he said.

Half an hour later he was sitting with Sunny in the hotel bar. They were
drinking ice-cold beers, Kronenbourg, sharp and clean-tasting and a thirst
quencher. He listened in silence as Sunny told her story again.

He said, "You know, whatever Krendler's up to, and I don't yet know what
it might be, if this really was him at the airport, then he's a very clever man.
He's chosen the perfect disguise. A wheelchair. No one would ever think to
look for Joel Krendler walking. He's disabled, he's always in that chair, always
needing help, even to ring for the butler, or to just sit in the darn thing."

"Except me. I'd look," Sunny said. "I saw him, Mac."

"Okay. Then we'll find out the truth."

Sunny was watching Laureen and Bertrand walk through the hall. "Look,
how cute," she said.

They disappeared together up the stairs and Mac turned back to look at
his woman. "What are we doing for dinner?" he asked.

"Sara's a wreck," she said.

"I wasn't thinking of asking Sara to dinner."

"Belinda too. She was really scared."

"Nor Belinda."

"So what were you thinking of?"

"You and me. How about room service?"

Sunny thought it was the best idea Mac had had since the Hôtel de Paris.

On their way to their room they passed Bertrand heading downstairs
again.

"Oh, hi, Bertrand," Sunny called. "If you want you could take Pirate for
a walk."

He stopped and actually looked at her, moon-eyed in his glasses instead
of skulking past. "I could?"

"Sure."

Just then Little Laureen came whizzing down. She was holding a pack of cards in her hand. "Oooh," she said, when she saw them. "I'm going to teach Bertrand to play poker. Texas Hold 'Em."

"Make sure she doesn't take you for every cent you've got," Mac warned as they went on their way.

"Maybe later with the dog, then, Bertrand," Sunny called. "Or tomorrow's just as good." She turned for a last glimpse. "Y'know what," she said to Mac. "I'll bet she knows all Bertrand's secrets by now. Little Laureen's unraveling that boy."

"I only hope she knows what she's got when he's finally unraveled," Mac replied.

56.

Laureen and Bertrand went and sat at one of the tables near the bookshelves where all the chess sets and the jigsaw puzzles and the games and DVDs were stored. It was cocktail hour and the bar was buzzing but their end of the big room was quiet.

"I can't stay long." Laureen hitched herself onto a chair and adjusted her tulle skirt, the raspberry calf-length one, like those worn by the ghostly Wilis in the ballet *Giselle*, now looking distinctly worse for wear but anyhow she still liked it. "Daddy wants to have an early dinner."

Bertrand nodded but made no comment. Laureen wished she had not said that about having dinner with her father because Bertrand had no one to have dinner with and she felt bad for him. She couldn't ask him to join them though, because she wanted to keep Bertrand separate, to keep him all to herself.

"Bertrand?" she said.

He looked at her, sitting opposite him at the card table. He had never heard his name spoken so many times in his entire life. Little Laureen prefaced everything she said to him with "Bertrand?"

"Yes?"

She shuffled the cards like an expert. He watched, fascinated as they slid silkily through her fingers.

"Do you really think we saw a ghost?"

"Of course not." Even though he believed they had, he would never admit to such a childish thing. "Everybody knows there's no such thing as ghosts."

Laureen dealt the cards, cut the rest of the pack and put it between them. She studied her cards, then peeked over at Bertrand's. "You have to go first," she explained. "Tell me how many cards you want."

"I don't know. All right, I'll guess. Four."

"Bertrand?"

"What?"

"If you were the art robbers where would be the best place of all to store the paintings?"

"I don't know."

"Why not Chez La Violette?"

He looked at her, surprised, and she said, "It's better than a sea cave. No damp and no octopusers."

"Octopusi," he said, then thought doubtfully that couldn't be right. "Anyhow, there are no paintings in Chez La Violette."

"How do you know?"

"Well, last time I was there, there weren't any. But that was before the robbery. Or anyhow on the night the robbery took place."

Laureen flung her cards triumphantly on the table. "You have to concentrate on this game. It's really easy if you do."

"How can I concentrate when you keep on talking?"

"I'm only talking about the art robbery. And about our reward," she added with a hint of longing in her high voice that got to him.

"I *wish*," he said, throwing his cards on the table.

Laureen stared at them. "Wait a minute. You won." She beamed, delighted. "Bertrand! You silly thing, you won! I had two fives and two queens. You had three twos."

Bertrand didn't understand the game and how he'd done it, but he beamed back at her. For a minute they looked like a couple of regular kids enjoying themselves.

Then Laureen said, "I have to go now. I'm having an early dinner with Daddy. I think he'd rather be having dinner with Belinda but she's confined to her room."

"Why?"

"Oh, you know, her husband wants to find her." She shrugged. "They say he's a bad guy and she has to stay hidden. That's why Daddy stays as close to her as he can." She eyed Bertrand. "At least that's what he says." Laureen was only eight years old but she would be a woman someday and was quickly learning the tricks of the trade.

"Okay." Bertrand knew she would not ask him to join them. Laureen kept her life compartmentalized, as did he. She and he were a separate entity. Together they were one. Apart, they were different people. Still, he was sad to see her go, leaving him at a loose end.

57.

Because Belinda had been "confined to barracks," there was no more jaunts into St. Tropez or Nice. She had successfully sabotaged her own safety and the infamous husband had been spotted clattering over the hotel in his red Bell helicopter, obviously alerted to her whereabouts. Mac had told Sara something would have to be done about Belinda, and soon. The paparazzo turned out to be a false alarm, but Lev reported that though the husband had scoured the entire coast he had not yet located the Hôtel des Rêves and still didn't know exactly where his wife was. What was certain was he would go on looking.

Sara had reverted to the old Sara, subdued after the previous day's events, back in her baggy beige shorts and white camp shirt, her shiny brown hair finally pulled back from her face in a ponytail. With her twiggy limbs, she looked like an overgrown schoolgirl, though in fact she was twenty-seven years old.

Flip-flops in hand, she walked barefoot along the edge of the water, stopping every now and then, gazing out to sea, searching the horizon like a woman looking for answers. From the opposite direction, Nate Masterson approached, also in beige shorts and a white tee and carrying his sandals. He called hello to her.

"Oooh, hi," she said, half-jumping out of her skin. She'd been so lost in her own thoughts she hadn't heard him coming.

"So, what are you up to today?" Nate asked.

"Well, you know . . ." Sara shrugged, avoiding his gaze. "Actually, nothing much. I guess I'll just hang out here with Belinda and the others."

Nate glanced speculatively at her. "You want to go for a ride? It's quite a long way, but I'll buy you lunch when we get there."

"Get where?"

"That's a secret. You'll have to wait to find out."

Sara turned back to contemplating the Mediterranean. "Oooh, I don't know . . ."

"Sara, please." Nate found himself suddenly pleading. He needed to tell somebody and Sara seemed the only one available. "I've something to show you, something really special and I'd like your opinion."

Surprised she turned to face him. "Really? You mean you want me to *help* you?"

"Just your opinion. I'll tell you more when we get there."

Sara turned pink with pleasure. Nobody ever asked her opinion, except at work of course, where she knew everything there was to know and was the arbiter on any decision making. "I think I'd like that, Nate," she said. Then with a doubtful look at her attire, "Should I go and change?"

"You look perfect." He grabbed her hand. "Come on, Sara Strange, let's go."

Sara rode most of the way with her arms snaked desperately around Nate's waist. Her knees were shaking when they finally roared up to a village perched on top of a sheer rock face.

"Where are we?" she squeaked, climbing thankfully off the back of the Ducati.

Nate led her to a café and without asking ordered two espressos. Standing side by side at the counter they downed the strong coffee, then he said, "Now what would you like?"

"Water," she said, still gasping for breath. Nate ordered it for her.

"Is this what you brought me to see?" Sara inspected the rugged little village with its narrow streets leading off the square. "And anyway, where are you taking me for lunch?" Her stomach was rumbling, she hadn't even had time for breakfast that morning.

"First let me show you my secret."

Taking her hand Nate led her out of the café and up one of those narrow streets. Thin alleyways ended in a sheer drop to the valley floor, and the houses were crammed close to each other, all in a row. Nate stopped at the one at the very end, at the top of the hilly street. Taking a key from his pocket, he unlocked the door and stood back for Sara to enter.

She threw him a puzzled glance. "In here?"

"Yes."

"But who lives here?"

"Nobody. Yet."

"Wait a minute, you didn't . . . I mean you're not telling me *you bought* this place?"

"I saw it yesterday and bought it immediately. And now I want you to tell me if I've done the right thing."

"You mean you bought it? *Just like that?* But it's out here, in the wilds. And you live in Manhattan. What about your job? I mean that's who you are, isn't it?"

"You know what, Sara Strange"—Nate pushed her up the step and into the house—"you and I have a lot more in common than I thought. Neither of us seems sure exactly who we are."

They stood in the small square hall, gazing round. Exposed stone walls; bleached beams; pale wood floors and a shout of color from a tiny red-tiled powder room. A modern white limestone staircase spiraled four floors to a skylit ceiling and together they circled up it.

There was one room on each floor. First a beamed living room that opened out into a graveled courtyard with a small iron table and chairs, looking like something from a French movie. There was a view over the whole of the valley, a mosaic of vineyards and once-upon-a-time farms, now made over into expensive villas dotted with dark blue swimming pools. The floor was pale wood and the low Italian sectional sofas were honey-colored with huge orange cushions.

The third floor consisted of a kitchen and dining room, fitted out immaculately in Bulthaup steel and with a large glass table and orange Eames chairs. The fourth had been divided into a smaller bedroom and a tiled shower, and the fifth and top floor was the master bedroom and bath.

Here a row of windows opened onto a small balcony with a pair of Philippe Starck foam armchairs in red, a small steel table, and window boxes hung with greenery. The low platform bed was black leather and the bathroom a modernist symphony in white subway tile. There were no rugs, no ornaments of any kind, nothing to soften the simple beauty of the new space in the original old setting.

Sara stood in the middle of the bedroom, turning round and round to take it all in: the different furnishings, the primary colors, the beams, the exposed stone walls, the wide windows; the magical view that extended beyond where she could see.

"I half-expect to find the Yellow Brick Road out there," she said, awed.

"Then you like it?" Nate was surprised how anxious he was for her reply.

"Like it? Nate, it's *wonderful*."

He heaved a sigh of relief and for the first time that day allowed himself to smile.

"Except . . . well, I mean, like, I just can't believe you actually *bought* it."

To tell the truth, nor could Nate. He shrugged a dismissive shoulder. "I fell in love," he said.

"So did I once, but that wasn't the answer."

"A house is less complicated than a lover," he said.

Sara laughed, twirling again, delighted. "Nate Masterson, I don't know you very well, in fact hardly at all, but I would guess this is the best move you ever made. It's just perfect." She turned to face him. "But what will you do here? I mean, like, all by yourself? In winter, and all?"

Nate was still smiling as he took her hand and led her back down the coolest spiral stairs he had ever seen and out onto the old cobbled street. He locked the door, pocketed the key and walked with her back to the Ducati.

"Let's talk about it over lunch," he said. "With my new friends."

It didn't take Sara more than a minute to fall in love all over again, this time with the miniature mill house set amid the trees, on the rushing stream with the waddling ducks and the simple restaurant. And with Malcolm and Roger, and their amazing hors d'oeuvres. By now she wasn't in the least surprised that Nate had bought the house.

"I was a waitress once," she said casually to Nate, as the dark-haired waitress brought more bread.

"You were? Where?"

"Hooters."

Nate's jaw dropped: he'd expected the local coffee shop.

Sara grinned. "Just kidding. It was a steak house. I was working my way through college. A business major. Imagine that."

In fact Nate could imagine that. There was a level head under all those insecurities.

"You've found your paradise," she said, tasting the tiny green lentils and dunking a hunk of baguette hungrily in the celeriac.

"I have," Nat said, watching her. For the first time she had lost her inhibitions and her self-consciousness and was simply enjoying herself. Perhaps it was this place, this more rugged bit of Provence that brought out the best in her, as it had him, even though he barely knew it yet. But he would. He would be here in the summer sun, like now, and back again in winter when the icy wind whistled and he knew the air would taste like wine, so clean and so pure you'd feel you could almost sail on the moon. Or at least on a star.

"You're the only person I've told," he said.

She glanced up, surprised. "Not even Belinda?"

He laughed. "Especially not Belinda."

Sara laughed with him. She knew that by now Belinda would have told everybody in the world Nate's secret. Or at least everybody she knew.

"Then let's not tell her," she whispered.

"Let's not." Nate grinned at her. He was enjoying himself.

"I plan on keeping my job, of course," he said, though in fact he had not yet given much thought to anything other than the impulsive purchase of the house. "It'll be different now, I won't be so almighty wrapped up in what I do."

"Now you can escape," Sara said, with a surge of longing in her voice that speared Nate's heart.

"Hey, what's up?" he said, gently for once.

"I have to leave soon. Next week in fact. Back to Kansas. It's not Kansas that's the trouble," she added quickly. "I love the place I was born. It's beautiful, the people are nice. Anyhow, everybody has to come from somewhere. So where do you come from?"

Nate shrugged, as though he didn't want to discuss it. "Born in Brooklyn, brought up in New Jersey," he said quickly. "Scholarship to Colgate, then business school. Parents died while I was there. Car crash." He shrugged again as Sara made a sympathetic face. "No family to speak of. Work became my reason for being. And I enjoyed it."

"Until now," Sara said.

"Until now."

Sara said, "I have a decent job and I'm very good at it. I'm in charge of admissions at the medical center, I keep everybody in line. You have no idea how bossy I can be." She laughed ruefully. "It's only in my personal life I'm such a dope."

"You're no dope." Nate poured her a glass of wine though he himself was not drinking. "You're a clever young woman, and a very attractive one. Trouble is you never allow either of those qualities to shine through. You cross your arms defensively over your chest; you hunch your shoulders and you let your beautiful hair hide your big brown eyes and your pretty face."

Shocked, Sara turned pink again.

"And I've never known a woman who blushed before," Nate said.

She pulled a face. "Left over from my childhood."

"So, what will you do, back in Kansas? Go back to the same old job, the same old routine?"

Sara nodded. "But not the same old lover."

Nate laughed. "Time to go," he said as Malcolm and Roger came over to say goodbye.

"See you soon," Malcolm yelled over the roar of the Ducati as they sped away.

58.

Bertrand was alone. Little Laureen's father had taken her off somewhere for the day and by evening they still had not returned. He missed her.

Unable to bear the idea of another early dinner alone without the prospect of seeing her, at his corner table under the scrutiny of the other diners and their curious children, he went to the kitchen and asked if he could please have a sandwich instead.

The sous-chef fixed it personally: chicken with tomatoes and a pesto sauce on a mini-baguette. A bottle of Orangina and Bertrand was on his way to his lair.

The lizards were out, basking in the last rays of the sun as he settled down. He had forgotten to bring his cape and binoculars and decided he would go back and get them later. He'd been neglecting his journal and it was time for some more Scientific Experiments, though not, he decided quickly, to Chez La Violette.

Chewing on the crusty sandwich, he thought about what Laureen had said last night. He knew there were no paintings at the villa, not even a print hanging on the wall. Still, maybe the robbers had hidden the stuff somewhere, until the excitement of the robbery had died down and they could be transported safely away to wherever stolen artworks were taken.

The sandwich tasted wonderful. He wished now he had more. The last of the light was fading from the sky, leaving that deep neon blue color that he knew later, when he was locked away in some cold northern boarding school, he would recall and be instantly transported from that bad world into this good one.

Bertrand loved the South of France, and he loved St. Tropez. There was just something about it that drew him. Maybe it was because he'd been coming here most of his life, though he was still only eleven. Because of his nocturnal Scientific Explorations, he felt he knew the inhabitants, their homes, their way of life. He only wished he knew whether there was really a ghost at Chez La Violette.

He lay back on the sparse grass. Small rocks bit into his back and he shifted until he found a comfortable spot. Then his eyes closed and he was fast asleep.

Bertrand wasn't sure exactly what it was that woke him, some sort of noise. He sat up and looked round. The luminous dial of his watch said it was five A.M. The horizon was just beginning to turn gray and the lights of the fishing boats had disappeared. Bertrand knew they would already be back in port, sorting, cleaning and marketing their catch. There was still one light out there, though. As he looked it came closer. A low, sleek, dark speedboat and, by the roar of its engine, a powerful one. It swirled inshore then cut its motor, idling close to the rocks beneath Bertrand's hill. He wished he had his binoculars. Curious, he crawled on his belly to the place where the hill descended into the sea.

The boat was a black beauty, fifty feet or more he guessed, with a small windowed saloon cabin. Steps led from the stern to a dinghy bobbing behind. The usual red and green riding lights had been switched off. In fact the only light came from the tiny cabin, through whose windows Bertrand could just make out two people. Then that light went off too.

He strained to read the boat's name but it was too dark, and anyhow it was swinging as though no one were in control.

Suddenly a woman emerged from the cabin, followed by a man. Her hair swung like the boat in the sudden wind and her long dress fluttered around her legs. The man stepped close to her. He grabbed her shoulder and she thrust him violently away.

She was shouting now and the wind carried her voice to the shore. "I'll tell everything I know," Bertrand heard her say.

The man laughed mockingly at her. "Here's your share of the guilt," he said, holding something out to her.

She hesitated, went closer, snatched it from him, and thrust it into her bag.

Then their voices were blown away and Bertrand did not hear what they said. But he saw the woman run to the stern, pull in the dinghy, hitch up her long skirts and climb clumsily into it. She tugged at the outboard motor and, without looking back, pushed off in the direction of St. Tropez.

The speedboat's engines came alive, roaring like a lion and making Bertrand jump. Then it too turned out to sea. In seconds it had caught up to the dinghy. Bertrand did not see what happened next but then the engines roared louder and it sped fast out to sea.

When the spray from its wake died down, Bertrand took another look. The speedboat was already far away, zooming across the horizon. The water was ruffled by the small wind that came with the dawn. There was no sign of the dinghy. Nor of the woman.

Bertrand drew a horrified breath. Had the man run her down? *Had he murdered her?*

He shook his head violently. No, no of course not. He'd probably picked the woman out of the water . . . Bertrand just hadn't been able to see that was all, it was too far away . . .

Bertrand took one last look, then terrified, he ran as fast as he could back to the hotel. He would never speak of this. He could never tell anyone what he thought he had seen. Because of course he had only imagined it. Hadn't he?

59.

Mac could not sleep. He was up before the birds, checking the hotel's newspaper stand in the front hall. It was too early for the papers even to have been delivered. He glanced out the glass doors. The sky was a chalky gray, not yet a hint of blue; too early for the sun to have risen. Still, a walk on the beach in the cool dawn would be invigorating, clear his befuddled head, give him time alone to think things out. Because things around here were certainly getting complicated.

He tugged on the dogs' leads. "Come on guys," he said, strolling toward the doors, just as young Bertrand Olivier shot through them, wild-eyed, ashen-faced, hair standing on end.

"Bertrand!" Mac's voice was sharper than he'd meant it to be, but he was alarmed. His first thought was what was the kid doing out at five-thirty in the morning? Then, what had happened to frighten him?

Bertrand hesitated. For a split second his eyes met Mac's, then he dashed past.

Mac grabbed his shoulder. "Hey, dude, what's going on?"

Panicked, Bertrand shrugged him off and ran for the stairs. He ran down the corridor to his room, fumbled with the key in the lock, finally got it open, slid inside and locked the door behind him.

He leaned his back against the door, heart thudding in his throat. He took off his glasses and threw them on the floor. If he were truly blind then he would never have seen what he believed he'd seen. He could never tell anyone about it. No one. Especially not Mac Reilly. The police would come, they would ask him questions, they'd take his binoculars, maybe they would even believe he had killed the woman. Her body was sure to come to the surface before too long, they would know she had been murdered. Then they would put him in jail, his mother would say he'd disgraced her . . . the stepchildren would take over . . . he was not part of their family . . .

Still with his back against the locked door, he slid to the floor, knees under his chin. He thought about Laureen. She was his friend. Perhaps there was somebody he could confess to after all. It was a risk, but one he decided he would have to take. If he lost Little Laureen's friendship, he would simply go to jail and never complain. There would be nothing left to complain about. No one left to talk to.

Mac walked the dogs all the way to the point, allowing them to run at will, tossing a ball in the water and watching Pirate struggle to swim, doggie-paddling with his two front feet as though he were normal, while Tesoro simply jumped back every time a small wave so much as touched her dainty paws.

The encounter with Bertrand had disturbed Mac. The boy had not even stopped to say hi to Pirate, who Mac knew he loved. Bertrand was badly frightened. Mac had seen it in his eyes, half-hidden though they were behind the big glasses; he'd seen the power of his fear in his tightly wound body; he'd seen the adrenaline moving him through that front hall as though demons were after him. Mac knew all about fear, he'd experienced it himself when confronted by a dangerous situation with seemingly no way out; and he knew it was that kind of fear he had seen in Bertrand.

He stood on the shoreline watching Pirate toss the ball into the air, and Tesoro daintily lick the salt off her perfect paws. Glancing over his shoulder he saw the roofline of Chez la Violette. The villa's windows gleamed a dull gray, not even reflecting the sudden burst of sunlight that illuminated the sky, changing it from pearl to opal to nail-polish pink. Then a hint of green, a touch of turquoise and finally a clean cloudless azure that met the Mediterranean in a lovely parabola. All that was needed was a rainbow and it would have been a landscape painter's fairy dream.

But this was no fairyland. And Chez La Violette was no dream. Somehow that house was at the core of all Mac's problems and as he started back down the beach, he determined to finally do something about it.

Back at the hotel, Renée was behind the reception desk again.

"Bonjour, Renée." Mac stopped to collect the newspapers that had been delivered while he was out. "You're bright and early today."

"*Oui, Monsieur Reilly.* Caroline is not back yet from Avignon and I'm substituting for her."

"You're a good friend, Renée."

She smiled. "Not really, *monsieur.* I don't know Caroline very well, but I'm sorry her mother is sick."

"Ah yes, her mother," Mac said thoughtfully, as he headed back to his room and "the sleeping beauty."

He passed Bertrand's room and stood for a minute wondering whether to knock and ask the boy what was going on. He could hear the sound of the shower running and decided to put it off till later; perhaps the boy would have calmed down by then and be more willing to talk.

Morning coffee, keeping hot in its silvery thermos, had been delivered on a tray outside their door, with the usual basket of small sweet buns and croissants. Sunny's downfall, he remembered with a grin as he carried them inside, then out onto the small terrace where the fresh morning scent of the roses hit him full force and the sparkle of the sea promised holiday fun.

Some holiday.

He went back inside. The antique painting was propped on the table next to the bed. He had to admit it did look a lot like Chez La Violette.

Sunny lay flat on her back, barely covered by a crumpled white sheet, arms over her head, pink palms facing out, head tilted to one side under a tumble of glossy back hair, frizzing slightly in the humidity.

Mac promised himself not to mention the frizzing; he knew it would drive Sunny crazy.

Her full lips were parted and her eyelids flickered as though she were dreaming, sending those long lashes fluttering. If you didn't know her, you would swear Sunny's lashes were false. But there was nothing false about his girl. Every part of Sunny Alvarez was real, including her sunshiny soul.

Leaving her to sleep, Mac went back out onto the terrace, poured himself some coffee, took a seat, put his feet up on a chair, bit into a sugar bun and opened his newspaper. For the moment, all was peaceful.

60.

Bertrand let the icy shower water spill over his face and over his swollen eyelids, cooling his head that felt about twice its normal size, it was so stuffed with bad thoughts.

Half an hour later, dried off and cool, he put on a fresh polo shirt, a white one from the clean pile the chambermaid had left on the chair. He looped the ragged blue-striped silk tie through his droopy gray shorts and tied it in a firm knot over his bony hips. He took a look at himself in the mirror. He did not look any different from the boy he had been yesterday. Except he knew he was. Something he had never before recognized as innocence was gone.

He brushed his wet blond hair flat against his skull, polished his glasses on a corner of the bedsheet, wedged them back on his beaky nose and slid his feet into his muddy sneakers.

He checked the illuminated green numbers on his watch. It was almost eight-thirty. Too early to wake Laureen? He thought about it then shrugged. No matter, he couldn't wait.

He opened his door and peeked into the corridor. The chambermaid a few doors down with her cart waved and he lifted his hand back. Locking the door carefully, he pocketed the key and walked as silently as he could along the corridor to Little Laureen's room. He put an ear to the door. He heard cartoon music. The TV must have been on. He tapped on the door.

Laureen answered in a flash. She was wearing Day-Glo orange pajamas, sort of like baggy shorts and a loose top, with the silver heart necklace that she never took off. It was the first time Bertrand had seen her in anything other than tutus. Except when he'd seen her in her underwear when they'd gone swimming, but that was different. Her hair stuck out in two mini-pigtails and her cheeks were pink from sleep.

She said, "Oh! Hi. What do you want?"

Bertrand blushed. He'd made a mistake. He should not have come, she didn't want to see him.

"I . . . I . . . w-w-w-wanted . . . t-to talk toooo you . . ."

He was stammering badly. Laureen sensed something was up. She looked closer, saw his red swollen eyes.

Turning back in to the room, she thrust her feet into her flip-flops, then came and took his arm. They walked down the corridor and the stairs, across the hall and through the open glass front doors.

Surprised, Renée watched the odd couple go by. Kids, she thought, smiling, and went back to her computer. More guests were checking in today and she was busy.

Marco, the bellboy, was on duty, standing on the steps, waiting for the checkouts, and later, the check-ins. He grinned when he saw the two of them, flitting past as though they expected no one to even notice. Weird, he thought, giving the glass doors an extra polish.

At the blue-painted Beach Bar, the cook looked up from fixing yet another espresso and saw them, as did his customer, a man from Paris and father of two children himself. Their eyes met and they smiled, glancing after the boy and the girl, wading through the water, still in their shoes. "Kids," they said.

Later, Laureen said, "Bertrand?"

"Yes."

"What's up?"

Bertrand couldn't bring himself to tell her. What if she didn't believe him? What if she said he'd done the murder and that was how he knew? Gathering his courage, he pointed to a large rock where the point of land near Chez La Violette met the sea. "When we get there, maybe I'll tell you."

Laureen nodded. She respected his silence.

Bertrand's steps slowed. The rock was getting closer and closer. Soon, he would have to confess.

"Here we are." Laureen arranged herself on a slab of rock sticking out over the water. "Oh look, Bertrand," she cried, leaning over. "Look, you can see all the little fish. Why, it's so clear you can even see the bottom."

Bertrand leaned over to look. Tiny fish darted in and out of the crevices and the sandy bottom was rippled like a woman's wavy hair.

Laureen wiggled farther out, with her head hanging over the water. "I feel like a mermaid," she cried, flinging her arms wide and flipping her legs in imitation of a fish-woman. Then she lost her balance. She clutched at Bertrand, who clutched at the rock. Together they teetered on the edge. Bertrand got a grip on the rock with one hand and on Laureen with the other. He gave her an almighty push backward that sent her reeling.

"Oww," she said, crossly. "That hurt."

Bertrand glared at her. She didn't care that he had saved her.

Then Laureen screamed. Her fingers searched for the necklace. Searched some more. She screamed again.

"Bertrand! *My necklace. It's gone.*"

Bertrand looked at her empty neck. Then into her empty eyes. Blank as the blue sky. Laureen had lost what was to her the most precious thing in the world.

He hung his head over the edge again. The water was clear as glass but there was no sign of the necklace. He lifted his head and looked at Little Laureen. She was still clutching her naked neck, eyes blank with panic.

Bertrand stood up. He stripped off his white polo shirt, his sneakers and his glasses. "I'm going in to find it," he said. And made a shallow dive off the edge.

"Oh!" Little Laureen yelled. "Oh, Bertrand!" Then she jumped into the water after him.

They met face-to-face under the clear water, which turned their skin green. Bertrand's long hair floated straight up. His eyes looked huge. He grabbed Laureen's arm and kicked hard, splashing them upward like corks out of a champagne bottle.

He held the necklace triumphantly over his head. "I found it, *Petite Laureen*," he yelled. "I found it."

Sitting on the edge of the rock, Laureen leaned over and kissed him on the cheek. Her tears mingled with the seawater. That necklace had been fastened on her neck by her mother. They'd bought it together in Tiffany the very last time her mother had been able to go out. Afterward, she had taken Laureen for lunch, triumphantly wearing her new necklace, and allowed her to skip the salad and just eat fries and a chocolate shake. Her mother had sipped lemon tea and they had chatted about everything. Well, not everything. Laureen knew that now. Two months later her mother was dead.

Laureen looked at Bertrand. "It was because I wasn't wearing my tutu," she said.

He shook his head, puzzled. "What was?"

"Losing the necklace. Mommy couldn't protect me because she didn't know where I was. Without my tutu, she couldn't find me."

Bertrand understood. Little Laureen really believed that her mother was looking down from heaven and that she could pick her out wherever she was by the brightly colored tutu.

He held out the necklace and said, "Let me put it on." Laureen bent her head and he slid it round her neck, straightening out the myriad fine silver chains, centering the heart perfectly in the hollow of her throat. After a struggle he got the clasp closed, then sat back inspecting his handiwork. Laureen gave a grateful sigh and smiled at him.

"I'm going in again," Bertrand said. "I saw something else down there." And he jumped off the rock.

Laureen crouched at the edge, peering anxiously after him. The sand was all kicked up now and the water was no longer clear. She was glad when she saw Bertrand's shape wiggling around. And then he popped up again, spitting water.

"Look what I found." He held something up.

She leaned over and took it from him.

It was a handbag. White, quilted and with the CC logo that, Texan child that she was, Laureen knew meant Chanel.

Bertrand hauled himself onto the rock next to her. Laureen twisted the fastener and opened the bag. Stunned, they looked at the contents, then at each other.

"Euros," Bertrand gasped.

"Tons of them." Laureen poked a finger at the wet notes. "Finders keepers," she said. "Sort of like a reward."

But Bertrand knew what this was. This was what the man on the boat had given the woman before he killed her. They were her "share of the guilt."

With a panicked cry he grabbed the bag from Laureen and hurled it down the beach.

He hadn't noticed Pirate galloping toward them. Eager for a new game, the dog got the bag in his teeth and began to shake it. Wet euros spun into the air, settling soggily on the sand.

"Hey, dude," Mac said to Bertrand. "What's going on?"

61.

It was the first time Mac had seen Little Laureen without the tutu. In fact she looked as though she were wearing pajamas. *And* she was soaking wet. So was Bertrand, who was wearing only his shorts. Mac grinned. At least they hadn't gone skinny-dipping.

But now it wasn't only Bertrand who looked frightened; it was both of them. They were avoiding looking at him, watching Pirate instead, who had a great game going, tossing bits of paper into the air.

Mac caught one on the way down, smoothed it in his fingers. It was a five-hundred-euro banknote. He looked at the rest of the money scattered on the sand like confetti at a wedding, then up at the two of them, staring warily back at him.

"Better get down from there and pick this up," he said. There was a cold edge to his voice that sent them scrambling quickly onto their knees, hands darting for the bills.

Mac stood, arms folded, silently watching as they came and knelt in front of him and deposited the wet pile.

"And the bag."

Bertrand ran to retrieve the white handbag from the rock where Pirate had tossed it. Thinking there was to be another game, Pirate whined and licked his face. Bertrand choked back the tears. He wanted to cry but he was a boy and boys didn't cry. At least, not often. He put the bag carefully next to the pile of notes.

Seeing his tight young face, Mac's heart softened. He didn't know what the hell the pair had been up to, but Bertrand was more frightened than any kid his age had a right to be.

"Okay, get up," he said. The two unfolded themselves and stood, brushing off the sand. Water dripped off the end of Bertrand's nose and from Little Laureen's skinny pigtails.

Mac took each by the hand. "Come with me." He walked them back to their rock. "Okay, so we'll sit here and you will tell me exactly what's going on. Let's start with you, Bertrand."

Bertrand gulped. He glanced at Laureen for support and she nodded. "Tell him," she said.

"I was in my lair," Bertrand began.

Laureen looked at him, surprised. She'd thought he was going to tell about the money. She translated for Mac. "Bertrand means his secret place, where he goes to be alone. It's on a little hill overlooking the water."

"I fell asleep," Bertrand went on. "When I woke the fishing boats were gone. The sky was dark, kind of gray dark and I knew dawn was coming. I looked at my watch. It was five o'clock."

Mac remembered Bertrand running, wild-eyed through the hotel hall at five-thirty that morning. "You saw something out there at sea," he guessed, wanting to make it easier.

Bertrand nodded. "A speedboat. Big, maybe fifty feet, black, or darker than the dawn anyway. And powerful. Its motor was what woke me, like a lion's growl."

"A lion boat," Little Laureen said, amazed. Her knees were hunched under her chin and she wrapped her arms around them, huddling into herself, trying to look smaller so maybe Mac wouldn't notice she was there. She wasn't sure what was going to happen but escape seemed like a good idea. And she was guilty, she *had* been about to steal those euros and help Bertrand get away from his mother.

"And then what?" Mac prompted, his eyes still on the boy.

"The boat came in close to the rocks. It had no riding lights, just a light in the saloon. I could see a man and a woman in there. Then she ran out on deck."

His voice wobbled as he told Mac how she'd stood there, with her long dress blowing against her legs, how the man had thrust something at her and she'd put it in her bag. "Here's your share of the guilt," the man had said, laughing.

Bertrand fell silent.

"And then what, Bertrand?" Mac prompted.

"And then she said she would tell everything . . . and she jumped into the dinghy and got the outboard going."

Bertrand put his hands in front of his face. "The speedboat went after her. Fast. It caught up to her. I didn't see what happened but then the speedboat took off and the dinghy was gone."

Bertrand gave Mac a helpless look. "I think he drowned her."

Laureen shrieked, then clapped her hand over her mouth. Her horrified blue eyes stared at Bertrand.

"We don't know that yet," Mac said, wanting to calm Bertrand. "Did you get the name of the speedboat?"

Bertrand shook his head. "I didn't have my binoculars and I couldn't see clearly with just my glasses and in the dark."

Mac picked up the quilted white leather handbag. He also knew a Chanel logo when he saw one. And anyhow, he'd seen this one before.

"Monsieur Reilly? Will they put me in jail now?" Bertrand sounded resigned. Little Laureen put a hand on his shoulder and squeezed it comfortingly.

Mac said, "Bertrand, nobody is going to put you in jail. You've done nothing wrong."

"We were thinking about stealing the money," Bertrand said.

"But that was only so we could pay Bertrand's hotel bill and then he'd never have to go to boarding school and never have to see his cruel mother ever again."

Laureen stood up for her friend and Mac liked that. He liked both these oddball kids. Meanwhile they had presented him with a dilemma. Obviously he would have to go to the police and tell them the story.

But first thing he had to get them cleaned up and into dry clothes. He would tell Sunny what had happened before deciding on his next move.

There was a flurry of activity back at the hotel. The two bellboys were hauling suitcases, and helping an old woman from the back of a large silver Mercedes.

Mac put a hand on each child's shoulder, holding them back, allowing the woman to be helped up the shallow front steps by her driver. She was very old, her face lined and yellowish in the bright sunlight as she fumbled her way up the two steps and into the hall, her gray chiffon scarf trailing like a pennant in the breeze.

Renée came out from behind the reception desk and kissed the old woman on both cheeks.

"Welcome back, Madame Lariot," she cried. "Summer is not complete without you here. Welcome back to the Hôtel des Rêves."

62.

Mac stopped. He turned to look at Madame Lariot. Tiny, thin, birdlike in her frailty, and ninety if she were a day. She was no rental scammer, scheming for a fast buck. This was a woman of means who obviously came every summer to the Hôtel des Rêves, where she was treated as an honored guest. *This* Madame Lariot was a victim, not a thief. A victim of identity theft. And he'd bet his last buck that Caroline Cavalaire was at the bottom of it.

"Go shower and get changed," he told the kids. "Then meet me in the courtyard. We'll have breakfast and talk about what to do."

They scuttled thankfully off up the stairs, and Mac got Sunny on the phone.

"Lover," she answered, with a purr in her voice. "I missed you."

"Can you be down here in five?"

Something in his voice alerted her to trouble. "Two," she said, clicking off.

The dogs were tangled in their leads. Mac unraveled Pirate. He picked up Tesoro, who was in one of her more understanding moods and gave him a quick lick instead of bared teeth.

"Thanks," he said. "I could use that."

Sunny was already running down the stairs toward him. She was in a blue halter top and white shorts with her signature red Dior daytime lipstick and large sunglasses. "Sorry, no time for a shower." She kissed him, leaving a kissy imprint on his mouth that she wiped off with her pinky.

"Nice perfume, though," he said, hugging her and hearing Tesoro, crushed between them, growl.

"It's the usual," she said. "Always good in a no-shower situation. So anyway, what's up?"

"Caroline Cavalaire."

Mac took her elbow and led her through the hall into the courtyard, already liberally dotted with breakfasters.

They took a seat at what had become the group's table, the long one by the fountain with a glimpse of the interior dining room, as well as of the terrace.

Sunny ordered coffee. *"Le plus fort,"* she told the waiter, *"avec du lait chaud à côté."*

"What does that mean?" Mac asked, mystified.

"Strong and with hot milk on the side. It's better than ordering a *crème*, you can judge exactly how much milk you'd like. So, why did you drag me out of bed because of Caroline. She been caught gambling again?"

"This time I think it was with her life."

Alarmed, Sunny clutched Tesoro closer. Pirate, as usual, was sitting on the edge of the fountain, taking a small lap here and there to keep cool.

Mac put the white euro-stuffed bag on the table. "Seen this before?"

Sunny stared but did not touch. "Caroline's Chanel bag."

He opened it and Sunny looked at the wads of wet banknotes. Then, blankly, at Mac.

"Bertrand was diving off the rocks, right here at the beach. He found it."

"But . . . but . . ." Sunny was floundering for an explanation but Mac told her not to bother. He told her what Bertrand had seen and about the woman run down in the dinghy.

"I believe that woman was Caroline," he said. "And this is her bag."

"Oh my God," Sunny said, horrified.

He held up a hand. "Wait until you hear what else I have to tell you. I just met Madame Lariot."

Sunny's chin jutted, her eyes were on stalks. *"What?"*

"The real Madame Lariot, all of ninety and a lady, and most definitely not a rental scammer."

"Then who is she?"

"She's the victim of stolen identity. And I believe our Caroline was the one who stole it. Listen, Sunny, Caroline worked here at the hotel, she had access to all old Madame Lariot's private information: her passport, her bank accounts, her credit card numbers. What she didn't have I'm willing to bet she conned Madame Lariot into giving her. An old lady like that, she'd been coming here for years, she would have trusted Caroline with anything."

He said, "Caroline knew Chez La Violette was empty. She opened bank accounts in the name of Madame Lariot, giving all the correct stolen references. There was no reason for anyone to suspect anything because Caroline never gave the address in the ad. And when we, the lucky ones, dreaming of our holiday in the sun responded and paid our money, she took it and ran."

"But Mac, our rental-scam Madame Lariot was middle-aged, dowdy, brown hair, glasses . . ."

"Yeah. And Joel Krendler is disabled and in a wheelchair with the purple-shadowed eyes and pale skin of a chronic invalid who rarely leaves his house. Don't you see, Sunny, the brown hair, the shapeless clothes, the glasses—it was all a disguise."

It suddenly dawned on Sunny exactly what a terrible thing had happened. "Oh my God," she wailed. "And now somebody killed Caroline."

"But not for our rent money. She probably has that stashed in a bank vault." Mac pointed to the damp euros. "I'll bet there's at least ten thousand dollars there. Somebody else gave this to her. 'Your share of the guilt,' Bertrand told me the man said. Obviously Caroline threatened to tell the truth. But he got her first, before she had a chance."

"You mean the man deliberately ran her down in the dinghy?"

Mac nodded. "And now I have to decide what to do about it."

He thought for a bit, then said, "Sunny?"

"What?"

"Our Madame Lariot went to Zurich and tried to sell a stolen painting, a Seurat, to a collector."

"Oh, my, God," Sunny gasped, remembering. "So she did."

"Caroline was more than a con woman. She knew how to get her hands on the stolen artworks."

"And was dumb enough to try to sell them."

"And, I believe, got caught by her accomplices," Mac said.

"You'll go to the police, of course."

Mac thought about it. "My problem is young Bertrand. He's frightened to death, terrified they'll lock him up."

"Of course they won't."

"But I want *you* to tell him that, then go to the police with us."

Sunny spotted the two children weaving their way through the tables. "Here they come," she said quietly.

"Bonjour, madame." Bertrand stood by the table until Sunny patted a chair and told him to sit down. Little Laureen was back in her orange tutu.

Sunny handed the Chihuahua to her and, subdued, the girl took the dog without a word.

"Okay," Sunny said cheerfully. "Let's order breakfast, then I'll tell you what we're going to do."

"You're not sending Bertrand to jail." Little Laureen's chin was firm and she held her mouth in a tight line, prepared to do battle.

"No, sweetheart, Bertrand is not going to jail. He's done nothing wrong. In fact, Bertrand, you're quite the hero. You saw something bad happen and you told Mac about it. After all, Mac's a famous detective. You knew he was the one to tell. Then you found the handbag." She pointed to it, still on the table and saw the boy flinch. Mac quickly removed it and put it on a chair.

Sunny said, "You gave Mac the bag and the money and he promised to take care of it. Now. All we have to do—you, me, and Mac—is to tell the police." She threw a glance at Little Laureen. "I don't think we'll be needing you, sweetheart, you can stay here and take care of the dogs for us. Mac and I will take care of Bertrand."

She smiled round the table. "There. Now that's resolved. Bertrand saw a very bad thing, something no doubt he will never forget. But it's also something very important that he cleverly helped to solve."

Feeling a little better, Bertrand polished his glasses on a corner of the tablecloth. "But who was she?"

Mac hesitated. He did not want to upset the boy by telling him it was probably Caroline. "We're not sure yet, Bertrand. That's for the police to find out." It was the truth.

"You okay with that?" he asked, and Bertrand nodded.

"Good, then let's order some eggs and toast. And how about some of those crispy hash browns or whatever they're called in this country?"

"*Pommes frites,*" Little Laureen said, cheering up. "And could I have some pancakes please?"

63.

Mac called a general meeting of the Misfits for nine o'clock that night, in the courtyard over dinner. Passing through the hall on their way there, he noticed Renée had been replaced by the man who usually acted as night concierge. The two bellboys were huddled in a corner, heads together, talking in low tones. The barkeeper kept a smile on his face as he mixed his drinks and served ice-cold beers, but the atmosphere was subdued.

Caroline Cavalaire's body had washed up on the rocks farther down the coast, near Hyères. Because she had no relatives, the hotel manager had been called in to identify her. A drowned person is not a pretty sight, swollen and bloated, the skin greenish tinged. The young woman was barely recognizable as the pretty blond receptionist. The manager had gone home to fortify himself with a double whiskey or two, and the news had spread round the staff like wildfire. No one knew what had happened, or why, only that the woman they had worked with was dead.

Mac's session with the local police had filled in a few gaps, but also posed a few questions. Bertrand, holding tightly to Sunny's hand, had told his story and, to his surprise, had been praised for his actions.

"Well done, my boy," the police captain had told him, slapping him on the shoulder. "You are a brave lad. Your mother will be proud of you."

Bertrand knew that wasn't so, but having gotten it all off his chest, he felt better.

Later that afternoon, Mac had accompanied the police to Caroline's apartment. The garments she'd worn in her role as Madame Lariot were hanging in her closet and the wig and glasses were in a box. Caroline wasn't too good at hiding things: all the documents, the leases, the canceled checks, the real Madame Lariot's personal information, her checking accounts et cetera, had been documented and stowed in a small desk under the window.

Caroline's closet was also stuffed with the expensive clothes she'd bought with the stolen money, and in a small wall safe they discovered a collection of fine jewelry, the emerald and diamond ring she usually wore to work, the diamond chandelier earrings she'd worn at the Caves du Roy, a diamond bracelet and other smaller pieces. Caroline was obviously a woman who liked the finer things and the temptation to get them had proved too strong.

"Much good it did her," Sunny said sadly, when Mac told her this, at nine as they walked out into the courtyard, where the others were already seated. Nobody smiled, not even Belinda.

"What's going on?" she whispered. "It's like somebody died in here."

Mac looked round, making sure Little Laureen was not there.

"She's having dinner with her friend." Billy nodded to where the two were sitting at Bertrand's corner table, eating large plates of spaghetti Bolognaise.

"I'm afraid somebody did die," Sunny said, and heard Sara gasp.

"It's Caroline Cavalaire," Mac said.

"The pretty receptionist?" Nate looked astounded. "A car accident?" he guessed.

Mac held up a hand, slowing him down. "Let's get some wine here, then I'll tell you exactly what happened."

Half an hour later, after he'd told them, they sat silently, sipping the Vieux Télégraphe Nate had recommended, trying to take in the events of the day.

"Okay, so I don't care about the money," Belinda said finally. "But why the hell did somebody have to go and kill her?"

"That is exactly what we now have to find out. Fortunately, the police are also investigating."

"So we're no longer on our own?" Nate said.

"Right. We're not. Let's just leave it up to them." Mac tested the wine again. Then, anxious to lift the moment, he said, "Wonderful wine, Nate. Thanks."

"I only discovered it a couple of days ago," Nate said casually. "When I bought my house."

Four pairs of eyes got him in their sights. Sara sat innocently back, hiding a smile.

"You did *what*?" Belinda said.

"Oh, you know, bought a house. In an old fortified village called Bonnieux."

"But I know it," she cried. "I've been there. It's adorable."

Nate had never heard a village called "adorable" before.

"Nate, I can't believe it." Sunny was smiling at him. He could see she was thrilled.

"I don't know how it happened," he confessed. "It just seemed meant for me."

"I so admire that," Sunny said. "Making a fast decision."

Nate gave a wry smile. "A decision that'll affect the rest of my life."

She leaned over and patted his hand. "For the better, I'm sure," she said softly.

"So when can we come and see this house?" Belinda was desperate to get away from the subject of the murdered girl. Inside she was trembling, thinking, *My God my God, that could be me, it so could be me . . .*

"Whenever you like. We'll organize an expedition." Nate was ordering another bottle of the good red and dinner was being discussed.

The two children were playing poker at their table, already into ice cream and watching them, Billy was glad they had not been told about Caroline. He determined they never would.

"Not a bad day's work," Mac said to Sunny, just as his phone rang.

"Hey, buddy," Ron Perrin said. "Wanna know some more about your boy Krendler?"

"Of course I do." Mac took another sip of the wine.

"Surprise, surprise, he gets around. On the quiet though. And in his own plane. Always takes his racing greyhound with him. A brindle. Never raced in its life. It's said to be the only thing he loves. There's been a succession of them, all exactly the same. Apparently Maria Callas gave him the first and he's had one ever since. Odd thing, though, his dogs never seem to get old. One day they're living the high life, eating off silver plates. Next there's a new one. Same breed. Same color. Just younger."

"Like rich men with their trophy wives," Mac said thoughtfully. "Trading them in for younger models."

"Rumor is he kills 'em off. Shows what a sadistic bastard he truly is."

"I never heard of anyone doing that with wives though. But as always, you're right on the mark."

"Keep me posted," Perrin said. "And remember, your room is waiting."

Mac was smiling as he closed his phone. The thing with the dogs was troubling though. And now he knew for sure it was Joel Krendler Sunny had seen in Nice airport. Who else would have a brindle greyhound?

64.

Later, Sunny and Mac sat on their terrace, holding hands, gazing silently into the deep blue midnight, hearing the soft swish of the waves hitting the shore, and catching the glimmer of phosphorescence on the water, like aquatic fireflies. They were both thinking about Caroline Cavalaire.

Sunny was the one who finally broke the silence with a deep sigh. "Poor, poor Caroline," she said sadly. "All that scheming, all those lies, and all for so little. You know what I think?"

Mac turned his head to look at her. "What do you think?"

"I think there has to be a man involved. Caroline wasn't dressing so fancy just for her own amusement. Remember Valenti at the Casino?"

Mac nodded. "I'd already thought of him, and how aggressive he was with her, how angry she was. And you know what else, Sunny Alvarez, Assistant Private Eye?"

Sunny grinned. "Tell me."

"A man like that, flashy, a player, man-about-town . . . a man like that, Sunny Alvarez, would have a speedboat. A fast one."

Remembering the sailboat and the excited look on Valenti's face as he sped through the water, Sunny agreed. "So why would he have a speedboat anyway?"

"For getting stolen works of art away from enormous houses on the water, instead of running the gauntlet of possible private security police on the prowl on the roads."

Sunny's eyes widened. "Wow," she said. "You really think Valenti is the art thief?"

"Here's how I'm thinking it happened. Valenti comes here to the hotel, for a drink, dinner, whatever. He meets Caroline, recognizes her for what she is, an attractive young woman on the make. My bet is he seduced her—not too difficult a task, he was attractive, rich. I'm sure she was willing. Then he used her to get information on wealthy guests and locals and to make the acquaintance of high-rolling punters at the Casino."

"But they couldn't all be art collectors."

"No, but I'm betting that Valenti had a nice little business on the side, in stolen jewelry and cash, similar to Caroline's, only bigger. How else did he keep his lifestyle going? A sailboat like his costs, and so does a summer season in the South of France."

"You think he works alone?"

Mac thought about that for a long time before he said, "No, I don't. Valenti's not the mastermind. Krendler is."

"Mac!"

"Alain Hassain at Interpol checked Krendler's flights out of Paris and Zurich. In the past three years he's flown here, or to airports close to here, at least a couple of dozen times. And six of those were around the time the art robberies took place. I think Valenti was part of an international gang, headed by Krendler, that met here in the South. They would arrive at night by boat, robbing rich houses of paintings and works of art, and others of jewelry and antiques. Usually the thefts went undiscovered until the owners returned, despite high-tech security that somehow or other had always failed. They used the speedboat to get their loot away. Then stashed it on Valenti's sailboat until the heat was off.

"By chance, Caroline found out about the bigger game Valenti was up to. Then, foolish woman that she was, she attempted to blackmail him. Instead he told her she could be a part of it, make far more money than she would working at the hotel, or working a scam. Valenti knew she was a thief, he must have implied that thieves always banded together, that Caroline was one of them. And she fell for it. When he dumped her, she threatened to tell all. Valenti invited her onto the boat, he was laughing at her, gave her her share of the 'guilt money' . . . then he ran her down in the dinghy."

"Valenti murdered her."

"He did. On Krendler's orders."

65.

Bertrand and Laureen were in the hotel parking lot and Bertrand was pumping up the tires of an old *vélo*, one of the half dozen bicycles available to guests. It had probably been there since the day the hotel opened. A small satchel was buckled to the back of the leather saddle. Inside was a tin box with fancy lettering, and inside of that was a puncture kit for fixing mini-blowouts while on the road. The pump clipped onto the inner strut and the handlebars were complete with a bell and a wire basket. All in all Bertrand considered it a fine feat of engineering along with customer satisfaction. He pumped some more and the flat tire grew rounder.

"I've never seen a bike like that." Laureen crouched next to him, gravely inspecting his work.

"I wish it were mine." Bertrand patted the old leather saddle the way Laureen might have patted a horse. He had never owned a bike.

Laureen handed him a straw hat and put on her own, bought at a shop on the Quai Suffren. She'd reluctantly replaced the "stolen" ones on the hatstand in the hall. Her hair was dragged into two bunches, one over each ear with the princess tiara on top, and she wore white sunglasses, almost as big as Bertrand's own. And, of course, the pink tutu.

"Let's go for a ride," she said.

"Where?"

"Oh, you know . . . anywhere . . ." She was vague but somehow he knew she was thinking of Chez La Violette. It was morning, bright and sunny.

"Okay. You take that bike." He pointed to the one next to his, the second best of the lot, and said, "Follow me."

Laureen straddled the bike, hitched herself and her tutu over the saddle and wobbled after him. Bertrand was already heading out the gates into the narrow lane. She waved hello to the stocky man leaning against the gatepost, reading his newspaper in the shade of a sycamore tree. It wasn't Lev but she knew he was one of Belinda's guards. He waved back and then she was pedaling madly after Bertrand. She knew where he was going, and why.

"Bertrand," she yelled plaintively. "Please slow down."

He glanced over his shoulder. Her plump legs were going at a terrific rate but she simply couldn't keep up and he slowed.

"We're off to see the villa," Laureen sang out suddenly. "The wonderful villa of Oz . . ."

"It's not the villa of Oz," Bertrand said.

"Of course not, silly. It just fits the tune that's all." She began to sing again. "We're off to see the villa . . ."

"The wonderful villa of Oz," Bertrand found himself joining in.

Cycling side by side they looked at each other and grinned. Quite suddenly the burden of everything Bertrand had been through lifted. Mac and Sunny had saved him from the police. He did not have to go to jail. He had told what he knew and been praised for it. Praise was rare in Bertrand's world and it made him feel good. There had been no word from his mother but now he had Mac, who he knew somehow would always help him. And Sunny, who had explained things to him. He had Little Laureen, his friend. And her father, who had asked him please to call him Billy from now on, and had given Laureen permission to spend time with him. "As long as you don't get into any more trouble," Billy had added with a grin. Now Bertrand was out bicycling and even dreaming maybe, just a little bit, of becoming a famous Tour de France winner one day. Of course he would have to start training right away.

He realized he was smiling and glanced sideways at Laureen. Her pink tutu fluttered in the breeze caused by their speed and her tiara had flattened against her brown hair so that now PRINCESS looked upside down. She too was smiling.

Laureen's smile was rare and Bertrand's grew even broader. In fact he burst out laughing, causing her to swerve in surprise.

"Bertrand!" she yelled. "You're laughing!"

He threw back his head and laughed some more, reveling in the sound of his own mirth. Laureen blinked then she joined in. Laughing giddily, the two sped toward Chez La Violette, with never a thought to any ghost.

This time Bertrand led the way through the almost hidden door into the kitchen garden. Laureen propped her bike outside next to his and followed him in. They stood for a moment, looking apprehensively around but today everything seemed normal. The bright sunlight left no room for shadows, except under the trees, and the crickets were chirruping loudly in the rosemary bushes. A pair of doves, startled by their presence, flew out of the bougainvillea where Bertrand pointed out they had a nest complete with two babies, all beak and as yet no feathers. Then, from round the corner of the house, padded a yellow dog.

"Ohhh," they exclaimed in astonished unison, looking apprehensively for its owner to appear. But no one did.

The dog was obviously some kind of Lab mix. Its yellow fur was rough and matted. Tongue lolling, it sat and waited for what they would do next. Its patience seemed to say it did not expect much from any human.

"What are you doing here, boy?" Bertrand spoke to it in French, which he knew would be its native language.

The dog's ears pricked up. It put its head to one side as though listening.

"See, he's intelligent," Laureen said.

"He's thin. I can see his ribs." Bertrand patted his own skinny ribs. They matched the dog's.

"Do you think he's starving?" Laureen's voice was as anxious as the dog's eyes. "Do you think he belongs to anyone?" she added, even more anxiously.

Bertrand thought about it. He and the dog looked at each other. He whistled and the dog lifted its head. *"Viens ici, chien,"* Bertrand commanded and the dog lumbered to its feet but didn't move.

"He's afraid." Laureen was full of sympathy now. *"Viens ici, chien adorable,"* she commanded, and the dog suddenly ran at them, stopping in a flurry of dust, just out of reach.

"No collar," Bertrand pointed out.

"He's nobody's dog." Laureen clapped her hands and the dog cowered back, frightened. "Oops, sorry, dear *chien*," she cried, on her knees now, hand held out to it.

Bertrand crouched next to her. He remembered he had a small piece of leftover breakfast baguette in his shorts pocket. It was stale but better than nothing. He fished it out, scattering fluff and crumbs and offered it to the dog.

It sniffed the air, then approached cautiously. Bertrand held his hand flat with the piece of bread still stuck with a few bits of butter and ham. With a sudden move the yellow dog snatched it from him. In about two seconds it was gone.

Bertrand stared longingly at the dog. It stared longingly back at him. "We can't keep him, of course," he said, because that was what his mother would have said.

Laureen sighed. "No," she agreed, in a small voice.

"We have to go inside now," Bertrand said to the dog.

The two walked carefully round it. It sat exactly where it was, twisting its neck to look after them.

"He's so pretty," Laureen whispered, turning to look and meeting its hopeful eyes. "I'll bet he's a good dog."

"Probably some holidaymakers abandoned him."

"Or maybe he just lives here. Maybe he belongs to Violette."

"You're crazy. He can't belong to a ghost."

Laureen stopped in her tracks. There!" she exclaimed triumphantly. "Now you've admitted it. There *is* a ghost."

They were standing on the steps outside the kitchen door. For a second Bertrand looked uncertain, then he stooped and searched for the key the janitor usually kept hidden in the terra-cotta pot of geraniums. This time it was there. "There is no ghost," he said, unlocking the door and pushing it open. As he stood in the silent shadowy kitchen, he wished he believed it.

He could hear Laureen breathing in back of him. "Okay, so there are no stolen paintings in here," he announced loudly, just to warn any possible ghost he was here.

He walked through the kitchen, hearing Laureen pattering after him in her ballet slippers. He thanked heaven it wasn't the cowboy boots today.

They were in the salon. Anything might have been hidden beneath the white shrouds covering the furniture but they were too afraid to look.

They went back into the hall. The door to La Violette's boudoir was shut. They hovered outside, avoiding looking at each other in case each saw the other was scared. Bertrand shoved his heavy glasses up his nose, ran his hands through his hair. He pushed open the door.

All was silent. And dark.

"Oooh, Bertrand," Laureen whispered, sounding scared.

He thought of her, laughing with him as they'd sped along the sunny lane on their bikes only minutes before. He knew he had to be the brave one and somehow that memory gave him the courage to step into that dark room and switch on the light.

A chandelier gleamed dimly. Only one bulb was lit but for Bertrand, it was better than none. He had boasted to Laureen that he'd been to Chez La Violette many times, that he knew it like the back of his own hand. It was true, he had. And he did. Only that was before he had suspected there was a ghost, and before he had believed the robbers might be using it to store their loot.

He turned to look at Laureen, still hovering in the doorway.

"You know what I think?" she said.

"What?"

"We should go to Monsieur François Reynaud, the owner of the stolen artworks, and tell him we believe the thieves took his paintings away on a boat. We'll say we think they're hidden somewhere at Chez La Violette, maybe even in the garden." The garden was wild enough to hide almost anything. "Then he'll give you the reward for being so clever."

"Okay," Bertrand agreed, relieved. "And then he can come and find the stolen paintings himself."

He switched off the light and closed the boudoir door, then they hurried back through the kitchen. Outside, the dog was still sitting where they had left it.

"Bertrand?" Laureen said.

"What?"

"Maybe the dog's a ghost."

"Ghosts don't eat old baguette."

"Oh. Well, I think he must have belonged to Violette."

He shrugged. "Violette was old, she died years ago. This dog is young."

"Well, maybe this dog is a great-great-great-great-grandson of Violette's *own* dog?" She wasn't giving up.

The two studied the dog. The dog stared back at them.

"Bertrand."

"What?"

"Why doesn't he bark?"

"I'll bet it's because he's afraid to."

Bertrand knew he was right from the way the dog was looking at him, half-afraid, half-beseeching. He knew exactly how that felt.

Steeling himself against that look, he said to Laureen, "We have to go now, and see Monsieur Reynaud, tell him what we believe."

"And get the reward," she said, brightening at the thought that soon Bertrand would be reprieved from his cruel mother. She put her hand to her throat, checking that the necklace was still there. Bertrand had rescued it and now she wanted to rescue him. "Let's go," she said, setting off briskly down the narrow overgrown path to the gate.

The yellow dog walked quietly behind them. When Bertrand turned to close the gate it slipped through, fast as any sleight of hand conjurer's dog. It sat again, watching them.

"He thinks he's yours," Laureen said.

Bertrand shrugged, steeling himself once again. "He's just hungry," he replied, climbing onto his bike and setting off, back down the lane.

With a worried glance behind her, Laureen set off after him.

"We can't just leave him there," she cried. "He's hungry."

Bertrand wobbled uncertainly, turned his head to look. The dog was trotting behind him, tongue lolling, eyes hopeful. When Bertrand stopped, so did the dog.

"Don't you see?" Laureen's voice was as hopeful as the dog's hopeful eyes. "He belongs to you now. Mac told me he rescued Pirate. Now you have to rescue this dog."

Bertrand imagined the yellow dog—his *own* dog accompanying him on his nightly Scientific Experiments. He imagined bathing him and combing him so his fur shone. He imagined swimming in the sea with his dog next to him. He would share his food with him, it wouldn't cost anything at all. He didn't stop to think what they would say at the hotel when he showed up with a large stray dog.

"What shall we call him?" he asked.

"Beauty."

He snorted disparagingly. "Too girly. Anyhow, he's French."

He remembered that first night at Chez La Violette, when all the strangers had arrived. The Riders on the Storm, he had called them, after the song by the Doors. "How about Storm?" he said.

Then Little Laureen said, "No. He's Yellow Dog." And somehow that was exactly his name.

And when Bernard called, "Here, Yellow Dog, *viens ici,*" the dog's tail wagged and its eyes lit up. It went and stood next to Bertrand while he tickled its neck and said "good boy." Then it trotted happily after him as he cycled down the lane, en route to François Reynaud's Villa les Ambassadeurs.

He and Laureen were singing again, "We're off to see the Reynaud, the wonderful Reynaud of Oz," as they went.

66.

Sunny was on her terrace with her open laptop. She didn't hear the cry of the peacocks or the children splashing in the pool, nor even the clatter, one more time, of the red helicopter overhead, flying even closer to the beach than before. Her attention was riveted on the information Google had just flashed on her screen.

Von Müller

A noble German family, barons from the fifteenth century. Later became major players in Bismarck's unification of Germany, thereby gaining themselves even more landholdings in Westphalia as well as properties in the cities of Hamburg and Düsseldorf, all of which were lost in World War II, as was the grand family home, a palace known modestly as Haus Müller. The family was never prolific and by the 1920s was reduced to the Baron Wilhelm August von Müller and his wife, the Baronin Lisel Hannah von Müller. There was one son, Kurt Wilhelm August von Müller (b. Jan. 8 1920).

Kurt von Müller was a musical prodigy and a career as a concert pianist was predicted but came to nothing. He achieved a small amount of fame as an accompanist to a well-known singer and actress, but this was not to last long.

In July 1944, Kurt von Müller was arrested and accused of spying and collaboration with the French. He was living in Paris at the time and was a German Army officer, working with the Reich. He escaped, it was said, with the aid of his lover, La Violette, but was caught and executed the following year.

The Baron and Baronin von Müller had been killed in an air raid on Hamburg a few months previously. Their only son, Kurt, was the last of the von Müller line. With his death the title of Baron died out. The family's much diminished estates were broken up into small parcels. Kurt von Müller had willed them to the workers on his lands, whose families had been working for the von Müllers for decades.

Sunny inspected the von Müller crest surmounting the piece. An eagle and a fox on a checkerboard shield. It was the same as the one on the ring.

She went into her room and took the blue velvet box from the top drawer of the chest, hidden under her cashmere sweater. She put the ring on her finger, thinking about Kurt von Müller, the German who had collaborated with the French, in a new twist on the old story. And about La Violette, who had loved him. Had Kurt, her lover, given her this ring before he died? To remember him by? Then, later, they had arrested her too. But for what? She sighed. There seemed to be no answer.

The gold ring felt cold on her finger, and, suddenly chilled, she took it off and put it back in its box. There must be an answer to what had happened to Violette, and the only place that answer could be was at Chez La Violette. Somehow, everything always seemed to come back to that.

Thinking of the villa, and about the way it must have been for Violette when all the world seemed young and everybody was in love, Sunny remembered that faint haunting scent that hung in the air. It was Violette's special perfume, she was sure of it. And since Violette had lived here, and since the best perfumers and growers of flowers for the expensive scents of the world were in nearby Grasse, surely one of those perfume makers would still have it? Or at least know where to find it?

Thanking heaven for the computer age, Sunny looked up perfume makers. Ten minutes later, she was on her way to Grasse. Alone again, because Mac was with Lev checking out the boat slips at Port Grimaud for the *Blue Picasso*, which had not been seen in the bay since the night Caroline drowned, and Mac wanted to know why. He said he knew Valenti was involved and he wasn't about to let him get away with it.

Sunny went first to say goodbye to Belinda and Sara, who she found playing bridge with Billy and a roped in middle-aged Frenchman with a bristly black mustache and sparkling blue eyes. At least they sparkled whenever he looked at Belinda, which Sunny noticed, even in the short time she was there, was quite frequently. Belinda looked despondent, though.

"I can't even go out on the beach now," she whispered to Sunny, at the same time holding up her cards carefully to show her her winning hand.

"You're not the only one," Sunny said, remembering she had not yet been out on the beach once. She was in St. Tropez and her new bikinis lay in the drawer, wasting away, while Mac sought out killers and she sought out perfume and an old woman's secrets.

"Where's Little Laureen?" she asked Billy.

His ten-gallon hat was back on his head, despite Belinda's best efforts, and Sunny noticed he was keeping a keener eye on Belinda and the Frenchman than on his cards.

"Little Laureen's gone for a bike ride with that French kid. He's her new best friend. Nice kid, though. Looks like he could use a friend or two. And so could my Laureen."

"Nate's gone to check on his new house," Sara added, looking as though she were wishing she was with him instead of playing bridge on the hotel's pretty patio. But it was her duty to keep Belinda company. Keep an eye on her. Make sure she didn't do anything crazy—like running off into St. Tropez again.

Sunny told them she was off to Grasse to look at the perfumeries, and Belinda advised her to stick to the single-note perfumes. "They don't get any better than at some of the small producers here," she said.

Of course, Sunny thought, driving the autoroute to Cannes one more time, then taking the turnoff that led into the hills high above the city, and to the famous perfumeries, that was exactly where she should go. To the smaller places, ones that had been there for a century or more.

The first she found was set back in a flower-filled garden, a splendid turn-of-the-century mansion with a stone portico and smart striped awnings over tall windows. The young man at the glass reception desk was very polite, very correct, and very sad that no they did not make a violet perfume. In fact there was only one place that did, as far as he knew, and he knew everybody in the Grasse area. It was in a village close by.

He directed Sunny to *Les Belles Auteurs, du Fleurs de Parfum,* a lofty title that turned out to be a tiny atelier, a studio on a small side street in a nearby village. She entered through a low stone arch, crossed a tiny cobbled courtyard and found herself knocking on the firmly closed wooden door that bore the stress and strains of age.

After a while there was the sound of footsteps, then the door opened a crack.

"*Qui est là?*"

It was a woman's voice. "*Pardon, madame.*" Sunny struggled to find the correct words that meant "I'm looking for a maker of violet perfume." "*Mais, je cherche un producteur d'un parfum particulier. Le parfum de violette. On me dit que votre établissement est* the sole *producteur.*"

She didn't think that was too bad for someone who had not really ever spoken French well, and who in any case had not spoken it for years.

Anyhow, this Frenchwoman understood because she said, "*Madame, depuis des années, personne n'avait demandé de parfum de violette.* Nobody has asked for violet perfume for years."

"*Mais madame, je m'appelle Sonora Alvarez. Je venais de Californie spécialement pour ce parfum. Je vous implore, madame, si c'est possible, aidez-moi.*"

Sunny was actually begging her, claiming she had come all the way from California in search of the violet perfume.

The door cracked a touch wider. A bespectacled eye met hers. "*Oui, c'est ça,*" the woman said, finally opening the door wide enough for Sunny to enter.

The hall was dark and smelled of about a thousand different flowers. And the woman was not old, perhaps in her fifties, tall, thin and elegant with her dark hair pulled back into a bun and wearing blue-rimmed half-glasses. Her eyes were dark and she had a Spanish look, with a fringed rose-patterned black shawl thrown over one shoulder and a chic slim black dress that, Sunny noticed, emphasized her very good figure.

"Pardon me for seeming rude," the woman said, now in perfect English. "But my father is ill and I did not want him disturbed." She held out her hand. "Geneviève Mouton-Craft. Now, tell me again, Madame Alvarez, how I can help you?"

Sunny apologized for disturbing her and told her what she was searching for.

"I don't work in the family business," Geneviève Mouton-Craft explained. "I live in Paris. My father is ill and that's the reason I'm here so early this summer. Normally, I would come with my children in July. Unfortunately, *mon père* is the only one left who knows this business. When he goes, then so will our *parfumerie.* It's been here for over a hundred and seventy years," she added with a sad look in her eyes. "But I have no talent for it, and my life took me in another direction, my own family, work . . ."

She shrugged and Sunny said she was sorry to disturb them, and of course, she would leave right away, but Geneviève Mouton-Craft put up a hand to stop her.

"*Mais non, madame,* let me see what I can find out for you. *Mon père*

worked in his business for almost sixty years. If we ever produced that perfume then he would know. Excuse me while I go and ask him."

Leaving Sunny in the hallway, she hurried away, returning five minutes
later.

"I have news," she said, smiling. "First, though, my father wishes to
know why you want this particular scent."

"Because I believe it was made for a very special woman, the chanteuse
La Violette."

Geneviève nodded. "If this were a quiz designed by my father, you would
have given the correct answer. This house made that perfume only for La Violette, oh so many years ago, more than even my father can remember. It was
a special blend of Parma violets, the rare variety first produced by an Italian,
the Comte de Brazza. Pure white blooms with pale blue tips and a sweetly
delicate perfume. Apparently La Violette decided she must have a scent that
matched her name, and when this house produced the Parma violet scent for
her, she fell in love with it. She used it all her life. It became, as they say, La
Violette's signature. When she left the room, they said her scent lingered,
tantalizingly so for the many men who were in love with her."

Sunny said, "Then you know the story of La Violette?"

"Only that she was a charmer with many lovers, and that she came to a
sad and lonely end. Her story is one of the legends of this part of France."

"Well, thank you, at least now I know about La Violette's perfume. And
you know what, *madame,* I could still smell it, in her old villa. That's how I
knew about it."

"You were in La Violette's villa?"

Sunny smiled. "Only briefly. It's a long story."

Geneviève held up her hand again. "One minute," she said and hurried
back into the dark interior of the house, leaving Sunny once more, standing
in the front hall.

A few minutes later, she was back. "My father asked me to give you this."
She handed Sunny a square cream-colored box, imprinted in deep purple
with the name of the perfume house, *Les Belles Auteurs, du Fleurs de Parfum.*
And the title *La Violette.*

"Oh my God." Sunny was stuttering, she was so overwhelmed. "Can this
really be it?"

Geneviève nodded her well-coiffed head. "My father wanted you to have
it. He said anyone who remembers La Violette well enough to speak her name
should have this. It's probably the very last bottle, kept more as a reminder of
the product than for anything else."

"How can I ever thank your father?" Sunny clutched the precious box to her chest. "You must let me pay for this."

"He wouldn't dream of it." Geneviève laughed at the thought. "He wanted me to thank you for bringing back a little of our past glory. That's all."

They shook hands and Sunny found herself walking, dazed, through the little cobbled courtyard, hearing the ancient wooden door slam behind her, through the low stone arch and onto the narrow street. Her car waited in the sunlight in the square at the end. She went and sat in it, then took a long look at the box.

Hardly daring, she opened the top flap and removed the bottle. It looked as pristine as the day it had been produced, right here in the little atelier down the street. It was obviously Lalique, a square *flacon* engraved with Violette's name, and with a beautiful frosted stopper in the shape of a Parma violet, each petal perfectly delineated. The perfume inside was the delicate pale color of the violets.

Sunny held the bottle to her nose. Even though the stopper kept the perfume tightly enclosed, she believed she could smell it. That faint, haunting scent of La Violette.

On her way back, she stopped at a smart florist in Cannes and ordered a large basket of Parma violets to be delivered to Madame Mouton-Craft.

"With my thanks and to rekindle old memories," she wrote on the card.

67.

Mac had found no trace of Joel Krendler. He had not checked into any of the grand hotels a man like that would normally frequent. He was either in a villa, or on a yacht.

"Like for instance, Valenti's *Blue Picasso*," Mac said to Lev.

They were on their way to Port Grimaud, the massive marina village complex farther along the coast. Through his contact, Lev knew Krendler was not in Monte Carlo, nor was he in St. Tropez. They figured Port Grimaud was just far enough away to be off the smart-yacht map, and big enough for him to stay out of sight. It was a long shot but Mac knew that in this game long shots were sometimes worth pursuing.

"Y'know what," he said to Lev, negotiating his way into the left overtaking lane and passing a Porsche with Spanish number plates, whose driver gave him the finger. He'd noticed Porsches did not like to be passed. "I've not even had time to take Sunny to the beach yet, and we've been here forever." Thinking of the events of the past few days he added, "At least it seems like forever."

"I guess I should say it serves you right for getting involved with all these people," Lev replied.

Mac overtook again. "I didn't get involved with them. They got involved with me."

"And of course you couldn't say no."

Mac knew Lev was right. That was his trouble. He never could say no. "Sunny thought we might get married out here," he said.

Lev threw him a surprised glance. "I thought you two were fine the way you are."

"So did I."

"Women," Lev said.

"You don't appear to have women problems."

Lev grinned. "If I do I keep 'em to myself. Take the next exit." He indicated the sign coming up.

Port Grimaud was off a very busy road with rental apartments and condos, town houses, shops, cafés, restaurants, ships' chandlers and yacht sales offices. It was a town in its own right and it was crammed with summer people and boats. Edging his way through, Mac was beginning to wish he'd never come.

"I could sure use a beer," Lev said as Mac squeezed into a parking spot that was too far from the waterfront but all he could find. Summer in the South of France was in full swing in this area, with tribes of children, distracted parents, backpackers and campers, all seeking sun and sea and probably he guessed, also a cold beer.

It was a walk to the waterfront where boats were stacked edge to edge, the owners sitting on their aft decks drinking iced martinis or champagne or beer, eating fresh shrimp and watching the people in the cafés opposite enviously watching them. The cafés also stretched the entire length of the harbor, with balconied condos rearing up behind them, taking advantage of the sea view. If you could get past the boat masts to the sea that is. Mac and Lev joined the crowd in a terrace café called, inappropriately, the Marlin.

"Didn't know they fished marlin in the Med," Mac said, remembering fishing trips off Baja, Mexico.

"They don't, but I guess nobody around here knows that, and if they do they don't care."

They took seats at a table in front with the passersby practically in their laps. The Marlin was a popular place, either that or it was lunchtime, and it was the only table free. Mac ordered a Kronenbourg and Lev a Stella, and they sat back looking at the boats through the constant passing parade. Mac ate a ham sandwich and Lev a cheese omelet. They had to admit that it was pretty good, and the icy beer cooled them down.

Mac said, "Krendler has a dog. And dogs have to be walked. He can't stay hidden on the boat all the time."

"Unless he kills off the dog." Lev glanced at him over his omelet. "You told me that was the pattern."

"I've heard it is. But he got off the plane with a brindle greyhound and that's what we need to look for."

"First, let's check the yachts. The *Blue Picasso* is big, a seventy-footer. There's only one place it might be."

They walked the length of the harbor to the deeper mooring. It wasn't easy spotting the *Blue Picasso* amongst all the big boats, and they walked all the way to the boatyard, where yachts were up on ramps, being refitted or painted, or fixed. The *Blue Picasso* was not up on a ramp. She was tucked away behind the boatyard, all by herself in a deepwater mooring. And on her deck stood a small brindle greyhound.

"Bingo," Mac said, high-fiving Lev and grinning.

"So what do we do now?" Lev asked.

"We wait and see what their next move is. Trust me," Mac said. "They're sure to have one planned. And it'll lead us to those stolen artworks."

"So you think Krendler's the mastermind?"

"I'm willing to bet the farm on it."

"Tell me, what made you think Krendler was involved?"

"It all gets back, as it always seems to," Mac said, "to Chez La Violette. Krendler bought that house over ten years ago. I believe he used it as his headquarters when planning the robberies. I think the fast black speedboat was brought in to transport the paintings by sea instead of by road from the robbery location to the *Blue Picasso,* then to a secret place. Where that is I don't yet know. And what I want now is for Krendler to lead us to it. I'm sure that's why he's here."

Lev nodded. He guessed no one would suspect they were transporting stolen goods by sea on a high-class sailboat.

Mac said, "I'll bet you that that black speedboat is here too, somewhere." He shrugged. "No matter, it's gonna turn up again and then we'll turn them over to the police."

"Why not now?"

"Because now, all I've got is a theory. And anything could happen."

"So why would they kill Caroline?"

"Y'know, I think it must have all started out as a simple seduction. And in her own way Caroline was as immoral as Valenti, with her rental scam, stealing old Madame Lariot's identity, including her bank accounts. We don't know yet how much was taken from those, by the way, but you can bet that's what she did. Caroline liked the good life and she was determined to get it."

Lev's face was expressionless. He'd heard stories like this before.

Mac said, "That poor French boy, Bertrand, was unfortunate enough to witness the murder."

"Valenti was paying her off," Lev said. "I guess he didn't expect her to get mad and make a run for it in the dinghy."

"So he ran her down. She's gone. Clean as a whistle. And Valenti is nowhere to be seen. Then Krendler shows up for the final act."

"So how will they sell the paintings?"

Mac shrugged. "There are collectors around the world, men—and women—obsessed with a certain artist, who will pay just to own a painting. They keep them in a secret room, or locked away in a steel walk-in safe where they go alone, to look at them, simply to feel them in their hands, to gloat over their mad possessions."

"There's no accounting for taste," Lev said.

"And that, my man, is what makes the crazy world you and I inhabit go round," Mac said. "And I'm willing to bet it's also why Krendler has no paintings of any value on the walls of his Paris mansion. He's not willing to share them with anybody. He wants them all to himself, in a place where, in the deepest night and the darkest depth of his soul, he can possess them."

"Jesus," Lev said. "Let's get outta here. I think I'd rather be looking out for Belinda and taking care of Jasper Lord than Joel Krendler."

"Six of one, half a dozen of the other," Mac said with a laugh. "Okay, let's go."

68.

Nate had left early that morning for Bonnieux, on his way to look at his house once again. Malcolm had told him it would be at least a month before he could take possession but he already felt it was his. It was a cash transaction and the divorced German wanted out fast, which was all to Nate's advantage. He'd never felt this excited about anything before. Possessions had never mattered to him, even though his Tribeca loft was, as the real estate woman informed him, the last word in desirability.

He hadn't *desired* it but he'd bought it anyway, and it worked for him. It was still as simple as the day he'd moved in: just a couple of plain sofas, a big bed and a giant flat-screen. There were no personal photographs, no memories in cute silver frames because Nate had none, and no vases either because he never bought flowers. It was only now, when he opened the door and stepped into the pale-beamed, old stone-walled world that had suddenly become his, that he felt he was "home."

He walked through his house, taking his time, checking out the showers—all multijet and functional—and stopping to admire the view from the master bedroom, even going so far as to lie on the bed to check if he could still see that checkerboard valley with the mountains beyond. And he could.

He liked his bathroom, the white subway tiles, the black mosaic floor, the dull pewter finish on the faucets. Even the mirror, embedded in slate seemed to offer a new look at his own smiling face, usually so serious, so preoccupied, always thinking of something else, never of the moment.

Now, he was thinking of the moment. On an impulse he walked down the street into the village square and bought a large bunch of giant sunflowers.

He put them in a big red vase and stood them on a stone window ledge with that green view behind. The colors of Provence hit him between the eyes with an almost physical impact. It was like looking at a van Gogh still-life. He finally knew what that artist was all about.

Later, he made his way down the hill to the mill, where he found Malcolm, surprisingly, in an apron, racing around, plates in hand and looking extremely flustered.

"Waitress quit," Malcolm explained, en route again to the kitchen. "Roger's cooking and I'm here all alone." He looked Nate up and down appraisingly. "Want to put on a pinny and come and help?"

Tying on the apron Nate thought of Sara telling him she'd worked at Hooters. That Sara was a dark horse all right. She'd surprised him a couple of times now.

After the lunch rush died down, Roger and Malcolm came and sat with him over a glass of wine and a hunk of fresh-baked bread and a couple of good cheeses, a St. Marcellin blue and a gentle Delices de Coeur that went well with the carafe of local rosé, a much darker wine than the rosés of the coast, with a fine berry taste.

"Tough day." Malcolm sighed deeply.

"It'll get even tougher," Roger said. "It's summer, everybody's already got a job and there's no waitresses to be found within a fifty-mile radius. If that."

"And I don't look good in an apron," Malcolm said, patting his belly.

Nate had already removed his own apron, and he hadn't in the least minded running in and out of the kitchen with plates of good food for the happy diners. But when Roger said they were thinking of expanding, adding a wing and turning the mill into a B and B, he was surprised.

"Maybe even a small hotel," Malcolm added hopefully. "You know, something simple, just a good restaurant with rooms above."

"Isn't that what every traveler hopes to be lucky enough to find?" Nate asked.

"You bet it is," Malcolm said. "But I'm afraid we have to do some number crunching and see what we can come up with. Neither Roger nor I is any good with figures, it's all we can do to keep the books straight. Sometimes I'm convinced there's more goes out than comes in. Still, we manage."

He grinned cheerfully at Nate, who looked thoughtful.

"I'm pretty good at numbers," Nate said. "Why don't you explain exactly what you've got in mind, and I'll look into it and tell you if it's viable?"

The two men brightened up. "We've never had an adviser before," Roger said, thrilled.

When Nate left, later that afternoon, it was with the accounts and the ar-
chitect's plans for an addition with rooms to be built out over the stream, like
a small bridge. The concept was so charming Nate almost wished he could be
part of it, but then he realized of course he could. He would be here often,
dining at the Moulin de Hubert (Hubert was the original owner of the mill).
He would be a part of it all.

69.

The yellow dog trotted behind as Bertrand raced down the hill on his *vélo*, through rows of vines hung with ripening grapes. He was freewheeling, feet off the pedals, legs sticking out on either side, hands off the handlebars except when he reached down to ring the bell. And he was singing at the top of his voice. "We're off to see the wizard, the wonderful Wizard Reynaud . . ."

Laureen's tongue stuck out with the effort as she too daringly removed her feet from the pedals, though she still clung to the safety of the hand brake. She lifted her hands off experimentally every now and then, and she also rang the bell frequently to make up for her lack of expertise. "We're off to see the wizard, the wonderful Wizard Reynaud . . ." Her voice trailed behind her as they rattled over the ruts, bouncing on the saddles and yelling out in fear.

Laureen saw the high white wall and the name Villa les Ambassadeurs above the gate and squeezed the brakes so tight she almost went over the handlebars. She propped her bike against the wall, said, "Come on," to Bertrand, then pulled the iron rod that clanged a loud bell somewhere inside the house.

Yellow Dog waited, panting, at Bertrand's feet. They jumped as a tiny security screen lit up and a voice said in French, "Who is it please?"

Seeing herself on the screen, Laureen said, "Laureen Bashford and Bertrand Olivier to see Monsieur Reynaud. Please," she added.

There was a long silence, then the woman's voice said again, "And why do you wish to see Monsieur Reynaud?"

"It's about his stolen art," Bertrand replied.

There was another silence. Laureen shuffled her feet in their worn ballet slippers, wondering what they would do if their plan failed and Monsieur Reynaud refused to see them.

"*S'il vous plaît, madame,*" she said in her best French accent. "*C'est très important.*"

That must have done the trick because the woman told them to wait a moment. The screen clicked off and they stood, shuffling their feet again, half-wishing they hadn't come.

After several minutes of silence the screen clicked on again. "I'm opening the gates," the woman said. "Follow the path in front of you to the main house."

The huge iron gates slid open silently and the dog whined when they swung back into place again, leaving him outside. The two walked down the wide driveway set with coral-colored pavers, past a small forest of trees, turning at a lawn with a view of the sea on the left, and turning again in to a wide circle in front of the house. The tall doors, almost as tall as the villa itself, were open and a pleasant-looking Spanish woman waited for them.

She inspected them as though she could not quite believe it. Then she asked them please to step inside, Monsieur Reynaud was waiting for them in his study.

François Reynaud was behind a large old-fashioned tulipwood desk that looked as if it had once graced some turn-of-the-century office, well-used and complete with scars and ink stains from some long-ago business world. The enormous burgundy studded-leather chair in which he sat, hands folded in front of him, looking at them over his spectacles, also bore the creases of time.

Bertrand's sneakers squeaked on the polished wood floors and Laureen skidded in her ballet shoes. They stood to attention, arms stiffly at their sides. No one spoke.

François Reynaud had difficulty holding back a smile as he took in the pudgy little girl in the grubby ballet frock with her hair poking out in two ragged bunches under the straw hat. And the skinny boy whose knees stuck out like doorknobs from his drooping shorts (were they fastened with an old tie?) and who was looking at him through oversize pale glasses. The boy ran his hands nervously through his hair. A mistake, François thought, unable to resist the smile now, as the boy's hair, chopped he guessed with a blunt pair of scissors, stood on end.

"Maria Dolores," he called the housekeeper who was waiting by the door to see if her boss was going to throw them out. "Lemonade for these children please."

He pointed to the two chairs in front of the desk and they sat in silence, waiting. Laureen sat on the very edge of her chair but it was still too high and her feet dangled. Without thinking, she swung them nervously, wondering why the Wizard Reynaud didn't speak to them.

The lemonade arrived on a big black tray in a tall crystal jug and was poured by Maria Dolores, clinking with ice and smelling deliciously of fresh lemons. Bertrand was too nervous to pick up the glass in case he spilled, but Laureen took a taste.

"*Merci, Monsieur Reynaud*," she said shyly. "*C'est très bon.*"

"*Ah, la petite parle français?*" Reynaud steepled his hands together, looking at her.

"Oh, well . . . not truly . . . I mean, well . . . sometimes I do . . ."

"It was a good effort. And your name is?"

"My name is Laureen Bashford. I'm from Texas."

Reynaud permitted himself another smile. "Of course you are," he said smoothly, turning his attention to the boy.

"*Et tai?*" he asked.

"Bertrand Olivier, *monsieur*. From Paris."

"Paris? Then I assume you are both here on vacation?"

"Yes, oh, yes, sir." The story came bubbling out of Laureen like the lemonade from the crystal jug. "It's about your stolen paintings, sir, we know what happened, we know how they did it and where they are . . ."

Astonished, Reynaud leaned across the big desk. "And how do you know that?" He looked questioningly at Bertrand.

"We figured it out, sir. Well, Little Laureen did."

"No I didn't," she objected, thinking about the reward for Bertrand. "We *both* guessed how it happened. I just thought about it when I was on a boat, looking at the land, how easy it must be just going in and out of a jetty and into a house . . ."

"And then we thought about it because of the ghost at Chez La Violette . . . ," Bertrand added.

Laureen flung him a triumphant glance. "Bertrand said there was no ghost but I knew there was, and that's why nobody goes there. Except the robbers, because it's empty."

"Nobody would ever see them, nobody would even think to look there . . ." Excited, Bertand picked up the story.

"Then you have seen these stolen paintings? At Chez La Violette?"

Bertrand's face fell.

"Well, not exactly," Laureen admitted.

"And the robbers? You've seen them?"

"Well . . . no . . . just the ghost light at night . . ."

François Reynaud got up from his big leather chair. He walked round his massive desk, picked up the crystal jug and poured more lemonade. "Maria Dolores," he called. "Please bring some of those *tartes tropéziennes* for *les petites*."

He perched on a corner of the desk, looking at them, unsmiling again, until the housekeeper reappeared with a basket of the tarts.

Laureen said *merci beaucoup* and took one. It tasted great and she sipped her lemonade, looking at Bertrand, who was chewing his carefully, trying not to make crumbs.

"Sir?" Bertrand said. "May I take one for my dog?"

Reynaud looked around the room, brows raised, as though he'd been missing something in the fantastical story they had come up with. He said, "I see no dog here."

"Oh, but *monsieur*, he's a *stray* dog. He's got yellow fur and Bertrand just named him Yellow Dog. And I know about Chez La Violette because my daddy rented it for a month for our vacation and then it all went wrong and it was all dusty and broken and haunted and we ended up at the Hôtel des Rêves where Bertrand is staying only his mother has just left him there, and he dived in and saved my necklace, and now he knows what happened and so you can pay him the reward and he'll never have to go away to boarding school and his cruel mother can stay in Italy with her new stepchildren because there's no room for Bertrand . . ."

Laureen paused for breath. Bertrand stared at her, glassy-eyed with shock. He hadn't expected all that.

"But Mac and Sunny are looking after Bertrand now," Laureen added. "And my daddy, Billy Bashford. We live on a ranch, the Glitter Ranch in Texas."

Bertrand said quickly, "Laureen's mother died. She wears the tutu so her mother can always find her, no matter where she is or how many people there are . . ."

"And the yellow dog belongs to Bertrand now," Laureen added. "And he's starving."

Reynaud held up his hand to stop the torrent. "Maria Dolores," he called the housekeeper again. "Please let the dog in and find him some food. I believe he's hungry."

He stood, looking silently at the pair of them. He had not been this moved by anything since his young friend had been killed.

"Let's go outside, shall we?" he suggested, leading the way through the open French doors to the beautiful pergola, tiled in blue and yellow, Moorish style. He watched as Laureen arranged herself on the blue cushions, hands clasped in her lap, knees apart, feet swinging. And Bertrand, tight with nerves, standing next to her.

"So, you know Mac Reilly," he said.

"And Sunny," Laureen said eagerly. "They're our friends."

"And do they know your story? About the boat and the robbers and Chez La Violette?"

"No," Bertrand admitted.

"We wanted to tell you ourselves," Laureen explained.

Reynaud nodded. "So you could earn the reward."

"It's to save Bertrand, you see." Laureen looked him in the eyes. "He has nowhere to go, his mother doesn't want him and if he gets the reward then he'll be free to do whatever he wants."

"Of course."

Maria Dolores appeared with the yellow dog tied to a piece of string. It walked sedately beside her, head and tail down. Until it spotted Bertrand that is, then it let out a yowl and galloped toward him, big tail flapping, almost bowling the housekeeper over.

"That's a fine dog," Reynaud said.

Bertrand smiled his rare smile. "Yes, sir, he is," he said proudly.

Maria Dolores came back with a bowl of food. It smelled like good chicken to Laureen, and the dog wolfed it down, never lifting its head once. A bowl of water was brought and it slurped lustily, splashing water everywhere, then sat back, scratching itself vigorously.

"He needs to learn a few manners though," Laureen said.

"I'll tell you what I'll do, children." Reynaud stood in front of them, arms folded over his chest, seeming tall as a tree as they looked up at him. "I'll investigate your story, check out your claims about the boat and Chez La Violette."

Laureen's face dropped. She had thought he would hand over the five hundred thousand euros there and then.

"And if what you say is true, then you will have earned the reward."

Bertrand knew it was all over. He picked up the end of the string attached to his dog. He said politely, "Thank you, Monsieur Reynaud," then nodded at Laureen to say goodbye also.

She looked at Reynaud for a long minute. Then, impulsively, she ran at him and threw her arms around his legs. "Thank you, Monsieur Reynaud, for the lemonade, and the tarts, and for Yellow Dog's food." Then she followed Bertrand out of the prettily tiled pergola.

She turned for one last look.

"You know what we were singing as we rode our bikes here? 'We're off to see the Wizard, the wonderful Wizard Reynaud.'" And, throwing him a smile over her shoulder, she was gone.

70.

Mac arrived back at the hotel before dinner, just in time to tell Sunny that he had found the *Blue Picasso* and suspected Krendler was on it. "Nothing I can do about it until Krendler or Valenti makes a move," he called from the shower where he was scrubbing off the long day's sweat.

He smiled, surprised as a naked Sunny pushed her way in and began to soap his back. "Well, thanks, I was almost too tired after that long drive to do that myself."

"Then why not let me help you?"

She massaged his shoulders and he let his head fall forward. Cool water dripped from his chin. "I think I'm in some sort of heaven," he murmured, turning and enfolding her in his arms.

"Mmmm, then let's get married," Sunny said.

He held her away from him. Tiny droplets beaded her lashes and her long hair fell back like a glossy black waterfall. "How can we find the time? I've been busy all day."

Sunny recognized the truth in what he'd said. So had she. "So, when this is all over, you and the Misfits, and me and La Violette, then we'll get married?"

"First we have to go to the beach."

"Why?"

"Because we've been in St. Tropez all this time and still haven't managed it."

She nodded, it was true, even though all the others had, including Little Laureen.

Mac's hands massaged the long lean muscles of her back, and her rounded behind, which fit into his hands like it was made for him.

The phone rang. He groaned and Tesoro yelped. It kept on ringing. Now Sunny groaned.

Mac's attention had shifted. He looked uneasily at her. "I have to answer it," he said, his mind already racing ahead to Krendler and Valenti. Grabbing a towel and dripping water, he raced to pick it up. Tesoro nipped at his heels and Pirate nipped at Tesoro.

"Reilly, this is François Reynaud."

"Sir, good to hear your voice. How can I help you?"

Reynaud laughed. "I don't know if you can help me, but you might very well be able to help two young friends of yours." And he proceeded to tell him of Bertrand and Laureen's visit, and their theory about the robberies.

"Jesus," Mac said, stunned. "I've been upstaged by a couple of kids. How did they figure it out? It's exactly what I've come up with myself, except for Chez La Violette being the place where they hide the paintings. My own thought is they were taken off by a speedboat. It met up with the *Blue Picasso* further along the coast and well out of the area, when the paintings were transferred. I'm willing to bet they're still on that sailboat, hidden behind all that fine paneling. In fact I've never seen a boat so covered in paneling."

"How do we find out?" Reynaud asked.

"It's a wait-and-see game right now. And it's no longer just about the robbery, *and* one murder. It's about the death of a young woman."

"A second murder, you mean?" Reynaud's voice was sharp.

"Exactly. And I believe I know who did it." Tesoro tugged at the towel and Mac tugged back. "I can't go to the police yet because I have no evidence, and neither do they. But when that moment comes, they will be there."

"Then I'll leave it to you. And you'll take care of those children? See what they are up to, that they're in no danger? We're talking murder, Reilly."

With a shock, Mac realized it was true, and that two interfering children could suddenly find themselves in peril. "Don't worry, sir, I will," he said.

Sunny had put Tesoro out on the terrace where she was yapping at the peacocks. Pirate lay peaceably at the foot of the bed, on the winning side for once. Now Sunny was lying on the bed.

Mac went and closed the shutters then lay down next to her. Cool sheets; half-light; the delicate upward sweep of her breasts; rough stubble, unshaven, the male smell of him, urgent hands, skin on skin. Was lovemaking ever as sweet before?

Later, they lay back, still entangled, her leg flung over his hip, his arm beneath her shoulders, breathing each other's breath, slowly tasting each other's lips.

"Let's run away together," Sunny said softly.

Mac's laugh rumbled from his chest. "Sunny Alvarez, are you suggesting we run away from *St. Tropez*? *This* is the place people run away *to*."

"Not when they have murder on their minds," she said, definitely not amused. Then she smiled forgivingly. "Anyway, I did a little investigating of my own." She reached for the bottle of violet perfume on the night table in front of the old oil painting and handed it to Mac.

He looked inquiringly at her, and at the cream-colored box, then he opened it and took out the delicate Lalique *flacon*. "Beautiful," he said, running a finger lightly across the petals of the stopper, listening while Sunny told him the story of her visit to the *parfumerie* in Grasse.

"It seems to me that Chez La Violette holds all the answers," she said, seriously. "A woman like that, a star, a beauty, a woman who loved and was loved, she wouldn't just leave. She wouldn't just die alone. Somewhere."

Mac wasn't so sure. Violette had been arrested after the war, accused of who knows what? Life, as she knew it had come to an end. What was left to live for?

Dinner was at nine with all the Misfits. He glanced at the golden sunburst clock on the wall, a midcentury relic that had found a new life here at the Hotel of Dreams.

"I guess she just lost her dream," he said.

71.

Mac was at the bar talking to Billy. They could see Laureen and Bertrand, who had a game of poker going at the far end of the room, while a few other children watched cartoons on TV, waiting for their parents to show up for dinner.

Mac had told Billy what his daughter was up to, and that it was now a dangerous game. "You might have to keep them out of it from now on," he said.

"Jesus." Billy was stunned. "And all I thought was thank the Lord, Little Laureen was finally coming out of her post-traumatic trance, and all due to her new friend."

"You can still thank Bertrand for that," Mac said. "And Bertrand can also thank Laureen. They needed each other."

Mac did not tell him that Valenti was a suspect in Caroline's murder, nor about Krendler. He'd given Billy just enough information to make sure that from now on Billy kept his daughter within sight at all times.

"I'll surely keep an eye on that boy also." Billy shoved his hat farther back and wiped his brow with a red, white and blue silk handkerchief. "Who the hell knew?"

"Not us." Mac slapped him on the shoulder as the Texan got up and went to tell the kids it was time for dinner.

Billy put his arm round his daughter's shoulders, and said, "Hey Bertrand, why don't you join us for dinner? I'm sure Laureen here would like that."

Bertrand's face, normally pale as alabaster from rarely going out in the daytime and only at night—like a vampire—flushed with pleasure.

"Before we go, though," Billy said, "we need to talk about your visit to Monsieur Reynaud."

Laureen gasped. She wondered how he knew. Nervous, Bertrand bit his lip.

"I'm gonna tell you kids, I think you've been very clever, putting two and two together. And Monsieur Reynaud appreciates that. He understands about the reward, but now he insists that you leave this alone. No more talking about robbers, no more guessing how it was done, or why, or who done it. Monsieur Reynaud does not want to put you in danger. And neither does Mac."

The two stared blankly at Billy. They were old enough to understand heartbreak but too young to know danger.

"Promise me," Billy said solemnly.

"Promise," they muttered in unison.

"Hand on heart," Billy insisted. And hands on hearts they promised again.

"Unless something exciting happens and we can get the reward," Laureen whispered to Bertrand as they followed her father out into the courtyard.

Bertrand walked proudly with Laureen to the long table in the courtyard where the Misfits were already seated, bottles of rosé—a new choice, Château St. Martin, peachy pink and crisp on the tongue—were already being poured and the menu's nightly specials being considered with the waiter, who now knew everyone by name and smiled as he saw the children.

Belinda made room for them between herself and Billy, and gave a gloomy hello to Mac and Sunny. Nate was in deep conversation with Sara about his new house and Laureen was telling Sunny excitedly about Bertrand's new dog.

"But where is he?" Sunny knew dogs were welcome in the dining room, as they were in most restaurants in France, and where they always seemed to behave like angels, half-hidden under their owners' chairs or under the tablecloth. Unlike Tesoro who always made her presence known, while Pirate, who never left Mac's side, behaved like a guard dog and as though he did not understand he was disabled.

"They wouldn't let me bring my dog in." Bertrand's face was long as he told them, shyly, that the manager had said the dog was a stray, that it was dirty, it must have fleas and could not possibly be allowed in, otherwise all the other dogs would be infested.

"I guess he's right, Bertrand," Billy said. "Tell you what though, tomorrow you and me and Little Laureen will find a dog beauty parlor and get Yellow Dog cleaned up."

"Can we really, Daddy?" Laureen was thrilled.

"And then maybe we'll all go for a drive somewhere, take your dog for a long walk, have lunch together."

It seemed to Sunny to be a perfect solution. In the meantime, she handed Tesoro to Laureen, who clutched the Chihuahua gratefully. Then Sunny ordered a plate of chopped steak and some kibble for Bertrand's dog. When it came Bertrand carried it out to the parking lot where Yellow Dog was tied to a tree under the wary gaze of Lev's duty guard. Bertrand waited while the dog ate, fast as a starving wolf. He watched it drink some water, patted it, arranged a beach towel for it to sleep on, patted it some more and returned to the table in the courtyard.

Lev's guard watched him go. He had never had a duty like this before; children were not in his orbit, though kidnappers were. It was peaceful here, at the Hôtel des Rêves. Too peaceful. He was bored out of his skull. He went back to the newspaper and tomorrow's racing form.

"I don't know what I'm going to do," Belinda said to Billy, talking across the bent heads of Laureen and Bertrand, who were busy with their fries, while she only toyed with a delicate fillet of sole, grilled simply with a brown butter sauce. It was delicious but she had no appetite.

Billy's eyes were filled with longing as he looked at her. It was the first time he'd felt anything for a woman since Betsy died, that stirring of the heart, and the belly. The new emotion was foreign to him. He didn't quite know how to deal with it. After all, he hadn't dated in years. All he was was a simple lonely Texan rancher with a young daughter. This exotic St. Tropez world was foreign to him, though he did admit to a liking for it. And after all, where else would he have met a woman like Belinda?

"You ride a horse?" he asked.

Belinda gave him a long appraising look. "Not yet," she said with a grin.

Billy knew she had understood what he meant; that he had horses on his ranch and she was welcome. No more needed to be said; they were on the same page.

He said, "You should eat that fish, it's wonderful."

Then Sara said, "Only two more days, then I have to go home."

"Sara! But you *can't* leave me," Belinda objected.

"So—stay," Sunny told her.

"I have to get back to work."

Nate said, "What if there were an alternative?"

"But there isn't. There has never been any alternative. I worked in high school, worked in college, worked all my life."

"You're twenty-seven," Nate said. "Old enough to know what work is all about, and young enough to change. And I might have just the thing for you. If you're willing to take a chance, that is." He looked at her closed face. "What d'you say, Sara? Are you a gambler?"

Sara's jaw set in a firm line. She had never gambled in her life, how could she start now? "No," she said.

"Then you don't want to know what I have in mind?"

The others were listening interestedly, eyes going back and forth between them, like spectators at a tennis match.

"At least listen to him," Belinda prompted.

"Okay, so I'm listening."

"I was at the Moulin de Hubert today," Nate said. "And Malcolm was running round with an apron on, serving the customers. Their waitress has quit."

Sara stared blankly at him. Was he seriously suggesting she become a waitress again?

"They're thinking of expanding, adding a few rooms, turning the place into a small auberge. But they have no business experience. Basically, Roger's a chef, and Malcolm fills in the gaps, but neither of them really knows what they're doing. What they need is someone with a business head."

Sara gaped. "You mean *me*?"

"You have the know-how, you told me you run your admissions office like a general, you studied business, and I believe you're not lacking ambition. The problem is Sara, you are bored."

"That's why you end up with the wrong men," Belinda added shrewdly. "Boredom's a killer."

"Of course you'd have to start out as a waitress," Nate added. "And of course you could live in my new house."

"Oh my God." Sara could not quite believe what she was hearing.

"Do not take the name of the Lord in vain," Little Laureen said, giving her a frown.

"Sorry." Sara stared down at her plate, lower lip caught in her teeth, long chestnut hair swinging over her face, hiding her. As it always did.

Mac's phone buzzed and he said "hi." He listened for a second, then leapt to his feet.

"Get the kids out of here," he said to Billy. Sunny felt trouble coming as Billy hauled them out of their chairs.

Mac said, "And Sunny, get Belinda out of here. Go through the parking lot." His voice was tense. *"Now."* Sunny and Belinda held hands, edging quickly round the table.

Just as Jasper Lord strode into the dining room.

72.

Everyone at the table froze.

All around them conversation went on as normal; dinner was being served, wine drunk.

Belinda had described her husband correctly: a burly fireplug in a cream Italian silk suit and black silk shirt. Dark glasses of course. And a mouth that smiled even though he was not smiling.

Behind him stood a couple of thugs, smart in South of France pastels. And behind them, was Lev.

Lev had been outside the hotel seconds ago when the long black Mercedes had drawn up, the biggest and most expensive Mercedes made. Certainly not the kind of car guests at the modest Hôtel des Rêves would own. But certainly a car he knew Belinda's husband did.

He'd called to warn Mac, but it was too late to get Belinda out of there. Now all Lev could do was protect her. His men were already in the courtyard, though he did not anticipate violence, not in the crowded dining room. What he did anticipate was that Lord would somehow try to get Belinda out and into the car.

"Well, good evening everybody." Jasper Lord was looking at Belinda. "Good to see you've made some new friends, sweetheart," he said, pulling up a chair and taking a seat.

Billy watched him, torn between staying to protect Belinda and removing the children from danger. The children won. He would have to trust Belinda to Mac. He edged them to the exit.

"So where you're goin'?" Lord demanded. "Sit back down, take it easy. Nice couple of kids you've got there."

Laureen clutched Tesoro to her chest, staring wide-eyed at the stranger. The dog bared her teeth in a growl.

Sunny had always known Tesoro understood men.

Mac was still standing next to his chair. Pirate was up now, and wary. So far Belinda had not said a word, just stared horrified at her husband.

"So, why do we have the doubtful honor of your presence, Mr. Lord?" Mac moved closer to him. Like Lev he knew there could be no violence, no guns in this crowded setting, and he kept his voice low so as not to attract attention.

Behind the two thugs, he saw Lev was on the phone. He also spotted Lev's guards standing at the perimeter of the courtyard.

Jasper Lord knew he was surrounded but felt no personal danger. He knew what the scene was.

"Belinda, sweetheart." The word *sweetheart* grated, making Sara flinch. Billy stood, still holding the children's hands, it was too risky to try to make a getaway and upset Lord. Nate and Sara got up though, and went to stand behind Belinda.

Belinda's face had lost its color but when she finally spoke her voice was clear and full of contempt. "I expected you to show up in a sleeveless undershirt. The kind they call 'wife-beaters,'" she said.

Lord eyed her silently from behind the dark glasses. He heaved a dramatic sigh. "Belinda, Belinda, why can't we just sort this out alone? You know how much I care about you. Let bygones be bygones, the past is the past. My love for you can overcome everything."

Looking at him, the funny thing was, that Belinda could almost believe him. She realized she was like Sara, after all. What is it with us women, she thought looking at the man who had courted her, married her, kept her a virtual prisoner and beaten her. What is it with us women, that we don't know how to let go of the dream? But Sara had. And now so did she.

"Get out of here, you bastard," she said, and heard Laureen's shocked gasp. "Put your hands over her ears, Billy," she warned. "She's not gonna want to hear what I have to say to this louse.

"I know you have a gun under that jacket," Belinda said in a low voice. "And I know you would not hesitate to use it on me. You'll do whatever it takes to get me back. Not because you care. Never that. But because you think I belong to you, and nobody—not anybody, ever—dumps Jasper Lord. Well, baby, I want you to know you are well and truly dumped."

Mac saw Lord's face flush purple with rage. He knew it was a hair-trigger moment.

"Reach for that gun and you'll regret it," he said, praying he would not have to do anything about it.

From outside came the wail of a police siren. Lord glanced round, startled, saw Lev standing in back of his own guards, knew there was nothing he could do.

"Let's go," he said to his guards. He pushed back his chair, leaned over the table, his face in Belinda's. "I'll get you back," he whispered. "You know that, don't you?" And then he turned and walked out of the dining room.

Around them, conversation and dinner went on as usual. No one had even noticed. Sunny found she was gripping the arms of her chair so tightly her hands hurt. She thought back to just a few hours ago, making love with Mac, and the tranquillity of those after-moments. The lull before the storm. Billy was clutching the children to him. Sara's face was white. Nate's eyes followed Mac and Lev as they stalked Lord through the dining room.

The police car was waiting outside, but even before he spoke to them, Mac knew there was nothing the cops could do for Belinda. The fact was her estranged husband had come to visit, to try to get her back. Nothing wrong with that. As far as anyone knew. Except intimidation was not a tactic the cops approved of. But it turned out they had more on their minds than Belinda.

There was a second police car now, and then a third. "Monsieur Lord?" The detective flashed his badge. "We have orders to escort you from these premises."

"Oh, and who gave those orders?"

"It is not my position to say, *monsieur*. But I am to escort you back to your helicopter. I think you will find that you are no longer welcome in this country."

Stiff with anger, railing silently against his situation, Jasper Lord got back into his magnificent car. He'd left the red Bell helicopter parked on top of a building in Cannes where he owned, but never used, a smart office. It would be a long ride back, even in such a luxurious vehicle, and Mac could hear him yelling at his guards as the chauffeur slammed the door and got into the driver's seat. The car purred away with its police escort.

Mac wondered what Jasper Lord's next move would be.

73.

Meanwhile, at the table in the dining room, no one spoke. Billy relaxed his grip on the children's shoulders. Nate and Sara still stood behind Belinda staring at the exit, as though expecting the husband to return.

Tesoro, in Laureen's arms, yapped pitifully, and Pirate hopped round, checking everybody was still there and all right. Mac and Lev had followed Jasper Lord and his thugs outside. Sunny looked apprehensively after them. Belinda breathed again.

"Sorry," Belinda said, unable to disguise the bitter edge to her shaky voice. "I warned you he was a bully, he's used to getting what he wants."

Sara sank into a chair. "All I signed up for was a little cruise," she wailed. Then seeing Belinda's pale face and trembling hands, she hugged her. "I wouldn't have let him touch you," she said fiercely. "Never. *Never*, you hear that, Belinda? That man will never hurt you, not while I'm here."

Belinda managed a smile. "Then maybe you'd better stay," she said, and Sara suddenly realized she hadn't even had time to think about Nate's idea that she work for Malcolm and Roger at the Moulin de Hubert.

Laureen stroked the Chihuahua nervously. "Daddy, why was that man so nasty to Belinda?"

"He's just not a good guy, baby, that's all. Nothing to worry about now. Mac has taken care of him."

"Then who will take care of Belinda?"

Billy thought that was a very good question. "We'll have to see about that, sweetheart," he said. He spotted Mac and Lev coming back and said, "Tell you what, why don't you both go to Bertrand's table and have some ice cream? I've heard they do an extra-special banana split, your own choice of flavors. And then how about a poker game?"

He took the playing cards from his pocket and gave them to Bertrand, who stood, silent and scared. He'd sensed violence in the air and did not understand what was going on.

Relieved, Bertrand took the cards. He said, "Come on, Laureen, I'll order the banana split. Which ice cream would you like?"

"Strawberry." She padded after him, still holding Tesoro, who had become a fixture in her arms. "Strawberry matches my dress," they heard her add.

"Jesus." Billy plumped onto the chair next to Belinda. "For a minute there I expected trouble."

Mac was back. "Too many people around for real trouble," he said. "Guys like Jasper Lord prefer to have no witnesses." He saw Belinda's still-shocked face and said, "I'm sorry, honey. I wish this hadn't happened, but now I know we have to get you out of here."

"But where?" She gulped back a threatening sob.

"There's my ranch in Texas for a start," Billy said. "It's surely a long way from Jasper Lord."

Belinda shook her head. "You can't do that. I mean, you can't just go home and take Little Laureen away from here. Don't you see how she's blossoming? No, you must stay." She shrugged. "I'll think of something."

"Well, I know it's not as far as Texas," Nate said, "but there's always my house in Bonnieux. I don't have full title yet, but I guess if I paid a bit more they would let me 'rent' it for a few weeks, until it's finally mine. It's a bit off the beaten track, stuck on a hilltop, nobody would know you, or even know you're there."

"I'd come with you," Sara said immediately.

Surprised, Belinda looked at her. "You mean you'd cancel your flight? You'll lose your money if you do. And maybe your job."

Fuck the plane fare, Sara thought. And fuck the job at the medical center. She was sticking with Belinda. For now, anyway. And *Oh My God*, she had just used the F-word—twice—in her own thoughts.

"I'm looking after you," she said stubbornly, and Belinda threw her a grateful smile.

"So that's set," Mac said. He had already spoken to his Interpol contact, Alain Hassain. Jasper Lord was persona non grata in France. Which didn't mean he wouldn't show up again, but at least they had breathing space.

He said, "Lev followed the police cars to make sure the husband left, 'back to San Remo,' the cops told me. And tomorrow I'll have Lev drive the two of you to Bonnieux early, so make sure to get your packing done tonight." He met Sunny's eyes, realized he was dealing with women and added with a wry smile, "Or at least before Lev shows up at dawn."

Nate had already gotten on the phone with Malcolm, giving him an edited version of the situation, and Malcolm told him he'd arrange it with the seller.

"Okay," Mac said. "Now I think what we all need is champagne."

"I'll vote for that," Sunny agreed.

"Me too," Belinda said, her old smile back on her pretty face.

Sunny thought it was amazing how pale someone could look beneath a tan.

Billy kept an eye on the children, busy with long spoons, digging through layers of banana split. Even from here he could see Laureen's pink satin chest was liberally dotted with blobs of chocolate. It didn't matter, the two of them were talking animatedly. He hoped they had put the ugly scene out of their minds.

"I'll miss you," he said to Belinda.

She looked at him, a clear, serious, contemplative look. "And you know what, Billy Bashford? I am going to miss you. You are truly a nice man, y'know that?"

Billy tugged at his Stetson and she laughed, reaching up and sweeping it off his head. "You don't have to hide your light beneath that bushel of a hat." She leaned to him and whispered, "You're too good-looking for that."

Billy grinned. "Then we're a matched pair," he said.

She patted his knee. "You're right, Texas."

Much later that night, when everybody had gone to bed, Bertrand slipped outside to the parking lot. The guard was no longer there but the yellow dog saw him and lumbered to its feet, long tail wagging like a flag. Tugging it on its string, Bertrand sneaked it up the back stairs and into his room.

The dog slept on his bed that night, curled up in a heavy lump at the bottom where Bertrand could feel it with his toes. They both slept dreamlessly till dawn.

Belinda, however, did not sleep. She sat alone on her terrace, listening to the soft slap of the waves, waiting for that new dawn. The husband had found her and despite her running away, she had no doubt he would find her again.

74.

The next morning, Sunny and Mac were up early to say goodbye. Lev pushed Belinda's Vuittons into the trunk of the Bentley, then squashed Sara's small carry-on, along with a flurry of shopping bags, onto the backseat next to her.

"I'm going to miss this place," Belinda said, already belted into the front passenger seat.

"You'll be back when it's all over," Sunny said encouragingly.

"Hey, sure I will." Belinda's smile hid her worry.

"Say goodbye to Billy for me," she said as they drove off, Nate leading the way on the Ducati, back in his bumblebee Lycra and the matching helmet and goggles.

"Just don't get mixed up with those Tour de France cyclists en route," Mac yelled after him. "They'll take you apart."

Laughing, Nate waved a nonchalant hand.

"Well!" Sunny leaned against Mac as the car turned out of the hotel driveway and was gone. "What do we do now?"

"Pray," Mac said grimly. He wasn't too sure the husband wasn't already back and on the trail. "Trouble is you can never trust a mobster."

"I'm praying." Sunny took his hand. The sun was just up and everything was peachy pink. "Let's go for a walk on the beach?"

They strolled hand in hand along the water's edge with Pirate dodging happily between their legs. It was too early for Tesoro who had opted to stay in bed.

"Well, we've lost two of our Misfits," Mac said. He threw a pebble, laughing as Pirate galloped after it, one ear up, one down. He was fast on his three legs. "That's my boy," Mac called. He loved that dog to pieces.

"I'm going to miss them." Sunny's arm was round his waist and she matched her own long-legged stride with his even longer one. She stopped to roll up her white capris. She was wearing an old T-shirt Mac had given her a couple of years before, with MALIBU NIGHTS in sparkly script across the chest. She would never part with that T-shirt, it would remain a tangible memory forever.

Mac kicked up some sand with his bare toes. "Funny how attached to them you can get. I mean, we came here for a quiet vacation, alone . . ."

Sunny laughed, remembering. "And Sara said all she signed up for was a quiet cruise."

"I'm willing to bet Nate Masterson is gonna change her life."

"Good luck to him." She tugged at Mac's arm. "How about changing ours, baby? Think we'll at least be able to spend time on the beach before we get married?"

He stopped and kissed her on the lips. Red lipsticky lips because even at dawn, Sunny would not be caught without her Dior Rouge lipstick; she said even a slick of color made a girl feel good. He ran his hand up under the back of her T-shirt. She did the same and they stood, face-to-face with the glimmering Mediterranean behind them and the dog edging his way between their feet.

"How could I ever be without you?" He kissed her some more, then stepped back. "But first, I have to deal with Krendler."

They walked on again, arms still round each other. They were at Bertrand's rock now, where he'd dived to rescue Laureen's silver necklace and come up with Caroline's white handbag full of sodden euros. On the right was the almost-hidden path that led between the umbrella pines and tamarisks to Chez La Violette.

They stood, gazing up at the villa's windows, a dull metallic gray, not even picking up a hint of the peachy sunrise.

"I wonder if those kids could be right," Mac said, thoughtfully. "Perhaps the stolen paintings are hidden at Chez La Violette after all."

Sunny shrugged. "There's nothing there. There's not even anywhere to *hide* anything." She was thinking about Violette though and wondering where the answer might be.

"Hey, let's go get some coffee."

She brightened up. "Breakfast?"

"You got it."

On the way back they encountered Bertrand with his dog on a string, sneaking out of the back entrance and through the parking lot.

He jumped, startled when he saw them. "Just taking my dog for a walk," he explained, as Pirate wagged his way up for a sniff.

Looking at them, Sunny thought it was a miracle what a dog and a friend could do. She was willing to bet there had been few smiles in Bertrand's life up to now.

But then a thought occurred to her. "I wonder what will happen to the dog when Bertrand's mother gets back," she said to Mac, suddenly worried.

75.

It was one of the best days Billy could remember in a long time. His daughter was smiling again.

He'd driven into St. Tropez with the two children in the backseat and the three dogs behind them—they had taken the Chihuahua and Pirate along to be groomed as well as the yellow dog.

When they found the beauty parlor Pour les Chiens, the woman in charge took one look at Yellow Dog and shook her head. "He must be full of fleas," she complained.

"I'd bet on that," Billy agreed. "Just give him your best flea bath and get rid of 'em all, otherwise we're gonna have a hotel full of 'em."

Leaving the dogs to their shampoos and grooming, they walked down the street where Billy found a café that served crepes, and Laureen said she was getting quite used to them without maple syrup. After that, they went back to the chic dog boutique where they had previously bought the ruby collar for Tesoro, and where Billy let Bertrand choose a sturdy collar for Yellow Dog and a matching leather lead. A couple of bowls for food and water, a brush for grooming, a plush padded bed with pictures of dogs on it, in case, Billy joked, Yellow Dog thought it was for someone else; a couple of bags of dog food, chew bones, a squeaky toy.

"Pirate and Tesoro are going to be jealous," Laureen warned, so they chose toys for them too.

After, they picked up the dogs from the beauty parlor. Billy said they smelled like they'd been dunked in women's perfume, so they took them for a long walk on a remote beach. They smelled much better after the wind had swept the glamour-dog aroma away, though Bertrand was still not sure about the yellow bow stuck on his dog's head. Laureen said it was cute though, so he left it there.

Neither child had mentioned the scene at the table the previous night and Billy breathed a sigh of relief. It must have gone over their heads: all they'd observed was a man talking badly to Belinda.

After that, the children devoured margarita pizza at a tiny open-fronted place on one of the narrow side streets, while Billy drank a Stella and marveled at how much a skinny kid like Bertrand could put away. Perhaps, like his dog, he'd been starving. And where was that mother of his anyway?

"What are you two gonna do now?" he asked as they drove back to the hotel.

"Dunno." Laureen shifted in the seat. Tesoro, who was on her knee of course, stuck her head out the window, sniffing the warm air.

Billy's arm lay along the open window; he too was enjoying the sun, gentler than the fierce Texan summer heat. Half of his mind was on Belinda, wondering where she was and what she was up to. He hoped she would be safe.

"Maybe sometime soon we can all drive up and visit Belinda," he suggested.

"Great." Laureen yawned. It had been a long day and a lot of food. Soon both she and Bertrand nodded off.

Back at the hotel, Billy decided a nap was in order. He hadn't realized how tired he was after a night of little sleep, worrying about Belinda and the husband, and he was glad to see the kids back to their rooms, then hit the sack. He thought he could sleep for about a week.

Laureen did not sleep though. She was worrying about Bertrand. She knew he would never be allowed to keep the dog at boarding school. Bertrand *had* to get that reward, but to do so, they must find the stolen paintings. They had told the Wizard of Reynaud they were hidden at Chez La Violette. She knew they just had to be. Didn't they?

Had there been enough space, Laureen would have paced her tiny room, but as it was all she could do was stride three steps forward then three back. She knew she had to do something! Okay, she decided. So she'd get Bertrand and they'd go to Chez La Violette, check it one more time. Even if they had to lift up those creepy white covers on the furniture and peek underneath. She shivered at the thought.

She checked out the window to see what was happening. It was too soon for dinner and all was quiet. A few clouds had climbed into the sky, muting the sunlight. She put on her orange tutu and her cowboy boots, then wondered if she'd done the right thing. Shouldn't she be wearing camouflage, like Bertrand did with his cape? Oh, and this time she would tell him to bring his binoculars so they could spy, see who was really there. Like, maybe a ghost.

She flung a blue beach towel over her shoulders so anyone noticing would think she was off to the beach, then she went and knocked on Bertrand's door.

He opened it and stared sleepily at her. Yellow Dog lingered behind him, eyes bright. Laureen thought he looked like a new dog, but maybe Bertrand was right and the bow was a bit girly.

Pulling it off, she said, "Come on, Bertrand. We have to go back to Chez La Violette and find those paintings."

She didn't have to explain further. Bertrand understood the urgency of the situation. He looked at her wrapped in the towel, and with her boots on, then he got his cape and his binoculars and his dog.

"Let's go," he said.

76.

Bertrand led the way along the quiet lane to Chez La Violette. He was wrapped in the camouflage cape, his dog at his heels, binoculars bouncing on his chest, stopping every now and then to peer importantly through them while Laureen waited patiently. He checked the lowering sky. Clouds had banked up on the horizon, blocking the sun. He said to Laureen, plodding flat-footedly along in her boots, wrapped in her beach towel, that he hoped there wasn't going to be another storm.

This time it had been easy to get out of the hotel without being seen. Lev was gone and so were the bodyguards, and everyone else had come in from the beach because the sun had disappeared. The back stairs and the parking lot made for a quick exit and now Yellow Dog was enjoying his walk, running ahead for a few minutes, then doubling quickly back to check that Bertrand was still there.

By the time they reached the kitchen gate at La Violette, the sky was electric blue and a deep silence had fallen. The birds had taken shelter and the rabbits had disappeared into their burrows. Even the crickets had stopped singing.

Bertrand opened the gate and stepped onto the overgrown path. Laureen hovered outside, wishing she hadn't suggested coming here.

"Come on, Little Laureen," Bertrand encouraged her. Yellow Dog sat at his side, tongue lolling, waiting for whatever was next.

"I don't think I want to do this anymore."

"But now we're here, we have to," he said stubbornly. "Anyhow, it was your idea, remember?"

Laureen remembered. Blue lightning lit the already electric blue sky and with a whimper, she ran after Bertrand, past the swans' head fountain to the kitchen entrance.

He fished in the geranium pot for the key and opened the door, then took off his cape and left it on the step, along with Laureen's beach towel.

"You first." Laureen hung back, but the dog dashed ahead, tail flailing, a growl in his throat.

"What's up, boy?" Bertrand called him back and the dog came and sat obediently at his feet. Outside, lightning flashed and thunder rolled. The dog's eyes rolled too.

"It's okay, Yellow Dog, no need to be scared," Laureen whispered, though her own heart was pounding and she was whispering so as not to make too much noise and alert the ghost. "What do we do now?" she asked.

Bertrand was already checking the kitchen cupboards, the pantry, even the old piano that stood, lid open, against the wall.

"Nothing in here," he said. "Let's try the salon."

Laureen thought of those big scary white shrouded objects. Could the stolen paintings really be hidden under them?

Bertrand read her mind. He said, "We have to lift up the covers and look."

She and the dog followed him into the salon. Everything was as they had left it except that one of the shutters was open, bringing welcome light into the big stuffy room. Bertrand decided the janitor must have left it open, and with Yellow Dog's inquisitive nose poking at the shrouds, he lifted up cover after cover. "Just furniture," he said.

Laureen breathed again.

"Next, La Violette's boudoir." Bertrand's voice was unexpectedly firm, but when he walked through the hall and opened the door, the dog sniffed the air, then hung back.

"Yellow Dog doesn't want to go in," Laureen objected because neither did she.

Secretly, Bertrand didn't blame the dog; there was something sad and silent about that room. "We *have* to go in," he said as bravely as he could. He turned to look at her, hanging back with the dog. "Unless you're scared of course," he added patronizingly.

Stung, Laureen stepped up to the door. Lightning lit the hallway but the boudoir was in darkness. She reached for Bertrand's hand, gripping it tightly as thunder rolled like a hundred railroad trucks directly overhead. Behind them the dog whimpered.

Bertrand pressed the light switch. Nothing happened. He tried again. Same thing. He peered into the darkness. The storm had probably taken out the electricity. He knew he would have to walk all the way through that big dark room and open up the shutters.

The house was silent after the great clap of thunder. Nothing stirred. "Bertrand?" Laureen's voice quivered.

"What?" His voice quivered too.

"Let's just go home."

"What about the reward?"

Laureen thought for a long minute. "All right," she agreed.

She took his hand and they walked together into the darkness, negotiating their way past dark clumps of furniture. It took a couple of scary minutes but finally they were at the bank of French doors. Bertrand unlatched the shutters and threw them back, breathing a sigh of relief. He flung open the glass-paneled doors. It was a gray stormy light but at least they could see.

Behind him, he heard Laureen say, "Bertrand?"

He turned to look at her. She was standing with her back to him, gaping at the wall. A large section of the dove gray paneling had been rolled back, revealing a space behind.

"A secret room!" he exclaimed.

"Just like in the movies!"

Bertrand's binoculars bounced on his chest as he rushed forward, all fear forgotten. "Come look, Laureen. *Just look.*"

The two of them stared at the stack of canvases propped against the back of the narrow aperture behind the paneling.

"We found them, Bertrand," Laureen whispered. *"Oh, Bertrand, we found them."*

"So you did, you little bastards." A voice came from in back of them. "And now what are we going to do about it?"

Joel Krendler stood there, a silver-topped cane in his hand and a look of complete malevolence on his face.

77.

An hour later, Sunny went out onto her terrace. The storm had passed and now every shrub and tree glistened with diamond droplets like Little Laureen's princess tiara. It was too much to hope for a rainbow because that would mean a pot of gold, and Sunny wasn't sure there would be one at the end of Violette's story.

She could not get Violette off her mind. Here she was, with all the clues: the legend, the ring, the lover, the disappearance. And still no clear idea of what had happened.

Tesoro climbed her leg, whining. Time for a walk. Mac had gone to Cannes earlier to talk to the police about Jasper Lord and make sure he'd really left. Sunny was on her own. Calling Pirate, she slid her still unsun-bronzed feet into flip-flops, put both dogs on their leads and headed downstairs.

Renée waved hello as they walked by. "*Bonsoir, madame,* a perfect time for a walk, after the storm, with everything so fresh," she said.

Renée was right and Sunny took deep breaths of that newly fresh air as they turned to the right outside the gates and strolled slowly along the lane. It had rained hard but not enough to turn the ruts into mud. She still had to dodge the puddles, though of course Pirate waded right through them, while Tesoro begged to be picked up. Sunny considered buying little booties for both dogs but thought better of it; Mac would never forgive her if he saw his Pirate in booties.

Of course her feet were taking her in the direction of Chez La Violette. Where else would she go when the legendary woman was constantly on her mind?

She let the dogs off the leads, stopping by the hidden path to the beach to let Pirate race round, chasing imaginary rabbits who, Sunny was quite certain, were not coming out until their grassy world dried up a bit, and certainly not with an exuberant dog crashing a warning. The horizon had cleared and a fresh breeze had sprung up. Through the still-dripping trees she could see the Mediterranean, sparkling sapphire, aquamarine, crystal-tipped.

And on it was a familiar boat. Long, sleek and black-sailed.

Sunny fumbled urgently in her pocket for her cell phone. She punched Mac's number. No reply. She tried again. Same thing. *Damn it. Where was he when she needed him?* She left a message.

"I'm here, standing outside Chez La Violette, and you'll never guess what I've seen. The *Blue Picasso* moored in the bay. Valenti is back. Call me."

She hesitated, not knowing what to do next. Then hoping Mac would call her soon she walked on to the villa. The back gate was open and the dogs sniffed happily as she stepped along the mossy path, slippery now from the rain.

Flip-flops were not the ideal attire for slippery paths and Sunny was so busy watching where she was going at first she took no of notice Pirate's sharp little *wuff*. When she looked up she saw the big yellow dog sitting on the kitchen doorstep.

"What are you doing here?" she cried, immediately realizing the answer. Of course, the dog would be with Bertrand. *And* Laureen. She saw the cape and a hotel beach towel and knew they must be here.

The yellow dog bent his head gratefully under her caressing hand, whining, wet tail flapping, sending muddy splatters over Sunny's bare legs.

"So what's up, boy?" she asked sympathetically. "And where's Bertrand? Come on, find him for me."

The dog whined again and Pirate ran to its side with a worried look. In her arms Tesoro gave a nervous little whinny, the kind Mac said sounded like police sirens.

The door was half-open and Sunny stepped inside, calling hello.

The silence was so complete it was almost deafening.

"Bertrand?" she called, still standing next to the open kitchen door.

This house had always gotten to her and now it was even worse. There was no scent of Parma violets this time, no rustling of small creatures in the wainscoting, no *chirrup* of stray crickets invading from the garden. Just an awful silence. The piano lid was still up, the mugs still upside down on the wooden draining board, the empty brandy bottle and the Nescafé tin next to them. It seemed so long ago since the night of the great storm, only a week and a half, when the Misfits met and came together and became like a small family, looking out for each other, caring. Now all there was was a silent villa falling into decay, still lost in the time warp of its long-dead owner.

"Bertrand?" she called, worried now, walking from the kitchen into the hall. A dim light came from the boudoir. Not the chandelier electric glow though. Somebody must have opened the shutters.

For once Sunny was not thinking of La Violette as she walked into the star's boudoir; she was smiling, thinking of course those incorrigible kids must be in here, looking for the stolen paintings.

The paintings were there all right, half a dozen of them piled in the center of the glow. And so was Joel Krendler, sitting on one of La Violette's silver-gray velvet sofas, legs nonchalantly crossed.

He lifted a gun and pointed it at her. It was not, Sunny noticed, a petite .22. This was a heavy-duty assault rifle. Krendler meant business.

"Mademoiselle Alvarez," Krendler said. "Please, come on in and take a seat. I think we need to talk."

78.

Sunny stared at the gun. You didn't need to be an expert to know that with one twitch of a finger it could take out her and the children and the dogs, and anybody else who just strayed into Krendler's orbit. Her heart thunked slowly somewhere in the pit of her stomach. Fear choked her into silence. There was no sign of the children.

Remember Mac, remember to keep your cool, she told herself, looking silently at the silent Krendler, who had an amused expression on his face, as though he enjoyed having a helpless woman at gunpoint, and was planning on some exotic torture. That coldness she had observed when they'd met in his Paris house was evident in his eyes; there was not a flicker of emotion as he looked at her, standing there, unable to speak.

"Better sit down after all," he said in a false kindly tone, pointing out a nearby chair.

Sunny sank into it because her legs would no longer support her. *Remember Mac,* she told herself again. *What would Mac do now? What would Mac expect her to do now? He'd expect her to keep her cool, right? You've been here before, in bad situations like this before,* she told herself. But not like this, she whimpered inwardly. Not *alone.* Tension crackled in the air between them. *And, oh God, where were the children?*

Still Krendler said nothing, enjoying the play of emotions across her face. It definitely gave him a buzz to have a woman frightened of him. He was a man who always had to be in control, whether it was in his public life, involved with the opera committees internationally, or his very private business dealings, especially the stolen art market, and in his control of Gianni

Valenti, a man who he'd found would do anything for money to enable him to maintain his rich playboy lifestyle; as well as the employees in the lesser chain of command who carried out his orders perfectly, silently. Or else. There had been more than a few casualties on the way but that was how Krendler ran his business. He would have no compunction at all in disposing of this rather beautiful and far too inquisitive woman.

"Too bad you happened to stray in here this evening," he said. His deep voice had a conversational edge, as though they were chatting over cocktails and not over the edge of a gun.

"Where are the children?" Sunny was panicking. Krendler was absolutely capable of killing her and the kids. Age played no role in his evil mind.

"Ah, the children." Krendler heaved a theatrical sigh. "Such *clever* children. Don't worry about them, Madmoiselle Alvarez, they will be well taken care of."

Sunny wondered what that meant. The phone in her pocket vibrated and she put a hand over it, hoping Krendler hadn't noticed. *It had to be Mac, please, please, pray it was Mac . . . If she didn't answer, surely he would come looking for her.*

"So," Krendler said, getting up and standing over her. "What do you think I should do with you now?"

"Now that I know you're the art thief, you mean? And a kidnapper of small children? And an evil man who is ruled by his own obsessions? Is that what you mean, *Monsieur Krendler?*"

He towered over her and Sunny knew she had made a terrible mistake. In a quick blur she saw his arm reach up, the arc of the gun as it crashed down on her head. Then nothing more.

In the sudden silence, faint cries could be from behind the closed paneling.

Krendler heaved another sigh. He'd thought he would simply get the stolen paintings out of here and onto the *Blue Picasso*. He and Valenti had planned to sail along the coast, putting in at Genoa. After that it would be easy to distribute the paintings to the appropriate clients, though he planned on keeping some for himself, one of which was the special small Seurat the stupid greedy little bitch Caroline Cavalaire had attempted to sell to a Zurich collector.

Caroline had followed Valenti to Chez La Violette, seen where the paintings were hidden and simply helped herself. She thought she'd been clever choosing the very smallest, not knowing that small was also valuable, especially personally to Krendler who loved his chosen artworks with a passion he could never offer a woman. With the exception, of course, of some of the female opera singers of the world, whose pure voices appealed to a sensual side of him only they could satisfy. But there was no time to think of that now.

Valenti appeared in the doorway. He saw Sunny Alvarez sprawled unconscious on the floor and heard the cries behind the paneling.

"Get them all into the dinghy," Krendler said harshly. "Take them to the *Blue Picasso*. We'll dispose of them once we're out at sea."

Valenti did not like it one bit. He'd killed Caroline on Krendler's orders, but he considered that justified. Caroline had betrayed them, stealing the painting and attempting to sell it and almost getting the police on their trail. Caroline was a petty thief who'd messed with the big boys. She'd deserved to die. But children?

He knelt down to inspect Sunny's wound. A deep gash split the top of her head. Blood spouted from it, matting her hair, running in a frightening torrent down her forehead. Her eyes opened suddenly and she looked at him through all that blood. He knew she'd heard what Krendler had said.

"Please," she murmured, "save the children, please just let them go . . ."

A look of pain crossed Valenti's handsome face. No sailboat, no rich lifestyle was worth the lives of two small children. He got to his feet. Krendler's wheelchair waited by the open French doors. It was his prop in the game of theater he played: one character was the bravely disabled rich businessman and opera lover; the other the privately ruthless sociopath who cared for no one. Not even his chief ally, Valenti.

"You'll have to help me with her," Valenti told him.

A look of distaste crossed Krendler's face as they lifted Sunny into the wheelchair, dropping her cruelly into it, making her cry out and put her hands up to her bloody head in pain.

In her pocket Sunny felt the phone vibrate again. She prayed it was Mac, that he'd got her message, that he would come to the villa, that he would save those children. But where were they? What had Krendler done to them? She could hear them calling. And then she passed out again.

79.

Billy knew he had slept too long. Normally he was a light sleeper and an early riser, but there was just something about the heat today, the storm and the soft tropical rainfall that had gotten to him.

He glanced at his sensible black Breitling chronograph watch Betsy had bought him years ago. He'd never worn any other. It had ticked away the minutes of their lives together, and eventually her death. He would never part with it.

Now though, it told him he had been sleeping for almost two hours. Leaping out of bed, instantly alert, and wondering what his little girl was up to, he showered, then in shorts and a cool fresh green plaid cotton shirt went to find her.

He was surprised when Laureen did not answer his knock. He opened the door and peeked inside. Not there. He thought about Bertrand, hesitated for a minute, not liking to disturb the boy's privacy, but guessed Bertrand would know where Laureen was.

He tapped on Bertrand's door and waited. Again no reply. He tapped again and tried the handle. The door was locked. "Bertrand?" he called.

The chambermaid coming down the hall with her cart said, "Bertrand went out. I saw him with your daughter a while ago."

Billy walked downstairs to the bar. People were grumbling about the storm and outside was wet with rain. He'd slept through the whole thing. He worried about the kids but guessed Laureen would have not gone out in the storm, she knew how dangerous lightning was. They were probably walking the dog and would be back any minute. He ordered a beer, sat back, relaxed.

A few minutes later Mac walked into the hall, cell phone in hand. He was staring at the phone with a worried look. Billy waved but Mac was already talking on the phone again. He held one hand over his ear, pacing back and forth, speaking rapidly. There was an expression on his usually genial face Billy had not seen before, a frown of tension between his brows, a tight line to his mouth, a firm snap as he shut down the phone.

Mac walked over to Billy, took the seat next to his, ordered a Grey Goose on the rocks with a twist.

"You haven't seen Sunny by any chance?" he asked.

Billy shook his head. "I just got up. Went looking for my kids but they've gone missing. Out walking the new dog, I guess."

"Sunny was doing the same thing. She called me a while ago, left a message. She said the *Blue Picasso* was in the bay."

Billy gave an astonished whistle. "Then Valenti is back?"

Mac took a slug of his drink. There was something wrong with this scenario. He didn't like that Sunny had not returned. And now Billy said the kids were missing.

The yellow dog bounded into the hall and skidded to a halt. It ran to Billy and shook itself violently, spattering him with rainwater. Then it jumped at Mac almost knocking him over. Its tail flapped furiously and it began to bark. It jumped up and down some more, then ran to the door, turning to look at them.

"Y'think he wants us to go with him?" Billy asked, mystified. Just as Pirate limped up the steps and leapt into Mac's arms.

"Whoa, whoa, steady my boy, steady." Mac got a grip on him but Pirate was barking frantically. He jumped down, ran to the door, stood next to Yellow Dog. Both dogs' heads were turned toward them.

Billy rammed on his hat. Outside the gates they turned right. Mac had already guessed where the dogs were taking them. On his left the *Blue Picasso* was moored in the bay.

"Valenti's gonna get away," Billy warned.

"Not this time. I've already alerted the coast guard. And the cops."

They were running now, keeping up with the dogs whose barks led them to their destination. In no time they were at Chez La Violette. The gates were open and so was the front door. Krendler was pushing Sunny in a wheelchair down the shallow steps. Her head lolled and blood streamed down her face. Slung over Krendler's shoulder was an assault rifle.

In a split second Mac took in his woman, bloody and looking half-dead, Krendler's powerful weapon, the gloating expression on his face.

"Get back, Billy," he warned, giving him an almighty shove into the bushes. He couldn't have Billy getting in the way.

"I'm gonna get him," Billy yelled, re-emerging. Mac shoved him back again.

"Let me handle this," he said.

Krendler was looking at them now, with that superior little half smile, if it could be called that, on his thin lips.

"*Eh bien,* if it's not the superdetective himself. I thought you might have done better than this, Mr. Reilly. After all"—he nodded at the barely conscious Sunny—"it's all over now but the crying."

He tilted Sunny's head forward so Mac could see the blood starting to coagulate but still running from the long gash across her scalp. "Too bad she stumbled onto something she shouldn't have." He shrugged. "But that's the price she has to pay. And now you too, Mr. Reilly. In fact I have all of you here now, in my power."

The assault rifle was in Krendler's hands, pointed at Mac. He meant business.

Mac could feel the bulk of the small-caliber gun under his armpit. It was no match for a heavy-duty weapon like Krendler's, even if he could get to it before Krendler opened fire.

"Where's my kids?" Billy bellowed, staggering from the bushes again, momentarily diverting Krendler's attention.

Sunny suddenly came to life. She jerked her arm up, knocking Krendler's rifle sideways. And then Mac had his pistol pointing at Krendler.

The assault rifle lay next to Krendler's right foot. Mac knew he could drop, grab the rifle, shoot. He could still harm Sunny, break her neck with one blow. He would kill him if he so much as moved a finger.

The *wha-wha* whine of police cars came from the lane.

With a sudden vicious push Krendler sent the wheelchair whizzing down the steps at Mac. The chair trembled on the edge, wobbled, tilted. Sunny went flying, face-first. Krendler reached for the rifle. In the split second given him, Mac had no time to take aim. He shot at a moving target.

Krendler's scream shattered the sudden silence. Mac shot again. Krendler was on the ground, moaning.

A police car growled up the drive, sirens blaring, blue lights flashing, followed by a second, then a third. Cops poured out of them like in an old Keystone Kops movie. The first group covered Krendler. The second ran into the house. Someone called for ambulances.

Billy ran past them, as did the yellow dog heading for La Violette's boudoir, where Gianni Valenti stood, a hand on each child's shoulder, looking at him.

"I wouldn't have hurt them," Valenti said, shoving the children away.

"Bastard," Billy snarled.

"Daddeeee," Laureen wailed as Billy hit Valenti so hard he heard his nose crack.

Valenti fell to the floor, hands to his face, blood everywhere. Laureen hurled herself into Billy's arms. The yellow dog wagged its tail anxiously at an alabaster-faced Bertrand. And the expensive paintings, propped against the sofa, toppled slowly, in a domino effect, to the ground.

"And all for that," Billy said bitterly, watching them fall, clutching his daughter to him, and putting his free arm round Bertrand.

Outside Mac was on his knees next to Sunny. He cradled her bleeding head, his pain for her in his eyes.

She looked up at him. "Well, if it isn't Colonel Mustard to the rescue." She was laughing at him, remembering the old Clue board game they liked as he folded her gratefully into his arms and kissed her.

"The children?" she asked. And then she passed out.

80.

Laureen perched on the edge of Billy's bed, a plump frazzled nymph in a ragged orange tutu. She wiggled her bare toes, wondering what had happened to her cowboy boots. Bertrand sat next to her. His glasses were lopsided and one lens was cracked. He gripped his hands so tightly together the knuckles showed white.

The pair had told their story to the police, who had been gentle and understanding, though very businesslike. François Reynaud had driven over to see what he could do to help. They had been checked out by a doctor, who found some bruises but nothing to worry about, and now they were waiting for Billy to tell them they shouldn't have done it.

"I know, Daddy," Laureen said, beating him to it.

"Know what, sweetheart?" He stood in front of them, arms folded over his chest, thanking God he still had them. He was certainly not about to give them a telling off.

"You feeling better now?" he said, beginning to pace the floor so he wouldn't keep on thinking about what might have happened, though the children didn't seem aware of the true danger. They had not seen Sunny bleeding on the step, not seen Krendler shot by Mac, not heard his screams of agony. Valenti had hauled them out from behind the paneling where Laureen told him they'd been for only a short while.

"Anyhow I always knew Mommy would find me," she said confidently, fingers busily smoothing out her ragged tulle skirt. "She always knows where I am."

"It wasn't really truly bad, Daddy," she said, though he did notice her slight shiver. "Besides, Bertrand looked after me."

"Bertrand is a hero," Billy said. "And so are you."

Laureen glanced sideways at her friend. He was sitting in that stiff soldier position like he did when there was bad news. She gave him a nudge, wondering what was up.

"It's okay, Bertrand," she said. "We found Monsieur Reynaud's paintings, remember? Now we get the reward."

Bertrand was remembering those scary moments when the big man, Krendler, had appeared. When Krendler had heard someone coming—it was Sunny he knew that now—he'd told Valenti to shut them in the secret room where the paintings had been stored. They hadn't been able to hear what was going on but had kept on yelling, hoping someone would hear them and let them out.

Then Valenti had come back and Billy had busted his nose and they'd been hustled out of there so fast there was no time to take in exactly what was going on. They were whisked back to the hotel in a police car, sirens blaring, which he and Laureen had quite enjoyed, but now he was worried about what his mother was going to say when she found out about it. Even five hundred thousand euros might not be enough to get away from her.

"You acted like a brother to Laureen," Billy said, watching the emotions play across the boy's young face. "You looked out for her, son, and I appreciate that."

"Thank you, sir. I mean Billy," Bertrand corrected himself.

"I'm hungry," Little Laureen said suddenly. "I think I need spaghetti and french fries."

Billy grinned at the two of them, thanking God for the resilience of small children. Kids would be kids. "Ice cream too, if you want," he said generously.

Sunny lay on her terrace, her head stitched and bandaged, sipping a Cosmo. The peacocks flew across the lawn with a great clatter of wings, making for the big cedar tree where they would roost for the night. "I needed something girly and pink," she said appreciatively to Mac.

"Anything you want," he replied, finally at peace with himself.

Krendler was in hospital in Nice with an armed policeman at his bedside, recovering from abdominal wounds and a shattered shoulder. And Valenti was in jail.

The coast guard had taken the *Blue Picasso* apart, ripping out the paneling, and found several more artworks stored in the space behind. The brindle greyhound had been taken to a safe place and would be found a new home—and a long life, as opposed to its probable fate at Krendler's hands.

Headlines had already flashed around the world. Both men were charged with murder; attempted murder; kidnapping; robbery and conspiracy for multiple grand theft. The French police had thrown the book at them.

Sunny was eyeing Mac from under the bandage that crisscrossed her eyebrows, giving her a kind of half-mummified look. "You know I'm a lot like you," she said. He raised a questioning eyebrow. "I'm an 'all-American' girl," she explained.

Of course, now he remembered telling her he was an "all-American guy" the night they'd dined at Le Grill in the Hôtel de Paris in Monte Carlo, instead of the grand Michelin three-star restaurant. "You want a steak," he hazarded a guess.

Sunny shook her head, wincing because she had forgotten the twelve stitches that crossed her scalp. "A hot dog." She sighed with longing. "Mustard and onions. Maybe some relish."

"You got it." Mac wondered where the hell he would find a hot dog in a small French hotel. "Anything else?"

She didn't shake her head this time, merely said, "No thank you. I think I'll just close my eyes for a few minutes while you're gone though."

Tesoro snuggled deeper on her lap. Pirate sat with his chin propped on her knee. Love radiated around. It was a picture Mac would treasure forever. He took a quick photo on his cell phone; his poor wounded brave Sunny had never looked more beautiful and he had never been more scared in his life.

"Hurry back, Colonel Mustard," he heard her call mockingly as he closed the door.

Downstairs he met Billy with Laureen and Bertrand and the yellow dog, all cleaned up and heading for their table in the courtyard.

"You're just the person I need to talk to," he told Bertrand. And then, because he couldn't speak enough French to explain to the kitchen exactly what it was Sunny wanted, he asked the boy to translate.

Of course the dog went with Bertrand, though it was not admitted to the kitchen. It waited outside till he came out then followed him back to the table. The yellow dog never left Bertrand's side.

"The chef says he will do his best," Bertrand said. "He says it may not be a genuine American hot dog, but he has mustard and he is making some relish."

"Homemade relish," Mac said impressed. He was also impressed with the two children.

Little Laureen was leaning against her daddy and his arm was around her shoulder. She wasn't sucking her thumb but she looked as though she would like to. She had changed into a fresh pink tutu—the orange one was pretty well wrecked, what with struggling when Valenti had pushed them into the little space behind the paneling and shut them in.

"I can't tell you how brave you were," Mac told them. "I think the French should give you both a medal."

Laureen perked up. "Will the Wizard Reynaud really give Bertrand the reward?"

"You bet he will," Mac said. "He's thrilled to have his paintings back. He told me he always knew you two would find them for him."

The children grinned at each other and the yellow dog settled under a chair the way a proper French dog that belonged to somebody should. The waiter brought a bowl of water and Bertrand sneaked the dog some chicken. He was so happy he wished this moment could go on forever.

Mac lowered his voice as he spoke to Billy, so the boy would not hear. "I discussed the reward with Reynaud. Because of the problem with the mother, we decided the five hundred thousand euros should be put immediately into a trust fund for Bertrand."

"Before she can get her hands on it, you mean," Billy said. He knew all about Bertrand's mother. Had he been in Texas, he would have set the child welfare services on her. No woman should be allowed to get away with what she'd done, abandoning her son, not even paying the hotel bill, which incidentally, he had taken care of himself. *And* telling her son he was not wanted. Billy's blood boiled at the thought.

Bertrand was no longer smiling though. He was thinking that, all too soon, Laureen and Billy would be leaving. And so would Mac and Sunny, and the rest of the little band he'd called the Riders on the Storm. He would be alone. Again. He wondered what he would do. He couldn't just stay here, at the hotel; in November they would close up for the winter months, opening again in the spring. And spring was an eternity away.

There was a sudden commotion and the dog lumbered to its feet. A young woman pushed her way past the waiters to their table. A photographer was with her.

"You must be the children who solved the Reynaud art theft," she said, as the photographer snapped busily.

Mac grinned. "Upstaged again," he said, just as the chef appeared with a tray on which resided a pale, whitish andouille sausage, a brioche split in half, a pile of chopped scallions, a small pot of dark mustard and a compote of figs and raisins in a little glass bowl.

"Alors, the pauvre Madame Alvarez's 'hot dog,' " the mustached chef said proudly.

Mac congratulated him on his new take on a traditional American theme and, leaving Billy to deal with "the local press," carried the tray upstairs.

Sunny was exactly where he'd left her. Tesoro was still on her lap, Pirate's head still on her knee. The Cosmo was finished though.

Mac removed Tesoro, who grumbled and attempted a little nip. He placed the tray on Sunny's lap.

"Voilà," he said, removing the dome with a flourish. *"Madame's* hot dog."

"Jesus," Sunny said, eyeing it warily.

Still, she ate that sausage in the brioche, smothered in mustard and scallions and fig and raisin relish. And enjoyed every last bite. Then she fell asleep in Mac's arms.

He was grateful the day was over.

81.

Lev was propping up the bar, something he seemed to do a lot of in his profession, only this time it was at the Moulin de Hubert. He was sipping a cold Perrier with lemon and keeping an eye on Belinda who, with a waitress's white apron over her jeans, flitted between tables delivering plates of Roger's nightly specials, the beef *daube*, as well as a *gigot*, roast lamb from the Alpilles hills that smelled wonderfully of rosemary and mint. Lev promised himself some of that later, when the rush had died down and the customers were drifting away into that warm clear Provençal night.

Looking at Belinda, simple in a T-shirt and jeans, unmade up, cropped blond hair gleaming, not a diamond in sight, he thought you'd never know she was married to a rich man.

Sara hurried light-footedly past him, five plates perfectly balanced, one in each hand, two up one arm, one up the other. Sara had obviously worked as a waitress before. He had to admit she looked cute, in white shorts, her now sun-bronzed but still skinny legs flashing beneath her big apron. She threw him a cheeky wink as she came back.

"You know something?" she said, hands on hips, taking him in from head to foot. "You look exactly like a security guard."

"Is that right?"

"Know something else? That tune you're always whistling? It's by the Pogues. 'Summer in Siam' it's called."

"God, Sara, you're right. It's been driving me crazy." Sara was not the kind of girl he would have expected to know a rarefied punk group like the Pogues.

"They were my favorite in college. I have every record they ever made, as well as the ones by Shane MacGowan himself. I happen to think they're very romantic."

It was not a word Lev would have applied to the raucous Irish group who could raise the roof and boost the beer level at any concert. Yet, when he thought about it, Sara was right. There were lovely melodies and gentle meaningful lyrics amongst their gritty streetwise Irish hearts. "Christmas in New York," Lev remembered another favorite.

"The best." They punched fists together and Sara went on her way. She turned at the kitchen door. "Hey, know what?" she said. "I'm having a *great* time." There was a big smile on her face as she swung confidently through the door.

Nate took a seat next to Lev. He had a new look tonight, more casual, more "Provençal," Lev decided with a grin. White shirt, jeans, flip-flops and a red cotton neckerchief tied at his throat. Nate's thick dark hair had grown longer and he had a tan from riding the bike as well as from the beach, yet despite it all, he still looked like the New York businessman abroad.

"Gotta try the lamb," Nate said, downing a glass of red wine, then going behind the bar and helping himself to more. "It beats any I've ever had."

"I'll get around to it." Lev was on duty; as long as Belinda was there it was his job to keep watch. His phone rang. He checked and saw it was Mac.

"Okay," he said, "what's up?"

He listened for a minute, then said, "You're kidding me." His eyes met Nate's inquiring ones.

"But she's all right," he said finally. "And the kids?"

He listened some more, then he said he would tell the others and get back to him.

"What?" Nate asked.

Lev looked at Belinda and Sara, running back and forth to the kitchen to speak to Roger. They were having a good time and for once not thinking of Jasper Lord.

"Later," he told Nate. "When they've finished and we can all talk."

It was almost midnight when they finally settled round the big table near the bar. Wine was poured and large plates of the rosemary lamb with mint sauce, tiny new potatoes and exquisite little sautéed bright orange and yellow squashes served. Everyone was hungry, chattering, happy. Lev hated to be the one to break the news.

Aware of Nate's eyes on him, he waited till they'd finished eating and were sitting back, sipping wine, sighing with pleasure.

"Okay, so I have some news," he said.

They listened in silence while he told the story of what had happened at Chez La Violette.

"Oh my God," Belinda cried. "Sunny could have been killed. And those poor children."

"Men are beasts!" Sara exclaimed, earning a wry smile from Nate. "I mean, sometimes they are," she added. "Like Krendler and Valenti."

"We can't just sit here and talk about it," Belinda said. "We have to go back, see everything's all right . . . I need to give Sunny a hug."

"And those kids," Sara added.

Lev noticed Sara looked pale under her tan and knew she was frightened. Violence was a long way from her calm routine life. The worst that had ever happened to her was that she had picked a dud boyfriend.

"I know what you're thinking," Sara said suddenly to him. "You think all that's ever happened to me was picking a dud boyfriend."

Lev stared at her, astonished.

"It's true," she said. "But I love Sunny. I love those kids. I love you, Belinda, and you, Nate." She looked at Lev. "Even you. And now Malcolm and Roger."

The chef sat back. He glanced worriedly at Malcolm, not quite sure he understood what was going on.

"I've come a long way," Sara said, "and I'm not going to let my friends down now. I have to go and see they're okay."

Lev checked the time. He said, "At least let's wait till morning." He knew there was no dissuading them but hoped that in daylight they might listen to reason. He wanted to keep Belinda here, under lock and key if possible, at least until Jasper Lord was taken care of.

"We'll set off at dawn," Belinda said.

Nate groaned. "Again?"

"We must see they are all right," Sara said stubbornly. "Then we'll come back."

There was no controlling them, Lev had to go along with it. "It's still dangerous," he warned. "The husband can return any time."

"Not now he's been kicked out of the country," Belinda said confidently.

Lev sighed. Didn't she understand there were no borders in Europe? Jasper Lord could enter by car from anywhere and be back in St. Tropez the same time they were. What Lev would bet on though, was that this time he would not use the red helicopter.

Despite her worry, Sara hated to leave. And so, she'd bet, did Nate. She'd noticed the bunch of giant sunflowers in the red vase on the stone window ledge. Only a man in love would do a thing like that, a man in love with a place.

She and Belinda were installed in the top-floor master bedroom. Below them, in the yellow room, was Nate, and below that, on the sofa in the living room was Lev.

Looking out of the bedroom window when they finally got back from the Moulin, Sara thought she had never seen such a dense darkness. No lights anywhere, just ink black countryside, sleeping, like the residents of the village. The silence, the very peacefulness, awoke a yearning in her and she knew she wanted to stay. She would talk to Malcolm and Roger later about becoming their permanent waitress. She told herself that after all, everyone had to start at the bottom, and besides she had enjoyed herself tonight, chatting with the customers, who hadn't grumbled, even when they'd been a bit slow getting food to the table.

Belinda was propped up in the black leather bed, still in her T-shirt, staring blankly in front of her. Sara thought she looked exhausted. How could she not, with a mad husband chasing her, ready to kill? He would never find her here though.

The window looked like a black canvas against the exposed stone wall. "A Rothko," Belinda decided. "And then when there's a full moon, it'll be a different artist. Imagine that, Sara, Nate gets to have a different painting every night."

They looked at each other, still not voicing what was uppermost on their minds. "Jesus, Sara," Belinda said shakily at last. "They might have been killed."

"They might," Sara agreed. "But they were not, and now we have to go back and tell them we love them."

"Kiss them better," Belinda said.

Sara eyed her critically. "You look as though you need some kissing better yourself. You need to get away from the husband permanently."

Belinda shrugged. "How to do it, that's the question."

"Divorce." Sara was practical.

Belinda laughed. "And here speaks the girl who less than two weeks ago walked out on the boyfriend. And what happened? He came looking for her. You and I have a lot in common, Sara, or at least, the same taste in men."

"I know." Sara did understand how difficult it was. "But I'm afraid for you," she said simply.

Belinda's sparkly blue eyes no longer sparkled as she said, "I'm scared too, Sara."

82.

"We're going the back way," Lev said, guiding the big Bentley out of the village very early the next morning. "Through a gorge, very scenic. Kind of a shortcut."

"A gorge? Does that mean like a twisty canyon road?" Belinda asked nervously.

"Kinda medium twisty." Lev didn't want to tell them he wanted to keep as far away as possible from the main routes just in case the husband was on the prowl. Of course eventually they would have to link up with the A8-E80, before cutting down the one and only road to St. Tropez. The same road where Sara had almost been hijacked. He was well aware it could happen again, and also aware it might happen anywhere. Jasper Lord was a high-powered mobster, he had money and pressure to spare. He would find his wife if it was the last thing he did, and Lev was now quite certain that if he did, it would also be the last thing Belinda did.

In the backseat Sara was pouring coffee from a thermos, slopping it over the sides of the paper cups as Lev took the curves.

"We could have stopped at a café and bought some," Nate complained, glancing over his shoulder at Sara mopping up the seat with paper napkins, while Belinda took a large bite out of a hefty sandwich.

"Turkey, ham and Swiss," she said, passing it over to him.

"This is Provence, not New York," he said. "Where d'you get turkey, ham and Swiss?"

"At the local Spar mini-market. They have everything there." She caught his tut-tutting frown and said, "Hey, I'm a junk-foodie at heart. Enough of all this fancy French stuff."

She was laughing at him and Nate knew it. He wished he could simply keep on being impulsive, the way he had when he'd bought the house. It was going to take time but he would get there. Look at Sara. God knows, if she could change, anybody could. He was sure within a year he'd be out of his Manhattan moneyman straitjacket and hanging out at the Moulin, with Malcolm and Roger. And he'd bet his life Sara would be running the place and have them making a profit for the first time.

"Good," he said, passing the sandwich on to Lev, who took an appreciative bite and passed it over his shoulder to Sara.

"Coffee?" Sara handed a paper cup to Nate, managing to spill it again as Lev curved round the ever-curving road.

"Oh my gosh." She peered out the window. "Belinda, will you just look at those cliffs?"

They were on a snaking white road leading through a narrow gorge, cliff on one side, sheer drop on the other. Only thing was, Lev hadn't expected to see so many trucks. Obviously, this was a route truckers also used as a shortcut. Keeping well back, he allowed yet another truck to pass.

Belinda hid her face in her shoulder. "I can't even look," she wailed, managing another peek at the boulder-strewn drop on their right.

"It's okay, Belinda, it'll soon be over." Sara looked up at the cliff. "Jesus," she muttered, then remembered Little Laureen would have told her not to take the Lord's name in vain. And you know what, she told herself, that child was right.

A helicopter clattered overhead. Lev peered upward. It was regulation silver color, not red. Still it worried him. They were coming to the end of the gorge, only a couple more miles to go, already the gradient had changed. The helicopter clattered overhead again. Alarmed, Lev glanced up again. Out of the corner of his eye he was aware of a large car approaching. It was maybe a couple of hundred yards away.

Instinct sensed danger. The car had Italian number plates. Now it was coming right at them. The bald, bullet-headed man in the passenger seat was aiming a black semiautomatic.

Maybe two seconds had passed.

"Get down," Lev yelled, ramming his foot to the metal.

"What . . . why . . . ?"

Sara shoved Belinda's head down and threw herself on top of her. Nate crouched forward, hands over his head, he wasn't sure why since a bullet would pierce anything.

The *rat-a-tat-tat* of gunfire echoed from the cliff, but instead of attempting to avoid the oncoming car, Lev swung the Bentley fast into its path. He saw the other driver panic, tug hard at the wheel, swerve to his left. The semi jerked upward, bullets ripped holes in the Italian car's own roof. And then it toppled, gently, almost in slow motion, over the cliff.

Trucks screeched to a stop. Men got out, stood at the edge of the gorge, looking down at the now blazing car, gesticulating wildly, telephoning the cops, running to the white Bentley, balanced precariously, one front wheel over the chasm.

Inside the car there was a terrible silence. The very air seemed to tremble. It felt as though even a breath would send them over the edge.

"Stay absolutely still." Lev's voice was quiet, controlled.

Nobody was moving anyway.

Sara was a lightweight but even now, when she knew they might be dead any second, she worried she was crushing Belinda, pinned underneath her. It was the first time Sara had known Belinda to be silent.

Nate remained crouched in the front seat, not even daring to remove his hands from over his head, even though now there were no bullets. He was thinking it was a pity that, when he'd finally found himself, he was going to die.

The big car shivered as the right front wheel slid a couple of inches farther over the edge.

Belinda waited for her life to pass before her closed eyes, the way it was supposed to just before you died. It did not. Instead she was swept by a terrible surge of anger at the husband. Her friends were going to die because he was an insane control freak. Goddamit, he'd even shot at them. The only consolation was that he must surely be dead now. But what sort of consolation was that when she was going to die too? Jasper Lord had achieved his last wish.

Lev kept his foot on the brake. Faces appeared in his window, yelling at him in French. Men flanked both sides. A dozen men were lifting the heavy car. Lev stared down into the chasm as the car trembled again, inches from the ground, floating for seconds in midair. Then it was lowered, like a giant beast, on all four great paws of its tires, back onto the highway.

"It's okay, you can breathe now," Lev said. Everything considered, he was pretty glad to be breathing himself.

Men were opening the doors. Belinda and Sara tumbled in a terrified heap onto the road. Nate took his head from his hands and looked round, stunned. Lev got out, reaching to shake the hands of the truck drivers who had saved them, just as police cars screamed round the bend, blue lights flashing.

Sara sat in the road, too traumatized to move, but Belinda scrambled to her feet. She peered into the car.

"Damn it, Sara," she said in a shaky voice. "You spilled coffee all over my leather seats."

And then she burst into tears.

83.

Hours later, the four of them were still sitting in the emergency room at the local hospital. No one had so much as a bruise. Sara had finally stopped trembling, Belinda had stopped crying, and Nate had finally begun to think he would live to see his new home again.

Lev was cool. It was all over now. The bodies were too charred to be recognizable, but he'd seen that it was Jasper Lord aiming the semi, and recognized the driver as one of the thugs from the nightclub. There had been two other men in the backseat. Now Lord and the others would be identified only by their dental records.

He'd made himself known to the police, told them the story, gone over the Bentley with them inch by inch until they found the GPS tracking device Lev had guessed would be there, planted under the chassis. Of course that's how Lord had known where to find Belinda. And this time he had not intended to let her get away, even if it meant putting a bullet through her himself. The silver helicopter was soon traced to a tiny local airport. It had been rented by one of Lord's men who had followed the Bentley's progress from the village to the canyon, keeping Lord informed while he drove up to meet it.

Obviously it was reckless behavior, even for a man as narcissistic, controlling and powerful as Jasper Lord, and it was that same obsessive behavior that had brought his end.

Sitting on a plastic chair, sipping a terrible cup of coffee with about six sugars in it, Belinda said, "I thought I cared about him, once upon a time, you know."

Sara patted her hand comfortingly. "Of course you did. You wouldn't have married him otherwise."

"Wouldn't I?" Belinda's bright blue eyes were bleak. "You've no idea how many times I've asked myself that question."

Nate sipped his own cup of bad coffee, no sugars. "So what was your answer?"

Belinda stared into the foam cup for a long moment. "I think it was the diamond necklace in the fish and chips newspaper that did it," she said finally. "It just, y'know"—she gave a little shrug—"it just seemed to capture the essence of who I was. I thought to myself, Well, here's a man who finally understands me. He knows I'll always be that Essex girl underneath the couture, and I thought that's what he loved." She shrugged again. "How wrong I was."

Sara tried a little comforting again. "I'll bet he loved you, once."

Belinda gave her a withering look. "For God's sake, Sara, of course he didn't. He just wanted to own me. I didn't understand it then, but he bought and paid for me. 'Love' had nothing to do with it."

Sara sank farther down in her plastic chair, staring wordlessly at the tile floor.

"Oh, *Saraaaaa!*" Belinda was on her knees in front of her. "The husband was never my friend. *Never.* Not like you. Do you think I'll ever forget what you did for me today? Do you imagine I won't go over and over again how you threw yourself on top of me to protect me? Without even thinking of your own safety? Sara Strange, I will love you forever. You are my best, my very dearest, my most wonderful friend."

Sara blinked away the tears, and said, "Even though I spilled coffee all over your leather seats?"

Belinda grinned. "Fuck the leather seats."

A look of shock crossed Sara's sweet face, then "Fuck the leather seats," she agreed, as they burst out laughing.

Lev had been on the phone to Mac for a long time. "Okay, let's go," he said finally. "A small plane's waiting at the local airport to take us back to St. Tropez."

The three looked at each other. "Wanna bet that Mac'll be waiting for us, at our table in the courtyard, bottles of rosé chilling, wanting to know what his Misfits have been up to?" Nate said.

"So, maybe now you can tell him you've found yourselves," observant Lev said, surprising them.

84.

Two nights later, Mac was surveying his little band of Misfits assembled once again around their long table in the courtyard at the Hôtel des Rêves. They were drinking a gorgeous champagne, vintage Billecart-Salmon rosé— Billy's treat, and the color of overripe peaches. Sunny's head was no longer bandaged but the two black eyes she'd gotten when she fell from the wheel-chair made her look like a raccoon. Mac still couldn't believe the others were unhurt. Especially Belinda.

"That's because Sara protected me," Belinda said. "*I* still can't believe she threw herself on top of me like that."

Sara blushed. "I didn't stop to think about it, I just knew the husband was out to get you."

"He could have gotten you instead."

"Not anymore, he can't," Lev said.

Belinda looked worriedly at him. "Why do I feel so guilty that he's dead?"

"It was you or him," he reminded her. "You're guilty of nothing." Lev knew that a dozen truckers had already testified the big Italian car had made straight for them, and started firing.

Silence fell. Mac's eyes met Sunny's swollen ones. "I think it's time we all thought of ourselves instead of the bad guys," he said. "A celebration is called for."

"More champagne?" Sara said, brightening.

Mac thought Sara had seriously improved since he first encountered her, timid and tearful, humiliated and possibly heartbroken in the driveway of Chez

La Violette. He also noticed that Billy had a protective arm round the back of Belinda's chair. And that Belinda didn't seem to mind. In fact she snuggled into Billy, giving him a plaintive upward glance every now and then that Mac knew was really getting to him. And also, every now and then, he saw that Billy checked the dining room, where Little Laureen and Bertrand sat together at his table in the window, no doubt consuming more spaghetti, though Laureen had now confided that she also liked her spaghetti with just ketchup. Sunny had almost gagged at the thought, but reminded herself kids would be kids.

Bertrand had on the new glasses Billy had bought to replace the big ugly ones with the broken lense. The boy had picked them out himself, plain wire granny glasses that blended in so you actually saw his angular face underneath the thatch of blond fringe. And tonight Little Laureen wore her palest pink tutu with her princess tiara and the cowboy boots—retrieved from the villa. As always, she had on her silver heart necklace, and her star-tipped wand lay on the table next to her. Tesoro was on her lap and Pirate on the floor next to the yellow dog. Despite the flea bath, all the dogs were scratching.

The two children were the stars of the show. Everyone in the hotel knew what had happened. Broad smiles were thrown their way and the other children had crowded round wanting to know all about how they'd captured the robbers.

Fresh bottles of champagne were called for. A chilled gazpacho had just been served when Mac heard Bertrand's name being called. He turned to look.

The big blond woman standing at Bertrand's table radiated anger and disapproval.

He saw Bertrand scramble to his feet, fumbling with his glasses, hitching up his shorts, spilling his Coca-Cola.

"Just look at you, boy," he heard the woman say, angrily. "How dare you go round looking like that, after all the time and money I've spent on you and your education? Get up at once and go pack your things. We'll be leaving first thing in the morning."

"Billy," Mac said, "Bertrand's mother is here."

The yellow dog lumbered to his feet and stood next to Bertrand. Pirate sat, ears perked, alert for trouble, and Tesoro gave her police siren wail.

Laureen jumped down from her chair and went and stood next to her friend. This mother was nothing at all like Cruella De Vil. She was all puffy: puffy eyes, puffy chest and puffy mouth. Laureen didn't see how a skinny rake like Bertrand could ever belong to her. She held tight on to his hand.

Billy was already at their table, followed by Mac. "You planning on taking this boy away, ma'am?" Billy asked, looking tall, wide and very Texan in his ten-gallon hat.

"What's it to you?" The woman eyed him dismissively. "I heard about the danger my son was in and I've come here to protect him, make sure he's all right."

"A bit late for that, ma'am, isn't it?" Billy moved a step closer. "I wonder if it was because you heard about the reward. The five hundred thousand euros?"

"Of course I heard about it." Her voice was very high up, cold, snappy, dismissive. "I read the newspaper, don't I? And I intend to make sure that money is properly invested. I'm having the documents drawn up this very minute. We'll see the *notaire* tomorrow to sign them."

"And no doubt sign over Bertrand's reward to you," Mac said. He had her number, though it didn't take much, she was so transparent.

"Taking advantage of an eleven-year-old boy," Billy added. "I think there are enough people round here who care about your son, and are willing to see that does not happen."

"In fact, *ma'am*," Mac added, with irony in the way he said the word *ma'am*, as though he couldn't stand even to give her the title, "Monsieur Reynaud, who gave the reward has already made sure the money is in trust in Bertrand's name. He will personally administer that trust and take care of your son's interests."

They could have sworn he saw the woman's blood boil. Her face purpled unbecomingly next to her bleached platinum hair.

At the other tables, people had stopped eating and were listening intently. They all knew Bertrand's story. They had gossiped about him being dumped by his mother, about the unpaid hotel bill, commented on his shabby appearance, his old-fashioned glasses and the uncut hair. Now Bertrand had become their local hero and there wasn't one of them who would see him done down by this uncaring woman who called herself a mother.

Madame Olivier, or whatever her new Italian married name was, turned a venomous look on Bertrand. "You ungrateful child," she hissed, smacking her fist so hard on the table plates rattled. Yellow Dog snarled and showed his teeth. "I'll work this out tomorrow. Meanwhile, get your things. We're leaving."

"I assume you plan on paying the bill before you leave," Billy said. "It must be quite a fair sum by now."

"Bertrand's trust can pay for it." She faced Billy defiantly. "And who the hell are you anyway, taking so much interest in my son."

"I am not your son." Bertrand spoke.

There was total silence in the dining room and at the tables in the court-yard. Waiters had stopped serving, the chef and kitchen workers hovered at the open kitchen door and Renée stood guard at the entrance.

"I . . . I am . . . n-n-n-n-n-n-nobody's-s s-son." Bertrand almost choked on his stammer.

Laureen squeezed his hand hard. "Bertrand is my friend," she said defiantly.

The woman gave her a contemptuous up and down look. "Another god-damn little freak," she said.

Billy stepped forward, towering angrily over her. Mac held him back. "You can't win this one in the short term," he warned. Then he said, "Ma'am, you left your son here alone for almost two months, with no contact from you. In fact you abandoned him, as everyone in this room will attest, in court if necessary. You told your son there was no place for him in your new family. You left the hotel bill unpaid, and mounting up, and you are only back here now to lay claim to your son's hard-earned reward. Let me tell you, Bertrand is a hero, but you have no praise for him. He's clever and you disparage him. He is a boy any man would be proud to claim as his son, and you belittle him."

"And you can bet my Texan boots he's never going back to you," Billy snarled.

Furious, Madame Olivier swung round, only to be faced by a roomful of diners, the men on their feet, faces glowering. She swung back again, stared at her son, lifted her hand as though to strike him. Pirate's and the Yellow Dog's hackles rose. She caught Billy's furious eye.

"I'll be back for you tomorrow, Bertrand," she said. "Have your things packed and be ready to leave by nine A.M."

The men did not move as she pushed past them, but their eyes followed her all the way to the door.

Renée put out a hand to stop her. She handed her a sheaf of papers. "*Madame.* Here is your bill. The hotel would like final settlement right away." She winked surreptitiously at Billy, who had already paid it, though Madame Olivier did not know that.

The woman glanced at the amounts, then threw Renée an outraged look. "This is way too much, and anyhow I already said Bertrand would pay this from his new trust."

"I'm afraid Monsieur Reynaud would not allow that." Renée was firm. "We shall expect full payment tomorrow, *madame,* or we will put it in the hands of the authorities."

Madame Olivier hesitated, not quite certain what that meant. Nor in fact was Renée, but it sounded intimidating.

Madame Olivier flung back her long blond hair and flounced in her high heels to the door where the bellboys stood guard. The yellow dog followed her and stood at the top of the steps watching as she stalked down them. Satisfied that she was gone, he padded back to Bertrand.

"Listen, kid," Billy said to Bertrand. "I heard you say that's not your mother. What did you mean by that?"

"She's my mother's sister," Bertrand said, finally able to speak again. "When my father died, and then my real mother, she took over. She got all my father's money. She told me to call her 'Mother.'"

Billy threw a paternal arm around Bertrand's shoulders. "Well then, son, we'll have to see what we can do about that. We'll go speak to Monsieur Reynaud in the morning, see what he can do to help us."

The other diners turned their attention back to their dinners.

"Better wave your magic wand again, Little Laureen," Billy said with a big grin. "And let's see if it can make your wishes come true."

The dogs were scratching again. "Fleas," he added, resignedly. "All the dogs must have 'em by now."

85.

Laureen and Bertrand met at the beach at midnight, then walked to his lair. Yellow Dog walked with them, head down, silent. Bertrand wore his cape and the binoculars, and Laureen her tutu, a beach towel and flip-flops. There had been no need to try to avoid the guards, because they had gone. Even Lev was no longer on official duty, and soon he would be gone too. Everyone was sleeping.

The lizards came out to check them, cautious this time because of the dog, who only sniffed warily and settled down to watch. They sat in silence.

"Bertrand?" Laureen said, after a while.

"Oui?"

"I'm sorry." She wanted to say more: how she had hated the way that woman had spoken to Bertrand; how she wished Yellow Dog had attacked her; how glad she was the woman was not his real mother. But there was no need. "Sorry" was enough.

"Thank you." Bertrand understood.

Silence fell again. The sea swished under the rocks at the foot of the slope, crickets murmured in the background, and with a whir of fast wings a night bird swooped momentarily overhead.

"I like your father," Bertrand said finally.

"And I know he likes you." Laureen glanced sideways at him, sitting bolt upright against his rock. He looked different in the new glasses, more grown-up somehow. All at once she didn't want Bertrand to grow up. She wanted everything to stay the same; she and Bertrand, friends, with their nocturnal meetings and their Scientific Experiments on human relations. Or relatives, or whatever. Soon, though, she would be leaving St. Tropez and her tiny room at the Hôtel des Rêves. She would leave this wonderful place and perhaps never come back. She reached for his hand. She couldn't bear that thought.

"Bertrand?" she said.

"*Oui?*"

"Texas is really nice you know."

He turned his head to look at her. Dark light glinted from his new glasses. "I know."

She said surprised, "But *how* do you know?"

"I've seen it on TV many times."

"Oh. Yeah. Cowboys. Texas is famous, I guess." He had moved his hand away and she touched it again, this time only with one finger. Then she lay back, arms spread, staring up at the sky. No moon, just a couple of fluffy clouds skidding slowly across the surface. She wondered if the sky ever really had a surface that you could touch. She wondered if her mother was there, behind the clouds, watching over her.

"Will your father really help me?" Bertrand asked after a long silent time.

"Of course. He said he would, didn't he? And Daddy always tells the truth. And the Wizard of Reynaud will help you too. I'm sure of it."

Bertrand wished he was so sure. All he was certain of was that tomorrow at nine his "mother" would come to get him. He shuddered at the thought, wondering how he could have wished for her return, all those long weeks after she'd disappeared, and before Little Laureen had come into his life.

"You can share my mother," Laureen said suddenly.

He stared at her, astonished. He didn't like to mention it, but her mother was dead.

Laureen had her hand on the heart necklace. "Don't worry, Bertrand," she said. "Everything will be all right."

Next to them, Yellow Dog snored gently. The lizards slid back into the rock crevices. The air smelled of the seaside and grass and rocks still warm from the sun.

Quite suddenly, Bertrand knew it would be all right.

86.

A few days later, life had calmed down again and Sunny had finally achieved her vacation dream of lying on a soft sandy beach in her best new bikini, the apple green one that tied in cheeky little bows low on the hip and under her breasts, though right now she was topless. Which made Mac nervous.

"You've seen me naked before," she said, lying back, enjoying the guilty pleasure of the sun on her body. Even though she was smothered in sunscreen old habits died hard.

"That's different," Mac said, eyeing the other couples lazing on the beach. Most of the women, like Sunny, were unself-consciously topless, strolling into the water, taking their children for a walk at the edge of the waves, drying off with blue-striped towels. To Mac, they didn't look quite real, more like women in a Bonnard painting, getting out of the bathtub. Only this was the sea and they were far more beautiful.

"See, it's okay," Sunny said. "It's just us being one with nature."

"Right," Mac said. He had to admit the view was pretty good. He said, "Here come Belinda and Sara."

Sunny lifted her head, shading her eyes with one hand. "Hi," she called and waved.

Belinda was topless like Sunny, and Mac averted his eyes. He suspected Sara was too, though now she had a shirt on. They flopped onto the sand next to them and Belinda said she was dying of thirst and Mac waved down a waiter, who had no compunction about looking at Belinda. Nor at Sunny. Did none of these Frenchmen even care? Was it only him?

"Oh don't be such a prude, Mac," Belinda said, giving him a nudge in the ribs. "Remember, you're in the South of France."

He said, "I'm only just beginning to realize it."

"So enjoy it then. We are."

Mac changed the subject. "How are you feeling today?"

She shrugged. "Good. I've gotten over it now, I tell myself it was the best thing that could have happened. It makes it easier to cope with *how* it happened."

"It was always you or him," Mac said. "Lev knew that."

"Wonderful Lev," Sara said, looking thoughtful. "He saved us all. I'll never forget that big car teetering on the edge and feeling that all it would take was one breath from me to send us over."

"I thought it would be my breath," Belinda confessed, and they laughed.

"I'll miss him, though, when he's gone." Sara looked away, and began busily buttoning her shirt. She knew Lev's life was a world apart from hers, and that he was a man who would never be owned. "I guess we'll never meet again, after tonight's dinner," she said sadly.

"The only time anybody meets Lev is when they are in trouble," Sunny said. "So it's better you don't."

The waiter came back with their drinks; no rosé wine today, just Diet Pepsi all round.

"I'm kind of missing Little Laureen and Bertrand," Belinda said, sipping the Pepsi through a curly blue straw. Her tone was casual but they got the message that she was also missing Billy.

Sunny sat up. Putting her sunglasses over her raccoon eyes, she took a sip of the icy drink. It felt as good as the sun did.

"Billy drove them into town," she said. "They took all the dogs for new flea baths. The kids just love those dogs."

Mac's phone was ringing again and Sunny raised her brows and heaved a sigh, because of course she knew he would answer it. He always did, even on vacation.

It was Alain Hassain from Interpol giving information on the clearing up of Jasper Lord's tangled international arms dealings. He said it would take a long time to sort them out, meanwhile all Lord's assets had been frozen and it would be an even longer time before it was decided what would be done with them.

He said he had more news, about Krendler this time. Mac listened in silence then said, "Jesus, Alain. Who knew?" sounding amazed.

He finished his conversation and passed on the information about Jasper Lord's assets to Belinda, who merely shrugged.

"As far as I'm concerned all his money should all be distributed to families in those war-torn starving countries he didn't give a shit about. I'm okay personally, I told you I'd already transferred my jewelry and some funds to the Bank of England. I reckon I'd earned it. After that, I don't really care."

"I have more news." Mac looked at Sunny. "This time it's about Krendler."

"Don't tell me he's escaped from jail?"

"He has not. And my guess is he and Valenti will be in there for life. Meanwhile, the police took apart his house in Paris."

Sunny said, "I remember that green-paneled drawing room, like something from an opera set."

"That paneling hid a secret room, exactly like the one at Chez La Violette only much bigger, and this one was steel-lined, with a computerized combination entry. Only Krendler knew how to access his secret room, and only he ever went in there. Until now."

"His own personal art gallery," Sunny guessed.

"He was selective, he kept only the paintings he loved, in a perfectly temperature-controlled environment, perfectly lit, each displayed like a hidden jewel behind black silk curtains that slid back at the push of a button. That way Krendler could gaze at each painting alone, no distractions, no one to bother him. It was only him and the dead artist alone in that room."

Belinda said, disgusted, "I knew he was bad but I didn't realize he was that creepy."

"Not only that." Mac looked at Sunny again. "You'll never guess what else they found in there."

"An opera singer? A butler? Fake paintings?"

"The mummified bodies of eleven greyhounds."

"Jesus!" Sunny choked on her Pepsi.

"We can only thank God it wasn't people," Mac said, "though we'll probably never know how many humans he took out along the way. Anyhow, the fame Krendler never sought has finally overtaken him. He's the talk of *tout Paris.*"

"A sociopath," Sara said, shuddering.

"A psychopath," Mac corrected her. "Mostly they start with killing small animals, then they progress to people."

"Let's not talk about it. Let's talk good stuff. Like what François Reynaud is doing for Bertrand." Sunny smoothed more lotion onto Belinda's back. Even Sara had taken off her shirt, though she'd kept on her top.

"Reynaud is really proud of that boy," Mac said. "He says he's been through a lot, that he's clever and brave and deserves a chance. Reynaud is prepared to give him that chance. He's applying for shared legal guardianship, with Billy. He has no sons of his own, and privately he told me it's a way of replacing the young man who was killed, who he'd known since he was a child. He says it's the least he can do, but more than that, he'll really enjoy being uncle and mentor to a boy like Bertrand."

"Little Laureen's gonna miss him, though," Belinda said, lying back next to Sunny, and sighing with pleasure as the sun swept her body with heat. "I know, I know," she said, as Sara whispered a warning, "Five minutes, that's all, just enough to give me a nice golden glow."

"She will," Mac said. "But Reynaud knows people in high places. He's pulling strings to get this through quickly, and meanwhile get permission for Bertrand to return to the ranch with Billy and Laureen. Until everything is finally worked out, and the woman who calls herself his 'mother' removed from the picture."

"Oh, boy," Sunny murmured, eyes closed. "Little Laureen's gonna love that. She'll be teaching Bertrand how to corral cattle and ride a pony."

"Hmm, I'll bet she will." Belinda looked thoughtful, remembering Billy asking her if she knew how to ride a horse. "What a very good idea," she said.

87.

That evening, Mac was watching Sunny vainly attempting to eliminate the black eyes with a concealer. It only made them look more raccoonlike and she threw it down in despair. "Now what?" she asked. "François Reynaud is giving a grand farewell dinner at Chez Tétou and I look awful."

Mac heaved an overdramatic sigh. "Imagine that, you looking awful, and probably Angelina will be there, with Brad, and maybe Johnny Depp . . ."

"Oh, stop it," Sunny said crossly.

"No, I mean it. Really."

He was laughing at her and she slumped on the bed, glaring at him.

"They go there all the time," he continued. "All the movie stars and celebs go."

"Only when the film festival is on."

"Uh-uh." He shook his head. "All the time. I have it on the best gossip."

"You never gossip." She ran her hands through her hair, thankful that the doctors who'd sewn up her head had not had to cut any of it off. It still hurt but it was definitely getting better.

"That'll teach me to go off investigating on my own," she said.

Mac gave her a long look. She had not mentioned Chez La Violette since that day, and he'd hoped she'd forgotten about it, and about the glamorous legend. He hadn't wanted to bring it up in case it upset her, but now he saw that he must. It was only fair.

He took a yellowed envelope from the bureau drawer and handed it to her. "It's for you," he said, when she looked inquiringly at him. "From La Violette. I found it in a box in the secret room, hidden under a bunch of dried flowers."

Sunny held it to her nose. Her eyes met his. "Parma violets," she said.

He'd guessed it would be. Sunny still sat with the envelope in her hands. "Aren't you going to open it?" he asked.

She looked at it, a small square envelope, yellow with age, smelling of violets. She said, "It's odd, but now I don't know if I want to. Somehow, it doesn't seem right, spying on another woman's private life."

Mac went and sat on the bed next to her. "But you see what it says on the envelope?"

"To those who might care" was written in small spidery script that had faded to the pale gray of Violette's boudoir, the color of her silken bed hangings, her velvet chaise, the odd little desk made from planks of driftwood where she must have sat to write this.

"You're a person who cares," Mac said. "I think she would know that."

"Yes. Yes, I do care."

Sunny ran her thumb under the V of the envelope. It had dried out over the years and opened easily. She took out the folded pages. They were like the ones still in the letter stand on Violette's desk, but these were filled with her small, tight script, an uneducated hand because, Sunny guessed, Violette had been brought up in an orphanage and probably had no formal education. All she had learned was what she had found as a girl on the streets and the stages of Paris. Violette was the woman the world had made her.

Sunny smoothed out the pages and began to read. Mac watched her silently. He hoped she would not get too upset.

"To whom it may concern," Violette began.

I believe that is the correct way to begin a confession of this nature, though I doubt there is anyone left who is "concerned" anymore. Except for my cats, of course, the tiny scoundrels who chase the mice and scare the local marauding dogs, and who sleep on my bed, all six of them. I tell myself at least they keep me warm at night, now there is no longer a man.

Sometimes, sitting out on the terrace of the house I built, a glass of cheap wine in my hand because I can no longer afford the champagne I used to serve so generously to my friends, I ask myself if I am unhappy.

Am I? I think perhaps I have recovered from being "unhappy" and now live entirely in a state of simply "being." Emotions are a thing of the past. "Fame" is gone, along with whatever beauty people saw in me, though in truth I always believed it was an illusion. I was merely a vital woman who could sing well enough and who was sexy enough to make men believe they really loved me. And some of them did. And I enjoyed many of them. Now the jewels are faded memories, like the men who gave them to me, for I made it a point of pride never to buy jewels myself.

I was a woman who had everything, even my own perfume, made only for me, from the flower that had given me my name. I smell it still, as I sit here; that soft, sensuous perfume that always left a memory of me in an empty room.

Clothes were my indulgence, and now look at me, in my dated chiffons and Chanels, and the long velvet medieval-style gowns, now with a blanket of cat hair. But I was sexy. I have to admit to an indulgence in that. Ultimately it was what brought my downfall.

Picture this, those who are concerned, if you will. A pretty girl, too tall for her fifteen years, a mane of long flame-colored hair, on the run from the prison they called an orphanage-asylum, bold eyes hiding her insecurities. Imagine how many tubs of laundry she had been made to clean, how heavy the stick with which she had to turn those clothes in the boiling water, how the steam seared her delicate skin. Ah, I know, I know, this sounds like one of the melodramas I starred in on the stages of France and Spain and Germany. But then of course, Germany was where it all started.

Skip a few months in time and imagine that girl, a runaway, so soon out of the laundry and now on the stage in Paris, half-naked in sequins and sparkles, ropes of fake pearls and diamonds around her neck. That was the young Violette, her hands still raw from that laundry, but now disguised with white powder.

Imagine, if you can, the most elegant man you have ever seen. Tall, impeccably dressed, hair smoothed back, a lean sensual face with light blue eyes that seemed to grip my own. And rich beyond belief.

That man became my first lover. I think now I will love him forever and beyond, though after him there were others. Not as many as people believed, though. I was selective in my affairs and I never slept with anybody for money, even though they showered me with expensive gifts. After all, I was successful, I was famous, I was rich in my own right. And oh how I enjoyed being "La Violette."

Another German, Kurt von Müller, came into my life when I was thirty-six and he was a mere twenty years. Oh, how everyone talked,

but we took no notice. He had such talent, young Kurt, far more
talent than was needed to be a mere accompanist to a music hall
star, but he had broken with his family and turned to me instead.
Those were the happy years. Then the war came.

Kurt was German. I was French. Kurt was recruited and became
an officer in a Nazi uniform. You will never know how much I hated
seeing him in that slick uniform, those smart shiny boots. Finally,
when the tentacles of war spread as far as the Riviera, I moved to
Paris, where Kurt was working for that madman Goering,
investigating the histories of the works of art Goering stole from the
French people to adorn his own castle, a temple devoted to his wife.

Then Kurt confessed to me that he was a spy; he was passing
information to the French and his life was in constant danger. He
needed to get away from Goering, who was suspicious. He needed a
façade to hide behind. He needed me.

He had a plan. I would go back onstage, sing for the Nazis,
entertain them, dine with them, "fraternize," they called it. I would
tell them I must have young Kurt as my accompanist. After all, that
was his job before the war came, and how could I manage without
him now?

Such was my fame, this was immediately allowed and I became
once again the toast of the town. And Kurt had his cover.

Why would I do this? you must be asking yourself. Putting myself
in danger for a young lover, charming though he was. After all, he
was still "the enemy," and there were plenty of other men.

Lovers come and go, but it was more than just that.

Remember the girl who worked in the laundry, all those years
ago? I certainly do. I never forgot her. Nor my first lover, the
handsome, charming Baron Wilhelm August von Müller, who
seduced me with my full cooperation and what I then believed was
true love. I still believe that. And when, a year later, our son was
born and named after his father, Kurt Wilhelm August von Müller,
my lover told me he had confessed his dalliance to his wife. Like me,
she was older, and she had never been able to bear children. They
needed a son and heir, and I, with a long and dreary future staring
in front of me, willingly handed over that child. I believed it would
give him, and me, a better life. I still believe that.

Callous, you might say? But do not judge so harshly. I gave my
gift with love to a man I loved. And after all, he was his son too.

So, in those later war years, when suspicion fell on my German son and he fled south toward Lyon where he hoped to contact the Resistance and persuade them he was not only part French, but also on their side, he was captured. Only a few days later, he was hung by the Nazis, in the city square as an example of what happened to German officers who betrayed their country.

I stayed, grieving, in my Paris house, alone for the first time in many years. Even my maid had left me. The end of hostilities came too late for my beloved boy, and I remember clearly standing on the streets of Paris, watching those handsome Americans with flowers stuck in their helmets, cheering and waving.

I was arrested a few days later, accused by the French of collaborating with the enemy. I chose to protect my son's name, not to tell my story, not demean Kurt's memory further by telling the world he was also "a bastard."

They cut off all my hair though, in that jail. My long beautiful red hair, that in truth was my one real claim to beauty. My humiliation was complete and I waited not too patiently, to be summoned to trial, and I welcomed the thought of death as an alternative to the living hell in which I found myself.

It was my own fault, of course. But I am a stubborn woman, always have been. I could face disgrace for myself but not for my son. Strangely, there were some who remembered, some who cared enough to pull strings, have me set free. I never asked who, or why. I simply put a hat over my naked head and returned to my one true home.

I had found the old ruined priory on the green hill overlooking the Mediterranean many years before, and, as always, had fallen passionately in love. I'd bought it immediately, even though I did not then have enough money to build. When I finally did, it was my dream home, the place I invited my friends, enemies, rivals. All of society came.

Oh, how I love this house. Even now, alone in its dusty, scented shabbiness, it means everything to me. How I would like to see it again, the way it was in the painting on the wall in front of me, filled with laughter, a child in the pool, friends drinking cocktails, myself draped over a chair, watching, listening.

It's all gone, and I am too tired and too old. I am wishing myself somewhere else, somewhere closer to that talented young man who gave up his family and a great career and returned to find his mother. How I wish now that he had not done it, though in truth, the end result would probably have been the same, and he would have died in the war anyway.

Such is the way it is.

I love the villa that bears my name. It has the imprint of my personality, my life, even my perfume. I love my darling cats who have kept me company these many years. I loved my life and everything that came with it. And now it's time to go.

So, to those of you who come later, and might even care, I am leaving this scrap of information, so that perhaps sometime, somewhere, someone will know the truth. And wish La Violette well.

Sunny looked up from the letter. Mac was watching her. "You must read it for yourself," she said, handing the pages to him.

She walked out onto the balcony and stood, with the breeze stirring her hair, looking out at the same view Violette had seen the evening she wrote her final letter. She clasped her arms round her shoulders, chilled.

When Mac finally came out to join her, he held her against him.

"What do you think she did?" Sunny asked, sadly.

"Maybe it's better not to ask what, or how. At least now we know why."

"She sounds so lovely, Mac, so real, so honest, so brave and vulnerable."

"She does," he agreed. "And now I think we should do what she would have wanted. We read the message she hoped some final person would find and understand. Now we should let it go, tear it into tiny pieces and scatter it to the wind."

"Violette would have wanted that, wouldn't she?" Sunny said.

88.

They were to meet the Misfits later, for the Grand Farewell Dinner thrown by François Reynaud, at Tétou in Golfe Juan. Sunny wore her favorite dress, a creamy silk splashed with gaudy red, pink and purple flowers, a low V back and front, cinched at the waist with a belt that ended in a beaded tassel. Purple high suede sandals, a tiny cream clutch that held the Dior Rouge lipstick, as well as the fifty-dollar bill she'd carried around for years in case of emergency—after all, a girl never knew when she might need a cab—a quick brush of her long hair, and she was ready.

Mac thought she looked beautiful, his golden girl, despite the two black eyes. But before the party, they had work to complete.

They drove to the place where a narrow azure creek ran inland from the sea, just beyond the villa. There was no sandy cove here, just the aquamarine sea, paler where the water rippled over the shallows. Somehow, Sunny knew this where Violette would have found final peace.

She took off her sandals and holding hands, she and Mac walked down the path. They stood, looking down at the water. Then, silk skirts bunched in one hand, Sunny waded into the sea.

She tore the confession into tiny pieces until nothing was left of the writing, then let the pieces flutter into that blue water to become like Violette, a part of the elements again.

"It's good now, isn't it?" she asked, looking back at Mac.

"It's good, baby," he agreed gently.

As they drove back they passed the villa where Sunny had arrived, alone, only a couple weeks ago, for a luxury vacation that had turned into mayhem and mystery. The place still drew her.

"I have to look, just one more time," she said.

Mac got out and opened the gates. They creaked now and wobbled on their big iron hinges. Together, they walked up the gravel drive, stopping to look at the ragged chamomile lawn, the empty neglected pool, the poplars whose leaves seemed to tinkle in the breeze. Crickets buzzed in the bougainvillea, and quite suddenly a small snake wiggled fast across the flagstone terrace.

Sunny shivered, remembering what happened to Eve. She felt no need to go inside, though. It was over.

The wrought-iron table and two chairs were still on the terrace outside Violette's boudoir, and the green shutters had been left unlatched. One of them swung, very gently, to and fro. The evening sun gleamed on the dusty window.

Was that the scent of violets in the air? And was that a pale shadow at the window?

Perhaps the scent was simply the jasmine, after all. Perhaps the faint gray shadow was merely dust motes, reflecting from the sun. Perhaps, perhaps . . .

"Goodbye, Violette," Sunny whispered. "I cared. Truly I did."

Then she walked back to join Mac. He closed the gates of Chez La Violette behind them for the last time, and they drove back to their Hotel of Dreams.

89.

Reynaud's yacht, the *Bellissima,* was large enough to cause quite a sensation when it put in at St. Tropez and sent its tender, complete with two striped-T-shirted crew, to pick them up with all their luggage.

The yacht was too large to berth in the port and lay offshore, gleaming in the setting sun, a private cruise ship that Reynaud often called "home." It was to take them across the bay to Golfe Juan and Chez Tétou, the famous fish restaurant Reynaud had chosen for their Grand Farewell Dinner.

All except Mac and Sunny were leaving the following morning. Tonight would be a time of celebration and of sadness at leaving new friends who would now become old friends. And of leaving Bertrand behind.

The women had dressed for the occasion; Sara in her Cavalli and the green wedge heels; Belinda in her red silk jersey wrap dress, though there was no risk of bullets tonight; and Sunny in her flower-splashed ivory silk with the tasseled belt. Little Laureen, of course, was in a tutu, an orange one this time because, she said, she was a bit nervous about going out to sea and wanted to make sure, in case of any trouble, that she would be spotted. No one needed to ask by whom.

She had brought along her wand and sat glued to Bertrand's side in the tender, letting the spray wash her hair, newly cut by Belinda so that it hung prettily to her shoulders with the princess tiara glittering on top. She wore the cowboy boots too, and was wiggling her hot toes because it was a warm evening despite the sea breeze. Of course she knew now to take the boots off on the boat.

"I'm glad Belinda's going to Texas with you," Bertrand said, over the buzz of the tender's motor.

Laureen nodded. "I'm glad she's coming too. She promised to cut my hair again, when it needs it. Besides, I think my dad's in love with her."

Bertrand looked worried, he knew how Laureen felt about her mother's memory. "Is that good?" he asked.

She threw him a soulful glance. "Of course it is. There's only one thing I would like more." She gripped her wand tighter, looking at its magic star.

Bertrand didn't need to ask what that was; he knew Little Laureen wanted him to go back to the ranch with her as much as he did, but the woman who called herself his "mother" was fighting against that in court.

"Here we are," the sailor in the navy-striped T-shirt called out as they bumped alongside the big yacht's steps.

Reynaud was waiting at the top to greet them. They were to spend the night on the yacht as his guests before flying home the next day.

The cabins were sumptuous, all nautical blue and white like Reynaud's Villa les Ambassadeurs, but with none of that ostentatious—and phony— paneling, like on Valenti's sailboat. Cocktails and lemonade were served on the afterdeck while the big boat cut through the water like a well-honed knife.

Billy was discreetly not holding Belinda's hand, though he would have liked to. She was barefoot, leaning against the deck rail, alone. He caught her glance and they smiled, one of those private smiles that meant something to each of them. He only wished he knew exactly what. Love had come back into Billy's life and he was afraid he would lose it again.

Sitting next to Nate, Sara nibbled caviar for the first time in her life and said out loud how marvelous it was.

"I like that things are a first for you," Nate said. "Most of the women I know act as though they've been weaned on caviar."

"I'm making the most of it before I become a waitress again."

"You serious about it?"

She met his eyes. "Maybe," she said with a grin.

Nate surely hoped she was. He was beginning to think his new house wouldn't be the same without her presence. And besides, she looked so cute tonight, a wispy waif in a smooth new Sassoon-type bob with a long fringe that finally allowed him to see her face properly. Again this was courtesy of Belinda, who was quite a magician with the scissors. She had also trimmed Nate's own hair into what was practically a buzz cut only with longer bits on top. He looked like a new man, except for the pale blue Brooks Brothers seersucker jacket of course. He was still a man in transition.

Sara caught Lev's eye. He gave her a wink and a wry smile. Sara sighed as she looked away. She hoped he would keep in touch, but she doubted it.

"Here we are," François Reynaud called as the big boat cut its engines and slid closer to shore. The small town of Vallauris gleamed in the low hills behind Golfe Juan, and Reynaud told them Picasso had once had a studio there, and there were now several museums devoted to his art.

The restaurant, Chez Tétou, had started life in the nineteen-twenties as a tiny beach shack owned by a local fisherman. Its reputation had grown over the years, though in essence it was still that same little beach shack, only larger now and nicely painted in white with black trim, casually elegant in its own simple way. It was comfortable, with big windows opening onto the sand and the sea, and it served the freshest fish in town. People came from all over the world for Tétou's famous bouillabaisse.

It was still run by the family of that original fisherman, and François Reynaud was greeted like an old friend. A long table had been reserved for them near the windows, and icy bottles of their favorite rosé wine, the Château Minuty L'Observatoire were poured.

Sara had never had bouillabaisse before, and neither had Billy, or Mac. "I guess we ought to try it," Sara said, game for anything.

"We should try it too," Bertrand said to Laureen.

She looked doubtful. "What about spaghetti?" she whispered.

He shook his head. "They don't make that here."

Her eyes were huge with dismay. "What about french fries?"

He shook his head.

Laureen sat back, subdued. "Okay then, I'll have the bouillabaisse," she said bravely. She wasn't quite sure what it was but the name sounded fishy. Only Sunny ordered the sole meunière.

Laureen wasn't hungry. She was thinking that she had to leave Bertrand behind the next morning. Her eyes met his. She wanted to hold his hand but decided against it in case the others were looking, afraid they might laugh.

The next table was being served their bouillabaisse. Laureen looked at the fishy soup and swallowed hard again. She took another gulp of water.

"Bertrand," she whispered.

"*Oui?*"

"I don't think I can do bouillabaisse."

His already alabaster face looked pale under his granny glasses and shock of hair. "Neither can I," he whispered back.

Belinda caught it and ordered lobsters for them. "And I noticed there's strawberry and raspberry tarte for dessert," she said.

Reynaud tapped his wineglass with a fork to get their attention.

"Messieurs, mesdames." He smiled at them. "Or may I now call you simply 'friends'? It has been my great good fortune to meet you, here in the South of France, in one of the most delightful places on this earth, St. Tropez. It was not always easy, but through disaster, has come joy. Especially for me, because now I am in the unusual position of having children in my life." He put a hand on Bertrand's thin shoulder. "Even though a French boy like Bertrand doesn't care for bouillabaisse," he added with a laugh. "Still, what counts, is that we are able to share this wonderful evening together before you each go your separate ways, though I am certain we shall meet again.

"I have one piece of news for you." He took a paper from his jacket pocket, unfolded it and held it up for them to see.

"This is official permission for Bertrand Olivier to travel to the USA under the guardianship of Billy Bashford. A passport will be issued tomorrow morning—although we will need a photograph of course."

Billy got up and went and stood behind Bertrand's chair. He gripped the boy's shoulders, too filled with emotion to speak. Leaving Bertrand behind would have left him with another crack in his already broken heart and now he didn't know whether to laugh or cry. Instead he looked at his daughter.

Laureen was certainly not crying. She was holding tight on to Bertrand's hand and beaming. Billy didn't remember when he'd last seen his little girl look so happy.

Bertrand allowed his head to rest against Billy's hand. His dream had come true and he belonged. He wondered if Laureen had really waved her magic wand. He believed in it now. Really he did.

Joy seemed to spread around the table like jelly on a peanut butter sandwich. Smiles were on everyone's faces. The bouillabaisse came and even Little Laureen tasted it and pronounced it "almost good." In fact it was wonderful, and so was the lobster that she and Bertrand devoured so fast they had to wait for the others to finish. As always, Laureen wondered impatiently why grown-ups took so long to eat, and why they talked so much, which meant she and Bertrand had to wait a long time for dessert. She surely hoped there was ice cream to go with that tarte.

"Bertrand?" she whispered.

He sighed exasperatedly and said, in English, "What?"

"I'll teach you to ride a horse, if you like."

His face lit up. "Okay," he agreed.

Sunny was smiling as she watched the Misfits, on their way to their new lives. "Now it's just us," she whispered to Mac. "We have one week left in St. Tropez."

Mac looked into her beautiful raccoon eyes. "One whole week," he agreed.

"Alone at last," she sighed happily.

"Apart from the dogs, of course," Mac added.

Epilogue

Two Weeks Later

Mac was on the deck of his cozy Malibu shack, feet up on the rail, contemplating the surging Pacific and life. Sunny had just arrived with pizza. A bottle of good Californian red, a Caymus, stood on the metal table between them. Pirate hung out in his usual spot, head stuck through the rails, looking out at the beach for something to chase, like a passing pelican or a seagull. Sunny was on the old Wal-Mart metal chaise she'd been trying to get Mac to replace for about three years, with Tesoro on her lap and a slice of pizza in her hand. Twilight deepened around them.

Mac gazed happily at his little family, at the glowering green ocean, at the string of lights threading along the edge of the long bay. He was used to the view but it always held magic for him. He was, at heart, a Malibu guy.

"Great vacation," Sunny said, in between bites and sips of the good wine.

"Great," Mac, said, looking at her.

She shivered as the cool evening breeze sprang up and he went inside and got his old denim shirt for her.

Sunny held it to her face, breathing in his body scent. "Why do boys' shirts always smell so *good*?" she asked, slipping it over her shoulders.

The phone rang.

Their eyes met. Silence hung like tension in the air. It rang again.

"Don't answer it," Sunny said.

Mac hesitated, his hand hovered. He just hated leaving a ringing phone, even though he knew it would probably mean trouble.

Twirling her beautiful heart-shaped pink diamond engagement ring, Sunny knew if Mac answered the phone it would be more work, more mysteries. She'd been convinced they would soon find time to get married, perhaps even go back to lovely St. Tropez and do it properly, the way they'd intended before the Misfits made a hash of their vacation. If only Mac wouldn't answer that phone.

But Mac was Mac. Smiling, he picked up the phone. He always did.

Post-Epilogue

Chez La Violette has been sold to a young French couple with five small children. The old villa will be torn down and a new one, suitable for such a large and happy family, is to be built in its place. Only the arched cloister, all that remains of the priory that first stood on the beautiful green hill, will remain. As will the name, Chez La Violette, in permanent tribute to a fallen star.

Valenti's Picasso, given to him in payment by Krendler and which he'd pretended was a fake, turned out to be a real fake. Krendler had fooled him. Both men are in jail and looking at life sentences.

Mac and Sunny are still in love, still engaged, and are thinking of getting married next summer, in an old church in the English countryside. Sunny knows exactly the place. Anyway, that's her plan for now. If only Mac doesn't pick up that phone.